Haunted by Secrets

SHADOWED SOULS SERIES

BOOK THREE

MADDISON COLE

DEDICATION

To the Anchor who weathers every storm.

To the One who never lets me fail.

To the Man who always believes in me.

Thank you for being my happy ending.

Note from the Author

Hi all! I'm not going to do the list of usual trigger warnings. By now, you know what you're getting into. Instead, please read this quick disclaimer before you tumble into the final book of the Shadowed Souls series.

I toyed with this plot line long and hard, writing the first half and then scraping it. Hence why, to my own dismay, I couldn't bring myself to include Meg's point of view in this story. I had to remind myself that this is Avery's story, and I need to continue it that way. In this book, you'll find the redemption arc, rollercoaster of emotions and closure you've been seeking for. There's a happily ever after at the end (for most). Please be rest assured, the plot has been keyboard bashed extremely hard by my blunt little fingers and everything happens for a reason!

On a tiny separate note, I am (*shock horror*) not a doctor. Although I have done extensive research into injuries that may or may not be sustained in this novel, ultimately this is a work of fiction. Some medical mumbo jumbo may not be one hundred percent accurate to real life, but it serves a purpose to entertain you. So please, go forth and be entertained, and I'll see you on the other side!

PROLOGUE

Eleven Years Ago...

Swinging my legs back and forth, the pool water laps against the side of the pool. I lean back, letting the afternoon sun soak into my skin. The manor feels so big and empty, with only the sound of the fountain splashing and the occasional bird in the trees to remind me I'm not completely alone.

My parents have been gone for weeks. Left on some urgent business. As usual, I don't know the details. It just sucks that it had to happen in the summer break and our trip to Mauritius was canceled.

"Master Wyatt?" A voice calls softly. I barely glance over to see Ms. Dee, one of the maids, standing a few feet away, holding a glass of lemonade. She's nice enough, although her missing fingers freak me out, but not much of a talker. Just like all the others who work for the Hughes. Silent, obedient, always there but never really here.

I take the lemonade and mumble a thanks. She smiles politely, then walks away, her low heels clicking on the patio tiles. Nothing seems right anymore. The lemonade's too sweet, and the sun is too bright. I'm sweating in my swim shorts, looking at the empty pool again. It's big enough for my entire class to fit in, which the many pool parties have proven.

But when it's only me, the pool is just a huge, lonely void. Sometimes I dive in just to make a splash, just to fill the silence, but today I don't even feel like that.

I wish they were home. I wish I had something to do, someone to play with.

There's only so much a ten-year-old can do in a house this big. I've already ridden my bike around the driveway more times than I can count, skimmed through the books in the library, and grew tired of playing video games in the theater room. When the end result is tucking myself into bed to stare at the ceiling, everything feels so pointless.

Maybe I'll call Huxley and see if he's finished with his photo shoot. Or practice gelling my hair back again. I find I like it that way, pushed back out of my green eyes. Or maybe—

The faint sound of a car engine breaks through the stillness. I sit up straight, bending to look through the french double doors. The unmistakable hum of my parents' Bentley drives into the underground garage. They're home. Finally.

My heart races as I jump up and dash across the patio, wet feet slapping against the stone. I don't even bother putting on shoes as I run through the sliding glass doors into the house, the cold marble floors a shock after the sun's warmth. I skid around the corner and head toward the internal elevator doors, where the staff were already gathering.

The metallic doors glide open, revealing my parents, dressed in their usual perfect way. Mom's in a sleek dress, sunglasses perched on top of her head, and Dad's in one of his tailored suits, his smile the same one I see in magazines. I grin, excited to tell them all about my day, even if nothing much happened.

But something's different this time.

They're not alone.

Standing just behind them, clutching the handle of a small, filthy backpack, is a girl. She's my age—around ten, I reckon. She's thin, her blonde hair pulled back into a slick ponytail, and her big eyes are wide with fear. Her clothes look brand new, a little too big, like they've been picked out by a personal shopper. She doesn't say anything; she just stares at the floor, avoiding eye contact.

I stop in my tracks, confused. I don't know who she is or why she's here. My parents don't usually bring people home. At least, not kids.

"Wyatt," Dad says, his voice warm and easy, like it always is when *he's about to announce something I'm not going to like. "We've got some news." I glance between them and the girl. I don't like surprises. Not ones I don't understand, anyway.*

"This is Avery," Mom says gently, stepping forward and placing a gentle hand on the girl's shoulder. "She's going to be staying with us from now on."

"Staying with us?" I repeat, dumbfounded. I can't figure out why, out of all the things they could bring home, it's this quiet, scared girl. I've been asking for a puppy for months.

"She's... well, she's our daughter now," Dad adds. As he looks at her, his smile softens in a way that makes my stomach flutter with unease. "We've adopted her."

Adopted? I step back, my guard instantly up. How could they do this? Make such a big decision without me, uncaring of my opinion. Maybe I don't want to share.

I continue to stare at the girl, Avery, wondering why she doesn't have a home of her own. What could have happened to pull on my parent's heartstrings so strongly? Actually, I don't want to know.

She's not like anyone I've ever seen before. Nothing like the girls in my class, with their perfect ponytails and expensive shoes. She's nothing like me either. She's... different.

But then something shifts. Maybe it's the way she's gripping that backpack strap so tightly, like it's the only thing keeping her grounded. Or maybe it's the way her blue eyes flicker up to meet mine for the briefest second, filled with uncertainty and fear. Everything inside of me washes away, cleaning the slate of what I thought I knew.

She looks like she needs someone. And for some reason, an instant protective feeling sets in. I take a step forward, not sure what to say but wanting to say something. Anything.

"Hey," I manage, my voice quieter than usual. "I'm Wyatt."

She doesn't reply right away; she just shifts on her feet, glancing at my parents as if waiting for permission to speak. Mom gives her a reassuring nod, and finally, Avery looks at me again, her lips parting as she whispers, "Hi."

It's just one word, but it's enough. Enough to make me feel like I need to do more. Be more. I've never had a sister before. I don't even know what it means to have one. But looking at her now, standing there so small in this giant house, I decide that I want to try.

"Do you wanna see the pool?" I ask, trying to sound casual, but there's an edge of excitement in my voice. I want her to feel welcome. To know that this place, my home, can be her home too. She hesitates, glancing back at my parents. Mom smiles and nods again.

Avery takes a deep breath, then nods slowly. She lets Ms. Dee take her backpack and steps toward me, her movements small and careful, like she's afraid of making a mistake. I lead her through the house, pointing out different rooms and talking a little too fast.

"That's the living room, but we never really use it. And over there's the kitchen, where Ms. Delores makes the best pancakes. The pool is this way." I step out of the open glass doors, the sunlight hitting us hard. The pool sparkles, and I can't help but grin as I gesture toward it. "Pretty cool, right?"

Avery blinks at the sight, her mouth opening slightly. I can see the wonder in her eyes—the complete awe. It's refreshing really, giving me a new outlook on the manor that seemed so boring to me just ten minutes ago.

"I-" Avery squeaks, her face going bright red. "I don't know how to swim." She shakes her head, trying to hide her blush behind the strands of hair falling free around her face.

"That's okay," I say quickly. "I can teach you." Her big, blue eyes flicker to mine again, and for the first time since she arrived, there's a tiny spark of something in her expression. Something close to hope, which rocks me.

"Okay," she whispers. It's certain now; I have to help her. Show her there's nothing to be scared of here—that I'll be her friend. Her brother, actually. It's got a nice ring to it.

We share a grin as I start to show her how to hold her arms out like she's swimming, even though we're both still standing by the pool's edge. She doesn't say much, but her eyes follow every movement, her tiny hands mimicking mine. So unsure and shy. I can't explain it, but it's like the need to protect her is already there, just sitting under my skin.

As I show her how to move her arms, a figure appears at the glass doors behind us. I glance up, thinking it's Mom coming to check on us, but it's Dad. He's leaning against the doorframe, arms crossed, his eyes fixed on us. Not in the usual, distant way, like when he's thinking about work or something else, but with an intensity that makes my stomach knot. I can't remember the last time he looked like that.

Avery stops mimicking my movements, noticing him too. Her shoulders tense, and I can feel her pulling back into herself, like she's worried she's done something wrong. The little bit of ease she had a second ago is gone, and that warm feeling I had earlier vanishes with it.

"Wyatt, can you come here for a minute?" His voice is calm, but I know the underlying note of seriousness. It's how he usually talks to me when I've disappointed him. He motions with his head for me to follow him back inside. I look at Avery again, trying to reassure her with a small smile, but she's already turned her gaze back to the pool, her arms wrapped around herself tightly.

As I step inside, I catch the last glimpse of her, standing there alone by the water, looking smaller than ever. I grit my teeth at the thought of leaving her out there, a tick beating in my jaw. What if something happens while I'm not there? What if she falls in?

Dad leads me to his study, out of earshot from the staff and far away from Avery. He stands there for a second, knocking his knuckles against his desk.

"Wyatt," he finally starts when I'm starting to fidget. "We need to have a serious talk." I swallow hard, bracing myself.

"What's going on?" His pale eyes meet mine, holding a weight in his gaze that I don't like. Not one bit.

"Avery has been through a lot. A lot more than any child should ever go through. She needs to be our focus now." Avery. I'd only just learned her name, and already it's like the air in the room shifts around it, making it feel heavier.

"Okay..." I say slowly, not sure where he's going with this. I glance toward the window, trying to angle myself to see the patio and failing. "What do you want me to do?"

Dad nods, but his face is still tight, his hands resting on his hips.

"There are some things that Avery's going to have to deal with in the coming months. We're going to be spending a lot of time helping her adjust. Protecting her." The word "protect" lingers in the air like an accusation. I open my mouth, but he continues before I can get the words out.

"She's fragile," Dad says, his voice laced with concern. It's unnerving. He pauses, his eyes locking onto mine. "So, with that being said," he sighs, "we've decided to send you to boarding school in the fall. Full time."

Boarding school. My chest tightens, the words feeling like I've been punched. They've mentioned it before, sure, but never like this. Never like a solution to something I didn't even know was a problem.

"You want me to leave?" I ask, my voice cracking. Dad lowers his head slightly.

"It's not about wanting you to leave, Wyatt. It's about making sure Avery has the best environment to heal. That's our priority. Keeping her safe."

Something sharp twists in my gut at the way he says it. Keeping her safe. Like somehow I could... what? Hurt her? No words make it out, my silence allowing Dad to keep talking. Keep making it so much worse.

"She's been through trauma. Real trauma. And right now, she needs stability. She needs calm. She needs..." He trails off, and I can feel it coming, whatever he's been dancing around this whole time. "She needs your mother and I, without distractions."

Distractions? My chest tightens as the realization hits me.

"You think I'm a distraction," I say quietly, my voice barely above a whisper. I look down at my bare feet, the weight of the words settling like bricks in my stomach. Less than an hour ago, I was secure enough to feel endless boredom. Now I'm being kicked out. No, I'm being replaced. "But I don't want to go," I snap, the anger bubbling up now, sharp and hot. "I want to stay here. I want to help her."

"I know you do," Dad says, his voice calm, but there's a finality to it. His decision has been made. "But right now, what Avery needs is space. And time. She needs to feel safe."

I angle myself to look out of the window, spotting where Avery still stands by the pool, her small figure outlined by the sunlight. She looks so alone. So lost. Maybe Dad's right. Maybe I don't know how to help her. But that doesn't make this hurt any less.

"You're sending me away," I mutter, the words bitter in my mouth. "For her. She just got here, and you're choosing her over me."

"We're doing what's best for both of you." Dad lets out a slow breath, walking closer to rest his hand on my shoulder.

I stare at her, and something inside me begins to twist. It's subtle at *first, like a knot pulling tighter with every breath. Dad's words echo in my head. I'm the distraction. I'm who she's not safe with. I'm the thing that needs to be removed because I'm not good enough for their precious, fragile girl.*

The warmth I felt when I first saw her, when I thought I could help, starts to curdle. What right do they have to push me aside for her? For someone who barely speaks, who just appeared out of nowhere, hijacking my world like a shadow creeping in? They expect me to leave, to disappear, so they can focus on her. Avery. The girl I'm supposed to feel sorry for. The girl I'm supposed to protect.

But something hardens in my chest, my heart twisting into something cold and unrecognizable. I can't stop staring at her. The longer I do, the more I realize that the feelings I have aren't soft or kind anymore. If I can't be her protector, if I can't have her attention the way I want it, then I'll make sure she feels me and sees me in every corner of her world. She won't be able to forget about me so easily.

That's the irony of it all. To keep Avery safe, it's been decided that I'm no longer good enough for the precious life my dad is building around her. No, not my dad anymore. My dad wouldn't have turned his back on me like this. He's just Nixon to me now.

WYATT

CHAPTER ONE

Breathe. Don't forget to breathe. Ignore the heartbeat hammering in your ears. Foot on the accelerator. Grip the steering wheel tighter. Forget the circumstances that led you to this point. Leave behind the person you were supposed to be.

Maybe this is what Axel experiences every time he has a nightmare. Except I can't wake up from this. I can't take my eyes off the road, nor can I turn around and go back. I've sealed my fate, and now I have to live with it.

A soft groan sounds from the backseat, followed by a high-pitched whimper. I keep staring straight ahead, focusing on the miles of tarmac propelling us further into the night. I've been dreading this since I drugged her, quickly packed our belongings into a duffle bag, and stuffed her into Huxley's SUV. The keys to my Nissan are in my pocket, stalling the guys from following us. It's better this way, safer for everyone involved.

"Mmmm! Mmph mmm-" the muffled outrage continues. Exhaling sharply through my nose, I answer the questions I imagine she's asking.

"This car is not stopping until I've convinced you not to do something stupid or I've run out of gas," I state clearly. The muted cries pick up a notch, feet slamming into the back of my seat, and when I finally glance over my shoulder, I can see why.

"Oh, Baxter! Come up front," I pat the passenger seat beside me. A bundle of molting gray fur, which has not stopped shedding all over Huxley's SUV, leaps through the center column. He instantly flops into the seat and drops his head onto my lap, whimpering again for me to stroke his head. In the rearview mirror, Avery forces herself upright, her hair a sticky mess of dog saliva around the bandana moonlighting as a makeshift gag. She glares at me, raging blue eyes amongst the imprints across her face from being passed out across the back seats for so long. I glare right back. "What? I couldn't leave him at the shelter. His days were numbered."

Another round of subdued screeching fills the car, this time much more animated. With her hands zip-tied behind her back, Avery jerks herself around, her shoulders rolling towards the rear window. I sigh, focusing back on the road and forcing my jaw to unclench.

"I know I left the Souls behind, but you didn't really give me any other option."

"Mmmm!?"

"Yes, you," I grit out, trying and failing to keep a lid on my anger. "If you'd had the courtesy to simply *knock* on my door instead of barging in, you wouldn't have seen the letters. And if you hadn't seen those, I would have been thinking more clearly before I needed to act."

A single thud of feet slams into the back of my chair. I inhale, allowing my chest to expand, slipping back into character. This is the version of me Avery knows—the one she needs to hate. It's how I've prevented shit like this from happening for so long. As soon as I let myself slip, as soon as my heart started doing the thinking instead of my head, I've condemned an innocent girl to a madman and kidnapped another who I haven't stopped fantasizing about for eleven years. Whoever said emotions don't make us weak had never met Avery Hughes.

Baxter shifts, letting out a sigh and curling himself into a tight ball on the passenger seat. I run a hand over his back absentmindedly, fingers tracing the rough patches of his fur, feeling the weight of the past few hours pressing down on me. I didn't plan for things to go this way; I certainly didn't plan for Avery to be dragged into it.

The thumping against the back of my seat may have stalled, but the heavy thrumming of my heartbeat is like I'm being kicked from inside my own chest. I grip the wheel tighter, feeling the leather bite into my palms as I force myself to stay calm. But as I glance back in the mirror, meeting her furious gaze again; I know there's no use apologizing. Words are empty, but her scowl isn't. Her voice rings around my skull as if she were screaming in my ear.

Meg is in danger, and everything that happens to her is on your conscience.

I wish I could say the guilt I feel has something to do with Meg and not everything to do with slamming the final nail in the coffin between me and Avery. She can't let herself get close to me now; the stone wall between us has been solidified.

"It really doesn't pain me to say this, but I told you so," I mutter, just loud enough for her to hear. Avery's glare hardens, her mouth working against the bandana. The fiery spark in her blue eyes promises to maim me as soon as she is able, but for now, I'm doing the talking for the both of us. "I told you that nothing good would come from you getting close to me. But you did it anyway."

Maybe it's pathetic of me to blame her for our current situation, but man, no one can say I didn't try to prevent this. To resist Avery's advances for as long as I did took the patience of a saint, and my right hand felt the burn of punishing my cock after each and every instance.

I'm met with silence from the back seat. However, Avery's silence is louder than when she's fighting and screaming at me. This way, there's nothing to distract me from the churning of my thoughts. I fight the urge to look at her again. The orange hoodie I paused to drag onto her body was a mistake. It's my favorite, and it looks so much better on her. A bitter laugh escapes my throat at the stupid sentiment, my shoulders easing.

"I mean, what did you actually think would happen? You'd seduce me, and I would magically fall into line like the others? Run you a bath after a hard day and massage your aching feet?" My voice quickly turns mocking. I roll my eyes and set my sights back on the road, an irritated smirk hitching up the corner of my mouth. If I wasn't so screwed, so far up shit's creek, I'd be laughing.

The moon slips through a coating of clouds, illuminating the road that never seems to end. It's been hours since I saw another car, given that it's nearing four in the morning. Only adrenaline is keeping me going at this point.

"Actually," Avery states calmly, and I hate the way that I flinch. I blame Baxter for shooting bolt upright in the passenger seat. My eyes flick up to the rearview mirror. That sneaky little devil has managed to shift her gag, the bandana hanging uselessly around her slender neck. "For some foolish reason, I thought you were as innocent in all of this as me. I thought you were," she pauses, looking for the right word, "redeemable."

"That was your first mistake," I grumble, gripping the steering wheel tightly once more. All of the tension I had previously shed hits me in an instant, and with it, the lingering shadow I've been keeping at bay creeps into my peripheral vision. The darkness is a cloak across the right side of the car, pale eyes glaring out from within. I shake my head, not needing any more distraction from the road ahead. I can't afford to be anything except on high alert.

"Speaking of mistakes," Avery sighs and draws her hands in front of her, rolling her wrists.

"How the hell did you get out?!" I toss a brief look over my shoulder, as if the mirror's reflection is lying to me. It's her turn to smirk.

"You are many things, Wyatt, but a criminal mastermind isn't one of them. I was taught self-defense for ten years. Zip-tying me with my wrists crossed leaves room for rotating and slipping my hands free."

"I suppose your self-defense tutor didn't tell you it's stupid to reveal your tips and tricks to the man who did it to you." I twist back in my seat, forcing air into my lungs. This is fine; I can handle this.

"He did, but you won't be restraining me again," Avery laughs softly.

"Oh?" I quirk a brow. Baxter stays sitting upright, his head ping-ponging back and forth between us. When she pauses, I forget how it's in my best interest to ignore her and look up at the mirror again. Her teeth are nibbling her bottom lip, a smile fighting against the movement. She's too calm, her shoulders too relaxed.

"Lesson number one was all about not fighting back, allowing your captor to become overconfident and careless. That's the best way to catch them off guard."

"What-" A flash of movement cuts across my peripheral vision, fast enough to snap my full attention back. Before I can process what's happening, Avery lunges forward, the zip tie I used on her aimed for my throat.

My foot slams on the gas reflexively, but it only makes the car jolt forward, the engine roaring as I grapple for the tie. Her hold is relentless, the plastic cutting into my skin and pressing down on my windpipe. In the mirror, her eyes are blazing with a fury I've never seen before.

"Take me back," she grits out. I writhe, causing Baxter to whine and howl.

"No," I choke out, gasping for air.

"Take. Me. Back," she growls again, her voice dark and unforgiving, each word punctuated by another squeeze. "You don't get to decide for me. You don't get to take me away from my Souls."

"Avery!" I gasp, but the words come out garbled, barely audible. Her grip tightens, and I lose any semblance of control over the vehicle. My vision blurs, the road becoming a jagged blur of black asphalt and oncoming shadows.

The car swerves violently to the left as I try to wrestle her away from my throat with one hand, my other hand struggling to control the wheel. We barely manage to stay on the road, but there's no chance of staying in a straight line anymore. Baxter lets out a panicked yelp beside me, but Avery doesn't shift, her body pressed against the back of my seat as she digs the tie into my neck.

The car skids, tires screeching as we veer too close to the shoulder. I can't breathe, each second draining what's left of my strength. The only thought in my mind is the faint, stubborn urge to stay alive. My free hand scrambles back to grip her hair, fingers prying and clawing, but she only presses harder, her face a mask of cold, determined rage.

"Let... go..." I manage to rasp, but my words dissolve into a pained groan. My foot slips off the accelerator, and the car jerks, screeching as it races dangerously close to the ditch on the side of the road. I can feel the wheels slipping as they hit the gravel.

The next moment is a chaotic blur. The car slams hard to the side, and suddenly, the world tilts. We careen down the ditch, metal crunching and glass shattering as the car flips, a violent cascade of jolts and crashes that throw me against the steering wheel and Avery against the ceiling. Baxter howls in terror as we roll, and then, as quickly as it started, everything stops.

Silence.

The taste of blood fills my mouth, coppery and sharp. The smell of gasoline and burnt rubber clouds the air, thick and suffocating. My chest heaves as I try to suck in a full breath, a strangled gasp escaping my bruised throat. A low whine sounds as I realize the weight on my chest isn't imaginary. I wrap my arms around Baxter on instinct, checking him over as best I can. He seems intact, aside from a case of shivers.

I twist where I can, barely able to see Avery through the shattered glass, her face scraped and hair tangled, but her eyes are still wide open, and they're locked onto mine. Where I expect to see fear, I find a sense of crazed victory. Her lip is split, a dark patch blossoming against her bright hair. It's the only evidence of an oncoming concussion as her blue eyes falter.

"I...win," she pants, her voice hoarse. "Call Dax. He'll take me home." She loses the fight against the arms holding her upright, crumbling into a heap before I get the chance to tell her I left our phones behind.

AVERY

The cold kiss of antiseptic stings as Wyatt presses a cotton ball to my temple. I watch him from a distance that's almost surreal, like watching a stranger handle me with reverent care. I don't recognise the empty expression on his face, devoid of anger or envy. In the very least, I'd expected waking to him screaming that I've wrecked Huxley's car. I'm glad he didn't, as my fragile head is on the verge of splitting in two if there happens to be any sudden noise.

He notices me staring but says nothing, continuing to apply gentle pressure to my head. We're sitting on the damp earth, the SUV nearby, its white glossy exterior camouflaged by mud and leaves. A heavy head lies on my lap, the heated breath of Baxter coating my thighs rhythmically. I don't have the energy to stroke him. I'm too focused on remaining upright. My cheek throbs where I feel glass has scraped my skin. My muscles are sluggish from exhaustion, no doubt the drug Wyatt used on me is still fighting to leave my system.

"I hate how easily I forgave you," I croak without any venom. My irritation over that fact has nothing to do with Wyatt and everything to do with myself. It doesn't matter that he was the secret writer of the letters I held dear. All I knew of Wyatt was that he spent years hating me and tormenting me. All the times he's allowed me to feel like I wasn't enough, like I didn't belong. And out of pure desperation, I was so willing to forgive everything for a taste of him. To know what it feels like to be held by him, to have his lips devour mine. "I hate that you make me so weak."

"That makes two of us," he replies softly, avoiding my gaze still. My heart thuds painfully. He could have lied and told me that I dreamt the whole thing. That Meg is safe, surrounded by her friends. But there's no escaping this. Wyatt's fingers lift to hold my chin, holding me in place as he works. "Stop squirming."

I don't know why I do just that, falling limp beneath his hold. I want to be plotting my next move, planning to dash into the shadows and disappear, but my mind can't grasp a thought before the next slips into its place. There's a throbbing pain in my neck which has been there since I woke in Hux's car, and has only intensified with the crash. The more my awareness comes back, the quicker my body sinks into shock, causing my legs to tremble and back to seize tightly.

I shudder, briefly closing my eyes. The image of the boys is there to greet me, the only thing I can hold onto. Axel's hazel eyes, Garrett's boyish smile, Huxley's crossed arms and Dax's quiet confidence. I lean into them, pretending I'm huddled in their arms instead of nestled deep in a thicket of trees under a sky that's teetering between twilight and dawn.

"You're lucky I found this," Wyatt says. I jolt back to reality and realize I was leaning against his shoulder, hindering his reach to my head. He waves at the red cross-emblazoned first aid kit on the ground like some saving grace. He's already covered a cut on his bicep with a slapdash bandage, and the redness around his neck only faintly shows the marks my zip tie left.

"I wouldn't be here if it wasn't for you," I retort, voice rasping as the words slip past my swollen throat. Wyatt's green eyes flash in the dim light.

"You think I wanted to crash? Or that I would choose this?" His voice is low, controlled, but there's something jagged beneath it, barely restrained. "You're not the only one with regrets here, Avery."

And there it is. The mask he pulls on whenever he's cornered. He lifts another cotton ball, disinfectant staining it bright red, and moves closer. His touch is rougher than before, as if he's punishing me away with every swab. I jerk my head back, but his hand on my jaw tightens, refusing to let me turn away.

"Sit still," he grits out. "Unless you'd rather I leave you bleeding in the dirt?"

"Don't pretend you care about me."

"That's all I've ever done!" he blares, and I wince, a throb pulsing through my skull. I waver, almost falling backwards if it weren't for Wyatt's quick grip on my arms. Catching himself, he exhales harshly and releases his hold, testing my balance to remain sitting upright. "You read those letters. You know exactly how I feel."

"Lies," I bite out, glaring at him with every ounce of defiance I have left. "You wrote those to toy with me, just another way to torture me when you weren't around. You knew when I finally found out, I'd be utterly crushed. Congratulations, you've succeeded." Wyatt lets out a mirthless laugh, a single, harsh sound.

"Sure. Whatever you say, Angel."

I clamp my mouth shut, watching his hands with narrowed eyes. I won't let him goad me, and no way in hell will I let him know how much I hate that pet name. Wyatt returns to my temple, carefully placing tape stitches on what feels like a gigantic bump. I look anywhere he isn't. Every tree is nearly gnarled with age, their roots spilling up from the ground like tangled fingers. The tarmac road slices through the treeline, harsh in comparison to the nature that surrounds it.

The crash replayed over and over again in my mind. The moment I lunged, the way his breath hitched when he realized I had him. And now we're stuck in this miserable dance of dependency, each of us too hurt to leave, both too furious to let go.

"The cut isn't too deep," Wyatt says suddenly, his thumb grazing the bruise on my head, "but I don't like the idea of you going to sleep anytime soon. For some reason, Hux's trunk was packed with camping gear. I'll set up a tent and we can rest until you're ready to start walking."

My gaze briefly drifts back to the SUV, also snagging on Huxley's need to hoard camping supplies. Then the memory of the safe house comes rushing back, and I realize he was preparing for the worst. An attack from Fredrick that would cause us to go off grid. Ironically, that's exactly what's happened, but not in the way any of the Souls could have anticipated.

I rip my chin free of Wyatt's hold, every inch of me screaming not to let him see any weakness. "I'm not going to be stuck here with you. I need to get back home. I need to help Meg."

Wyatt's expression shifts, and for a split second, I think I see something break beneath the cold detachment. He recoils, pressing his lips into a thin line, and he begins to pack up the first aid kit. The cold bites harder as his warmth pulls away, leaving only the hollow echo of our shared breath in the stillness. When he finally breaks the silence, his tone is almost resigned.

"Stay with Baxter. I'll look for level ground."

I grit my teeth, every part of me wanting to argue, to run, but fatigue pulls at my limbs, settling into my bones with a relentless ache. The fight drains from me, leaving only raw tension and the dawning reality of our situation. Getting one up on Wyatt seemed like all that mattered in the car, but maybe I should have waited until we were near some sort of civilization.

Curling my arms around Baxter, I half drag us both towards a tree trunk and slump against it. The large hound shifts his way up my body until his warmth seeps into my front, his head on my shoulder. His breathing is easy to mimic, deep, and soothing. I stroke him absentmindedly, my eyes drifting closed.

"Hey!" Wyatt throws a packaged brioche at me. "Eat, and no sleeping!"

Despite Wyatt's orders, I rouse to the feeling of a wet tongue on my uninjured cheek. I come around much slower than usual, lazily blinking upwards to a green tarp covering. Below me, the ground is cushioned by what I imagine are sleeping bags layered on top of one another, a blanket over my front. I shake my head, grumbling at Baxter. The hound retreats, jumping over my body to get to Wyatt instead. I flinch, the low tremor of a headache slicing through me, much to Wyatt's amusement.

"Told you not to go to sleep." His face is now being attacked with long strokes of Baxter's tongue, but he's not brushing them away. He welcomes them, a soft smile on his mouth as he ruffs up the fur around the dog's neck. I lie there, just watching. Am I still asleep? Have I woken up in a different reality, where Wyatt is just a joy-filled guy with a soft spot for mutts? He's certainly never shown the same affiliation for me.

Giggling bubbles from my lips. As if I want Wyatt fawning all over me, calling me a good girl, and fluffing up my hair. The thought gets more ridiculous, and I convince myself I am indeed still asleep. Or dead, possibly dead.

"What's so funny?" Wyatt cuts through my laughter. I don't respond, gently pushing myself up onto my elbows.

A small package lands on my chest with a soft thud, that same brioche bouncing off my blanket before resting on the ground. I stare at it, fingers itching to tear it open even as resentment builds. Wyatt sits in the corner, his green gaze trained as if daring me to ignore him. I want to tell him I don't need his help and that I'd rather starve than accept anything from him. But my stomach betrays me, twisting with the pangs of hunger that have been gnawing at me since we crashed.

Reluctantly, I reach for the brioche, peeling back the wrapper with shaky fingers. It's absurdly sweet, the taste settling like syrup on my tongue, and I try not to imagine him smirking at my compliance. Wyatt watches in silence, releasing his hold on Baxter so that the pup can settle beside him. Large brown eyes track the brioche, a low whine escaping him. Breaking it in half, I feed him whilst altogether ignoring the fact that Wyatt might be hungry too. He made his terrible choices; he can fend for himself.

"Feel better?" Wyatt asks after a beat, his voice a shade gentler.

"Do you want me to thank you or something?" I snap, surprised at the bitterness that laces my tone. He doesn't deserve it, at least not right now, but I can't help it. The anger that simmers beneath the surface refuses to die down, lingering in my veins like a toxic burn. Although who I'm mad at is blurry, and I fear the answer might be myself.

Wyatt only sighs, cracking his neck side to side. "No, Avery. I don't want your thanks." His eyes, normally sharp and calculating, appear reserved as he looks at me, a flicker of something unreadable crossing his face. "I've spent years harboring your hatred for me. I'm not going to shy away from it now."

"Such a martyr," I huff and clench my jaw tight. I can't speak for harboring hatred because I'm a sap for a lost cause, but he's done a fantastic job at fucking with my head. I don't know what I feel for him anymore. I don't know what I want from him, except for the space to pull myself together. An idea begins to take shape in my mind. The same one I started in the car and executed poorly. I need to take back control.

After a few minutes of silence, I shift, pulling myself fully into a half-seated position. Wyatt's eyes track me, wary but calm. "What now?" he mutters, his tone tired. I keep my voice low and casual, forcing myself not to look at him.

"I need to pee," I say simply.

"Seems like Huxley thought of that too." Following Wyatt's gaze, I spot a stack of small boxes beside some heavy-duty torches, each one labeled as a 'personal toilet.' My nose scrunches up, then I scoff out a ridiculous laugh when I realize Wyatt is serious.

"I hardly think we're on peeing in front of each other terms." I watch Wyatt's nostrils flare, dreading what his response might be. Something along the lines of seeing me in many other compromising positions before. The heat hits my cheeks, twinging slightly, but thankfully Wyatt doesn't comment on it. Instead, he shrugs, nodding toward the dense line of trees just outside the tent.

"Fine. But don't take too long. It'll be dark soon," he says. I stutter to a halt.

"Dark?! How long was I out?"

"All day," Wyatt huffs as if I'm a huge inconvenience to him. "Just think, you could have been in a nice warm bed by now if you'd let me take you where we were heading." I don't ask where exactly that is, refusing to let Wyatt bait me.

Keeping my expression blank, I push myself to my feet, carefully testing my balance through the tent, which is easily large enough to sleep six. I don't miss the way Wyatt's eyes track my every move, cautious as ever. Trust will never be something that comes easy with us, and for good reason.

Stepping outside, the cold grips me in its firm hold, stealing a puff of visible air from my mouth. I'm struck by the winter air colliding with a layer of sweat coating my body, thanks to being swaddled in a blanket, sweatpants, and a very familiar orange hoodie. Beyond the cold, my muscles scream in protest, every bruise and scrape from the crash making their presence known. I stumble slightly, exaggerating the limp. Upon glancing back, I note how Wyatt's gaze softens just a fraction before he turns his attention back to Baxter.

My steps start slow. As I reach the tree line, I glance back, ensuring he's preoccupied, before slipping into the cover of the forest. I make sure I'm out of sight before attending to my needs, dignity flying away on the wings of a bird bursting through the branches. I flinch at the sudden sound, righting my clothing and taking a step back towards the tent. Then I pause. It's quiet out here, a frozen moon-coated landscape in the middle of nowhere.

I have no idea where I am, but there's a road cutting through the forest nearby. Roads lead to towns; towns have people. Wyatt intends to walk us towards civilization, no doubt refusing to let me out of his sight for a single second. I'll be his pet without a leash, firmly under his control for as long as I'm in his overbearing presence.

The question is, how much do I trust him? Wyatt has vowed to keep me safe, in his own demented possessive way, but I don't care about staying safe. I care about saving Meg from an evil she doesn't understand. I know Fredrick. I know his ways. His cues. I've spent the last ten years failing to forget them. I survived him once, and I can do it again.

My eyes track the direction the bird flew. Endless tree trunks, a forest floor littered with dead leaves. I don't think. I don't second guess myself. I just bolt.

AVERY

My legs pump as I weave through the dense woodland, the sting of branches slicing at my cheeks barely registering. Every shallow breath claws its way out of my lungs, my head pounding in rhythm with my thundering heart. Along with the rashness of my decision, the forest seems to have come to life and is actively conspiring against me. Roots jut up like traps; shadows play tricks with my eyes. I push through, my only focus being on getting far away. On my only shot at taking back some control.

The forest floor crunches beneath my sneakers, every sound amplified in the silence. I try to lighten my steps, but being stealthy is impossible. Panic claws its way through my straining limbs, unknown traumas from the crash deciding to now present themselves. I become vaguely aware of an insistent tug in my ribs, pain blossoming across my hip on the same side. The side I fell on when the car overturned. It doesn't matter right now. All I can think is, I can't let Wyatt stop me from saving my twin.

Veering right, I sense the road is close. The tree line chasing me comes to a sudden halt up ahead, the stark emptiness beyond that of a manmade design. I don't want to breach it yet, revealing myself to anyone who might come looking, so I just keep moving. Keep running, using the cover of the forest as my camouflage. I can't hear anything beyond the chaotic symphony of my own body. Gasping breaths, racing pulse, blood roaring in my ears. Then, the stillness shatters.

"Avery!" Wyatt's commanding voice echoes through the trees. The sound sends a spike of adrenaline through me. I don't look back. My body screams for rest, every muscle burning, but I force it to keep going, driven by sheer will. Becoming careless, I skid over loose rocks, my footing faltering for a moment before I caught myself. Behind me, the sound of his footsteps grows louder, steadier, and unrelenting.

"You can't outrun me!" Wyatt's voice pierces the air again, closer this time. I duck behind a massive oak, pausing for a split second to press myself against its rough bark. My chest heaves as I try to silence my breathing, to listen past the pounding of my heart. The trees around me hum with an unnatural stillness. Then, just as I think he's lost my trail, I hear the crunch of leaves. Deliberate, careful footsteps, moving closer.

Panic flares white-hot in my chest. In less than a minute, he'll be passing by, seeing me scared and shivering. Wyatt is right; I can't outrun him, but my body doesn't get the memo. I break cover, darting toward a patch of denser trees ahead, the promise of thicker shadows urging me forward. But the open stretch is a trap, every step too exposed. I risk a glance over my shoulder and regret it instantly.

He's right there.

A flash of broad shoulders and clenched fists. Bathed in moonlight, his focus centered on me. A figure cutting through the trees with terrifying ease. His zip hoodie hangs open, flapping like dark wings as he steadily closes the gap. Wyatt is fast, his strides calculated, and his focus unshakable.

Desperation claws at me. I push harder, faster, the undergrowth tearing at my legs. The road ahead looms closer, the thinning trees a cruel betrayal. The choice is to stay in the woods with Wyatt hunting me down or running out into the road and hoping a car isn't going too fast to stop. My lungs burn, my vision blurs, but I won't allow myself to stop. I won't let him win easily.

Behind me, Wyatt has broken into a run. His footsteps thunder, each one louder than the last.

"Don't make this harder than it has to be, Avery," his voice carries, sharp and cutting. I stumble, my foot catching on a twisted root. Pain explodes in my ankle, sharp and unforgiving. A cry rips from my throat as I go down, hitting the dirt hard. For a moment, the world tilts, and I feel the cold bite of hopelessness.

Wyatt's arms wrap around me like steel bands, wrenching me upright. I scream, thrashing wildly, my nails clawing at his arms, but his grip is immovable. He spins me to face him, his eyes blazing like twin emerald fires.

"Enough," he growls, his voice low but carrying the weight of finality. "I'm not your enemy here."

"Yes, you are!" I fight harder, twisting and kicking, but it's like trying to break free of a storm. His hands shift, gripping my wrists and pinning them between us. The first touch of wetness seeps into my cheek. I twist my head aside, desperately trying to free my hands for another reason now. I won't let Wyatt see me cry. Yet he's unmovable, slowly leaning over me. His breath brushes against my ear as he whispers, softer now.

"I'm not letting go." Something in his tone cuts through me, a raw edge that drains the last of my strength. My knees buckle, and he catches me, his hands steadying me as I sag against him, trembling.

"Please," I rasp the plea, my voice shaking as much as my body. "I have to get to Meg. I have to save her." Wyatt sighs, his grip loosening just enough to let me breathe but not escape.

"You know I can't let you do that." His words hang between us, heavy and suffocating. For a long moment, neither of us moves. His forehead rests against mine, the heat of his presence overwhelming. My breath hitches as I realize there's no escape. Not from him, not from whatever this damaged and unnurtured thing is between us.

I almost concede. Until Meg's face flashes before my eyes in the dark. Has he got to her yet? Is she terrified and alone? My jaw aches with the desire to scream until my lungs burn, but I manage to hold it in. Just. Wyatt's hands have loosened on my wrists, the weight of his forehead on me lulling me back to the present. I inhale, count to three, and bring my knee up between his legs. I might not be able to outrun him, but I can hurt him.

Except Wyatt wasn't as unaware as I'd hoped. He jerks back just in time, his hands clenched around my wrists painfully. Those eyes blaze now, furious and somewhat disappointed.

"Fuck you, Wyatt!" I scream into the night, twisting with renewed vigor. I don't stop this time, I give him everything I've got. "You can't keep me prisoner forever."

"I don't need to," he grinds out, his voice winded by my elbow meeting his sternum. "Only until you're safe from harm." On a quick spin, he wrenches my arms behind my back and starts to drag me in the direction of the tent. My feet dig for purchase in the earth, to no avail. My struggles are to my own detriment, wearing me out quickly. I'm doing half the work for him, subduing myself until I'm panting thick clouds of air before my face.

"Why do you choose now to have a moral compass?" I whimper, not receiving an answer. My thrashing isn't as vigorous now, the cold seeping into my bones. Adrenaline subsides, causing my body to be racked by more shivers. The bump on my head refuses to be ignored now, and it begins to throb insistently. I don't want to lean into Wyatt's warmth to feel the heated breath fanning my ear, but I find myself doing it anyway. He's a poison, and I'm addicted.

The silence stretches a thick, oppressive weight between us. Wyatt's grip is firm but no longer bruising. My sneakers skid against the leaves, but the more compliant I become, the more gentle Wyatt is. He turns me to face forward, his hold more like a hug from behind. Each stride of his legs guides mine forward like some kind of dance. As if I'm not relenting to his decisions.

Baxter is pacing around outside the tent, howling and uneasy from the commotion. Wyatt releases one of the arms banded around me to stroke Baxter's head, reassuring him. I'm in half a mind to use the distraction to my advantage, but what's the use? I'll just be dragged back by my hair next time.

Breaching the tent, I expect Wyatt to shove me inside. Instead, his hands grab the hem of the hoodie, and he drags it over my head.

"What the hell are you doing?!" I gasp, slapping his hands away when he reaches for my T-shirt.

"You slipped in a mud patch," he grunts. I blink rapidly, only now noticing the smeared mud over his front. As if nothing happened outside beyond a moonlight stroll for lovers, the corner of his mouth hikes upwards into a smirk. "Plus, I'm going to need your body heat if we're going to make it through the night."

Then he whips my T-shirt up and over my head, quickly shoving down my sweatpants. Luckily, he doesn't seem bothered about removing my underwear because my puckered nipples have everything to do with the cold and nothing to do with him. Baxter tilts his head and whines as if he can detect the lie on me. Dammit.

Leaving me to attend to my sneakers and the rest of the sweatpants now pooled at my calves, Wyatt undresses, tossing our soaked clothes aside. He layers the sleeping bags on top of one another to soften the hard ground and unzips the top one, gesturing for me to get inside.

"Good thinking of Hux to get two-man sleeping bags." He's still smirking, and I feel my nostrils flare. I don't know who I despise more. Morally grey Wyatt or smug bastard Wyatt. A beat of stubbornness passes, my arms crossed over my front. With the fall of night, a blistering cold has settled, rooting itself into my very being. Huffing in defeat, I slip into the quilted sack.

"Don't get any ideas," I narrow my eyes before rolling onto my side. I listen to the double-zipping of the entrance, the rustling of Wyatt settling Baxter into a sleeping bag of his own, and the shuffle of him scooting in behind me. He doesn't hesitate, wrapping his solid arms around me and dragging us together, skin to skin, my back to his front. His crotch is nestled against my ass, a little jolt coming from his cock. "What did I just-"

"Relax, I'm only human. I've had more visceral reactions to spooning Axel."

Like a slice of tension through the air, we both suddenly tense. My eyes sting with unshed tears, the effort to be strong all of a sudden was too taxing for my body. Is Axel having a nightmare right now? Fearing where I am or what's happening? Are the others crowding around to comfort him, or are they arguing over who should have been there, who should have stopped this? It's the not knowing that hurts the most.

Before long, rain patters steadily on the tent's roof, masking some of the noise from the forest. I can still hear the occasional crack of a branch or rustle of leaves carried on a light wind. It seems like the world is at war with itself, while my mind does the same. Every second that passes, I feel like I shouldn't be here. I should be out there doing something productive. But the thought of moving again so soon causes my limbs to weigh heavier into the makeshift mattress Wyatt has made for us.

"I left a note," Wyatt murmurs quietly, like a confession meant only for the rain to hear. His voice disarms me for a moment. "I told them it's best this way. That I'd look after you until it's safe to return."

The weight of the blanket suddenly feels like it's made of lead. His chest rises and falls in a controlled rhythm that contrasts sharply with my own erratic breathing. His calmness infuriates me, despite the way I try to mimic it. To channel it. Swallowing against my head, Wyatt chooses his words carefully.

"And I'd really like to keep that promise, if you wouldn't mind pressing pause on running away or trying to get us killed." Oh yes, his words were delivered so gently, yet they've sparked something sharp in me. I glare at the tent's rippling wall.

"Why should I make any of this easy on you?" I huff a bitter laugh, caught up on his audacity. He's making out this is all my fault, my choice. As if I wasn't blindsided, drugged, stuffed into the SUV against my will, and catapulted into who-knows-where.

Wyatt leans back slightly, his hands braced on my hips. I ignore how warm they feel and the large span of his palms that I've craved to pass over my body for a long time. Longer than I care to admit.

"That's fair," he says at last, devoid of his usual edge. Silence falls over us once more, the rain filling the void like a metronome to our shared tension. After a while, I convince myself he's fallen asleep. His heart beats against my back. His limbs are perfectly curled into mine, lending as much warmth as he is taking. A small yawn tugs at my mouth, and I allow my eyelids to droop at last.

"Would it help if I told you I tried to offer myself to Fredrick first?"

The whisper jolts my eyes back open. Nothing in Wyatt's position has changed, not even a twitch of his fingers. His breathing is level, and his heart rate has the same annoying steadiness. I must have dreamt it. A trick of my mind, constantly trying to redeem Wyatt. The biggest form of self-sabotage I've ever experienced, I think to myself as I let the draw of sleep pull me back under again. As if Wyatt would take Meg's place. As if he would sacrifice himself for me.

WYATT

CHAPTER FOUR

I lie still until Avery's breathing evens out, soft and steady against my chest. I hold her until I no longer have a convincing reason to, until sharing warmth is no longer a justification to keep my hands on her flawless skin.

She doesn't stir. If she heard me, she doesn't show it. It doesn't matter either way. My confession doesn't reverse the damage I've done. The harm that lurks in the quiet, that manifests in the dark corners of my mind, curls its fingers around my throat like the bind I can never escape.

Avery may be safe here with me, but that safety is a fragile illusion I've stolen. Ripped from the hands of men who once called me brother. They won't take me back now. I burned those bridges to ash when I stole their girl.

She wasn't even supposed to become one of us, and damn, I tried to prevent it. I've betrayed her trust more times than she can comprehend. I've sabotaged her happiness in the name of protecting her, when really, it was just about keeping her for myself. A woman I never planned to pursue but couldn't watch my men seduce her either. Selfishness. Pure selfishness.

The tent walls feel smaller with every passing second. The air becomes heavier. A shiver shudders down my spine, and I instinctively know he's back. I don't turn my head, already knowing what I'll see. A figment of Ray, his body shifting and warping like smoke. He rarely has a face, but those pale eyes haunt me regardless. I suppose it goes hand in hand with how far my sanity is slipping on any given day. He doesn't speak, as he never does. He only watches. Waiting. Expecting.

Since Avery burst into my room and decided sedating her was the best option, Ray has been distant. It's as if my focus on her blocks him out. Yet, the longer I'm with her, the less comforting his presence feels. Imagining him doesn't bring me any closer to the man I didn't get a proper chance to know. It's become a twisted mockery of what he never had. I grip Avery tighter. She's real. The only thing that's ever felt real.

The shadow pulses as it closes in, causing the air to grow colder. I try to blink back the image, knowing that it's not real, but a clawed hand reaches toward Avery's sleeping form regardless, hovering just above the bare shoulder that's slipped free of the cover. My breath hitches.

Not her.

I shove the words down, refuse to speak them aloud. I won't give this broken part of my mind that much power. But the weight of its presence presses on my chest, drumming against my ribs like a war cry. Avery shifts slightly in my arms, murmuring something unintelligible in her sleep. I focus on her warmth, on the rise and fall of her breath. On the way her fingers twitch against my arms.

She belongs to me.

The shadow recoils, twisting in on itself and writhing like a dying flame. I don't let go of Avery. Not even when my limbs start to shake. I won't let anything or anyone take her from me.

When I brave a look over my shoulder, I find that we're alone once more. The only shadows lurking around the tent are the ones cast through the gnarled fingers of trees outside, bathed in moonlight. I suck in a sharp breath, squeezing my eyes shut. The tent is calm again, and Avery is still safe in my arms. The air isn't thick with rot and regret, but resignation. Deep down, I seem to know that he isn't coming back. Ray is gone, but I don't mourn his loss this time. I just hold Avery closer, tethering myself to her world. The one I keep falling further and further away from.

One thing is for certain. Things have changed. Just as Avery molded herself into our small family like she was always supposed to be there, she's infiltrated my being. Forced her way in, revealing fissures I didn't know I had. Issues I'd been too comfortable to ignore, but have now been brought to the lift where I'll have to deal with them.

These thoughts tumble through my mind for what feels like hours, to the point where I don't know if I'm awake or asleep. Usually, when I'm plagued this way, I would be hunched over a notepad, writing until my mind was empty. Avery doesn't even know the worst of it. She's only seen a tiny fraction of the words I write. The polished, finessed versions. And now that she knows I'm the man she calls Mr. XO, she won't accept any more of my letters. She won't listen to my words. I'm stuck with them.

I've never appreciated it. The form of therapy, the mental release. Like siphoning the poison from my brain. In the wilderness, holding the woman of my darkest desires and knowing she's never been further away, I withhold a bitter, self-directed laugh. She was never supposed to see me like this. Raw and unmasked. She was supposed to see *him*—the version of me I could never truly become. The man she imagined I was.

But there's no hiding anymore. No pen and paper to shield me. Just this crushing, unbearable truth. I love her more than I hate myself, and that terrifies me. Because there are no lengths that I won't go to to ensure she lives another day. I need her alive to keep punishing me, to keep reminding me of the shit I've done.

Apologies won't take back Meg's identity. Letters can't prevent the damage I've caused. Words can't convince Avery that it was the only way to protect her. None of these words matter anymore.

Words are empty without action, and my actions are unforgivable.

AVERY

CHAPTER FIVE

The sun filters through the barren canopy above, gnarled branches causing the dappled light to cast patterns across the forest floor. We left at the buttcrack of dawn, actively ignoring the way we woke up. I'd turned in the night and draped myself over Wyatt's body with my face in the crook of his neck. I didn't have time to be mortified at my drool against his skin because my hand was gripping his cock through his boxers. What's even worse is that he was hard and responsive to every twitch of my fingers.

Not thinking about it. Nope, no thank you. A quick change into our hastily packed sweats and a few cubes of gum shoved into my mouth, and we were out of there.

A caw sounds overhead, a crow igniting my jealousy with its ability to fly off into the wilderness. Shouldering my pack higher, I try to distribute the weight of supplies evenly. My legs ache, my back protests, and the damp chill that had evaded me overnight has returned with a vengeance. What I'd give to eat something that isn't a packaged brioche.

Ahead of me, Wyatt trudges along, his broad shoulders squared as though the strain of his pack doesn't bother him. He's managed to shake the foul mood he woke up in, claiming to have had a nightmare, but I would honestly rather he was pissed off because I am. I'm sore and tired, the little sleep I had doing nothing to revitalize me, and looking at him soldering on with infuriating ease is making my headache even worse. Baxter trots between us, his tail wagging, seemingly oblivious to the tension radiating from me.

"Would it kill you to slow down?" I snap, swatting at a low-hanging branch before it smacks me in the face. Wyatt glances over his shoulder, his expression as bored as ever.

"Would it kill you to keep up? I thought ballerinas were meant to have stamina." I glare daggers at the back of his head, my steps quickening just enough to draw level with him.

"And I thought basketball players were meant to be about team spirit. I must say, my morale is scraping across the ground beneath my sneakers right now."

"Would a pep talk stop you from whining?" Wyatt smirks, the kind that makes me want to throw something at him.

I open my mouth to retort but am interrupted by Baxter letting out a low bark. He bounds ahead, his nose to the ground, tail wagging furiously. Wyatt and I exchange a glance before following him, my boots crunching over dry leaves and twigs. It's the most excitement we've had all morning, and for a brief, fleeting moment, I dare to hope Baxter's found something useful. A sign telling us where we are perhaps? Anything to signal the end of this endless sea of trees.

Instead, we find him pawing at a moss-covered log, thoroughly enthralled by a family of ants. I sigh, rubbing at the bridge of my nose.

"You must be hungry, old boy. We'll get you some food soon." Wyatt crouches beside the dog, scratching behind his ears. I drop my pack with a dramatic thud, crossing my arms.

"Will we, though? You have no idea how far we are from anywhere," I sigh, planting my hands firmly on my hips. There I go, straight back to whining, apparently. Wyatt straightens, towering over me as his smirk fades into something sharper, more serious.

"We just need to keep following the road." He growls, his eyes quickly dropping to my split lip and then up again. My gaze strays to the left, where I know the road to be at the top of a grassy back. I'm not sure why we have to navigate the uneven forest rather than walk along the smooth tarmac, but alas, Wyatt is in charge. For now.

Tilting my head back, I look at him properly for the first time today. His eyes are a darker green today, shrouded by the dark circles surrounding them. His ruffled hair is desperately lacking the styling products he would normally use, but that doesn't detract from his overall appeal. To someone else, not me. I couldn't give two shits that his head is tilting forward, bringing his sharp nose and occasional smirks closer to my level. Or that the smudge of dirt on his jaw could be considered endearing.

"Lead the way. I don't want to have to camp out here another night." My voice cracks, an unwelcome memory surfacing at that moment. Wyatt must have the exact same one, because his eyes flash and a sharp inhale is drawn through his parted lips. *Fuck.* Is it too much to ask the universe to make him ugly? It would make my life so much easier if I could hate him without my libido popping up to say hi every time he looks at me.

Wyatt strides away, and Baxter nudges my leg, breaking through my thoughts. I let out a shaky breath, reaching down to ruffle his fur.

"Come on then," I mutter, grabbing my pack and hoisting it onto my shoulders. Wyatt has stalled by a trunk, casually waiting for me to catch up this time, rather than trailing me around on an invisible leash. I stop to tilt my head up and ask him something that's been on my mind. A simple hope I hadn't dared voice, but whether I like it or not, Wyatt is currently my only companion.

"Do you think, if we're out here long enough, Nixon might come looking for me?" My voice is small, careful not to insinuate that Nixon might look for him too. Regardless, Wyatt chuckles under his breath and we fall into step along the uneven ground.

"I don't know if you've realized," he muses, shoving his hands into the pockets of his sweatpants, "but Nixon doesn't give a shit about you anymore." His words slam into me harder than the cold ever could. My steps falter with the cracking of twigs.

"Of course he does," I frown, irritation flaring back to the surface. It's as if Wyatt is always searching for the easiest way to piss me off and he succeeds every damn time. His eyes roll, landing on me with a condescending tilt to his head.

"Nixon practically signed your death warrant when he forced you to join Waversea. If he was really concerned about your safety, he'd have sent you straight to that pretty little safe house. Not enroll you in a school where your name was listed on the registry for anyone to find."

My sneakers scuff against a moss-covered root as my mind whirls, a string of weak protests leaving my lips. Wyatt doesn't bother backtracking to save my feelings. He never does.

"There's something I can't dispute," Wyatt rolls his shoulders, as if his next words might pain him. "And that's Nixon's love for his wife. Cathy shattered him when she had that affair, and despite the many he had in retaliation, he loved her endlessly." His breath clouds in the cold air as he exhales. "I've thought long and hard about the day they brought you home, and the sudden shift in Nixon's demeanor. You gave them hope. A reason to try and be a real family again. And I do think they got that, at least for a while. The Christmas portraits were practically sickening to receive each year."

I sense, rather than see, the eye roll that follows, Wyatt's voice dripping with disgust. But I don't stop him, savoring the truth from his perspective at long last.

"I know you won't like hearing this," he mutters, stepping over a fallen branch, "but Nixon's love for you died when Cathy did." The words punch through my chest, hollowing me out from the inside. "You remind him of her betrayal. Of the very man who killed her and has been chasing you ever since. He's tried to protect your feelings, all while pushing you away. I'd consider it his parting gift if I were you." Wyatt's pace remains steady, his voice unwavering. "It's a much softer approach than he took with me."

A small rock rolls behind my shoe and I lurch sideways, directly into Wyatt's arms. He stares down at me, so many secrets hidden within his emerald eyes. My fingers tighten around the sleeve of his hoodie.

"You know exactly where he is, don't you?"

The branches overhead whisper the answer Wyatt refuses to give me in the breeze. The damp earth shifts beneath my sneakers as I right myself, pushing away from his hold. With it, Wyatt takes the little warmth I had. I decide to drop the topic, refocusing on walking and getting the hell out of here.

The day stretches on, the monotony of the forest broken only by our occasional bickering and Baxter's enthusiastic detours. It's taxing, both physically and mentally, but it's better than the silence. Silence gives me too much time to think about the time we're wasting. About what could be happening to Meg, what the Souls are doing. I suppose that's what caused me to start an argument about the fact Die Hard is *not* a Christmas movie.

"You clearly haven't seen it," Wyatt tries to brush me off.

"I have seen it, and I stand by my opinion." I hold my head high, stepping over a twisted root crossing our path.

"The soundtracks are Christmas songs. It takes place at a Christmas party, for fuck's sake! It's a Christmas movie." Wyatt quickly sounds exasperated, his hands flicking out in a stressed movement. I find I'm quite enjoying how easy it is to rattle him.

"It's an action movie, which, for your information, was actually released in July. No one releases a Christmas movie in July."

"There's snow at the end! John McClane's wife is called Holly-"

"Shh," I hold up my hand.

"Did you just *shush* me?"

"Shhh!" I say again, putting my hand in front of his face. "Listen!" I stop mid-step, my ears straining to catch onto the foreign sound. It's faint beneath the rustling leaves and distant bird calls, but it's there. A low rumble in the distance. My heart leaps.

"A car!" I gasped, the word exploding from me like an answered prayer. "Wyatt, we're saved!" Without waiting for him, I lunge forward, dropping my pack to scramble up the muddy bank. I'll pick up my stuff later. For now, I just need to stop that damn car and put an end to this torture.

My hands claw at the earth, dirt packing under my nails as I drag myself higher, desperate to reach the road before the sound fades. The rumbling grows louder, fueling my adrenaline. Salvation is so close I can taste it.

Then, out of nowhere, a crushing weight slams into my back, driving me face-first into the slick ground. The impact knocks the wind clean out of me, and before I can process what's happening, Wyatt has me pinned in a full-body hold. He drags us both down the slope, away from the road, away from the sound, away from help.

"What the actual hell, Wyatt?" I wheeze, writhing beneath him like a live wire. He flips me over and claps a hand over my mouth before I can say anything else. His green eyes lock on mine, wild and frenzied, an edge of something that almost looks like fear. The sound of the car grows deafening, and I freeze beneath him. My mind races. This isn't just panic. It's something worse. The vehicle roars past above us, the noise receding as quickly as it came, leaving us alone in the suffocating silence of the forest.

I go limp, the fight bleeding out of me. Only then does Wyatt release his hold, his chest heaving with effort as he retreats, putting distance between us.

"What was that?" I demand, pushing myself upright.

"Nothing," he replies too quickly, rushing to collect our discarded bags from the ground. I close the gap between us, shoving his shoulder.

"No, seriously. What is going on? Why wouldn't you let me hitch a ride to the closest town?"

"We don't know who's in that car," Wyatt cuts in, voice clipped. His back is to me now as he shoulders both of our bags, his movements jerky and tense. I narrow my eyes.

"Who do *you* think was in that car?" My tone is slower now, deliberate, as I stalk after him. Baxter is whining, brushing up against Wyatt's leg and looking up at him for comfort. The following silence is thick; Wyatt's expression pulled taut. I watch the tick in his jaw beat several times while he struggles with his own thoughts. Tentatively, I reach a hand out and place it on his bicep. "Wyatt, who are we running from?"

"Everyone," he says without taking his eyes from the ground. Strolling towards a thick, fallen trunk, Wyatt drops down, pressing the heels of his palms into his eyes. I ease down beside him, my chest seizing painfully.

"When I met with Fredrick, he wasn't alone. There was a whole room of thugs, ex-convicts," Wyatt sighs, dropping his hands. "Fredrick spoke of owing favors and losing control. He said his men were becoming restless, and if he didn't get a resolution, they would start acting out. They were bored of the cat and mouse. They wanted..."

"What did they want?" I ask quietly, edging closer.

"They wanted to take you for themselves. I saw the gleam in their eyes, Avery." Wyatt finally turns his head to look at me, his eyes swimming with defiance and misery. "I will not let them have you."

"And even now that you... that they possibly have Meg, do you think I'm in danger?" My pulse thunders in my ears, and Baxter lays his head on my thigh. Wyatt's stare is unmoving, unnerving, as I swallow hard.

"I do." He nods slowly. Suddenly, I'm on high alert. Every crack of a branch, every flap of a bird's wing. My eyes dart around the forest as if I'm in enemy territory, and I shuffle in closer to Wyatt. He tracks the movement, staring at the spot where my arm is now pressed against his, but he doesn't comment on it.

Somewhere amongst this new information is the sinking reality I don't want to face. Wyatt's arm shifts, resting over my back and opening his body to me. It's a simple gesture that I accept, while the small voice in my mind screams even louder.

"You were always going to take me away, weren't you? The sedative... you had it all ready." I piece it together like broken fragments of a puzzle. The resulting picture is framed by Wyatt short huff.

"Not as ready as I'd have liked. If you hadn't burst in, I could have finished my letter to the Souls explaining everything. I could have packed your belongings. I thought I had at least until morning."

"You were telling them the truth?" I plead, begging for something to hold onto. I don't want Wyatt to always be my villain. Fuck knows I've tried my hardest to paint him as anything but. He gives a single, jerky nod, and my whole world spins.

This wasn't some last resort Wyatt thought up on the spot—to whisk me away from the ones I love because that's simply who he is. The man who can't stand to see me happy.

No. I see him clearly now. Every sharp word, every secretive glance, every maddeningly frustrating decision. It was never about control. It was fear. It was a desperate man drowning in his own darkness, willing to burn his bridges and break his bonds just to keep me alive. To keep me safe. In that aspect, he is the same as the rest of the Souls, despite his actions being less than favorable.

I search his face for something, anything, to suggest this is another one of his cruel jokes, but there's nothing there—just raw, unfiltered conviction. Wyatt just watches me, his face like stone. The realization is suffocating. He's sacrificed so much—his loyalty, his crew, maybe even Meg—all for me. And the sickest part? He doesn't even expect me to forgive him.

He doesn't care if I hate him, as long as I live.

My chest tightens, and my hand instinctively grips the fabric of my shirt, desperate to anchor myself to reality. Baxter whimpers again, his head pressing into my thigh as though he can feel the storm brewing inside me.

"Wait. My...my belongings," I whisper, playing his words back on a loop. Beyond the sentiment, I see the cracks now. I see the fear that lingers just beneath the surface, the way Wyatt's fingers twitch against his knees. Parting my dry lips, my voice cracks as if saying the words will seal my fate. "You make it sound like I'm never going back."

A low, heavy sigh escapes him as he pulls me closer. My face leans into the rise and fall of his chest, into the tender kiss he places on my head. I know it's coming, but if I bury myself into his body, perhaps I'll be saved from hearing it. Or at least, save myself from Wyatt's probing stare when the first tear escapes my eye.

"Avery. You're never going back."

WYATT

CHAPTER SIX

Despite Avery's reservations, I wasn't lying when I told her tonight would be colder than before. I could sense it as night fell. The sweat coating my skin quickly became a straightjacket, encasing me with the bitter cold biting at my limbs. And with the blanket of darkness came another set of problems involving the lack of sight and the stirring of nocturnal creatures. It was time to stop, even if we desperately wanted to keep going.

Now I'm lying in that darkness, actively listening to the broken silence beyond the walls of the tent. Avery is facing away from me, curled in the sleeping bag with her back pressed against my front. She didn't fight me this time. I know my admission has rattled her, but it's better this way. At least she won't keep trying to run off and jump into a random vehicle just to get away from me.

I slip into a light daze, my thoughts growing muffled. Avery's hair tickles my nose, the curve of her back following the length of my torso. She has no right to feel this good after two days of being stranded in the middle of nowhere. I made a vow with my dick to behave tonight, but she isn't helping.

My stomach rumbles, a hollow sound that can't be filled with brioches and protein bars. We need real food. Even though we've been walking all day with exhaustion weighing us down more than the bottled water on my back, and we've covered a huge distance, it wasn't quite far enough. Tomorrow. We'll reach civilization tomorrow.

A soft whimper sounds within the tent. I suck in a breath, instantly on alert. It wasn't Baxter, who's quietly snoozing in his own sleeping bag in the corner. It sounds again, punctuated with shallow and erratic breathing. Avery's body shudders, small tremors rolling through her frame as if she's fighting something invisible. Shallow, uneven gasps slip through faint, broken whimpers. Her hands clutch at the sleeping bag, tightening and loosening in a rhythm that mirrors her jerky movements.

She shifts against me, her legs kicking slightly, as if trying to run but unable to get away. The barrier stopping her is my arm curled around her middle. She scratches at my skin, throwing her head back and forth.

"Avery?" I whisper, giving her a small shake. To push myself up, I have to withdraw my arm from beneath her head, and this makes her nightmare worse. "Avery," I try again, leaning over her trembling frame, probably exactly like the monster of her nightmare is currently doing.

"I don't..." Her lips mumbling, forming words I can't quite hear but can feel. The look on her face, pinched and desperate, sends a shiver down my own spine.

"Avery, it's Wyatt."

"Wyatt," she mutters, and her voice trembles. "I don't want... I don't want you." Swallowing hard, I breathe against the sudden slice of pain that slams into me. Lowering my gaze, I absentmindedly stroke her damp hair.

"I know, Angel." I continue to stroke her, trying to comfort her through the subconscious hell she's been dragged into. No matter how many times she jostles or how many times she tells me she doesn't want me, I don't push away. I can handle the pain, just about. But it's the weight of her distress that presses down on me. The drive to stop her from hurting that brings on the sharp, undeniable urge to pull her out of it, to make it stop.

"Avery, wake up." I say roughly, a command she can't deny. Her eyes fly open, wide and disoriented, as she sucks in a sharp breath. For a second, she looks like she doesn't know where she is or who I am, but then her gaze locks on mine, and some of the panic ebbs away.

"Wyatt," she whispers, her voice trembling. "What happened?" Everything taut and raging inside of me stalls, a frozen abyss while she's looking at me like that. Not like the monster. Not her villain, but her hero. She's quick to blink away the admiration, shutting down before me. It takes every shred of my control to not crash my lips against hers—anything to bring that look back. To rid myself of her rejection.

"Hey," I say softly instead. "You're okay. It was just a bad dream."

Her breathing is still uneven, and she doesn't move. Tension holds her jaw prisoner, her hands clutching the edge of the sleeping bag like it's the only thing keeping her tethered. Her eyes are sunken, her skin too ashy. We must reach civilization tomorrow. There's no other option.

"You want to talk about it?" I ask gently, even though I know she won't. Avery's not the type to open up unless you pry the truth from her. She shakes her head, confirming my suspicion. Instead, I lie back, wrestling with the pounding of my heart. There will be no sleeping for either of us now, but I can at least give Avery a distraction. Shift her focus onto something else.

"What do you see in the guys?" I ask casually, my voice even. I feel Avery's interest pique, her head twisting upwards. After a beat, she rolls onto her back too, finding my arm beneath her head again.

"Why?" she probes. I smile in the dark. Avery is anything but easy, and damn if I don't enjoy the fight.

"I'm just curious, that's all. They're just as fucked up and damaged as... Well, me. What attracted you to them?" There's a double meaning somewhere within my words, one I didn't intend, but I can't take it back now. Avery exhales harshly through her nose.

"Well, for starters, they have never tried to scare me, harm me, or actively spent years pushing me away."

"I've never tried to harm you," I instantly bite back. My brows furrow as I quickly catalogue the past few months. Avery snorts a laugh.

"Oh yeah? What about the Fall Ball? You literally pressed a blade against my thigh." I wince, scrunching my eyes and nose tightly. Swallowing, I toy with my response, wondering if she'll even believe me.

"I'm fairly certain someone spiked my drink that night," I answer in a small voice. One that causes Avery's ears to strain for the rest of my confession. "I felt fine, although admittedly a bit pissed off, when I went outside. Next thing I know, I'm waking up in bed with flashes of what happened. Your body pressed against mine, the way you looked up at me, even when I felt the knife in my hand and you were pressing closer. You're so...defiant."

I struggle against those images now. How willing Avery was to take whatever pain I gave her, believing it's what I desired. I've never wanted anything less, but the reaction of my body to that memory shames me. Those huge blue eyes dilated, consuming me whole. Her parted lips and flushed cheeks. She looked beyond beautiful that night anyway, but those few snippets I remember—she was exquisite. It led to many dreams of knife and blood play that I refuse to think about right now, with her heat pressed against me, lost in the woods.

"Anyways," I clear my throat, "I felt fucking terrible, so I got those compression socks you needed. I'd overheard you talking about them on the phone. Do you know the kind of ads I still get after searching for 'petite ballet compression socks near me'?" I finger quote in the air despite her not being able to see me. She can feel the shift in my bicep though. "Not to mention, I have to duck my head walking through the local high street now. The sales girl in the uniform store thinks we're best friends."

Avery stifles a tiny laugh. My chest explodes at the sound, yearning for more of it. For once, it's not her hatred and her tears. Smiling to myself, I huff a short laugh, replaying that night in my mind.

"I watched you dance for a while in the studio. You get so lost in your head, you didn't even notice I was there, and when you were stretching, I snuck the socks into your bag and got the fuck back home before anyone noticed. Then you came bursting into the frat house, telling me you're being stalked, and I just... left it at that. It was easier that way."

She's quiet now, listening intently. Thinking too hard. Licking my lips, I wrestle for something else to add, just to fill the void of my heart bleeding out. Luckily, Avery beats me to it.

"I thought the piano guy was trying to kill me," Avery breathes. It's my turn to force my chuckle to stay down.

"Theo? Nah, he's a nice guy. I was his partner in Business Studies last year." It's the truth; Theo is a nice guy, and it helps that he's scared shitless of me. He's been texting me updates of Avery's movements and moods for months.

Although he completely left out the fact Avery had a male partner for the Winter showcase, which caught me by surprise while I was sitting in the audience. I don't care that he is gay. He had fingers trailing all over her thighs and her ribs. He lifted her at one point, keeping her elevated by a hand on her crotch, and I saw red. Everything that followed in the dressing room had as much to do with removing his touch from Avery's skin, as it did with punishing myself for being so jealous.

"Well, as it turned out, I was being stalked. Just not by you." Avery sighs, shifting the mood. My heart slowly sinks, growing heavier by the second.

The way I handled Avery's concerns was naive. I thought, since she was safe from me revealing myself, there was no need to fret. I brushed off her concerns and let the Souls pander to her every whim. But I was wrong. I should have looked a little closer and realised she was in danger earlier. Long before Hux was shot. But that would have meant getting closer to her, and I couldn't afford to do that. I couldn't let her uncover my secrets and discover just how much I craved her. How possessive I can be.

Now that's all gone to shit.

"I miss home," Avery murmurs into the dark, her voice cracking slightly.

"Me too," I admit quietly, my voice rough with fatigue. "More than you know." Instinctively, my arm tenses beneath her head, the desire to drag her close taking over. I manage to keep myself in check until Avery whispers, "Do it."

I move before I've fully decided if it's for the best. Draping my arm over her waist, my hand settles on the warm fabric of her T-shirt. Avery's abdomen shifts, adjusting to my weight; I'm now wrapped around her lithe body. Avery will never understand how something so simple can steady the storm inside me, just a little.

Avery shifts, twisting her face into the crook of my neck. Her fingers brush over my chest, tentative and unsure. It's dangerous territory we're treading, whether through desperation for comfort or, dare I believe, that she might have forgiven me. Just a little bit. It's more than I expected. More than I thought I'd ever get from her. I can take the sex—the mindblowing, incredible sex—while still keeping myself protected. This is different.

All bets are off now. I'm exposed. My feelings are known. And god, I don't think I've ever spoken so much in one day. Not even to the Souls. They talk to me and around me, but I tend to keep my thoughts to myself. Keep the barrier up so no one can slip inside. Well, here comes Avery with her sledgehammer. My barrier is a pile of rubble now, and my heart feels like it's going to beat out of my chest.

"So," I play with my tongue between my teeth, "back to my earlier question. I truly want to know what you see in the Souls." Avery lifts her head slightly, glimpsing my profile through the shadows. I can't see her eyes, but I imagine them large and unblinking. "Humor me."

"I just think they're perfect." She shrugs, lowering back down against my neck. A shift against my collarbone gives the impression of a small smile creeping onto her face. "Damaged, yes, but perfect still. Axel is so beautiful, inside and out. He's precious, you know? You just want to protect him from the world, but you also need to give him the freedom to live."

I close my eyes, inhaling against Avery's hair. My chest swells at her description of Axel and how she sees him. Of how protective yet understanding she is of him. I don't respond; I just listen.

"And he has to be like that, because only someone truly incredible could bring Garrett out of himself. Garrett is hilarious. Considering these past few months have probably been the worst of my life, they've also been the best. He makes me laugh, but he also challenges me to look deeper beneath the surface. People can shrug him off or think he's just full of shit, but when I'm with Garrett... I just know everything is going to be okay."

She's right again. I'm floored by how perceptive Avery is, and I want to hear more.

"And Hux?"

"Huxley struck me as quite basic when I first met him. That stereotypical jock, maybe a bit shallow. He's had a rough time, and I know he wouldn't have been injured if it wasn't for me bringing out family drama his way. But I'm glad I could be with him in his recovery. He's so strong, yet so stubborn. He tries to battle his demons alone, but it's the moments when he cracks and lets me help; that's when I feel the most connected to him. We've built a bond through his struggles. His willingness to fight, and to fight for me, shows me what kind of man he really is. I'm indebted to him, but that's not why I fell for him."

A trickle of emotion rolls through my spine. I can't name exactly what it is, but it's a visceral reaction to the admiration in Avery's voice. The depths of what she feels. Any pretence I had of her surface-level feelings has been shattered.

"And then there's Dax," Avery breathes, the smile evident in her voice. I don't need to hear the rest; it's evident in the way she speaks. In the way she sighs, "I love Dax."

I don't say anything; just adjust the sleeping bag around us and let the silence settle again. Her hand presses lightly against my chest, and for once, I don't think about how awkward it is or how much I shouldn't enjoy this moment. I just let her drift into a peaceful state, keeping watch over her in the dark. I toy with my final question for a while, unsure if I'm pushing my luck. If I really want the answer. In the end, my willingness for self-sabotage wins out.

"Dare I ask... what do you see in me?" Avery hums lightly, rousing to look up at my jaw. The movement presses her chest further into my side, the entire length of her touching some part of my body. I swallow and press forward, somewhat awkwardly. "You're cuddling up to me, despite being here against your will. There must be a reason."

The question lingers in the air, and for a moment, Avery doesn't answer. Her breathing evens out, soft and steady against my neck, but I know she's not asleep. I feel her body tense slightly, her fingers brushing absent patterns over my heart, and I wonder if she's stalling or just doesn't know how to frame her answer. Each second of silence feels like a weight pressing down on my chest, compressing my ribs until the quiet isn't just uncomfortable; it's unbearable. I regret asking, wanting to take it back.

"You really want me to answer that?" Avery asks, her voice low, almost fragile.

"Yeah," I lie, too far gone to leave it alone now. The answer can't be good. I'm just the guy who's trapped her here, a means to survive. The outsider. The interloper. The one who took her away from everything she cares about under the guise of protection. The Souls have her love, her trust, and her admiration.

I let the silence stretch between us again, suffocating and heavy, while Avery settles back against me. Her body fits perfectly against mine, but the space between us feels like a chasm. I clench my jaw, staring into the darkness. I have no right to be mad; I've done all of this to myself. But then she speaks, sending me into a spiral for the remainder of the night.

"Well... for some reason, even though I hate that I still believe it, I see potential in you, Wyatt. I can't bring myself to think you're beyond redeemable."

I hold my jaw in a squared position, a numbness creeping through my face and spreading south. I might be having an epitome or a seizure, but I don't let it show outwardly. She thinks I'm redeemable after everything I've done. After the hurt I've caused. I close my eyes, pushing the unfurling emotions aside with one single thought left in mind.

We must reach civilization tomorrow. For her, we have to.

AVERY

Deja Vu carries me through the forest. The sun still filters through the trees in patches, those same patterns tracing the leaf-ridden ground. Our supplies are lighter today, a vague reminder that they're starting to run low. My legs still ache, my stomach growls with hunger, and my feet are blistered from miles of trudging over uneven ground, but none of it feels as hopeless as before. Because Wyatt is openly talking to me.

"Your hair's a mess," Wyatt teases, his voice breaking through the quiet. I throw him a glare, and he nudges my shoulder.

"Thanks for the update," I shoot back, a grin tugging at my lips. He's as disheveled as I am, maybe more. His shirt is rumpled, his jaw covered in scruff, and his hair is pointing in about six different directions. "You're just annoyed you woke up spooning the dog instead of me."

I hold his gaze, referencing how I slipped out of the tent this morning to pee, and Baxter promptly took my place in the sleeping bag. Wyatt got a mouthful of fur as he whispered secret words into Baxter's ear. I wish I knew what he said.

After a moment, a full-bodied laugh escapes Wyatt, scaring away the nearby birds. It shocks me too. I'm treading this newfound commodore as tentatively as the snaking roots camouflage across the forest floor. He lightly shoves at my arm, seeming to find these excuses to touch me, playfully telling me to shut up. Setting his green eyes ahead, I allow myself another moment to look him over. He appears different today. Lighter, somehow.

We continue on, minutes turning into hours, the day becoming more lost than we are. My feet are dragging; my calves have long gone numb. Leaning against a tree trunk, I open my mouth to demand a break when a distant noise gives me pause. Instead, a raspy croak of my dry throat causes me to cough. Wyatt looks back, retracing his steps to hand me a bottle of water from his pack. I wave him away, signalling to the air. Baxter heard it too, his ears pricked high.

"Did you hear that?" I rasp, my voice still rough. Wyatt freezes, his head tilting slightly as he listens. The forest seems to hold its breath. Then the sound comes again, faint but unmistakable. His eyes lock on mine, and I see the same spark of hope flaring to life in his expression. Far away, a carhorn blares, and another responds.

"We made it?" Wyatt asks quietly, like he's afraid saying it too loudly might scare the sound away.

I'm already pushing off the tree, exhaustion forgotten. My legs carry me forward faster than they have all day, weaving between the trees. Wyatt is right behind me, his sneakers crunching the undergrowth, and Baxter barks once, dashing ahead as though he knows exactly where to go. If the horns blare again, I wouldn't know since my pulse is thundering in my ears.

We don't stop until the trees thin out and then halt altogether, our aching feet stumbling onto a paved sidewalk. Before us, lines of buildings border parallel roads that all lead to a large church in the town's center.

"We fucking made it!" I shout, excitement bubbling over. A few people look up from their local businesses, wide-eyed and wary of the dirty, disheveled couple who have appeared seemingly out of nowhere. Baxter trots back towards us, rubbing against Wyatt's leg while his tail wags vigorously. He leans down, ruffling Baxter's fur.

"Good boy," Wyatt mutters, his voice low but tender. I stall, waiting for Wyatt to lead the way, but instead, he straightens and turns to me. A flicker of indecision crosses his face, and then his arms are banding around me in a crushing hug. I don't even consider my own arms wrapping around his body; they just do.

"You did good too, Avery." Wyatt lets out a breathy laugh—the kind of sound that's filled with relief. Baxter barks once, most likely wanting the attention back on him, and we slowly break apart. The warmth of Wyatt's chest doesn't retreat far, his hands hesitant to withdraw from my waist. As he slips away, my heart lurches at the same time as my hand, grabbing his in a sweaty hold. I can't explain the need for it, but I don't want to lose this connection to him. Not when we've just found it.

Wyatt doesn't object, his thumb passing over the back of my hand. He inhales deeply, taking in the town in one sweeping gaze. Then, without another word, we're moving again, directly to the closest diner.

The building is small, nestled between a hardware store and a barbershop, with a flickering neon open sign in the window. The scent of frying bacon and freshly brewed coffee hits me like a wall, and my stomach growls so loudly that Wyatt snorts.

Pushing the door wide, we're met with a jingle from the little brass bell above. The hum of conversation inside goes quiet as we step in, our bedraggled appearance earning more than a few curious stares. A waitress, somewhere in her forties with a kind face and her blonde hair piled into a messy bun, approaches cautiously. Her name tag reads *Linda*.

"A booth for two, is it?" she asks, her gaze flickering over us before landing on Baxter, who's salivating all over the floor. "I'll see that your pooch has some food and water set out by the door. Follow me," she smiles. Briefly stopping by the counter, Linda asks a colleague to attend to Baxter, and the young girl's face lights up. She bounds off to make a fuss of him, both happy for the company.

"I'll bring some water and menus," Linda says, seeing us to our table. We collapse into the booth, the cracked vinyl cushions squeaking under us. Our backpacks are forgotten by our feet. The locals are still staring, whispering quietly around us. Disheveled or not, it won't be long before Wyatt is recognised and they start snapping photos for the papers.

Linda returns quickly with glasses of water and a basket of complimentary rolls, and I swear I've never tasted anything as good as the first bite of warm bread. Wyatt watches me tear into a second roll with an amused expression, though he's not far behind, stuffing his face with the same resolve.

"Where are you two coming from?" Linda asks when she returns with the menus, her curiosity getting the better of her.

"The forest," Wyatt answers vaguely but not rudely. Like a ton of bricks, it hits me that he is being cautious of how much information we reveal. That I should also be careful who I speak to and what I say. "We had a little accident with our car and were left stranded. You wouldn't happen to know a mechanic? And a place we can stay until we can get back on the road?"

"Oh, you poor dears!" Linda clutches her chest, looking between us with large brown eyes. "Let me make some calls and see what we can do. For now, rest and know that we serve the best burgers in town right here." She winks before walking off to take another table's order.

I glance at Wyatt over the rim of my glass. He's watching her closely, a sliver of tension rippling through his shoulders. For someone I pegged as a materialistic man, the dirt smeared across his T-shirt and his chipped fingernails are the last thing on his mind. He's thinking, calculating. Slowly returning to the version of Wyatt who puts himself on the outside of a conversation, who sees too much and overthinks constantly.

"What are you going to get?" I ask, pushing a menu his way.

"Everything," he says without missing a beat. I laugh, earning a sideways smirk from him. Finally, Wyatt sighs and his shoulders lower, the tension ebbing. I'm not going to think too hard about why I want to hold onto him being this way for a while longer. To keep him smiling, to stop the weight of stress from settling back in. We may have been lost in the forest, but somewhere along the way, I feel like I found Wyatt, and I'm not quite ready to let that go.

Linda wasn't lying about these being the best burgers, but after days of protein bars, anything hot, cheesy, and greasy would be the best thing I've ever put in my mouth. Garrett would have plenty to say about that sentence. Wyatt and I moan our way through burgers, fries, sides, and large sodas until we're complaining about stomach aches. Totally worth it, though.

Once Linda has collected our plates, Wyatt follows her to settle the bill. He keeps me in his eyeline at all times, not that I'll be going anywhere. I've never felt so full, and my ass has molded to the seat. Instead, I stare out of the nearby window, taking in the quaint little town. Residents go about their business, unaware of the outsiders who have entered their solace and the drama that we bring. Hopefully we'll be merely passing through without incident.

"Ready to go?" Wyatt asks when he returns. He has no right to look as good as he does in crumpled clothes, all tousled hair, and sharp green eyes. I blink a few times, slow to compute. "Linda has called the mechanic; he's bringing a tow truck around."

"We're going straight back out there?!" My voice rises a few pitches. Wyatt blinks a few times, as if he thought I would jump up and follow his lead. We've covered a lot of ground, both physically and emotionally, but I'm still me, and me thinks I have forest PTSD. "What if the tow truck runs out of gas and we're stranded again?"

Perhaps I'm being irrational, but Wyatt doesn't scoff and shrug off my concern like he once would have. Instead, he exhales and nods slowly, picking at the edge of the tablecloth.

"Okay. I'll go."

"Really?" I ask, despite it being what I wanted. "You're leaving me here alone?" I find myself shrinking in the booth, suddenly aware that everyone nearby can hear and see me. I don't know anyone in this town except for Wyatt, and the thought of him leaving is like ripping away my safety blanket. And that's exactly why he needs to go. Since when did I start seeking safety and comfort in Wyatt? Yeah, time apart is exactly what I need to get my thoughts in check.

Wyatt continues to nod, each word pulled from his lips with visible effort.

"Someone needs to show the mechanic where the SUV is. I won't force you to come, but if you don't mind, I'd really like it if you talk to Linda about some accommodation." My brows raise, surprised at the request. I do need a shower and to sleep with real pillows. I just didn't think Wyatt would consider my needs above his own desires. "And then go there and lock the door."

I chuckle to myself. That sounds more like it. A tow truck passes by the window, honking twice. I feel each blare like juddering heartbeats, slicing through the tension radiating from Wyatt. Something is going unsaid, but I'm not quite sure what it is.

Movement shuffles at my side, presumably Wyatt leaving until a warm thigh nudges mine to shift up the bench seat. I obey, frowning as Wyatt crowds me against the window, his hand along the back of the booth. His heat falls over me, that blanket of comfort settling once again.

"Look," he sighs. I'm frozen in place by his other hand lightly lowering on my thigh. "I know what the likelihood of you being here when I get back is. And for what it's worth... I'm glad you got to see a different side of me. I'll probably have shut it down the next time we meet."

My gaze shoots up to his green eyes. A storm of feral emotions swirls just beneath the surface. I'm hyperaware of the weight of his hand on my thigh, the way his thumb brushes absent patterns against the fabric of my sweatpants, as though trying to ground us both. His presence is all-consuming, pulling every ounce of air from my lungs.

I should push him away. I should tell him to go, to take his guarded heart, and leave before I'm in too deep. But I can't. I'm trapped by the vulnerability etched into every line of his face, the words I'm hesitant to speak.

"What's changed?" I breathe close to his face. "I... I thought you said I couldn't go back." Wyatt swallows, and I track the movement of his Adam's apple. Tilting his head, Wyatt looks down at his hand.

"I've come to realise that protecting you and suffocating you are two very different things. I thought I could handle your hatred if what I was doing was the right thing. But controlling you... preventing you from being yourself... that's not something I can live with."

The heat radiating from his body seeps into mine, and for a fleeting moment, the world outside this diner doesn't exist. Just us. Just Wyatt, holding me in place as if he's afraid I'll disappear if he lets go. My pulse thrums wildly, echoing the silent plea in his gaze. *Stay.*

"I'm not going to cage you anymore, Avery. It hasn't served me well this far. I want to earn your trust, despite it being against my every instinct to walk away from you right now."

"This feels a lot like a goodbye," I whisper, hindered by vulnerability. My breath stutters as his hand tightens on my leg, the silent tether between us pulling taut. A thousand thoughts war in my head, but all I can think is, *beg me to stay.* And yet, I know he won't. Wyatt will shut me out, because when emotions run too high; that's what he does. Leaning closer, Wyatt's lips brush my ear, the hand from the back of the booth shifting to gently hold my head.

"I wish you the best. Be safe, Angel, whatever you decide."

My mind scrambles to make sense of the chaos unfurling between us, but all I can focus on is the sharp, searing awareness of him. The weight of his hand gripping my thigh. The faint scent of pine and muck clings to his clothes. The faintest kiss touches my cheek, and then he's moving to leave me behind.

"Wait!" I shoot my hand out to grab his wrist. Wyatt regards me stoically, already blanketing over his emotions. Lowering my voice, I cast a quick glance around. "What about...Fredrick's men?" Wyatt stills for a moment and then softens, gently prying my fingers free from his wrist.

"I trust you can look after yourself," he replies. My mouth drops open.

"I think that's the nicest thing you've ever said to me." The hint of a smirk shadows his mouth before he turns away. I watch Wyatt leave without looking back, Baxter hot on his heels. Avoiding looking out of the window, I wait until the tow truck has pulled away before breathing properly again. I'm alone. Hauntingly alone for the first time in months. More than that, I'm free.

"Did you want me to set you up with a room, dear?" Linda appears just in time. My body was about to throw me into a tumbling panic attack. "My sister owns a local Bed and Breakfast. I can give her a call if you like." Call. Phones. Through my starvation, I'd forgotten we weren't in some mirage but back in reality.

"That would be lovely; thank you." I rush to say. "Would you mind if I used your phone as well? I need to check in with some people." Linda nods, fishing a smart phone out of her apron. She tells me to take my time and heads out back, returning once to give me a free slice of apple pie.

In that time, I'd successfully stared at the screen, berating myself for not knowing anyone's numbers off my heart. Shaking my foot nervously, I go out on a limb, calling my own number in the hopes that someone is nearby. The dial tone is tedious but only lasts for three rings.

"Hello?" A male voice answers. A stupid, strangled sound escapes me, and I clamp a hand over my mouth. My eyes squeeze shut as I hunch over, clutching the phone like it's my lifeline. "Hello? Who is this?"

"Dax?" I breathe. I hear his sharp inhale.

"Avery," Dax gasps down the phone. The weight of feeling behind that one word is enough to break through the tough facade I've been putting on, a defense mechanism that slips in place around Wyatt. Numerous voices perk up in the background, and Dax quickly hushes them all. "Holy shit. Swan, where are you? Are you safe?"

"I'm okay. We-" I stop myself, leaving out the crash. They don't need more reasons to worry. "We've stopped over in a small town; I'm not sure where to be honest. But I'm fine, I promise."

I expect to be bombarded with questions, asking where Wyatt is taking me, why he took me, and how he's treating me. I don't really have any answer for any, but that's not what comes. Dax sighs, a hitch in his breathing. Is he crying?

"Oh Aves, I'm sorry. I'm so sorry." I stop twitching my foot, slowly sitting upright. My hair falls away from my face, and I frown, confusion knotting in my chest.

"What could you possibly be sorry for?" I frown. Maybe the guys searched and are feeling guilty that they weren't able to find me yet. Not that it matters anymore. I'm free to come home now.

"I...There's..." Dax stumbles over his words, each hesitation twisting the knot tighter.

"Dax, you're scaring me. Whatever it is, just say it."

"We're at the hospital, Aves. There was an... incident." The blood drains from my face, my hand holding the phone starting to shake.

"Who?" is the only word I say, a swift demand.

"It's Axel." The breath is ripped from my lungs. Those two words hit me like a physical blow.

"Give me the address," I state, forcing the words past the lump in my throat. "I just need to wait for Hux's car to be fixed—"

"My what?!" A voice shouts from a distance. I realise now I'm on loud speaker. Dax sighs, rattling off the name of a hospital in a completely different state. What the hell are they doing so far from Waversea?! I shove my questions aside, wanting to focus on what's important.

"Give Axel my love. I'll be there as soon as I can."

"No, Peach," Garrett pitches in. It takes a second to place his voice. Stripped of his usual humor, he just sounds... broken. "If you come here now, it undoes all of Wyatt's efforts to keep you away. He was right to take you from us."

My mind reels. There's no way they're condoning Wyatt's actions of drugging and kidnapping me in the dead of night. The only explanation is that something has gone very, *very* wrong. I straighten, my resolve hardening like steel.

"Tell me everything," I say, my voice cold as the tough facade slips back into place. It's the only thing keeping me from falling apart.

CHAPTER EIGHT

The Day Before

"What's taking so long?" I huff and strain my head to look through the reception window. I knew letting Garrett go in alone was a mistake. Not that he gave us much of a choice. When deciding who'd be the most charming to head in and find out which dorm Meg occupies, he stormed in before we had time to talk it through.

"This is fucking stupid," Huxley leans against the lamppost, arms crossed, his jaw tight with frustration. "If she'd just answer her damn phone, we wouldn't have needed to drive all the way up here." I bite my tongue, refusing to get into this fight again. Meg might not be in a position to answer her phone, but stating that won't help ease the tension between us. The fury rolling off Hux already has everyone on edge.

"If the police had taken us seriously, we wouldn't have needed to drive all the way up here," Axel corrects. He's sitting on the curb, knees drawn up, absently spinning Avery's compass bracelet on his wrist. It's true, the police brushed off our concerns. Apparently they checked in on Fredrick and found nothing of concern, which ultimately lost us a few days of twiddling our thumbs. I turn away, angling myself to spot Garrett through the glass.

Spotting his head of shaggy dark hair, I track the way he's leaning over the desk, tattooed arms on full show. The girl behind appears to be politely refusing him with small shakes of her head. I drop my head back to look at the night's sky. Somewhere out there, Avery is beneath the same sky. I hope for Wyatt's sake that he's keeping to his word, his letter burning a hole in my pocket.

Meg's the next target. Protect her, leave Avery's safety to me.

It seems, much like the rest of Wyatt's plans, the note was hastily put together. The night we returned to the frat house from Midnight Madness, it looked like an atomic bomb had gone off in both Wyatt and Avery's rooms. In fact, if it wasn't for the letter Garrett found on the dining table and the text I noticed on Avery's phone, we'd have thought Fredrick took them both.

After hours of talking Huxley down from a ledge and convincing Axel it wasn't his fault for sleeping through the entire ordeal, we came to the conclusion to trust Wyatt. He's our leader, and we used to follow his word blindly. Now that he's carrying our precious cargo, it's harder for some to take his orders so easily.

"I'm going to fucking kill him," Hux mutters, not for the first time. At present, I'm not sure which 'him' he's referring to, as Garrett skips down the outer steps.

"Receptionist isn't budging on her GDPR rules. She must be into girls," he shrugs. His conclusion spurs Hux to stride forward, and I quickly put myself in the way.

"Focus. We don't have time for this." I raise my hands and stare Hux down until he grunts and turns away. Garrett drops onto the curb, hugging Axel to him. I frown, worried about our fragile friend. Axel continues to blame himself; his nightmares are an every night occurrence, and he doesn't bother hiding his wince when he pulls too hard on his ribs now. I suppose he doesn't feel the need to put on a strong front anymore. Catching Garrett's eye, a rare moment of worry slips through. Someone needs to do something. Without Avery to keep our spirits up, we really need a win right now.

"Gare, stay with him. Hux, let's go." I don't hang around for more arguments on how we should and shouldn't do things, but I breathe a sigh of relief when I hear footsteps following. Rounding the reception building, I find a cut-through that leads into a maze of pathways. The campus is quiet, even for this time of day.

At Waversea, students would be hustling from dorms to the library, the canteen to the gym. All the night owls who can't rest until their minds and bodies are exhausted. At Hollowbrook, it's eerily quiet, as if there's a curfew that no one dares to break.

The university layout feels like a cage, with twisting alleys that are framed by huge structures that block out the moon's light and leering windows that are too dark to see inside. Shadows hang like thick drapes, leaving us exposed in too many places. I suppress a shudder, but my eyes are flicking from one potential alcove to the next in a bid to remain on high alert. The dim lights from the lampposts do little to help.

Eventually, we resurface in a courtyard with a tall building looming in the background. It's a tall, rectangular monolith of pale bricks and the only one with almost every light on. I'd be willing to bet that's where the dorm rooms are. We seem to share the same thought, as Huxley's long strides quicken. We cut through overgrown hedges, pass by a cluster of bicycles haphazardly chained to a rack near the entrance, and slip inside.

So, this is where all the people are.

Students linger in small groups, some lounging on mismatched sofas near the stairs, others perched on the edges of tables, laughing softly or scrolling through their phones. A girl with bright pink hair glances up as we pass, her eyes narrowing slightly before she goes back to her conversation. Most of the faces are disinterested, but there's a subtle shift as a pair of outsiders stroll into their midst.

The lobby is well used, with scuffed tiles and walls plastered with faded posters for campus events. Along one wall, vending machines hum in a low, almost comforting rhythm, their flickering lights casting uneven glows. Opposite them, a wide staircase curls up toward the dorms above, its banister polished in patches where countless hands have gripped it over time. A faint scent of sweat, laundry detergent, and something vaguely greasy hangs in the air, clinging to the space like an unwelcome guest. Speaking of unwelcome guests...

Beside me, Huxley shifts his weight impatiently, crossing his arms over his chest as his sharp gaze darts around the room. His jaw clenches and unclenches, and I can feel the frustration radiating off him. "So, what now?" he mutters, voice low and taut. "Are we just going to knock on every door until we find her?"

I roll my eyes and suppress a sigh, shrugging off his sour mood. "Relax," I say, forcing a tight smile. "I'll figure it out." Hux snorts quietly, clearly unconvinced, but doesn't argue further. I pull Avery's phone from my pocket and tap it awake to pull up a photo of Meg.

A group of students lounges there, sprawled out in various states of relaxation. "Excuse me guys, sorry to interrupt." I step up to the sofas, halting the conversations happening within the room instantly. Every set of eyes turns to me, the air thick with curiosity and mild annoyance. "Does anyone know where I can find this girl?"

"Who's asking?" A girl with a buzzcut snaps closed a battered textbook, while another two others whisper quietly, their eyes not leaving my face.

"Just a friend. I really need to talk to her."

A lanky guy with curly hair who is draped over one armrest squints at the screen, then leans back with a dismissive snort. "Nice phone, dude," he says, a grin tugging at the corner of his mouth. A quiet laugh bubbles up from the other end of the sofa. I lower the pink device and stuff it back in my pocket. This is pointless.

Hux shifts behind me, the weight of his glare enough to make the group fidget. Before he can step in with whatever sharp comment is brewing on his tongue, one of the quieter students, a girl with glasses perched low on her nose, clears her throat. "You're looking for Meg?" she asks, her voice soft but clear.

I turn to her, nodding quickly. "Yeah. It's important. Do you know where she is?" The girl hesitates, glancing at her companions before speaking.

"She'll probably be at the stadium, running lacrosse drills. She's usually there this time of night." I didn't anticipate the flood of relief that hits me. A physical weight lifts from my shoulders. Meg is here; people have seen her. I couldn't fight the niggling worry that was creeping in, but now I don't feel as helpless. I can protect Meg, just like Avery would want me to do.

Hastily typing out the directions, I thank Glasses Girl and head out to find Garrett and Axel. They're waiting just outside the entrance, passing the time by passing saliva. I manage to break up their lip-lock and usher them back to the main parking lot.

Now comes the hard part. Convincing Meg to pack up and leave with us. We discussed the plan on the way over, which gave us a break from arguing over who drove Wyatt's sports Nissan. I won in the end, too worried that Huxley would total the car in revenge for Wyatt stealing his SUV. We've already lost precious time waiting for a replacement key to arrive, so Meg is our only priority right now. First we ensure she's under our protection, then Hux can do whatever he likes with Wyatt's car.

Following the directions to a tee, we roll up to the stadium and stride inside, finding the place conveniently unlocked. Garrett doesn't miss a beat, planting himself at the front of our small group.

"Axel, hang back. You're not in any fit state for this," he states. Axel chuckles, devoid of all humor, and steps into Garrett's side.

"Like fuck. I'm not weak," he flashes a heated glare out of the corner of his eye. Garrett's tensed jaw loosens, his head whipping aside.

"I know that, but you're injured. I promised to not let anything happen to you again." Hux grunts, as if he doesn't really believe Garrett's sentiment, but it goes ignored. Turning into Axel's body, Gare reaches up to clasp the back of his lover's neck. "I can't go into this if I'm worrying about you. Be our lookout, but the first sign of trouble, I want you to get in that damn car and floor it out of here. Promise me." Pressing their foreheads together, Axel sighs, tightening his lips.

"No."

"We don't have time for this," I huff, rolling my eyes. Tapping Huxley's shoulder, I jerk my head to step around the two, embracing each other, leaving them to quarrel about who should do what and creep through the building. The long hallway is framed by darkened windows either side; the low hum of vending machines met with the buzzing lights overhead. At the far end, a pair of double fire doors gleam, slightly ajar for a harsh wind to slip inside and curl around my spine. Low, gruff voices can be heard amongst the muffled sound of resistance.

Huxley curses under his breath but follows as I press myself against the cold wall, peering through the gap. Outside, a dimly lit pitch is shrouded by shadows, overlooked by empty stands. Three men are clustered near the stadium steps, crowding around a female figure as they successfully gag her with what might be a kneehigh sock. One tightly grips Meg's arm, her face pale and tear-streaked, her sports uniform twisted and torn. She's put up one hell of a fight, but it wasn't enough. Her other hand is clenched around her phone, which one of the men snatches away with a growl.

"Bit too late for that, don't you think?" He tosses the phone to the ground and stamps on it, shattering the screen. The other two laugh menacingly, dragging Meg away by her arm and hair. The other hangs back, placing a quick call in which he calls his mission a success, before following through another exit.

Hux and I wait for the quiet to settle before ducking out onto the pitch, keeping close to the stands as our feet move swiftly. Garrett and Axel are right behind, our heated breaths creating clouds of pale smoke in the air. I manage to catch the far door just before it slams closed, a jolt of pain crunching along my fingers that I ignore for now.

The moment we step inside, the coppery tang of blood hits me. It's faint but unmistakable, mingling with the sterile scent of fresh paint and old wood. My stomach drops. Red streaks skid across the polished floor, scuffed with a struggle. They've hurt her.

A labyrinth of cold concrete hallways stretches ahead, each turn blindly leading us into a stilted darkness. The faint sound of Meg's muffled cries bounces off the walls, haunting and disorienting like a cruel game of hide-and-seek.

Huxley stays close to my side, his eyes sharp and scanning, every muscle in his body coiled tight like a spring ready to snap. Garrett and Axel trail behind us, their hushed footsteps falling in sync with ours. No one speaks. The weight of the silence presses down on us, heavier with every hallway we pass, the sound of Meg's cries growing faint and then vanishing altogether.

Slowly, the reddened scuffs on the floor become a singular line, and I can almost pinpoint where Meg has passed out, forcing her to be dragged the rest of the way. The coppery scent increases, leading us to a metal door labeled *Locker Room A.* My heart thunders in my ears as I share a small nod with Hux, reaching out for the door handle.

Suddenly, a door to our left bursts open, slamming against the wall with a thunderous crack. Four men step out of the next locker room, their necks branded with thick, black numbers. Prison tattoos. One carries a crowbar, its metal glinting under the flickering fluorescent lights behind them. Grins are plastered across their scarred faces. They knew we were here.

"Looks like we've got company," Crowbar sneers, his voice rough and guttural. His gaze rakes over us, landing on Garrett when he steps in front of Axel. "Back down, kid. We've got what we came for."

"Where have you taken her?" Garrett's tone is dangerous, his fists already clenched. I'm glad he can pretend we're not hugely out of our depth, because the tremble to my sore fingers wouldn't have managed it. The man with the crowbar chuckles, tapping the weapon against his palm.

"Too late. She's ours now. But you can join her if you're feeling brave."

I don't know if Garrett is still riding the high of being Axel's protector or if he felt the need to prove a point. But something causes him to lunge first, his fist colliding with the man's jaw in a loud crunch. The crowbar is dropped, skidding away as Garrett is half dragged into the room, their bodies grappling for control. The distinctive slam of bodies hitting metal sounds as Axel kneels to pick the crowbar up, feeling the weight in his hands. When he blinks up at the man slamming Garrett into the lockers again, there's a deadly determination to his hazel eyes.

I barely have time to react as another guy charges me. He's massive, his shoulders wide enough to block out the light. I duck under his first swing, his meaty fist whistling past my ear. Using his momentum, I drive my shoulder into his ribs, but it's like hitting a brick wall. He snarls, grabbing the back of my jacket and carrying me into the locker room, effectively cornering us inside before tossing me into a nearby bench.

Pain blooms in my side as the wood splinters beneath me. He advances on me before I've got to my feet. A heavy boot slams into my gut, robbing my lungs of air. Around the tears springing to my eyes, I see him turn towards Axel.

"Wait-" I fumble with his ankle, feebly trying to cling onto his trousers. I can't be sure my hand even closes into a fist, the pain splintering through my fingers and across my torso stealing all of my focus, but it's enough to garner his attention. He lifts me again, pinning me up against a metal grate to level punches into my side. I grunt, throwing rogue swings that don't connect, all the while keeping the others in my eye line.

Huxley moves like a storm, fluid and unstoppable. He dodges a knife aimed at his stomach, twisting his attacker's wrist with brutal precision until the blade clatters to the floor. Without missing a beat, he delivers a sharp elbow to the man's temple, sending him crumpling to the ground. Behind him, Axel approaches the man struggling with Garrett, and with a wince, lifts the crowbar high into the air. It comes down with a sickening sound I don't think I'll ever be able to forget.

Metal meeting flesh, dull, wet, and final. The goon crumples to the floor with a thud, his body limp and unmoving, his head split and oozing around the crowbar still embedded in his skull. Axel's hazel eyes widen, his breath hitching in sharp, shallow gasps. Blood splatters his face, masking the horror that blossoms underneath.

"Fuck. Holy fuck," Axel's voice is twinged with disbelief as he stares at his own hands, as if they're foreign to him now. His chest heaves, and for a moment, it's as though the world has frozen around him. This isn't what we signed up for. We're not killers; we're basketball players for fuck's sake.

The moment shatters when the man holding me up releases my jacket and roars in rage, his boot crashing into Axel's side and sending him sprawling to the floor. "Axel!" Garrett shouts in protest, surging forward, but he's intercepted by Huxley's assailant, who drives a fist into his stomach and forces him to double over.

Huxley's voice cuts through the chaos as he scrambles toward his friend, but the two goons left are on a warpath, not letting either him or Garrett close to a gasping Axel on the ground. A trembling hand hovers over his left ribs, not daring to touch himself through his hoodie. Fuck, his ribs. I army crawl across the tiled floor, outstretching my own hand. A heavy boot quickly stamps on my fingers, crushing them beneath the sole and twisting. I scream, the pop of bones reverberating through my entire arm.

Axel is hauled up by his shirt, delivering a brutal punch to his face. The impact sends him crashing into the lockers, his head bouncing off the unforgiving metal, and his body drops right in front of me. Within reaching distance, but I don't dare try to touch him again. It'll bring too much attention to both of us. Instead, we stare into each other's eyes, Axel's becoming more distant by the second. Blood trickles from his nose and the corner of his mouth, pooling beneath his face. His eyes flutter shut, and an eerie stillness settles over him.

"Enough," a thick voice booms. Whoever has entered has enough authority to halt the goons in their revenge. "Leave them. It's time to go."

The assailants retreat as quickly as they'd appeared, leaving devastation in their wake. Garrett stumbles free of his attacker and collapses to his knees beside Axel. His hands shake as he reaches out, gently cradling Axel's face. "Axel!" Garrett chokes, his voice breaking. Tears spill freely down his cheeks, landing on Axel's bloodied shirt. "Come on, wake up. Please, just...just wake up."

The room is eerily quiet now, the only sound being Garrett's desperate pleas. He leans down, pressing his forehead to Axel's, his shoulders shaking as sobs wrack his body. "You promised me," he whispers, his voice trembling. "You promised you wouldn't leave me."

As I work to pull myself up into a sitting position, cradling my broken hand, Huxley kneels beside them, his expression grim as he checks Axel's pulse. A flicker of relief crosses his face, but it's fleeting. "He's alive," he murmurs. "But we need to get him out of here." Garrett nods wordlessly, his grip on Axel tightening as if letting go would make him slip away for good. I wobble, attempting to stand and failing twice. The third time, Huxley's there to hoist me up with his shoulder.

It provides little comfort. My sense of gravity was unbalanced, and my body was protesting against every tiny moment. But none of that matters. We failed. Meg is gone, and Axel is hurt. Our spirits are beaten, and we've lost more than we've gained. I wanted to be the man Avery could rely on when she's not here to fight her own battles. I wanted to be her hero.

CHAPTER NINE

The drive back to town somehow seems longer than the walk. I'm twisted towards the passenger window, watching the forest pass. It's surreal that only this morning we were waking up for another day of trekking. Now we're back to reality, and I can take a moment's pause to realise what actually happened between these tree trunks. Avery and I bonded. Solidified something that's been disjointed between us for years. At least it was good while it lasted.

Since hoisting Huxley's SUV onto the back of his truck, Jimmy the mechanic has been harassed by Baxter constantly trying to sit on his lap whilst driving. Jimmy doesn't seem to mind, chuckling and stroking Baxter's head with one hand, the other lazily tossed over the wheel. He seems like he's a decent man, about middle-aged, wife, and kids. He wears a white wife-beater despite the winter and has faded tattoos trailing his arms.

"You don't talk much, huh?" Jimmy asks over the sound of the radio. I shrug, not sparing a glance away from the window.

"Just thinking is all."

"About your girl waiting for you?" Jimmy reaches over to elbow my arm, bobbing his eyebrows rapidly. I clench my back teeth together, not bothering to explain how much Avery is *not* my girl. Clearly, this small town doesn't read the tabloids often.

"She's probably long gone by now," I sigh, scratching a hand over my jaw. Jimmy's smile fades but his curiosity is piqued.

"Why's that?"

Looking up, I search for patience and find little. "I told her to. She's better off without me." A solemn atmosphere settles in the cab, punctuated by a small humming sound from my temporary companion.

"Hmmm. Well, they say the best way to love someone is to let them go and see if they come back."

"I don't love her," I answer far too quickly. Surprised by my own reaction, I settle back into the seat, deciding I need to take a long, hard look at myself in the mirror later. Probably followed by an hour of screaming in the shower until I have no voice left to say stupid shit to strangers.

"Fair enough." Jimmy chuckles low, the sound rumbling through the cab. His attention shifts back to the road, but I catch the faint smirk still lingering on his face. I tighten my jaw, my fingers twitching against my thigh. The silence between us feels heavy now, only interrupted by the hum of the engine and the occasional excited bark from Baxter.

The forest blurs past the window, and my thoughts circle back to Avery like they always do. I try to focus on the trees, counting them, measuring the distance between their trunks, anything to avoid the gnawing ache in my chest. But her face creeps in, her wide smile and large eyes gleaming with affection. I've seen her look at the others like that. I make sure it's never meant for me.

"Doesn't seem like you don't love her," Jimmy says after a beat, his voice casual but probing. I whip my head toward him, but he doesn't look at me. His gaze stays fixed on the road, one hand still lazily stroking Baxter's fur.

"What do you know about it?" I snap, all of my irritation flaring back up in a second. Jimmy finally glances my way, his expression calm, almost pitying.

"Not much," he admits, "but I've seen enough men like you to know when one's lying to himself." My chest tightens, the truth of his words landing harder than I want to admit. I shift in my seat, turning back toward the window, the reflection of my face barely visible against the darkened glass.

"She's better off without me," I repeat, this time quieter, as if saying it softer will make it true. Jimmy doesn't press further, and for that, I'm grateful. The drive stretches out in silence, my thoughts growing heavier with every passing mile.

Love. What would be the point of loving her? In fact, it would be the worst thing I could do. It would drag her down and smother her in my darkness until she couldn't breathe. Avery deserves more than that. She deserves light and softness—things I can't give her no matter how much I want to. I dig my nails into my palm, the pain a welcome distraction.

"Irish wolfhound, I reckon," Jimmy says after a good long while. I glance over and raise a brow at the sudden announcement. "Your dog. From the fur, I'd say he's part Irish wolfhound. We had a mutt when I was growing up, same wiry fur. He was a fantastic dog, boundless energy, extremely loyal. My pops never let me have any pets, but one day this dog started following me home from school. I called him Wolfy and fed him my sandwich crusts so my mom thought I ate them. Then Wolfy started coming in the house, stayed in my bedroom."

Maybe it's the need to talk about anything else, but I find myself contributing to the conversation. "And your dad, he let you keep him?" Jimmy grins again, his eyes dropping to meet with Baxter's.

"He didn't know. Too busy with his affairs, see. By the time he noticed a scruffy dog wandering around the kitchen, I was about ready to graduate from high school, and it was too late by then. Wolfy was only with us a few more months, but I sure loved that mutt." Jimmy smiles at Baxter and gives him a stroke between his ears. I turn back to the window, giving them their privacy.

Before I know it, we're pulling into the garage, and my nails have embedded half-moon bloodied marks into my palms. I have an idea of what I'll find when I hop out of the truck, or rather, what I won't find. I gave her an out. She'd be a fool not to take it and run while she can.

Pulling myself to stand straighter, I plaster on a blank expression and follow Jimmy into his small office. It's more of a storage cupboard, with spare parts and paperwork covering what I presume is a desk underneath. He shows me to a chair and grabs a notepad before leaving me alone with my thoughts once more. It's a dangerous place to be, so I latch onto the distant radio instead. There's a segment on about trying to reconnect old, jilted lovers through the phone lines. Fuck.

"So, damage isn't all that bad," Jimmy returns some time later. I'd lost myself to the bubbles running through the water dispenser. Dropping into a chair hidden by coats, he shoves things around for some space on the desk to show me his scribbled list. "Mostly cosmetic. The rear panel will need replacing. I can bang out the side doors and that big dent in the hood, and replace the windows, no issue. Will need new tires on the right side. You're lucky all that rain didn't do any internal damage with the car left on its side like that."

"Do you have the parts here?"

Jimmy looks around and then strains to peer back towards his workshop. "I have a few odd bits I can piece together, but they won't be the same color or official BMW supply. If you wanted those, I'd need to order them in." I quickly wave my hand. At this rate, I think I'll order Hux a brand new SUV and scrap this one once it's got me to where I'm going.

"That won't be necessary. Just enough to get back on the road."

Jimmy nods, jotting down some prices and notes. "Alright then. Give me a few days, and I'll see it done." He stands, and I quickly follow suit. There's no point delaying the inevitable. I may have arrived as half of a pair, but I expect I'm leaving alone. She'll be long gone by now.

"Name your price to have it ready by tomorrow morning." At this, Jimmy smiles a wide, toothy grin. We settle up our business, and I grab my backpack from the cab. There's barely anything left in it now, except for a few spare clothes that need washing, my toothbrush, and a blank notepad. I didn't think too hard on the reasons for grabbing it at the last minute. It just feels soothing to have one nearby.

Heading out of the open garage, Jimmy rushes up behind me, his smart phone in hand with a message open on the screen.

"Looks like you're in luck," he smiles, his eyebrows dancing again. I peer at the message, although Jimmy gives me a playful shoulder barge. "She's stayed after all."

"What are you talking about?" I frown, brushing down my shoulder as if I'm not in a sweatshirt that's grubbier than Jimmy's wife beater. Producing a handful of business cards from his pocket, he flicks through them until he produces the one he's looking for.

"There's a room sorted for you at Bonnie's Bed and Breakfast. Ask at the reception for details. They don't accept pets though, I'm afraid." Jimmy gives Baxter a forlorn look that doesn't look anything like regret. Another situation that appears out of my control.

"Do you know of a place Baxter can stay?" I sigh.

"Oh, I'd be happy to look after him for the night. My girls will spoil him rotten." Baxter barks, jumping up at Jimmy and reveling in all of the fuss he's being given. I look to the concrete ground, swallowing past a lump in my throat.

"You know what, Jimmy. Why don't you keep him safe for me?" On a long exhale, a weight is lifted from my shoulders. Whistling sharply, I call Baxter over and kneel down, accepting his licks on my face. "Be a good boy, okay?" I whisper a silent goodbye and let him return to an elated Jimmy, knowing it might possibly be the last time I see him.

It's better this way. Baxter's an old dog, sentenced to die, forgotten in a shelter before I found him. At least this way, he'll be loved and cared for. He'll have a stable home, which isn't something I can currently provide. More importantly, he won't be with me anymore. No one prospers when they're with me.

But dare I dream that there's someone willing to try?

With the pack on my shoulder, my feet swiftly carry me to the address listed on the business card, which turns out to be on the opposite side of town. At the far end of a gravel driveway, I walk up the wooden steps of a charming two-story building. Ivy creeps up one side of weathered brick walls, framing the windows with its pale leaves. The front porch is adorned with rocking chairs and overflowing flower boxes. A wrought-iron sign hanging above the front door reads *'Bonnie's'* in looping cursive.

I take a steady breath and push open the heavy oak. A bell jingles overhead, and a woman emerges from behind the reception desk. She's older, with a kind face and silvery hair pinned into a loose bun. She appears to have a keen resemblance to Linda, the diner waitress. Her smile widens as I approach.

"You must be Wyatt," she says, her voice warm. "Your friend said you'd be along shortly. Room three, upstairs. She's waiting for you." Her words hit like a punch to the chest. Jimmy wasn't lying—Avery's here. She's actually here.

Nodding mutely, I accept the brass key she hands me and climb the narrow staircase. The dimly lit hallways smell of lavender, due to vases of the flowers on low tables, mingling with the faint aroma of freshly baked cookies wafting from somewhere below. The wooden steps creak under my weight, my shadow cast across the floral wallpaper as I approach a door at the end of the hall, labelled with the number three.

Pushing the key into the lock, I twist slowly, unsure if I'm ready for what's waiting on the other side. Why hasn't she run at the first opportunity? Then I grow a pair of balls and push the door open.

Avery stands by the window, facing outwards. She doesn't turn at the sound of the door, lost in her own thoughts, permitting me a moment to just stare at her. Her hair is loose, tumbling down her back in soft, golden waves. She's shed the baggy sweatpants and sneakers, dressed in a simple knit sweater and leggings that cling to her slender frame.

There is a pile of folded clothes on the edge of a queen-sized bed, seemingly for me. The room for two is small and cosy, with a small bathroom off to the side. A pair of armchairs sit by the window, with a small table between them holding another vase of lavender.

I pause, unsure what to say. Whether I should disrupt her at all. But then, impatience for answers gets the better of me, and I step further into the small room. "You're here," I say softly, my voice barely above a whisper. Avery's head whips around, her expression unreadable. Clearing my throat, I clarify, "I didn't think you'd stick around."

"Wyatt," Avery replies, a quiet plea that wrings my insides. In the dim light of the lamp, her eyes are red and puffy. She's been crying. All pretences that I've guarded myself against her charms fall away. Crossing the room in a few strides, I reach for her, and she comes willingly. Crashing against my chest, I hold her there, stroking her hair and letting her tremble against me.

"Is it Fredrick? Did something happen? Fuck, I never should have left you." I chastise myself. Avery shakes her head, turning so her cheek is pressed against me.

"It's Axel. He's in the hospital."

My world tilts until I'm dropping on the bed's green quilted throw, taking Avery with me. Just like that, our private world has shattered. Reality has come crashing back in.

I don't immediately ask the questions burning my throat, as if delaying the knowledge of what happened will make it any less my fault. Once again, as always, I was tunnel visioned. Avery's safety was my priority, and now visions of Fredrick's men storming the frat house and becoming enraged at her disappearance fill my mind. Perhaps they took her disappearance out on the Souls. I was stupid to think they could defend themselves against convicts and thugs. I've been stupid in so many ways. There is nothing I can do now, but the temptation to put my fist through a wall is strong.

Instead, I focus on what's right in front of me, bundled in my arms as if she belongs there. "Why did you wait for me? Why haven't you gone to be with him already?"

Avery pulls back slightly, just enough to look up at me. Her blue eyes, glossy with more tears, search mine as though the answer is hidden somewhere between us. She opens her mouth, hesitates, then closes it again. I brush my thumb over the healing split in her lip from the crash, giving her all the time she needs. The air is thick with her indecision, her pain, and her haunted whisper.

"Because I didn't want to go alone. I... needed you."

I nod, not trusting my voice. The admission twists something deep inside me. Avery, who's always been so self-assured, so steady in the chaos, is admitting she needs me. She chose to wait for me.

Her words crack something in me that's been brittle for too long. I cradle her, soothing her as if I have the right to. The urgency to leave and be by Axel's side is crushing, but there's that small, selfish side to me that always seems to speak a little bit louder than the other voices in my head. She needs me. The car won't be fixed until tomorrow. We have tonight, thanks to some sort of divine intervention. And maybe, just maybe, I need her, too.

AVERY

CHAPTER TEN

When I managed to stop crying for long enough, I relayed everything Dax told me. How the boys went to Meg's university and were a fraction too late. How Axel's ribs were re-broken and punctured his lung. Surgery has managed to repair the damage, but he's yet to wake up. They're all in limbo, not knowing what to do or where to go, waiting and suffering in silence.

My heart cracks all over again, and the tears come back tenfold. I should have been there. I should be with them now, and regardless of Wyatt being the reason I'm not, he's the only thing keeping me upright.

Yet to say a word in response, Wyatt lifts me into his arms, my body limp against his chest. Walking us into the bathroom, he doesn't put me down until we're in the shower cubicle. Turning the knob, a dose of ice-cold water shoots from the shower head before it warms. We gasp and cling tighter together on instinct, shuddering laughs prying us apart when there's no reason to keep holding each other.

He reaches for my knitted sweater first, giving me every chance to smack his hands away. I don't, despite the vulnerability seeping from me. I'm waiting for the switch to flip, for Wyatt to revert back to the man I thought I knew and take what he wants. A shameful part of me knows I wouldn't stop him either. I just want him in any sense of the selfish word. It's all want, want, want.

His fingers linger, growing braver, knuckles brushing my collarbone as he pulls the sweater over my head. My breath hitches, and he's given a brief reprieve from my careful gaze. Then they're back, ever curious, all seeing. I'm standing before Wyatt in a black lace bra, the first one I picked up at a small clothing store in town. I wasn't hanging around to peruse the racks, wanting to be out of the public eye as quickly as possible after hearing Axel's news.

First choice or not, Wyatt seems to approve. A tick is produced in his jaw, his clenched teeth a testament to how much he's restraining. How much he wants this to last. His hands lower to my leggings, until mine flash out to stop them. I'm almost trembling with the need for him to continue, but I manage to lower his arms to his side.

Then I take the hem of his shirt and lift it upwards. I'm slow, cautious, and testing, and Wyatt lets me cross this bridge in my own time. It becomes a game of like for like. We're equals in this give and take. One piece of clothing at a time measured and mirrored movements. There's no stronger hand, but a common ground we walk together.

Standing before one another fully naked under the spray, I can't say who kisses who first. It's a mesh of lips colliding, our desperation to be in this moment visceral. It's raw, unhurried, yet urgent. The kind of kiss that anchors you and sets you adrift all at once. Wyatt's hands slide to my waist, long fingers pressing into my skin as if to remind himself I'm real. The water cascades over us, washing away the grime of the forest and the tension from days of uncertainty.

This is not like the last time we showered together, when we were both using each other for gain. Both trying to rid ourselves of the demons that fuel this attraction, hoping it would fizzle out afterwards. It didn't fizzle at all and has only proven to stoke the flames higher.

Is this an escape from all the shit happening outside this B&B? One hundred percent. And I'm going to take that escape before the world comes crashing down on my head.

I'm the girl he's not supposed to have, who he can't want. He's the asshole who's given me every reason to walk away—the reason I hate myself for still being here and giving myself to him like this. But I can't stop. I walk into that fire, willing it to burn me to ashes.

My fingers tangle in his wet hair, tugging gently, pulling him closer. Every shiver of his body against mine feels like a revelation. We're not just touching. We're unraveling each other, piece by piece, barrier by barrier. The water is warm, but it's his body against mine that sets me alight.

I break the kiss, gasping for air, and his forehead drops to mine. His breath fans across my lips, uneven and heavy, green eyes searching mine. There's an unspoken question in them, one I answer by threading my fingers down his arms and lacing them through his.

Wyatt swallows hard, his throat bobbing with the effort. His expression seems to say, *'you're everything I've ever wanted'*, though no words pass his lips. He presses his palm flat against my lower back, guiding me under the full force of the water. The spray beats down on us, encasing us together and silencing out everything else.

I brace my hands upon his chest. His dragon tattoo breathes with him, rising and falling, shifting with the pull at his ribs. My hands trail down his chest, water pooling in the dips and lines of his muscles. I memorize them with my fingertips, each tremor of his body another page written into the story we're creating. I find myself wondering how he would write this and what words he'd use to describe how he's feeling.

Revealing he is Mr. XO gave me the answers I wanted but also cut me off from his thoughts. The connection I didn't even know we had has been severed, and I'm only just realising its lasting effects.

Wyatt's fingers skim over the curve of my shoulder, tracing a trail of water running down my arm. His hair falls forward, his eyes becoming shielded. He uses this to his advantage, as if cutting off our eye contact allows him to push forward with his most hidden desires. The kiss reignites, possessive and deliberate. His lips part against mine as his hands slide lower, framing my hips, his touch firm and grounding.

I press closer, not permitting any space between us as the warm water cascades in a curtain, parting only for our joined limbs. My palms glide along his sides, over the ridges of muscle and damp, smooth skin.

Wyatt explores just as much, brushing soaked strands of hair from my face, his fingers lingering near my temple before trailing down my jaw. His thumb grazes my lips, his chest heaving against mine with the weight of restraint. Slowly, his hand drops lower, teasing the path down my ribs, his palm flattening against my stomach. Every touch ignites a spark that is quickly catching fire. I'm too hot, too taut.

I meet his gaze, the water streaking between us doing nothing to blur the intensity of his green eyes locked on mine. Then he reaches down, deftly sliding his hand between my thighs. I gasp at his touch, and he seems to breathe it in, his lips hovering over mine. My pleasure is his drug of choice, speared on by his fingers rolling over my clit. Wyatt roams in steady circles, pushing me to the edge of sanity. I roll my hips, trying to urge him further south, but he's not having it.

The kiss resumes, hungrier this time, his mouth capturing mine with a fervor that seems to say everything he refuses to put into words. He craves me, and that thought drives me higher and higher. I arch into him, holding onto his shoulders. My nails lightly graze his skin, relishing how his muscles tense beneath my touch, a quiet shudder betraying the tension he's holding back.

The room is filled with the steady rhythm of water hitting tile, but it's the sound of my ragged breaths and the low, throaty growl from deep within him that drowns everything else out. He tilts his head, breaking the kiss, only to press his lips to the hollow of my throat. The sensation pulls me under, my hands threading into his hair again. The slide of skin against skin, slick and heated, binds us in a way that feels primal, raw, and unapologetic.

"Angel," Wyatt mutters, a cracked sound that strips me bare. "Go lie on the bed. I'll be there in two minutes." I hesitate, not ready to leave his heat, but knowing the quicker we get out of this shower, the quicker we can connect in the way we want. The way we need if we're going to be able to face the world as a united front. Clearly, fighting against each other isn't going to get us anywhere.

Wiggling the rest of the way out of my leggings, I leave the soppy heap in the corner of the cubicle and leave, grabbing a towel on my way out. I roughly shake it over my hair, leaving the ends damp and crinkled. I'd already showered before Wyatt arrived, but I wasn't going to deny seeing where his passions would go. Closing the curtains, I leave the lamp on for mood lighting and wander back towards the back. The shower soon shuts off with a dull echo through the pipes.

When Wyatt appears, a towel is pinned around his waist, and his eyes zeroed in on me like a target. He picks me up mid-stride, one hand gripping my thigh and lifting me effortlessly. Instinctively, my legs wrap around his waist.

"I thought I told you to be lying on the bed." He grumbles, his mouth against the curve of my neck. The vanilla body wash clings to his skin, colliding with my senses. Droplets from his hair roll down my chest and collect in my bra. I bite my lip, smirking at the feel of his messy kisses against my skin.

"That would be counterproductive to me disobeying you."

"Which would also be counterproductive to me making love to you," Wyatt retorts. I fall still in his arms, stunned into submission. His mouth doesn't stop moving, speaking between kisses. "I can't throw you around and spank you tonight."

"Can't? Or won't?" I ask, gripping his sharp jaw so he will look at me. Bags hang beneath his eyes, speaking of days without real sleep, but it doesn't seem to phase him.

"Stop testing me and let us have this." Wyatt groans somewhat painfully. I push his wet hair aside so I have an uninterrupted view of his eyes and the plea held within. "We need this." The walls he's built falter briefly, and in that fleeting moment, I see a crack in his armor. Something vulnerable, almost tender, before it's replaced by the all-consuming intensity of his next kiss.

I'm lowered onto the mattress, quickly pushed down by his weight. Given that my legs are still wrapped around his hips and the towel from his waist is now missing, Wyatt slides into me without hesitation. There's no barrier between us; his intrusion is like a claim that leaves no room for doubt. His breath catches, a hopeless sound that mixes with mine as he pushes deeper, his body fitting against mine perfectly.

Wyatt props himself on his forearms, his green eyes locking onto mine, the intensity of his gaze making my chest tighten. He moves deliberately, as though mapping every reaction, every shudder that escapes me. The weight of him pins me to the mattress, grounding me in the moment, while the slow, hypnotic rhythm of his body against mine pulls me into a haze.

His lips find mine again, softer this time, almost reverent. His lips melt against me with every careful thrust of his hips. His fingers splay across my waist, gripping just enough to hold me in place as he shifts his weight slightly, angling deeper. The change makes me groan, my nails finding purchase on his shoulders. Wyatt moans in response, the sound vibrating through his chest and into mine.

But it's his face that has me enthralled. I can't close my eyes, drinking in the sight of him. He's beautiful normally, but when he's this raw, he's breath-taking. Pressing his bruised lips together, his eyes become more glazed, everything centered on where his body joins mine. Our movements fall into sync, a slow build of tension winding through every nerve. He refuses to pick up the pace, remaining steady whilst I'm trembling beneath him.

The room feels smaller, the dim light casting shadows over the planes of his body, accentuating every taut muscle, every bead of water still clinging to his tattooed skin. Wyatt presses his forehead to mine, his eyes fluttering closed for a moment as his rhythm falters, a telltale sign that he's holding himself back.

I lift my hips to meet his, wordlessly urging him to let go and to stop holding back. His restraint finally snaps, and his rhythm grows faster and more erratic, the intensity between us reaching its peak. Wyatt's hand slips beneath my lower back, lifting me into him as he drives deeper, the coil of tension finally unraveling in a rush of heat and electricity that leaves me gasping his name. His own release follows, his body trembling above me as he buries his face in the crook of my neck, his breath hot against my skin.

"Come for me, Angel," he murmurs that nickname again, his voice strained, his grip tightening on my hips. His lips find the edge of my jaw, trailing kisses down my neck. I arch beneath him, the friction pushing me closer to the edge until I tumble over it. He's right there with me, free-falling without a parachute. His groans cancel out mine, vibrating against my skin as his body tenses, adding to the climax rushing through my core. His heat pours into me, his movements slowing but not stopping as we ride out the last waves together.

His hand slides from my back to cradle my face, thumb brushing gently over my cheek as though he's afraid I might disappear. "I'm going to miss you."

"I'm not going anywhere," I vow without thinking about the ramifications of such a sentence. Only that it feels right.

Wyatt finally leans down, pressing a final lingering kiss to my lips. "We'll see." Then he shifts, pulling away just enough to roll us onto our sides, his arm draped possessively over my waist.

We stay like that, tangled together, the world outside this room forgotten. The rise and fall of his chest against my back is so similar to the sleeping bag we've been sharing for the past couple of nights. I shiver just thinking about the damp ground, the whistling wind, and the lack of hot food. Wyatt reaches over, pulling the quilted throw over the both of us and snuggles in further.

"Wyatt?" I ask into the silence, my heart finally returning to a normal beat. He hums in response, a graveled sound of exhaustion. "Was that the first time you've ever made love to someone?" I bite down on my lip, my eyelids falling closed as I wait for the answer that never comes.

CHAPTER ELEVEN

Warm arms cradle me, rhythmic breathing skating across my nape. How can something so wrong feel so damn right?

I was never supposed to crave Wyatt the way I do, but last night, he barrelled through my defences and left me bare. Now, there's no going back to how it was before. I can't pretend to hate him. I can't keep punishing him for his terrible choices, and the man I saw last night doesn't expect me to. Wyatt is unraveling for me. Untangling years of false truths and misguided beliefs for himself. The man who made sweet love to me last night wants to fix the harm he has caused, and I'm going to make sure he does. Starting with saving Meg.

The sun creeping into a pink and orange sky doesn't bring the regret I'd expected to feel; instead, a strange contentment has me sinking deeper into his hold whilst staring out of the window. I can almost imagine this is how life could be if he'd been honest from the beginning. If the letters he wrote me were voiced instead of hidden under an alias.

Wyatt's fingers twitch against my stomach, hinting that he's waking. I've been awake for hours, wondering what his mood might be. Will he deny what happened between us and slam down his barriers again?

Evidently not.

Trailing his fingers up my torso between my breasts and stopping at my jaw, Wyatt twists my head into a passionate kiss. Slanting his lips across mine, longing mingled within their soft caress, he turns me into the curve of his body. Tugging, pulling, and silently begging. His cock juts between us, his morning glory living up to its name and pressing into my hip. I groan against his mouth, allowing his tongue to slip in to coax mine out. Our limbs tangle, unable to get close enough.

Much like last night, he's in no rush. His movements are calm and purposeful. There isn't a place he can't touch, physically or otherwise. I'm laid bare on this bed for him to take, use, and ruin. Whatever Wyatt wants, I'll accept, which in itself is both terrifying and freeing. If there's one thing I thought Wyatt would never earn from me, it was my trust.

Every inch of my skin tingles as tongue drives into my mouth, wringing an onslaught of emotion to the surface. I feel him everywhere, even in the curling of my toes. Shamefully thrusting against him in the bleak morning light, his emerald green eyes give me their full concentration, as if he doesn't want anyone else.

Lifting my leg in the crook of his arm, he slides into my wetness in one easy movement with a moan like he needed that as much as I did. Languid strokes of his dick grazing my G-spot, gently kneading my breasts without releasing my mouth long enough to breathe properly. I dive into the escape he's offering and beg him with my reactions to leave his mark. To cherish and fuck me simultaneously. To make this last as long as we have before the sun fully rises today.

Rolling us, Wyatt looms over me. His broad shoulders and thickly muscled arms block the rest of the world out of view, only me and him existing for now. I run my fingernails down the length of his spine, his firm ass clenching with each steady thrust. A choke rises in my throat, thoughts of this possibly being the last time with him churning in my mind.

Reaching up to grab a handful of his brown hair, I yank his head aside and hiss into his ear. "Faster." I demand, desperate to break the intimacy. I don't want his affection, not now I know how much it will hurt to lose it. I'd rather my last experience with Wyatt was harsh and unfair, helping to ward my heart against him.

"No," he replies simply.

Gripping my wrists, he lifts them either side of my head and watches me intently. His hair flicks forward, but he doesn't break our gaze, watching me moan and squirm beneath him. I try to kiss his enticingly close lips, but he deflects me with a grin, refusing to be distracted. A flutter in my lower abdomen builds to an intensity that has me gasping, my limbs prickling in anticipation. I pointlessly wriggle to break free from his stare, biting back a groan at my building orgasm.

"Look at me," Wyatt says softly. I shake my head, clenching my eyes closed instead. My thighs lock around his waist, trying to slow his steady rhythm. Withholding my pleasure seems like the only power move I have left.

"See how much you affect me," he steals a quick kiss, driving me to blink up at his handsome face. His stubble is becoming more of a permanent feature, making his square jaw and green eyes more prominent. Strain pulls at his features a moment before I feel him erupt inside me, his climax triggering mine like a bulldozer ploughing through my centre.

Refusing to look away, we hold each other's gaze as we groan in unison. As he releases my wrists, I immediately latch onto his body and ride the waves, giving me a new lease of life with each roll of my core. My walls clamp around him with an impossibly tight squeeze, milking his every drop as my nails pierce his chest. Sweat lines our bodies as we pant together, goose bumps covering my flesh. My breath shudders as we come down together, melting back into the bed whilst locked in an embrace.

We stay like that for a long time, Wyatt's mouth opening a few times to say something, but the words don't come out. Eventually, I relieve him of whatever torment his mind is battling and go to shower. Wyatt's fingers tighten on mine as I try to leave, instinctively clinging on. I smile, stroking his cheek.

"I'll be right back," I promise, and he releases me. Thankfully, he doesn't follow, allowing me the time to wash off and mentally prepare for today. I'm torn. The change in dynamic between Wyatt and me is so fresh, yet I'm about to walk into a situation where I might have to choose between shunning him or defending him. I don't know which I'll choose, but I do know I'll face scrutiny for either option.

How can I forgive the man who sold out my own twin? Regardless of his reasons, the damage can't be undone, and anything that happens from here on out isn't just on him, but on me as well. I know Meg's alive; I can feel it in the pit of my soul, but that's where my certainty ends. The lengths Fredrick will go to in hopes of fulfilling some twisted sense of revenge.

Yet I'm going back to my Souls today. One step back to hopefully take two forward. My heart has to return home to those I've come to consider my family and those who will stop at nothing to help me. They've already tried to save Meg once, and they'll do it again because we're on the same page. We have an understanding that my life doesn't come before hers, and I can't carry on without knowing she's okay. That information is all I need, then Wyatt can do whatever he damn well likes with me.

CHAPTER TWELVE

Hux's car is a sorry sight, a matte black bumper highlighting the dark scratches in the rest of the white paintwork, but it runs. Baxter saw us off from the garage as best he could with a small girl wrapped around his neck. His tail didn't stop wagging the entire time.

Avery sits up front in the passenger seat, her socked feet crossed on the dash. She hums and bobs her head to each song playing on the radio, pitching in with random chatter every so often. She's been this way for the entire drive, bottling up her grief to face the long hours on the road. I refuse to stop longer than a mere toilet break or to refresh the snacks, and she doesn't want to hang around unnecessarily either. We have somewhere to be.

Holding onto the memory of last night, of how I woke up with my arms wound around her beautiful body, I push my foot harder on the accelerator. Dare I toss around the vicious L word, but there is definitely a driving force pushing me onward. A need to get her back to the men she's missing. I get it now, although it's painfully too late. She's too precious for one heart, too loving to be caged to one man—even if I wish it wasn't so.

Suddenly, Avery withdraws her long legs and sits upright, turning to me with wide eyes. "Do you know what I've just realised?" I can't explain how my heart lurches and how I'm hanging on her every word and apparent revelation. "Meg's birthday is in May." I spare her a quick, confused look, feeling the slam of guilt at the mention of Meg's name. Each time it hurts a little harder, cuts a little deeper, as my feelings for Avery are unleashed. But it's not pain in Avery's expression, it's a mix of curiosity and wonder.

"Yeah, so?"

"Sooooo, she's my twin. We share a birthday. Fredrick knew my birthday since he took me from the hospital, so they must have lied about hers to keep covering up their secret." There's no need to ask who 'they' are. Our incredibly deceptive parents who used every weapon in their arsenal to keep up this pretence. I slide my eyes back to the road, although there's something unusually cute about watching Avery piece it all together. Playing detective with her own life like it's a live TV drama. "Meg thinks she is three months older than me. That's the end of her summer pool parties, I suppose."

Avery lets out a small laugh, the sound light but tinged with a trace of something else. I continue to slide glances her way, trying to decipher it until she notices. "What? I'm trying to be optimistic." Despite there being no harshness to her voice, a gut-punching sensation levels me anyway. Just another way Avery is fighting to keep her head above sea level, and I'm the sole cause of it. I grip the steering wheel tighter, the familiar surge of anger bubbling under my skin.

"Sounds exhausting," I huff. Avery forces a smirk, leaning back into her seat and tilting her head toward me.

"Why wasn't there a big celebration for your birthday?" she asks. "I know it's just before mine, since Cathy was always so desperate for you to come home for it." I drum my fingers on the wheel, pretending her nonchalant tone fools me. She's deflecting, switching the conversation before the hurt settles. Although whether she's trying to protect herself or me, I can't be sure. At least for now, I can help maintain the distraction.

"Well, I don't really care for mine but Garrett forces me to throw that fresher's party every year as a guise to celebrate." Just the mention of it brings back a flood of unwanted memories.

That party where I was furious to find her in the middle of our team's groupies, looking delectable despite being mostly covered up. My fury wasn't directed at her for crashing it though, but because that was the first moment I saw Axel defending her. He tried to hide her from me, and I sought to send a clear message.

It backfired of course, the guys instantly standing against me and taking her side. I hated how quickly they turned when they knew, *they knew*, the torment I suffered because of her. I'm certain they became her bodyguards from that night, shielding her from me and truly, I haven't felt so betrayed since Nixon kicked me out of my childhood home. It's all about her, and it always has been.

Avery's attention turns back to the open stretch of freeway ahead, her fingers idly playing with the hem of my oversized hoodie swamping her small frame. She made sure the few clothes we had were dry cleaned whilst we ate breakfast in the diner again, and that orange monstrosity was at the top of the pile. It feels a bit too late to tell her I never even liked the damn thing and that she should probably just keep it, but my stubbornness shines through. I just can't help but love the small fights.

"What about the guys? When are their birthdays?"

Her question seems innocent enough, but something about the way she asks makes me glance over, catching the faint crease in her brow. I raise a brow of my own.

"You don't know?"

Her little pink tongue quickly pokes out, moistening her lips as if she's embarrassed by my question. Or maybe I said it more as an accusation. I really can't keep myself in check when I'm around her.

"It's never really come up," she admits, giving an awkward half-shrug. "You know, what with running from a madman and all. We haven't exactly had time to slow down and...date properly."

I nod my head, processing her words. Jealousy and regret toys with the clench of my jaw, but I'm swift to tuck away the ugly emotions for reflection another time.

"Fair enough. Well, Dax's is March fourteenth. He'll tell you it's the best day of the year since it's also Pi Day. He bakes himself a birthday pie and forces us all to do trivia. Spoiler alert, he always wins."

Avery grins, her posture relaxing as I continue.

"Garrett's June fifth. He's a very proud Slytherin because of it. Movie marathons and themed snacks are a must. Axel's a summer baby, August second, and—" I pause, glancing her way with a slight wince. "You missed Huxley's. December twenty-seventh."

"What?!" Avery bolts upright in her seat, so fast I worry she'll give herself whiplash. Her expression is equal parts shock and outrage. "Why didn't he tell me? We could've celebrated at the cabin!" I snort softly, flicking on the indicator as I guide the car toward the next exit.

"We never celebrate. He hates his birthday. He'll do anything to avoid it."

"That's stupid," Avery pouts, crossing her arms like she's ready to stage an intervention. Shrugging one shoulder, I let her words hang for a moment before responding. There's so much to Huxley the world doesn't see or doesn't care to try. I know with Avery that isn't the case, and like she said, they just haven't had the time for these sorts of conversations. I just didn't think I'd be the one having it with her.

"He finds it superficial. Part of his '*running away from being a rich kid*' thing. He grew up being given everything he could ever want, except the two things he really needed."

Avery's crystal blue gaze sharpens, curiosity causing her to twist back towards me. "What's that?" she asks tentatively, possibly afraid of the answer.

"To be loved and to be taken seriously," I say simply. "All that blonde hair and charisma? It was a gift for a child model and movie star. But no one cared to look beneath the surface. He was told what to say, how to act, how to dress. And after years of appeasing his parents, they stole everything. Every cent of the money he made. To them, he was just a piggy bank."

Avery's expression shifts, her earlier indignation melting into something softer yet heavier. She sighs, dropping her head back against the seat. "I take it back. That's not stupid at all."

Falling into a thoughtful silence, Avery refocuses on the road and realises where we are. With a sharp intake of air, her fingers start fidgeting as she looks up at the large hospital coming into view. It's heaving with cars trying to park near the building, horns blaring with impatience to see loved ones. I pull over a few meters from the rear ambulance bay and reach across her to pop the passenger door.

"You head in. I'll park and be up in a minute."

Avery turns to me sharply, her small hands gripping my arm, so I'm stuck leaning over her. "No, you won't," she accuses, her cheeks staining pink. I swallow, finding myself far too close to her all-consuming eyes.

"You really think after these last few days I haven't gotten some insight into your mind? Did you seriously just drive me all the way here just to turn around and leave?"

Her words hang in the air, daring me to argue. I don't. Instead, I just hang there, wondering how she's managed to crawl beneath my defenses. Then, when her stare becomes too intrusive, I move. Twisting the arm she's holding, I grip the back of her neck and crash her lips against mine.

The kiss ignites my soul, spreading like a wildfire. She consumes me in an instant, eradicating who I thought I was and replacing it with who she needs me to be. My hand tangles in her hair, anchoring her to me as if letting go would break me. Her lips are soft but desperate, drowning out the rest of the world outside. The blaring horns, the chaos of the hospital, even the frantic thud of my own heartbeat. It all disappears until all that remains is her.

Her hands slide up my chest, fisting the fabric of my T-shirt as she pulls me closer, her breath mingling with mine in a frantic exchange. I pour everything into that kiss. The anguish, the longing, the unspoken words that I've been too much of a coward to say aloud. My thumb brushes her jaw, the fragile curve of her face fitting perfectly in my grasp, and I can feel the faint tremble in her body as if she's holding back tears.

I won't let her shed a single tear for me. I'm not worth her sorrow. Slowly taking her clawed hand in mine, I pry her fingers from my T-shirt. Carefully, gently, relieving her from keeping me here. I doubt she notices, too caught up in the clashing of our lips and the battle between our tongues. Even when we made love last night, which was indeed my first time, I didn't allow this depth of emotion to seep through. I suppose that's because this is a goodbye.

When I finally pull back, I don't go far. Our foreheads touch, her shaky breath mingling with mine, her lips red and swollen. "Tell Axel I send my love," I whisper hoarsely, my voice breaking under the weight of everything I can't say. Pulling away, I will her to get out of the car. Leave whilst we both still can. Of course she doesn't.

Avery's arm snaps out, hitting me square in the chest. I take the hit, figuring it's what she needs to vent, but I didn't count on the hand that slams down on my crotch, takes a whole handful of cock and squeezes. Hard. I squeak, flinching a few inches out of my seat. Her grip is unrelenting, despite the genuine fear in my eyes. Leaning closer, Avery's nostrils flare, and when she speaks, it's with the most threatening tone her sweet voice can manage.

"Tell him yourself, asshole." Jerking her hand, she traps my balls against my thigh and drives her fist down deeper. I try to twist in the seat, but there's no release, and another small squeal that I'm ashamed of escapes me. "Park the car and I'll see you inside."

Whipping her hand away, I gasp at the release. My hands are hovering over my privates, hesitant to touch myself. The door slams, and she's gone, leaving my heart punching against my chest and my tender cock recoiling into my body.

"Oh, Wyatt Junior. Why is it always you that pays the price?"

GARRETT

Pacing around the tiny waiting room I've been forced into while the doctor performs his morning check-up, I can't stop replaying that night in my head. Like a scratched record that plays the same song, glitches, and jumps back over and over. Axel's body limp in my arms, the warmth leaving his body, the words I should have said lodged in my throat. His life was literally slipping away, and no amount of praying or crying could bring him back to me. I can't even consider if the air ambulance hadn't shown up when it did; I refuse to travel down that path knowing a part of me won't come back.

My fingers clasp into fists, my body shaking with the need to be back at his bedside. It's been two fucking days, and not a single doctor can tell me why he hasn't woken up yet. Dax and Huxley have been staying at a motel on the edge of the city, returning during visiting hours like one of the nurses suggested I also did. Like I told her, either I'm allowed to stay with Axel at all times or she'd better get a second bed ready in his room, 'cause I will jab a scalpel into my throat if that's what it takes.

Funnily enough, not only was I permitted to remain, but we now have security standing guard by the door, and I got a complimentary evaluation from a psychologist. Nothing like a mental sweep of my childhood trauma to get the juices flowing, and I know where to direct all of that unearthed murderous intention. Fucking Fredrick.

That same nurse who called security on me walks past the glass door, rounding the safety of her desk before nodding for me to return. I fly into the hallway, making her flinch as I jog back to Axel's room, my footsteps echoing down the corridor. Nodding to today's guard with a cocky smile, I slip into the room, and my heart finally settles at the sight of his sleeping form. The steady beep of the heart monitor is the only reassurance I have that he's still here, still mine.

"Sorry that took so long," I murmur, like he can hear me. Like he's just sleeping and not locked away in whatever place his mind has gone. Talking to him is the only thing that keeps me from losing it. Crossing the room, I fluff his pillows out of habit, fingers trembling. The private room, with its simple comforts and muted light, is the best thing Huxley's money has ever bought.

I kick off my shoes and jeans, slipping under the covers beside him. The sterile smell of the hospital is a stark contrast to the warmth of his skin. I burrow closer, resting my head on his shoulder and tangling our fingers together.

"I was thinking," I sigh, melting back into his body. "Dangerous, I know, but I had to do something. Anyways, I was thinking that after you're all healed and I've painted my bedroom walls with Fredrick's blood, we should go away. All of us. Somewhere far away."

I let the words spill out, trying to sound casual, like I'm not terrified he'll never hear any of this. Like I'm not deciding to pour my soul of all the shit I shouldn't have held back.

"Italy, maybe. Florence first, to see Michelangelo's David. Then Venice, because you'd look ridiculously gorgeous in a gondola. We could hit the Sistine Chapel, rave it up in Vatican City, and finish off with a villa in Rome. Just us, the Souls, and an obscene amount of pizza."

The dream feels fragile as it leaves my lips. That's a new development—dreaming. I haven't bothered holding onto hope in the longest time, because what's the point? I only trust what I can see and feel in front of me. But while being met with only silence, the mind wonders. No, worse than that. It fractures.

Leaning into Axel, I let the words keep coming. "You don't know this, because I've never told anyone, but I kinda really like history and architecture. When I was a kid, I used to lose myself in books from my dad's study, imagining I was away on their travels with them. Like they hadn't left me behind. I taught myself that as long as there was that connection and the fridge wasn't empty, I was fine."

The confession comes without warning, raw and unfiltered, surprising even me. This is the reason I hate therapists, and psychologists are even worse. I've been mentally battered open like an egg, encased in cracks. Well, might as well keep going. My gooey center might pour out.

"Until they abandoned me for that month-long cruise. I was nine, left with a wad of cash and a list of takeout numbers. I didn't call a single one. Gave up, I guess. I wanted to see how long it'd take someone to notice I was gone." My throat tightens, the memory sharp and bitter. "Eleven. Days. It took eleven fucking days, Axe. I barely remember being scraped off the floor by a police officer, the blue lights flashing beyond my eyes, waking in a hospital bed with a tube down my throat. *Force-feeding me.* Can you imagine?"

I chuckle, a rough and hollow sound. As if I haven't been catching the food trolley three times again when it's being wheeled past, ensuring I'm eating Axel's fair share. It's included in the room cost, and I'm not one for wasting Huxley's money. Alas, I digress.

"That was the last time I gave a shit about being loved, until you. I never ever thought I could deserve you, but I swear if you come back. If we can get Avery back, I can show you both. I can make you both so happy."

Axel doesn't stir, but his presence continues to ground me. I reach for the remote hooked to the bed, pulling the TV closer. I flick through channels until a Planet Earth documentary takes my fancy, leaving it on silent. When words fail me, when I've run out of things to say, I take to reading the subtitles. Hopefully the cadence of my voice, something steady and familiar, is soothing to Axel. A bit of familiarity to latch onto and pull himself back to me.

Or he's cursing me inside his head to shut the fuck up, but until such a time that he is screaming it in my face, I will keep going. This is all I have to offer him right now, and it's all that's stopping me from falling apart.

"Hey, I've told you before. You can't be in the bed with him," a deep southern drawl cuts through my blissful Italian reverie. I wake with a startled snort, my cheek pressed to Axel's shoulder.

A broad woman with pale skin and a mischievous smirk looms over me, her blue-and-white dress valiantly struggling to contain her ample curves. She jabs me in the side with a playful poke. "C'mon now, sugar," she teases.

I swat at her hand like she's a fly. "Back off, Mamma. Don't you know I'm a taken man?"

Sitting upright, I stretch my arms over my head, earning a satisfying crack from my spine before swinging my legs off the bed. The nurse, who has insisted I call her Mamma ever since Axel was rushed into surgery, grins and scoops up my discarded jeans, tossing them at me.

"Boy, you better put those chicken legs away before Dr. Breeson comes back. One more strike, and he'll boot your behind out of this ward faster than you can say 'fried okra.'"

I catch the jeans and glare at her, indignant. "First of all, we're paying Dr. Breeson's annual salary to keep Axel in this room. And second of all, I do not have chicken legs."

Mamma arches a brow as I glance down at my thighs, noticing the lack of definition I've been studiously ignoring. Huffing, I hop off the bed and yank on my jeans. She cackles as she smooths the sheets around Axel, artfully disguising the evidence of my illicit cuddle session.

On the other side of the bed, I take Axel's hand in mine, careful not to jostle the cannula. My shirt clings to my chest, damp with stale sweat, and I'm pretty sure I smell like I've spent a week marinating in regret. My mouth tastes like something crawled inside and died. A fitting reflection of how I feel inside.

"Mamma," I say, dragging a hand through my disheveled hair, "can you stay with him for five minutes while I grab a shower?"

She pauses, adjusting the IV with practiced efficiency, before her eyes crinkle into a warm smile. "Course I will, darlin'. Go on now."

Leaning down, I brush a kiss against Axel's forehead and run my hand over his cropped hair. He's going to lose his mind when he wakes up and sees it growing out like this.

"He's lucky to have you," Mamma muses softly, her voice carrying a surprising tenderness as she folds the blanket over his chest.

I glance back at him, my throat tightening. "No," I murmur. "He's really not."

In the bathroom, I strip off my rumpled clothes and twist the shower dial all the way to scalding, knowing damn well it'll barely reach lukewarm. Stepping into the spray, I grab the cheap hospital shower gel and lather up my chest, the faintly medicinal scent doing nothing to improve my mood.

The distance between us, even just these few feet, feels unbearable. My heart aches like a wound that refuses to heal, bleeding fresh every time I look at his face. Distracted, I forget about the bruises lining my ribs until my hand brushes them, and I hiss in pain.

Cursing under my breath, I rinse off and twist the shower off with a sharp jerk. I reach for what has to be the world's smallest hand towel and attempt to dry myself, the thin fabric doing little more than smearing water around. Pulling on clean clothes from the bag I'm living out of, I brush my teeth and take a moment to lean against the sink, staring at my reflection in the mirror. Dark circles shadow my eyes, bruises lining my cheeks and throat, my jaw tight with unspoken fears. Let's not talk about my hair.

With a steadying breath, I push off the counter and step back into the room, where Axel waits in peaceful silence. Mamma quickly ducks out when I reappear, leaving me to another day of sitting here, holding his hand, and staring at him. I understand he needs time to heal, but if he could just open his hazel eyes or give me any hint that he's going to be okay, that would be fantastic.

A soft knock sounds at the door, and I ignore it. My eyes are set solely on the man I nearly lost—the one I'll never let come to harm ever again. I might not be much, but he can have whatever he deems worth saving. Just open your damn eyes, Axe.

"Garrett?" a soft feminine voice sounds from just inside the door. My hand on Axel's instinctively clenches, anticipating the trick that my mind is about to play on me. "Garrett," the voice calls again, more insistent this time, and there's a shuffle of footsteps approaching the bed. She's a ghost, dredged up by exhaustion and longing. I don't dare look up; don't dare let the hope sink its claws into me. My throat tightens as I grit my teeth, focusing all my energy on Axel's steady but maddeningly silent form.

"Garrett, look at me." Well, here goes nothing. I whip my head up so fast I feel the crack in my neck. And there she is, standing a few feet away, her hands clasped nervously in front of her. *Avery.*

Her hair is slightly messy, like she's been running her hands through it for hours, and her eyes are red-rimmed but alive with determination. She's dressed in that vibrant orange hoodie she loves, the one that should look ridiculous swamping her black leggings, but instead she is the definition of adorable. And she's here.

"Peach?" My voice cracks on her name, disbelief warring with the tidal wave of relief that crashes over me.

"I got here as soon as I could," she says, her lips trembling as she steps closer. Her eyes scan over the state of me before they flick to Axel, and her breath catches, her expression crumbling. "Oh, Gare..."

Before I can stop myself, I'm on my feet, the chair scraping loudly against the floor as it's shoved backward. I cross the space between us in two strides and pull her into my arms.

She lets out a quiet gasp but doesn't hesitate, throwing her arms around my neck and holding on like she's afraid I'll disappear. I bury my face in her hair, breathing her in, grounding myself in the reality that she's here, warm and alive and real.

"You came back," I manage to choke out, my voice thick with emotion. I feel her shaking against me, her lithe frame pressed against the length of my body, and her face in the curve of my neck.

"I had to be with him," she whispers, her voice breaking. "Why does it have to be him?" I don't think she meant to say it so bluntly, given how her body tenses. I tighten my arms around her, trying to anchor myself, trying to keep from falling apart completely.

"Trust me, Peach. I'd switch positions in an instant." For a moment, there's nothing but the sound of her soft cries muffled against my chest and the steady beeping of Axel's heart monitor. When she pulls back slightly, her hands cup my face, her thumbs brushing away the tears I hadn't even realized were falling.

"You look like shit," she says, her lips curving into a faint, watery smile. A strangled laugh escapes me, and I shake my head.

"I feel like it."

Her smile falters, and she glances past me to Axel. The air shifts, the weight of the room pressing down on us again.

"How bad is it?" she asks softly as she steps closer to the bed.

I can't speak, can't find the words to explain how close we came to losing him, how his lungs were filling with blood by the time we got him here, and how helpless I've felt these past two days. So I don't. I just reach out and take her hand, guiding her to sit in the chair I'd been occupying moments ago. She sits gingerly, her eyes glued to Axel's face, and reaches out to brush her fingers over the short hair on his head.

"He'd hate that," she echoes what I was thinking. I resolve then to do something about Axel's hair before he wakes. "Hey, Axe," she whispers, "it's me. I'm here. We're together now." Watching her cup Axel's cheek, cradling him with such vulnerability, shatters something inside me. The boys can come and go, containing their emotions to visiting hours, but Avery understands. I'm not alone in this anymore. She'll stay with me, talk to him with me, and feel this crushing, unbearable pain with me.

Dropping to my knees, as if my legs have been holding on just long enough for someone to take over, I kneel beside her, lowering my head onto her thighs, and for the first time in two days, I let myself cry.

AVERY

I hold Garrett until his shoulders cease to shake, holding up the weight of everything crashing down on him all at once. His hands are fists in my lap, being brushed lightly by my thumb running over his white knuckles.

"Garrett," I whisper. He flinches slightly but doesn't pull away. His head drops forward onto my thighs, dark strands of his hair falling across his face as he chokes out a shuddering breath. "You gonna be okay?"

"I'm not-" His voice cracks, raw and broken. "I'm not used to feeling this way."

"I know." My hands shift to his hair, running through the damp strands. "I'm sorry I wasn't here."

"It's okay," Garrett murmurs.

My eyes rove over the man in the bed. He doesn't look like himself under the harsh lighting, his skin pale and his hair longer than I've ever seen it, in short, gray spikes covering his scalp. On his wrist, just above the hand I'm holding, is a very familiar compass bracelet. My chest tightens so sharply, I forget how to breathe, but I don't let Garrett know it. He has enough to worry about.

The heart monitor beeps routinely, the only reminder that Axel is still with us. He's so still, his lashes fanning his cheeks and his mouth slack. I'm praying behind those eyelids that he's not suffering. That he's not stuck in his own version of hell with us helplessly waiting on the outside.

At some point, as my mind ping-pongs between overthinking and becoming a blank slate, Garrett twists. He places himself between my legs, facing the bed. His head lies back, still being massaged by my hand while the other holds Axel's. Garrett can't see him, so his eyes find me instead.

Endless dark pools of emotion, swirling and staring. I succumb and tilt my head downward, drawing my hand over his cheek. His face presses against my palm, his warmth a contrast to Axel's cool touch. A touch of wetness seeps through my leggings, rogue, silent tears seeping from Garrett's eye. the curve of my neck, and I feel the damp warmth of his tears soaking into my skin.

"I'm here," I remind him, rubbing his jaw in soothing strokes. "I'm not going to let you go through this alone." His breath hitches, and then the dam breaks. A gut-wrenching sob tears from his chest, his hands clenching onto my arm and wrist like he's afraid I might disappear. I tense my thighs around his shoulders, holding him as tightly as I can, rocking us gently in place, whispering soft reassurances even as my own tears threaten to spill over.

But I refuse to let them fall.

Garrett's pain is palpable, heavy in the air between us. It's in the way his body trembles, in the raw sound of his cries, in the desperate way he clings to me. He's been shouldering this burden, carrying a weight that no amount of humor can penetrate. His heart is breaking.

After what feels like an eternity, his sobs begin to subside again. His breathing evens out, though it's still shaky, and his hold on me loosens just enough to turn himself into my thigh, hugging my leg. I don't try to shift him from the floor, figuring it's where he wants to be. Where the ground is a solid presence, he can't fall through, and I'm this anchor. I keep my hand on his face, grounding him, as I look down into his tear-streaked face.

"Right, come on. We can't have Axel seeing you like this," I tell him, firm but gentle. Garrett's glistening dark eyes meet mine. I offer him a small, tentative smile, despite the wave of sadness that strikes everytime I see his bruises. "The best thing is to be our usual selves; give him a sense of normalcy. I've been here for almost an hour, and I've yet to see you eat anything." His lips twitch upward in the faintest response. There he is, simmering under the surface.

The quiet is shattered by the sudden thud of a bag hitting the floor. Garrett and I both jump, startled, and our heads whip toward the door. Dax is standing in the doorway, his arms hanging loosely at his sides, and his blue eyes wide and rimmed with exhaustion. One of his hands is bandaged around a splint holding his fingers straight. His usual softness is nowhere to be seen, replaced by something hard and sharp. I swallow, watching it pass as he blinks, clearly expecting me to disappear like a mirage.

"Avery," he gasps, seeming rooted in place. Huxley crashes into his back, the pair of them narrowly avoiding tripping over the duffle bag on the ground. Hux's brown gaze hits me like a sledgehammer, my resolve threatening to crack again. Although that's not what straightens my spine and steers my voice to sound so steady.

"Where have you been?" I raise a brow. Garrett remains curled against my leg; his arms slack now, his breathing slow and steady. I feel him shift slightly, angling himself away from the door like he's not ready to face them with his face stained and eyes puffy. My free hand continues to stroke his hair, my touch soft and rhythmic, grounding him and myself.

"Us?" Huxley frowns around a split lip, a scoff of disbelief escaping him. I get the irony, but my body remains tense, taut with accusation.

"Yes, you. I walked into an absolute mess in here. Someone should have stayed with Garrett."

"Well, *excuse me*," Huxley flies into full defensive mode. "If any more of us demanded to stay overnight, security would have had us all escorted out in handcuffs. We had to make a truce and stick to visiting hours. What else were we—" Dax places his good hand on Hux's shoulder, settling his rant down to a muttered simmer. Stepping over the bag, Dax slowly crosses the room. His head is nodding, his eyes sunken.

"You're right, we're late. We ran into town for supplies. We don't usually take this long." Lowering onto his knees at my side, he leans into my side, breathing me in. Warmth stirs at his presence, and as I open my arm to hug him, he presses his face against my ribs. "I've missed you."

Dax's quiet admission sends a ripple through me, his words laced with exhaustion, relief, and perhaps guilt. My arm tightens around him while I shake my feet from my shoes and cross my legs over Garrett's middle. All the while, Axel has my outstretched hand.

"I've missed you too," I reply, threatening to fall into the sea of blue blinking up at me. Somehow, the edges of my memory had forgotten just how beautiful he is in person. How viscerally my heart reacts to him. He's here. They're all here, barring one who seems to have lost his way.

Huxley stands frozen just inside the doorway, his eyes darting between me, Garrett, and Dax. His jaw works, tension etched into every line of his face, but he doesn't say anything. Not yet. Instead, he steps forward, his movements slow and deliberate, like he's not sure if he's welcome.

"We've been through hell this week," Hux mutters, tinged with concern. His gaze locks on Axel, silently sleeping, and then slides to me. "For multiple reasons." Coming to stand just behind me, Huxley lets out a weighted sigh, raking a hand through his blonde hair. "Sorry for being away so long, Gare. I could lie to you and say town was busy, but truth is I wasn't in a rush to get back. I can't stand looking at Axel like... this."

Like a siren on the shore, Garrett blinks out of the numb ravine he'd slipped into. I feel him startle at how close everyone is. There's a long pause before he lifts his head slowly, his eyes bloodshot and heavy-lidded as he briefly meets Hux's gaze.

"It's fine, man. I get it."

Huxley's hands lower to my shoulders, rubbing out the tension settled there. He works his way down, his thumbs brushing against my neck and collarbone, eventually folding himself over to hug me. His hair tickles my face, his deep breaths skating over my front. I cling to them all, rooted to that single chair and connecting us in the only way I know how. I've been missing for a week, but it's enough for the fractures to grow. Enough for the Shadowed Souls to splinter from the inside out. At least now, we're together and we can rebuild. We can find our ways back to each other.

"The fuck—" a harsh curse slices into the room as Wyatt trips over the bag still in the doorway. Huxley's hold around me tenses, and he whips upright. Within a flash, I've released Axel, dodged those on the floor, and I am standing in front of Huxley's heaving chest, making an effort to hold him back.

"Step aside, Swan," he demands, devoid of the gentle tone he'd only just found. I stand firm, giving him a little shove to look at me.

"No," I set my jaw. "it's not what you think. Wyatt was protecting me, in his own barbaric way," I grumble, wondering why my instincts are screaming at me to defend him. I guess our relationship really has come far in the past week. Huxley tries to push me aside into Dax's waiting arms, but I refuse to budge. "Huxley, I won't let you hurt him."

"It's fine," Wyatt sighs dramatically from across the room. He's paced to the foot of the bed, lifting Axel's medical notes and scanning through them. "I deserve it."

"Oh my god, will you stop?!" I hiss over my shoulder, narrowing my eyes with as much venom as my fragile heart can muster. "This pity party bullshit is done. You don't deserve it, and we don't need to pretend we hate each other anymore. Those days are done."

Something akin to pity sparks in Wyatt's green eyes. Mourning the old days when it was easy. Push me away and hide from his feelings. Not anymore.

"Aves," Dax clears his throat, tentatively brushing my arm. "Let them hash it out. It'll be okay."

I only realise now that I'm trembling. The strain of trying to piece them all back together to fix the bonds that have been broken, is too much for me alone. I close my eyes to exhale, and Huxley's small nudge on my hip eases me in Dax's direction.

Opening them, I look back to Garrett, now planted in the 'hand-holding' seat. He nods before returning his attention to Axel, reminding me of why we're here. Of what's really important. I stumble into Dax's arms, allowing him to hold me up in the hug I've been needing. His bandaged hand is careful to remain untouched.

"I've missed you," he whispers into my ear again, pressing a kiss against my neck. "I've needed you." I melt into Dax's body, my arms wound tightly around his neck. There isn't an inch of space between us, our hearts syncing and erasing the past week of separation. In Dax, I find my home, as I do in all of them.

Twisting to look over my shoulder, I watch Huxley approach Wyatt with bated breath. I wait for the fist clench, the first swing, but it doesn't come. Instead, when Hux raises his arms, it's to engulf Wyatt in a similar hug to the one Dax has me caged in. Shocked, green eyes catch mine, Wyatt's face falling slack and then twisting in confusion. Words I can't hear are muttered, emotions filtering through Wyatt's features I'm not accustomed to seeing.

Dax shifts against me, his head lifting slightly as he looks over at Garrett. "We brought food," he says, looking to fill the silence around the heart monitor. "Not great food, but it's something. Figured you'd be starving."

"Starving," Garrett mutters. His tone lacks its usual enthusiasm, but when he finally sits back, scrubbing a hand over his face, I can see the faintest hint of gratitude in his expression.

Dax pulls back, his warmth leaving my side as he reaches for the bag he dropped earlier, unzipping it and pulling out a stack of sandwiches and bottled drinks. Setting the food on the small table by the window, he pulls out a packaged object and carefully places it down.

"And we got this."

Garrett's eyes drag across the room, settling on the chrome-handled razor. He vaults himself out of the seat with more energy than I reckon he actually has. Dax's head tilts, hiding a small blush. "I know there's not much we can control in our current state, but I thought this is something we can do."

Garrett steps around me and Dax, his jaw tightening as he crosses the room. For a second, I think he is going for the razor, but instead, he turns away and pulls Wyatt into a rough, almost desperate hug. I suck in a sharp breath, not realising how much it meant to me that Wyatt was accepted back into his brother's fold. How much it matters that we're all connected and no one is left behind.

"Don't ever fucking disappear like that again," Garrett growls, his voice thick. "She's all of ours, and we all get a say in how to keep her safe." Dax nuzzles against my neck, unable to let me go quite yet.

"Or you know, I could just decide for myself," I raise a brow. Wyatt and Garrett look at me like that's the stupidest thing they've ever heard and start to chuckle, rubbing each other's backs. Despite being the unwilling cause of their comedy, the tension has broken, and for that I'm thankful. A small smile tugs at my own lips.

Garrett breaks away, ignoring the food in favor of picking up the razor. He beckons us all to come over to the bed, taking my hand in his.

"Up you go, Peach," he directs. Huxley and Dax take care to lift Axel's sleeping form upright so that I can slip in behind him. His weight is crushing, despite the lack of definition in his muscles. Wyatt ducks his head, feet shuffling towards the window, when Garrett catches him by the collar of his shirt. Planting the razor in Wyatt's hand, he has no choice but to join us.

Dax fetches an overbed table from across the room. On it, he places a water jug, plastic cup, and can of shaving foam one at a time, whilst Huxley grabs a few hand towels from the bathroom. With careful, measured movements, we all work to lay the towel across my stomach and lower Axel's head back in his new upright position.

Without much discussion, we all fall into our roles. Wyatt swallows thickly, dipping the razor into Dax's cup of water, watching the ripples spread across the surface. Garrett is in charge of foaming. Wyatt stands beside me, steady and focused, his movements deliberate as he begins shaving Axel's head. Huxley has a towel ready to gently wipe the path Wyatt's razor takes, presenting freshly shaved patches. Before me, Axel comes back into view.

When Wyatt hands me the razor, Dax and Garrett move in to lift Axel's head and shoulders again. My fingers wrap around the handle, and Wyatt's fingers close over mine. I don't dare blink up at him the way I want to, intent on gliding the razor up the curve of Axel's neck. Wyatt leads me through it, each stroke removing the uneven growth and revealing the smooth, pale skin beneath. It's not perfect, but it's good enough. We're working together to care for him. He'd love it.

Section by section, we pass the razor around, each of us contributing to the slow transformation. Garrett hovers nearby, his brow furrowed in concentration as he angles the razor awkwardly around Axel's temple. Dax steps in to help, tilting Axel's head to reveal the delicate spot behind his left ear.

We tilt his head this way and that, all intent on watching the smooth glides until his extra scalp is exposed. My hands are steady, but my chest feels tight, Axel's weight pressing down on me. He's still so motionless, his breaths shallow but steady. I swallow hard, pushing the thoughts aside and focusing on the task at hand. With a final brush of the blade over his forehead, Garrett withdraws and smiles. Finally smiles, like his heart is about to burst. It eases everything tight in me.

Dax gathers the towels beneath his arm and the hair-filled cup in hand, disappearing into the bathroom. Garrett takes the razor back to the bag while Huxley and Wyatt help to hold Axel and I slip out. As the boys find chairs to settle into, I stay by Axel's side, running my fingertips lightly over his newly shaven head. He looks... lighter somehow. The sharp angles of his face stand out more now, and there's a soft reminder of the Axel I know.

"So," Hux opens a bottle of water and takes a long swig. "You gonna tell us what you did with our Little Swan?" He looks back to Wyatt, leaning on the window sill. Wyatt's eyes meet mine, a slight panic in his tightened lips. Where would he even start?

"I hope you weren't gentle," Garrett pitches in from his chair. "We weren't in any of our practices." I feel a blush rush to my cheeks, and I throw a dare stare in his direction. Garrett chuckles, throwing his legs up to cross his ankles on Huxley's thigh and taking a large bite of a sandwich.

Wyatt opens his mouth to respond but is thankfully cut off by the clicking of high heels echoing in from the hallway. Glancing towards the door frame, I see Garrett's face fall. The smile he'd only just found disappears, his sandwich forgotten on the table. I grip onto Axel's hand protectively, anticipating a threat advancing on us.

A doctor steps into the room, followed by a woman dressed for a business meeting rather than a hospital visit. A navy jumpsuit clings to her curves, pink detailing around the bust to a matching sash tied tightly to cinch her waist. Her neck and ears are dripping with expensive jewellery, her dark hair pulled back into a chignon bun.

"Who are you?" Huxley stands and confronts her. There's barely any height difference between the two with her six-inch heels. Ignoring the question, the woman's pale brown eyes drag over Axel lazily and come to rest on our joined hands. Her perfectly painted red lips lift in a sneer, the true reflection of her ugly personality coming to the surface. Straightening my shoulders, refusing to be intimidated, I latch onto Garrett's answer, dripping with venom.

"Although she doesn't deserve the title, this is Axel's mom."

AVERY

CHAPTER FIFTEEN

"Oh, my poor boy! What have you done to him?" Axel's mom saunters across the room to inspect the botched shave job we just finished, reaching out to run her finger across a few missed longer hairs. Garrett's hand shoots across from the other side of the bed, snatching her wrist tightly in his grip.

"Don't pretend you give a shit about him, Sharon," he hisses her name through his teeth. "He doesn't belong to you anymore." Garrett's dark eyes are blazing with fury, his arm trembling from the firm hold that has the slender woman whimpering.

After a tense second, which has even a doctor hovering in the doorway frozen with anticipation, Garrett releases her with a shove and moves to sit on the bed. Sliding his arm beneath Axel's neck, Garrett tenderly pulls him close like a lion protecting his sleeping mate from outside threats.

With a roll of her eyes, Sharon turns around to face the rest of us and holds out her palms expectantly. The doctor, whose name tag reads as Dr. Breeson, jerks into action. Rushing forward with a brown envelope I hadn't noticed he was holding, he pulls a pen from his jacket pocket and hands them both to Sharon.

Pulling the papers free, her eyes roam over the typed words, lips pursing before scrawling an elaborate signature with her manicured fingers. The glint of an outrageous diamond fixed to her skinny wedding finger catches Garrett's attention. His eyes narrowed as he tracks the jewel back down her side.

"There," she hands the paperwork back to the doctor, his forehead dripping with sweat, making his black hair look even greasier. "I've already made the necessary arrangements." He nods quickly, his eyes flicking back to Garrett before ducking out of the room like a bomb is about to detonate.

"What arrangements?" I ask when clearly no one else is going to speak. Dax's muscles are bunched by the bathroom door, his locked jaw matching Huxley's, who has edged around and slyly stepped in front of me. Sharon's pale eyes light up further as she takes in Huxley, scanning his handsome features and broad frame and pausing over his crotch for a beat too long.

"Axel's coming home with me."

"Like fuck he is!" Garrett roars, gently placing down Axel's head before leaping from the mattress to join the rest of us by the foot of the bed. "I refuse to let him out of my sight, especially around the likes of you. You're not beyond pimping out his unconscious body for the right price." His chest is heaving, fists clenched, ready for a fight that Sharon doesn't seem interested in having.

I clearly don't know as many details of Axel's past as everyone else in this room, but I know enough, and the woman before me isn't the monster I envisioned. Axel has her full lips and heart-shaped face, although that's where the similarities end.

Her hair sits perfectly at the back of her slender jewel-covered neck, her breasts too perky to be natural in an expensive pantsuit. She easily could have been a model or boutique owner, but I suppose marrying into money was more her speed. Twisting her lips at Garrett's comment and checking her watch, she looks to the ceiling as if her patience is being tested.

"I don't like this anymore than you do, but both the hospital and Waversea have been insistent. There aren't enough beds to keep him here indefinitely, and since Axel is still a minor by law, he needs to return to my care whether I want him to or not. I've got enough on my plate without babysitting a houseful of overgrown delinquents. By all means, tag along and play happy couples or whatever this is," she waves her hand vaguely between all of us. "He's being transported within the hour, with or without you."

Her heels click loudly across the floor as she moves to leave, my mind whirling with questions and concerns. My mouth opens, but it's not my voice that fills the room.

"We're all coming with him," Wyatt states coldly. Sharon halts at his demanding tone, looking back over her shoulder, although she isn't looking in his direction. A smirk pulls at her lips as she holds Huxley's gaze and raises a brow.

"As you wish. A bit of extra eye candy hanging around is never a bad thing," she winks at him and leaves, her hips slinking with much more vigour than before. Huxley visibly shudders. *Well, that was disturbing.* No one moves for a while, watching the empty space in the doorway.

I'm the first one to turn, finding Dax's blue eyes fixed on me with a note of longing in them. For a split second, I could have easily run into his arms and allowed his spicy scent to wash away my worries. His gentle touch and soft lips to take control of my pain and wipe it from existence. But that won't help Garrett, who is quickly spiraling back into the panic that consumed him earlier.

I close the space between us and take his trembling fists in my hands. Garrett stares over my head; his neck is so taut it looks like it might snap itself at any moment. "Hey, look at me." I beckon his head to tilt downwards. "Nothing will happen to him. You heard her, she'll be preoccupied."

"I promised he'd never go back there," Garrett's eyes shift between mine, the glassiness from earlier reappearing. I cup his jaw, feeling the weight of the others all pressing closer.

"None of us wanted this, but our hands are tied," Dax says from my side. Huxley swallows hard beyond my shoulder.

"The least we can do is make sure we're there for him when he wakes."

"She won't get within ten feet of him," Wyatt growls, his shoulders tense and jaw tight. I blink over at him, but he doesn't spare me a glance. His expression is murderous and set on the empty doorway. "I'll make sure of it."

Something about Wyatt's certainty breaks through Garrett's rising panic. Nodding slowly, some of the tension ebbs from his shoulders, his concerned gaze flicking back to Axel. On a heavy sigh, he whispers his agreement and shifts back to the bedside, brushing his fingers along Axel's jaw. Peacefully sleeping Axel, blissfully unaware that he's about to return to the place of his nightmares.

No time was wasted. Security quickly evacuate most of us from the room to prepare Axel for transportation. As expected by all, Garrett refuses to leave. Luckily, Dax and Huxley are in the habit of keeping their belongings close, and Wyatt left ours in the trunk so no time is wasted gathering our belongings. Within just a few minutes, we are ready to go, settling in for yet another long journey.

Watching through the SUV's windscreen, the gurney is pushed into the back of an ambulance in the hospital's layby. Garrett is also on the bed, his arm and leg hoisted over his lover, hissing at anyone who gets too close like a pissed-off cat. The two porters struggle to move the extra weight on the silver ramp, using their shoulders to stop it from rolling back down. I have to snort at the ridiculousness of it all.

Finally managing to secure the gurney in place and slam the back doors closed, one of the porters raps on the side of the ambulance for the driver to pull away. Huxley doesn't waste a second, keeping the SUV right on their tail as the van merges into traffic. His jaw is tight, hands gripping the wheel as he weaves through the busy streets, refusing to let any cars slide between us.

Wyatt sits in the passenger seat, for once relinquishing control. His elbow rests on the doorframe, his sharp green eyes fixed on the ambulance ahead, though the occasional twitch of his knee betrays his impatience.

In the back, Dax and I sit huddled together. I could have taken the seat against the other window, but the space between us seemed too vast. An urgency to pull him close and not let go shifted me into the center. The anxiety churning in my chest is quieter with his presence anchoring me. My legs are draped across his lap, where his injured hand lies carefully and his free fingers trace patterns on my calf through my leggings.

"So," Huxley starts when we can't handle only the sound of the engine humming through the cab. Not even the radio is playing. "Does someone want to tell me why my car has a black bumper and a grey passenger door? I'm not even going to ask about the left-side windows not being black-out glass like they should be."

Wyatt's jaw twitches, but he doesn't turn around. I swallow hard, shifting against Dax, who seems to find the whole situation amusing. A low chuckle rumbles in his chest as he glances at me, his hand stilling on my leg.

"I was wondering how long it would take him to bring it up," Dax snorts beside my ear. I was hoping Huxley was too distracted in the parking lot to notice the mix-match parts making up the SUV's exterior. I should have known better. The silence stretches until Wyatt flicks his green gaze over his shoulder at me.

"This one is all on you," he says unhelpfully, before turning his attention back to the ambulance in front. I roll my eyes, not knowing why I expected anything different.

"We had an accident," I finally mutter. The events of that night replay in my mind like a stuttering film reel. Wyatt's cold demeanor, the twist of the wheel, headlights slicing through the air, the screech of tires, the crunch of the metal hitting the ground.

"An *accident*," Huxley echoes, a slow nod of his head. "I think I'm going to need something more specific. My baby looks like she's been driven through a demolition derby, and I'm not even going to mention the animal hair and the *smell*. Seriously, what the fuck guys?"

Wyatt shifts in his seat, brushing said-dog hair from his sweatpants. I must admit, Baxter definitely has left his stench as a parting gift. "Avery swerved us into a ditch in the middle of nowhere." My mouth drops open. As if Wyatt is going to blame this all on me?! Huffing through my nostrils, my eyes narrow to slits. Dax is trying to smother this laughter behind his hand now, my barely concealed frustration leaking through clenched teeth.

"In hindsight, I may have been a little rash. But in my defence, my decision making was warped by the drugs in my system and Wyatt blaming me for his terrible choices. Plus, I was bound, gagged, and covered in dog drool. So yeah, I totaled the car, and I'm sorry."

Dax sobers, both his and Hux's eyes darting to Wyatt. He has the audacity to shrug, unaffected. "I'll have the SUV fixed up as new." The atmosphere in the front becomes charged with the bunching of Huxley's shoulder.

"I don't give a shit about that," he grips the wheel hard. "Was Avery hurt?"

I can almost hear Wyatt's eye roll. "Nothing serious, and I'm fine too; thanks for asking." That same instinct from the hospital room arises in me to smooth everything out. Especially as we're about to walk into Axel's old home. He's going to need us, minus the petty squabbles.

"Wyatt actually took good care of me."

Real good care if the previous night and morning are anything to go by.

Huxley's eyes flick up to the rearview mirror, narrowing at the blush that coats my cheeks. I clear my throat and put on a sweet smile for his benefit. "Thanks to your forward planning, we had everything we needed." I lean forward to stroke the tension from his shoulders, earning a brief brush on his jaw against my knuckles. Wyatt tracks the motion, careful not to reveal whatever he's thinking.

Looking to distract myself, I reach into a crumpled snack bag nestled in Dax's car door, plucking out a pink Starburst. The wrapper crinkles in my hand before I pop the candy into Dax's mouth, and unwrap myself a second. Despite the weight lingering in the car and the pain he must be feeling in his fingers, Dax gives me a small smile as he watches me chew.

I sigh against his shoulder, tugging the sleeves of Wyatt's oversized hoodie over my hands, the familiar scent of him bringing a sliver of peace. It's become my comfort blanket these past few months, a shield against the weight of everything crashing down around us.

My gaze flickers to Axel's silhouette, just visible through the ambulance's rear windows. I can't shake the image of him lying so still in that bed, his chest barely rising and falling. He would hate this, being carted back to a place he's tried so hard to leave behind. For the first time, I'm glad he's not awake to experience it. Even with Garrett's body draped across him, probably muttering reassurances into his ear, we're delivering him back to the one place he swore he'd never return.

Hunting for an escape from my thoughts and finding none, I suddenly sit upright and turn to Dax. "Do you have my phone?" He reaches into the duffle bag at his feet, pulling out Wyatt's first and tossing it into his lap, before retrieving a pink device from the side pocket. I inhale sharply, the screen lighting up to greet me.

"I kept it charged in case Meg tried to call," Dax looks away guilty. His focus turns to the countryside beyond the window. "I'm sorry we couldn't get to her in time. We really did try."

"I know," I press against him until I'm sure he's being crushed. His arm tightens around me as I flick through my apps, not really sure what I'm looking for. A message from Nixon maybe, a few missed calls. There's nothing. Instead, I open the photos to scroll through photos of me and Meg. Camping trips, movie nights, college parties. Memories we might not get a second chance to enjoy together, the future looking bleak for both of us.

With my phone clutched in hand, my mind whirls with new options I didn't have before. If I contact Fredrick, maybe I can convince him to take me instead and let me pay the debt he feels he's owed. A thought I keep locked inside my head. Wyatt is straight on his too, typing Sharon's name into a search engine and reading out the top result.

"Sharon Barrett, surviving widow of Matthew Barrett, has recently tied the knot to a man twenty years her senior after the pair met at his law firm. Mrs Barrett has been working as a secretary at the practice for the last four years, after speculation that she was running low on funds. She has not recently been seen in public with her son, Axel, following an alleged family dispute, nor was he present for her wedding. In an unconventional twist, Mrs Barrett insisted that her new spouse took on her last name-"

My stomach rolls, and I tune out the rest of the article. I hate her already. Turning towards the window, the countryside stretching out before us intensifies the feeling that I'm going to throw up. It's starkly different from the cramped chaos of the city we've left behind. Rolling hills and sparse clusters of trees replace the endless maze of buildings and streets. We're drifting too far away. Like a thread being pulled from a jumper, I feel the chasm between Meg and I pull taut, barely hanging on. I don't know where she is or what's happening to her. I love Axel and will see him safe too, but this is a step back I wasn't anticipating.

Huxley keeps looking at me in the rearview mirror, keenly watching my mind tick over. "Axel's is the last place Fredrick or any of his goons would look for any of us. We can regroup and search for her from there. We'll make it work." He tries to reassure me. I twist my face out of his eyeline, not liking how easily he can read me, even in the reflection. "We won't stop until she's safe."

The words settle in the air, a fragile promise wrapped in uncertainty. Wyatt and Dax make no comment. I know neither of them are the type to make vows they don't intend to keep, and their silence is damning. I lose myself to the horizon once more, lowering further into Dax's hold until my head meets his shoulder. The ambulance remains firmly in my sights, the orange and white flashing light perched on top drifting out as I let the veil of sleep carry me away.

CHAPTER SIXTEEN

I hang back, watching from a distance as Axel is quickly but carefully taken up the grand staircase. Garrett and Hux carry his gurney between them, the ambulance driver carrying the IV drip and bag of equipment right behind. We're told by an elderly butler that a doctor has been contacted about temporarily moving in. He will arrive in the morning.

That leaves Dax to gingerly help a sleepy Avery ascend those same stairs with one arm, her head lolling against his neck, her bag slung over his shoulder. She's slept the entire way, her eyelids glued shut whenever I snuck a sly look into the backseat.

I'm not buying it.

Pushing off the damaged SUV, I unfold my arms and stride through the entrance. The uniformed butler, who has been not-so-patiently waiting for me, closes the huge door and clears his throat.

"Do you need an escort to one of the guest bedrooms?" He raises a gray brow, his expression the opposite of helpful. It seems he didn't want us here as much as we didn't want to come. Shaking my head, I grab my duffle bag from where it's been dumped in the lobby. He's gone before I've straightened, leaving me to brood. I truly thought the next home I stepped into would be my last.

A loving home with the woman who's been desperate to love me for my entire life. I suppose my only saving grace is that I hadn't warned

Rachel we were coming, or she would have been going stir-crazy when we didn't show up. The Perelli's manor was the only place I thought might be safe for Avery, a place of sanctuary until we could ensure Meg wasn't in danger. Until I came up with an alternative for all of the Souls and the girls. I'm just playing puppet master until the day I feel relieved of duty.

I drag my feet toward the stairs, the echo of my footsteps swallowed by the grandeur of Axel's family home. The place feels suffocating, with its vaulted ceilings and heavy drapes that block out the moonlight. It reeks of wealth and sordid secrets—the kind of place that makes my skin itch with the knowledge of what's happened within these very walls.

As I climb, I replay the look on Avery's face when we arrived, the way her lips parted as she took it all in, her arm tightening on Dax's arm. She put on a great show, if I didn't know better than to fall for it. That's why I'm not surprised when I catch the soft rustle of movement in one of the rooms just down the hall.

Carefully, I set my duffle bag down and creep toward the sound. The door is cracked open, and through the sliver of light, I see her. A curtain of golden hair and lean limbs crouched near the foot of the bed, her bag open on the floor and her fingers working frantically. Behind her, drawers in the dresser are left open, clothing hanging over the wood from her haste. She darts to one bedside cabinet, then another, digging around before returning.

Avery checks the time on her phone; her face is suddenly illuminated by the glaring light. I inhale sharply at the pink tinge of her cheeks and the way her blue eyes are blown wide as she frantically twists to Dax's bag. I watch her decide which of his belongings may be of use to her with quick, efficient movements. Down the hallway, a toilet flushes, and I know the moment she does, she's nearly out of time.

"Going somewhere?" I lean against the doorframe, folding my arms across my chest. Avery freezes, her shoulders tensing as if bracing for impact. Slowly, she straightens, but she doesn't turn to face me.

"I don't have time for this, Wyatt." Avery's voice is sharper than usual. Whatever she's spent hours thinking about whilst feigning sleep in the car, she's come to the wrong conclusion. I bite back the harsh retort that slips onto my tongue. What about the men in this house, the family she chose to build? Don't they need her? Don't I?

"And you know I'm not going to let you run off in the middle of the night," I go with instead. Pushing the door open wider, I step inside to block her exit. "Especially when you know damn well it's not safe."

Finally, she spins around, her eyes flashing and fists clenching with defiance. "You know I can't just sit here when Meg needs me. And I don't need your permission to leave. I'm not your responsibility."

"Like hell you're not." My voice is low and steady, but anger simmers beneath the surface. I vaguely hear the shower down the hall switch on, the thunder of water hitting the floor, buying me a few more minutes of time. Dax won't stay away for long, but it will have to be enough. Closing the door with my back, I look upon the woman I let creep beneath my defences with daggers in my eyes.

"Did yesterday mean nothing to you?" I growl, the sound barely audible to my own ears. Avery gasps, most likely reliving the way I kissed every inch of her body, how I held her and pushed into her with maddening slowness. "Did I not prove that I'm willing to do whatever it takes to look after you? And now, with Axel unconscious somewhere beneath this roof, you want to leave and rip us all apart again?"

My accusation strikes just as intended, a direct arrow to the heart. Avery hardens her features, mirroring back the mask she's used to receiving from me.

"I'm just leading by your example," she snaps, her voice rising. "We agreed to stay with Axel, but this," she throws her hands up and gestures around the room. "This is a prison. I thought I could wait until he was better, but every day we wait is another day she suffers. I can't just sit around, going insane, while—"

I close the distance between us in a few strides, gripping her shoulders before she can retreat. "Stop. We all need to sleep, then we can discuss this as a group tomorrow." I swallow, the words unfamiliar to myself. I'm trying to do this whole team thing, trying to become comfortable with being open and honest, but Avery jerks against the hold of my fingers, shoving at my chest. I don't move an inch.

"No! This is my fight. Fre..." her breath catches. "Fredrick is my monster. I know what to expect; Meg doesn't." A sickening twisting of my stomach results in my grip tightening. Avery winces, and I instantly loosen them.

"You survived him, and you were a child. Not even out of single digits. Meg is stubborn and headstrong. She won't just survive him. She'll make him pay." I truly believe that, and by the way Avery whimpers against my chest, so does she. Her body is warm, trembling under my grip, but she doesn't pull away. I can feel the heat radiating from her skin and the rapid pulse at the base of her throat.

We stand together, wallowing in our own helplessness. Avery knows leaving tonight without a clear plan is foolish. Just as much as I know that holding her close like this, comforting her when I can't give her the love she needs...well, that's just dangerous for the both of us.

Blue eyes lock on mine, glistening with tears she refuses to let fall. "Wyatt," she whispers, her voice soft now, almost pleading. "What if you chose wrong? What if I'm not worth saving?"

I should let go. I should leave this conversation to someone else better suited for her. There's enough of them nearby, but my feet don't shift. The selfish bastard in me just can't seem to let her go. My hands slide down from her shoulders, brushing her arms through my garish orange hoodie, tracing the curve of her knuckles until our fingers are intertwined. Her lips part, and I swear I can feel her heartbeat echoing mine.

"You don't get to decide that." I murmur, my voice dropping to a husky whisper. It barely takes a tilt of her head, the straightening of her spine, and her mouth is hovering against mine. Her breath hitches, a fragile sound that stokes the fire already burning in my chest. Closing that last inch of distance, her soft lips tremble slightly, parting with permission. The faint taste of her, sweet and familiar, devastates me.

My tongue is in her mouth in the next second. Without thinking, without reason, I pull her closer, our tangled hands slipping apart as my palm cups her jaw. A soft moan sounds, and I don't know who it came from.

This is not a kiss. It's a surrender. A reckless, desperate rush of everything I've buried. The anger, the fear, the unbearable ache of wanting her and never knowing if I'd deserve her. Her fingers twist into my shirt, pulling me closer as though I might disappear, and I let her. I let her take all of me because I don't know how to stop. Now I've given her a piece of myself, the rest is pouring out, and I don't have the tools or the willpower to stop it.

Cradling her gently, despite the storm raging inside me, I kiss away her fears until the door down the hall opens. I hear the click, the slapping of bare feet against marble. I'm out of time.

It takes more effort than I realised to pull myself back and break the connection between us. The drugs I briefly dabbled with at the safe house are nothing compared to the addiction that is Avery. Had I known simply tasting her lips would give me the same euphoric high and that she could vanish the shadows from my mind so easily, I wouldn't have spent so long resisting her.

Those footsteps grow closer. Against my better judgement, I pull back, exhaling sharply and dropping my hands to my sides. Avery steps back too, hugging the hoodie around herself. Her bag sits half-packed at her feet, a silent witness to her attempt to flee.

"Look," I say, softening my tone. "I know you're scared. I get it. But I was wrong to think we were better apart." I swallow, releasing the true meaning of my words before she does. "The Shadowed Souls are not separating again. So the question is, are you with us or not?"

Her jaw tightens, and for a moment, I think she'll argue. But then her shoulders sag and the fight drains out of her. "I hate this," she whispers.

"Join the club," I mutter. Just outside the door, Huxley calls Dax's name, the pair falling into a hushed conversation. Carefully and silently, I step around Avery, crouching to pick up her bag. I upturn the contents onto the floor and zip the bag closed, keeping it clenched in my fist. When I straighten, she's watching me, her expression unreadable.

"Go to bed, Angel," I say, brushing past her toward the door. Her fingers reach for my arm, a tentative brush that causes me to pause. Dropping her gaze to the floor, Avery nods, and she bites her bruised bottom lip.

"Goodnight, Wyatt," she murmurs. I swallow hard, lifting my head to hold it high as I step into the hall and stride away before Huxley or Dax can comment. I find myself in the very same bathroom Dax vacated, steam billowing all around me. Shutting the door, I slump against the wood, releasing a shaky breath.

She's still here. For now. But keeping her safe feels like trying to hold back the tide. With that thought in mind, I slip Avery's pink phone out of her bag, delete Fredrick's message and attached phone number, and toss it aside.

I meant what I said; I was wrong to separate us from the Souls. I was stupid to think it wouldn't take all of us to look after her, especially when Avery seems intent on getting herself killed.

HUXLEY

Warmth presses against the line of my back. I shuffle along the mattress slightly, tucking my pillow beneath itself to raise my head slightly. A hardback by Truman Capote rests awkwardly in my hands, a stream of morning light causing me to squint at the small text while my companion snoozes gently.

Apparently, after whatever happened in the room next door, Wyatt felt the need to stay close to someone last night. He wriggles again, pressing his back against mine and leaving me with around two inches of space at the edge of the four-poster. I give up on trying to read through the early hours, replacing the book on the bedside table and slipping free of the covers, giving him the kingsize to himself.

Stretching, I crack my neck and back, taking in my surroundings. It seems this particular guest room is being used as the storage space for all of Axel's late father's possessions. I didn't meet Mr. Barrett while he was alive, but the framed portrait against the wall holds too many resemblances to Axel to be anyone else. Boxes of classic literature and ornaments fill the space, some of the finest suits I've ever seen line the opposite wall, collecting dust. A whole life packed up and stashed away as if he never existed.

Another shuffle followed by a groan sounds to my left, Wyatt seeming unsettled. I stare down at him for a moment. His eyes are clenched, a pained expression pinching at his brows. He shifts again, his breathing uneven as his frown deepens.

For a moment, I consider waking him, but something stops me. In all the years I've known him, Wyatt has always slept soundly. Always been certain of himself. But whatever happened with Avery this past week has changed him. There's a vulnerability I don't understand—a dent in his armor. But like with all of Wyatt's struggles, this feels personal. The kind of battle fought behind closed doors.

Grabbing a fresh set of clothes from my bag, I sneak out into the corridor and close the door with a soft click. The bathroom is along the hall, and I stroll slowly, letting my eyes roam over the interior bathed in daylight after arriving in pitch black last night. As far as mansions go, I would say this is the grandest I've seen. A complete contrast to Axel's humble soul.

The ceiling is a masterpiece of intersecting wooden beams, the geometric pattern mirrored in the marbled flooring. Suspended at the heart of the lobby ahead is a glimmering chandelier, its cascade of crystals scattering spots of light across the winding staircase below. Pointed archways rise at either end of the hallway, their curves framing the passageways and echoing the character of thick, wooden doors set every few feet apart along the hall.

As my fingers trace the smooth mahogany bannister, the sharp tang of paint fumes drifts through the labyrinth of corridors, mingling with the faint scent of aged wood and varnish. The butler who showed us to our rooms last night briefly spoke of the recent renovations in an irritable tone that matched the way he spoke about Sharon and her new husband.

After a quick wash in an equally lavish double bathroom, I change into jeans and a black T-shirt and go in search of breakfast. Not that I'm hungry in the slightest, but I promised myself to make the effort and restore my strength. The time might come where Avery's life depends on it. I need to be ready.

Turning towards the wide staircase, a door at the end of the hallway catches my eye. Not because it's white, unlike all the rest, which are a range of the deepest and richest browns, but because there's a small rectangular sign on this one. Creeping forward, curiosity filling my veins, the sign comes into focus. A starry background sits behind a suited astronaut with 'Axel's Room' scrawled in the centre. It appears to be handmade.

I instantly feel sick, turning away from the innocence of a boy who endured so much torture behind this door. Who is back in there now, unknowing of what we've brought him into. Should we have fought harder? Will our being here be enough?

Shuffling sounds within just as the door swings open, an exhausted Garrett appears in the doorway with a towel clutched in his hand. His hair is long enough to cover his eyes when he allows it to flop forward, a yawn pulling his mouth wide open.

Scrubbing a hand over his face, he pulls the door closed behind him and almost crashes into me. The bastard didn't even look up. Jumping out of his way, he continues up the hallway without any acknowledgement. My gaze flicks to the door handle, wondering if Axel might be awake yet.

"Don't even think about it," Garrett shouts back, entering the bathroom and slamming the door shut. *Asshole.* Maybe I should be happy that some things never change and that Garrett is the same possessive dick as always. At least he's taking care of Axel the way he deserves now, not pulling him along on an invisible leash and dropping him like yesterday's trash whenever he felt like it. Axel always came right back despite my hushed warnings. I can only hope he's finally got what he was hoping for.

Jogging downstairs and emerging in the kitchen, I'm stunned to find a whole team of house staff lifting their heads to greet me kindly. I blink through their chorused 'good morning', flicking my gaze between their sex-shop style maid's and butler's outfits. They're nothing like the elderly gentleman who greeted us last night. They're much more *youthful*.

A guy around my age with a top knot grins at me while stirring a huge pan of pasta. A black jacket hangs open around tanned abs, a tie hanging from his neck with no shirt. The belt of his slacks is dangerously low, revealing a dark tuft of hair trailing south.

He beckons me in, gesturing to the kitchen island. Beside him, the group chats easily as they make subs in a production line. Another pair is preparing tubs of salads on the far end of the same island. I slowly lower onto a stool, watching their easy going dynamics as if it's surreal.

"You guys know it's barely eight in the morning, right?" I finally ask. "Isn't breakfast on the menu?" Top Knot widens his grin, whereas a young woman to his right fumbles with her apron.

"Of course, sir. Whatever you need," she rushes off to the fridge, whipping out the eggs and bacon.

"Oh no, I didn't mean-" I start, but Top Knot chuckles.

"It's cool, man. Whatever you want, we can do it. Anything for a friend of Axel's." The hair on the back of my neck stands up. Axel has never mentioned having friends back home.

"You know Axel?" My brow raises. A round of sniggers rotates around the kitchen.

"Not yet, but we've heard so much about him," Top Knot's eyes glisten into the distance. "He's the original. Like Steve Jobs, and we're his apples." Feeling eyes on me, I glance around to the others, who quickly drop their awe-filled gazes and giggle like schoolgirls, even the men. Licking my lips, the heat of that gaze intensifies, and I quickly catch myself.

Top Knot turns off the hob and puts aside his pasta pot. "To answer your question, it's Sunday. We prep our lunches and meals for when we're back at college during the week and return on Fridays to stay through the weekends. Although Sharon requested extras to be made while you and your friends are staying." I narrow my eyes at his first-name basis with Axel's mom, feeling like I'm missing something obvious.

"So you work here? All of you?" I drum my fingers on the surface, my other hand propping my chin up. Top Knot shrugs, fetching a stack of freshly-washed tupperware.

"Sort of. We're the Lots." When I don't respond, he tilts his head and speaks as if I'm a bit slow. "For the auctions. We keep a cut of what we make, and the tips are great." Another round of laughter bursts through the air at his innuendo. I suppress a shudder, and he continues, pretending not to notice. "Free lodgings when we like, and the parties are something else. You should join us on Friday. It's thrilling."

"You're whores," I blurt out. No one is offended or even surprised. They're too busy working in sync and smirking with hidden messages being passed through their side glances. Leaning across the counter, Top Knot reaches out to brush my blond waves behind my ear.

"We're whatever you want us to be, handsome." I quickly pull back. What the fuck have I just walked in to?

The words echo back now in context. Axel is the original. By the time a plate of steaming eggs, bacon, and pancakes is pushed beneath my nose, I'm fighting a gag. On second thoughts, I couldn't eat now, not even for Avery's sake. Sharon is still pulling this shit, running a brothel of sorts. All based on what she did to Axel.

Dax slips into the stool beside me, sliding his arm around my shoulder. I flinch, but relish his quick hug before it's gone. I hadn't realised how unnatural it's been without Axel initiating the hugs and gentle touches between us. I'm glad Dax isn't allowing the void to keep growing in his absence. Several pairs of eyes shoot our way, but not with judgement. Hints of jealousy and encouragement flare to life in their faces, Top Knot frozen in place with a look of longing. I swallow, turning to Dax's ear to keep our conversation private.

"Tell me Avery isn't on her own," I command roughly. Dax's blue eyes catch mine with a strange look, but he recovers quickly.

"Wyatt's with her." I nod, not knowing if that's better or worse. I keep my head twisted away from the rest of those listening in.

"Do not leave her alone for a second in this house." Dax's mouth tightens into a firm line, and he agrees instantly, not needing an explanation. He can sense the tension radiating from me. I slide the plate of food towards Dax, letting him eat one-handed in my place.

The staff refocus on their tasks, busying themselves with the various meals before packing them into individual portioned boxes. Each container has a white sticker with today's date placed on top and is stacked neatly into the double refrigerator. Dax's thigh remains pressed against mine out of sight, a silent reassurance that we're alright, as long as we stick together.

After taking the plate and washing up, most of those in the kitchen head out. A few hang back, Top Knot included, pottering around with his smirk cemented in place. I don't attempt to make conversation with Dax. Who knows what is being passed back to Sharon, and by the Rolex on Top Knot's wrist, I can only imagine he's one of her favorites.

A throat is cleared in the doorway, the butler from last night staring directly at me. His thinning dark hair is combed over, a grey speckled moustache lining his upper lip. He's the only member of staff I've seen who is above college age, his pressed white shirt, black slacks, and shiny shoes showing years of professionalism.

"Mrs Barrett has requested your presence." I square my shoulders, wondering why Axel's mom thinks I would come running because she clicked her slender fingers.

"Are you sure it's me she wants?" I pass a glance at Dax, my blood running cold. The butler makes a humorless noise in his throat.

"Positive, *Sir*," he drawls sarcastically before turning and leading the way.

"Do you-" I stop myself from asking Dax to tag along. I'm a grown ass man; I don't need protection from a predator. He seems to read my face, standing to slap me on the shoulder.

"I'm going to take some food up to Garrett. Catch you after?"

I nod with a sigh. Yeah, sure, I'll be the bait and will report back later. I'm forced to run to catch up to the butler before he disappears down the hallway. Beyond floor-to-ceiling windows lining this side of the mansion, an idyllic green setting sprawls across the landscape, rows of automatic sprinklers spraying across the manicured lawn. At the far end, a metal cage is just visible, which houses the tennis courts.

Passing through a barely used living area, hammocks swing gently in the breeze on the patio beyond. The butler leads me through the spider web of hallways, passing various rooms before turning sharply and opening a door at the far end.

The space inside is dim, with electric lanterns descending alongside a hidden staircase. Sulphur tickles my nose, and a brush of humidity sinks into my jeans. They immediately feel too tight, too constricted, and I'm sure that's the point.

The butler ushers me towards the steps before closing the door, leaving me in almost complete darkness. I really should have insisted Dax came along. Squinting and trying not to fall, I feel each step with my bare foot before stepping down until I find myself in an underground chamber.

The room has been decorated to look like a cave, the bumpy walls and curved ceiling are painted stone grey. Sounds of the rainforest echo from hidden speakers, insects chirping, and frogs croaking between hollow droplets of rain. Two leather massage tables sit to the left, below shelves of small bottles and rolled towels. Artificial vines have been draped around blue lights, which reflect on the water filling the centre of the room. At the back of the round jacuzzi, Axel's mom is eyeing me hungrily.

"I thought you could use some relaxation. I can see from a mile off how tense you are." Once again, I'm struck by the lack of consideration of the early hour. Does no one sleep in this house?

Sharon licks her cherry-red lips and unashamedly tracks each of my biceps with her pale brown eyes. Fighting the impulse to cross my arms defensively, knowing it would only make me appear more muscular than I really am, I stand loosely with unhidden hatred filling my features. If I wasn't worried she would kick us all out and Axel would be trapped in a house alone with her again, I wouldn't have been able to restrain my tongue from spilling every curse word and name I have rolling around my mind.

"I'm good." I shrug and turn to leave, splashing behind, telling me she's rushing to stop me. I manage to jerk back before her wet, slender hand lands on my shoulder, growling for her to step back. In no version of this world would I have ever found her attractive, regardless of the things she's done. A black bikini top barely covers her huge, clearly fake, breasts, and her stomach is unrealistically slender. Her thigh is covered with black ink in the shape of a large cat, its body on the prowl and fangs exposed in a hiss. I'm almost certain it's supposed to be a cougar. *Shudder.*

"You seem so stressed. Why don't you let me help relieve you?" She tiptoes to whisper into my ear but is careful not to touch me. Yet.

"What about your husband?" I huff, putting further distance between us. She follows, her chest brushing mine. Bile rises in my throat.

"Oh, don't mind him. He's banging his secretary."

"You are his secretary," I deadpan. She giggles like life is some big fucking joke. She can screw who she wants, abuse who she wants, and will never face any repercussions.

"Handsome and intuitive, what a catch. Seriously, have a massage on me." She winks, sashaying her hips across the room to stroke the massage table. Her talons lightly scratch the leather, the cocky smile on her face showing she actually thinks I'll be persuaded. That she can bat her lashes and have any man in the palm of her hand.

Reaching over the table, pushing her ass high into the air, she pushes a button on the wall I didn't notice. The whirring of a door opening reaches my ears, although I can't see it from this angle, until a man appears a moment later. I recognise him instantly as Top Knot.

For the love of fuck, what have I just walked into? And how many secret tunnels does this mansion have? I, for one, will not be sleeping soundly anymore.

He doesn't spare me a glance, his eyes trained on Sharon like a lovesick puppy. His fingers deftly slide off his jacket and reach for his belt. Underneath his slacks, he's wearing a tiny pair of purple briefs. My eyes nearly explode in my head, seeing that he's already half-hard and reaching for the oils. Sharon holds out her hand for me, leaning her body against the massage table in a way I'm sure she considers to be sexy. I'm too busy trying not to vomit at the audacity of it all.

"You really are a vile creature, aren't you?" Her practiced smile falters. Top Knot swings his eyes to me now, a look of disappointment swimming in his features. Was this all some ploy, and I'm supposed to be the prized pig? No, thank you.

Jogging up the stairs, I shake off the vile desperation clinging to my skin. I can't stop shuddering, tripping over myself multiple times until I finally make it back to the staircase. Locating Avery's room, I burst in, ignoring the scene before me. Avery is curled up on the bed, staring at Wyatt pacing across the room, deep in thought.

"Hux, you okay?" Avery asks, just shifting her legs aside before I drop heavily on the mattress. She looks as relieved as I am to see each other. Her fingers instantly sink into my hair, massaging my head. Wyatt hovers on the edge of my vision, standing over the bed with a frown. A tremor rolls through my back, my stomach twisted in knots as I lean my head further into Avery's lap.

"I told Dax that he's not allowed to leave you alone in this house." I swallow hard. "I've changed my mind. I think I'm the one who needs protecting." And while Avery laughs into her shoulder, I retell the last hour of my life in vivid detail.

CHAPTER EIGHTEEN

"I've never been concerned about my anal virginity before," Huxley shudders as the door opens. Dax becomes the newest addition to the mattress.

"I seriously doubt that. You've lived with Garrett long enough," Dax chuckles under his breath. Finally, the glimmer of worry leaves Hux's chocolate brown eyes, and he concedes with a small smile. His blonde waves slip through my fingers as he twists to see Dax.

"How are they?"

Dax's arm slips around my body, cradling me close. "Axel's the same. Garrett is being insufferable. Made me spoon feed him so he didn't have to let go of Axel's hand." Dax leans against my shoulder.

"We should be with them," I decide, trying to move. Dax keeps me rooted in place, slowly shaking his head.

"Garrett thinks it's best that we're not all crowding Axel when he comes around. Not here."

Hux snorts and returns to stare at the ceiling. "And all it took was major surgery for Gare to finally start putting Axel first." I scowl, jerking my thighs beneath his head.

"Hey, they've come really far lately. Just because Garrett isn't professing his love from the rooftops doesn't mean he doesn't care." A stilted silence follows where we clearly agree to disagree, a joined heavy exhale bringing the three of us back into a relaxed huddle.

Like the rest of the morning since Wyatt permitted himself entry into the bedroom, he has returned to pacing, lost in thought. He doesn't seem to want anything other than to keep me in his sights. Maybe he has visions of me tying together bedsheets and abseiling out of the window after my moment of weakness last night.

"Wyatt," I call out, ceasing his steps. He flashes his green eyes my way, the mask of indifference firmly in place. "Are you going to talk to us today, or are you just going to wear track marks into the carpet?" I'm not sure he will actually listen to me, but I've decided there's no point tiptoeing around. I might as well see if he's going to continue opening up or revert back into himself again. Dax and Huxley go perfectly still, watching our newfound dynamic play out.

Wyatt exhales slowly, the tension in his shoulders giving way as he leans back against the window frame. His gaze drifts to the glass, his reflection distorted by the pale light filtering through. "I'm... struggling," he admits at last, the words heavy, as if dragged out of him. His posture sags, the usual air of command slipping away like smoke. "Normally, I can step back, remove myself from the situation, and see it clearly. But this time, I'm stuck. I don't know how to protect you from Fredrick if he changes his mind, or how to protect Axel from his mom, or if we'll ever truly get either Axel or Garrett back. I just don't know what to do."

My chest tightens at the sight of him like this. Uncertain, vulnerable. It's a side of Wyatt I've never seen before, and judging by the way Dax's and Hux's brows shoot up, they haven't either.

"Where do we go from here?" Wyatt's question hangs in the air, not directed at anyone, but it's a question that demands an answer. The room is silent, the weight of uncertainty pressing down on all of us. No one speaks because no one knows what to say. We're all grappling with the same truth. We're out of our depth. But sitting here, wallowing in uncertainty, isn't going to help anyone. I take a deep breath and set my jaw.

"Let me get dressed." I pat Huxley's shoulder to shift his head from my thighs. "We can't make any decisions until we know what we're working with." He shifts up onto his elbows with his lips slightly parted.

"You want me to go back out there?" There's a slight hitch in his voice, and I feel Dax twist away to hide his sniggering. As hilarious as

I'm sure it is to watch this 'Top Knot' come onto Hux, it's not going to help me navigate the mansion until Axel is able to leave.

"I'd like it if you came with, but I'm not going to force you." His brown eyes search mine for a moment, his hesitation clear in the way he swallows. I lean in and press a light kiss to his cheek. "I won't let anything happen to your anal virginity. There's strength in numbers," I wink. Hux leans his face into mine, breathing in my skin and strength.

I clamber over Dax, rooting through the pile of clothes Wyatt left heaped on the bedroom floor. I would have folded them, but Dax appearing in the doorway last night, dripping with water droplets and giving me those '*fuck me*' eyes took president. As if he knew I needed the distraction, his mouth and his good hand worshipped every inch of my skin until I was panting and begging for him to fill me.

Licking my lips at the memory, I pull out some sweatpants and socks, helping myself to Dax's duffle to fill in the rest. First matter of business, washing or acquiring fresh clothes. He kneels beside me, handing over a pair of brightly colored boxers and a sweatshirt. My heart stutters when I turn the material over in my hands, revealing the lacrosse team's logo for Hollowbrook. *Meg's.*

"I thought wherever we found you, you might want it." He smiles faintly, a small curve of his lips, and I can feel his presence beside me, steady and grounding. My fingers tighten around the soft fabric, and I force myself to swallow the lump rising in my throat. Dax doesn't push. He just lets me sit with it for a moment before he stands and moves toward Huxley, who's groaning as he swings his legs off the mattress. I gather the clothes and excuse myself to the bathroom to quickly shower and dress.

When I return, the three of them are waiting, hungry eyes dragging over my body as if I'm not wearing the baggiest of clothes and my hair is thrown up messily. I never did manage to slip into the heiress role. Wyatt breaks eye contact first, pushing off the window frame. Dax reaches for my hand, Huxley's arm rounds my shoulders, and Wyatt trails behind as we move around the mansion, cataloguing each open room. Upstairs doesn't present anything other than guest bedrooms, lavish bathrooms, and a few unused offices that I presume were Axel's dads.

As we reach the lower level, the noise increases. Conversations, laughter, movement, all coming from the left of the grand foyer. We head right first. This side of the mansion is untouched, seemingly for appearances only. The formal living room is purely white with gold accents, each piece of furniture perfectly angled towards large bay windows facing the back gardens.

Beyond this, we find a library, an elegant dining room, a ballroom that Wyatt hastily moves us away from, and the entrance to an underground wine cellar gleaming with vintage wine bottles. Before long, we've arrived back at the foyer and face what I have decided are the living quarters.

Guys and girls around our age pace the halls, all smiles and flirtatious looks. This living room has a distinctively different feel, swarming with energy. It's cozier in here, oversized leather couches and mismatched pillows, a massive TV mounted above a stone fireplace currently playing some car racing game. The scent of freshly baked pastries wafts through the air, mingling with the laughter and overlapping voices of the group sprawled across the space.

An expensive coffee table is piled high with snacks, while someone strums a guitar near the window. A few heads turn as we enter, curious eyes scanning us briefly before they return to their conversations. No one seems particularly interested in us, yet the vibe in the room feels oddly territorial, like we're treading on unspoken boundaries.

Dax's grip tightens on my hand, his body language protective as his gaze sweeps the room. Wyatt stays behind, silent but watchful, as we move between the groups of people. Escaping without incident to pass the kitchens, laundry room, and a number of storage cupboards, we find more people in both a games room and a home theatre.

Despite Huxley's warning, I wasn't prepared for how many of them there were. The uniforms he spoke of are nowhere to be seen. Instead, a sea of fitted tees, crop tops, short denim shorts, and jeans pass by, designer labels on most. We finally reach the end of the house, stepping into a conservatory. The glass walls are lined with potted plants, a distinct winter chill seeping in through the cracked rear door. On that breeze, travels the scent of smoke and weed from those hovering outside.

"Huxley!" a man calls from behind. Hux's arm tightens slightly around my shoulders. "You missed all the fun." I turn, although his hold tries to prevent it, to see a lean man approaching. His smile is all teeth and charm, his earlobes stretched with circular plugs and a piercing glints between his brown eyes. Upon his head, dark, wispy hair has been pulled into a top knot. *There he is.* Extending his hand to me, his eyes sparkle as I accept it, despite the rumble in Huxley's chest. "Or perhaps you were having some fun of your own. Who is this beauty?"

"She's absolutely none of your business," Huxley drags me a step back to sever the connection of our hands. Wyatt and Dax grumble something to the same effect, and Top Knot grins wider.

"Has he always been a selfish lover?" He gestures his head to Hux, earning himself a stern glare. I meet his boldness head on and smirk right back.

"Yes," I laugh. "I'm Avery, and you are?"

"Taylor," he replies smoothly, offering a mock bow that brings him eye level with my chest. The action does not go unnoticed. Huxley spins me sharply, only his large hands on my waist stopping me from toppling over. Dax and Wyatt instantly close ranks, their broad shoulders blocking Taylor's view.

"What are you doing, Swan?" Hux whispers, his face pinched. I reach up to smooth the frown out of his brow.

"Recon. We can't protect Axel if we don't know what's happening around here."

"Which involves you flirting?" Hux bites back, his fingertips twitching against my sides.

"I literally shook his hand and told him my name. I've flirted more with Mrs. Russell, the elderly librarian." I narrow my eyes, looking up at him with steely determination. "We're strangers in a house they clearly have the run of, and we don't need to make any more enemies. Someone is going to have to play nice."

"Fine," Hux bites out after a tense pause, his jaw tightening. "I will." I raise a brow as he releases me and rounds the two acting as our bodyguards. Taylor is still standing there, his grin in full effect. Not that Wyatt will let me get within arm's reach of him again. His arm bands around my waist, holding me back as Huxley plants himself directly in the way.

"Relax, big guy. I'm just being friendly." Taylor holds up his hands in mock surrender. His tone is light, but his eyes flick to me again, their gleam suggesting otherwise. "Avery's off limits. Got it. But you," Taylor reaches out to drag his index finger down the center of Huxley's chest, "you should come hang out with us next weekend. House rule, Sunday is Fun Day."

"Good to know," Hux replies, although I can hear his teeth grating together. Taylor retreats with lingering looks over where Wyatt's arm is band around my middle and gives me a wink before he disappears from the room. The three around me exhale heavily. I shake my head, breaking free of Wyatt's hold. I suppose I forgot that their ease with each other doesn't mean they aren't still possessive and jealous.

Heading out of the conservatory with the intention to head back upstairs, the clicking of heels against the marble catches my ears. I turn my head just in time to see Sharon disappearing around the corner with a man, a stethoscope hanging loosely around his neck. My feet are moving instantly, and the guys are quickly racing behind. It's easy to follow that clicking sound through back hallways we've yet to explore, halting in an office with tropical canvases instead of windows.

Sharon is leaning against a large desk in a tight skirt and a cropped blazer. Her hair is slicked back into a perfect ponytail, jewelry dripping from her ears, neck, and fingers. She is hitching a perfectly shaped brow at the doctor sitting in front of us.

"Give it to me straight, Marcus. How long until I can get rid of him?"

"I'd be interested to know as well," I permit my own entry, shadows filing in behind me. The doctor peers over the high back seat and clears his throat.

"I, um, I can't discuss Mr. Barrett's care with anyone except his guardian," the doc stammers. Wyatt strides around the room, placing himself a few feet from Sharon. His sharp, green eyes pierce the room, his stance strong and powerful. The mask of indifference slips to reveal an air of authority. He'd make a ruthless businessman.

"I'm Axel's guardian. Answer the question. How long before I can get him out of here?"

Hux, Dax, and I fully enter the room, adding to Marcus' unease. He pulls the stethoscope free from his neck and tugs at his navy sweater, looking to Sharon for instructions. She sighs and nods, lifting a hand to inspect her nails.

"Well, it's hard to say. There's no telling how weak his muscles are or the effects his mind will have in relation to his delayed responsiveness.

Not to mention the trauma his lungs have suffered. Any labored breathing, panic attack, or crying could induce more strain, making the healing period longer." Sharon snorts to herself, but our eyes narrow on the middle-aged man, ignoring her completely. The Doc taps a thumb on his trousers and relents. "Hypothetically, if Mr. Barrett were to wake today, perhaps he could be ready to move elsewhere within a week. But it all depends on-"

My mind fades out. A week, minimum, depending on what state he wakes in. I raise a hand to my forehead, trying to breathe through the rush pounding in my ears. A week, minimum, that I could possibly get out there and start searching for Meg. What might she be subjected to in that time, and how much can she endure? Dully, I realize my back is being rubbed, and I lean further into Dax's side.

"Why is he asleep in the first place?" I interject sharply into whatever conversation is happening around me. "Surely at this point, alarm bells are ringing." Marcus blinks a few times, caught off guard, and scratches his chin in thought.

"There are a few possibilities," he begins, his voice carefully measured. "It could be a prolonged reaction to the anesthesia, though that's less likely at this stage. Another possibility is that his cerebral metabolism has been affected. It's uncommon given the nature of his injury and surgery, but not entirely out of the question."

"And the other option?" Huxley huffs, his frustration palpable as he moves closer to Wyatt. Dax and I step in, taking the silent stance of Axel's real family. Marcus hesitates, his gaze flicking between them all.

"Axel isn't waking up simply because he doesn't want to." The words hit like a punch to the gut. A sharp silence fills the room as the weight of the statement settles over us. Huxley's jaw tightens, Wyatt's hands ball into fists, and my heart twists painfully in my chest. Dax remains close, stroking circles over my back and whispering into my ear that it's going to be okay. I don't see how he can remain optimistic, but I'm thankful that he is.

The doctor stands to leave, revealing the truth of his size. He rivals Huxley's height, although that's where the similarities end. Marcus' size is not toned muscle, but that of a man who stress eats and spends longer typing up reports rather than treating patients. His hair is dark, although thinning, and there are white tufts in his five o'clock shadow.

Sharon dismisses him with the instruction to keep her informed, leaving the five of us in a stare-off in her office.

"So this is how it's going to go," she says, her voice laced with a subtle edge I immediately don't like. "The students will be going back to college this evening, and my husband returns home once they've left. He isn't currently aware of the *situation* we've found ourselves in." Her eyes flick to Wyatt at his low hiss. I feel that same sentiment. "I trust you can all handle yourselves discreetly and stay out of the way when needed."

"And when would that be?" I set my jaw and tilt my head to meet her pale eyes. Sharon pushes off the desk to round it, settling into her leather chair. She assesses us all with sharp scrutiny.

"You can have the run of the mansion during the week. Our Butler, Evans, will see that you have whatever you need. However, I run events every Friday night with high-profile guests who value their anonymity. Don't be present during this time, and we won't have any problems."

Events. A dull thud of my pulse beats in my ears. She means the auctions that she started with Axel and has not only continued but built upon. The hoards of students, the high-profile guests. This is a fully fledged organization.

"Good to know," Wyatt replies coolly, his tone nonchalant, but his posture remains rigid. "You don't have to worry. As soon as Axel is ready, we'll leave and you will never-" Wyatt takes a step forward, "ever-" he presses his fists against the wood, "see him again." Sharon's gaze lingers on him for a moment before a cruel smile spreads across her face.

"Excellent."

Wyatt shifts back, reaching for my hand on instinct. I don't even know if he's aware that he's clutching onto me and dragging me out of the door, but Sharon sees it. Her eyes spark to life, taking in the hands gently pressing against my back, the way I'm caged in by possessive muscle.

As we slip out of the office and back into the lively halls, I can't help but glance over my shoulder. The energy in that room felt stifling, dangerous like a powder keg waiting for the right spark.

Sharon isn't just a monster. She's a black widow in more ways than one, weaving silky threads of manipulation. Anyone who dares to step too close will become entangled and trapped, and what's worse is that they're enjoying it. They're encouraging her, dulled to the venom she seeps. It's no wonder Axel has struggled with nightmares of her for so long or that Huxley was jarred this morning.

Blinking up at Wyatt, I squeeze his hand, grounding us both as his jaw tightens, a storm brewing behind his green eyes. "We'll keep him safe," I promise, my voice steadier than I feel. Wyatt doesn't answer, but his grip softens slightly, a silent promise passing between us. An understanding that neither of us are running from this. We're going to do whatever it takes to look after Axel and keep us all together.

# DAX

"Hey, I might have found something," I call out to Avery. She pokes her head out of the bookcases, her hair falling to one side. Hope flares in her blue eyes, and she crosses the library to join my side. I lay the book on my crossed legs, using my good hand to hold the pages open for her to see over my shoulder. "Metabolic encephalopathy is the most frequent cause of disordered consciousness. It's a chemical imbalance in the blood; side effects can include not waking immediately after a surgery or trauma."

Avery lowers to a crouch beside me, her eyes flying from left to right. I watch her chew on her lip, a frown forming between her brows.

"It also says it's caused by global brain dysfunction or the organs not working properly. This can't be it, Dax. We've got enough problems without diagnosing Axel with phantom illnesses." Shaking her head, she stands and retraces her steps to the bookshelves, leaving me sitting in front of a flickering fireplace. Just before disappearing, Avery pauses with a hand on the shelving unit, a long sigh rattling through her chest. "I'm sorry, that was really snippy. I'm just tired and stressed."

I let out a low chuckle, unfurling my legs on the thick carpet. "You? Snippy? Never," I tease. She peeks at me from under her lashes, her lips twitching upward despite herself. Then the frown returns as she remembers she shouldn't have anything to smile about, and she slips into the aisle. I leave her for a short while, barely reading the rest of the medical journal before snapping it closed.

Ironically, we came to the library as an excuse to get away from the crushing weight of the morning and proceeded to research headaches into ourselves. It's not a healthy tactic, but it's how I dealt with my mom's sickness. I was young, but not as naive as the doctors made out. After every appointment, I'd go home and research the terms they used, doing whatever it took to understand what was happening. As if that would make the outcome any different. It wasn't long after her passing that I switched to fiction and never looked back, and now I remember why.

Pushing to my feet, I stretch in the fire's warmth before going in search of Avery. I find her nestled between the stacks, in a small alcove she's created for herself. Surrounded by the fortress of books she's been working through, she absentmindedly picks at her lip. Titles on eating disorders, trauma recovery, men's mental health, and the psychological aftermath of accidents cover a coffee table, a low velvet sofa, and the floor. Unlike me, she's focused on issues she might actually have a shot at helping with.

I tiptoe through her stacks, finding a small space I can just about squeeze into behind her. My legs are bent by her waist, the small of her back shifting to press against my crotch. I swallow, forcing my attention to remain on my hand rubbing her shoulder. The fingers on my other hand throb like they always do, especially just after Hux changes my bandages, but it's bearable. There are more pressing issues to distract me with.

"You're allowed to be stressed, you know. We all are. And researching conditions I know nothing about probably isn't helping, but it's filling the time. Stopping me from going stir crazy."

"I get that," Avery nods, leaning back to rest her head on my shoulder. She remains there, her face turned up to the ceiling. I stare openly, tracing her features with my eyes. These are the rare moments I wait for, when the need to fight is stripped back, when the fire simmers to a low burn and Avery can just *be*. She should get to be like this more often, able to put her faith in us. To let us carry the weight for a while until she finds the strength to pick herself back up.

Before my very eyes, I watch those bricks start to layer back up. Her lips press together in quiet defiance, her eyes burning with determination even though she's exhausted. Mentally exhausted from caring so much, trying to keep us all together by purely holding on so tight. I fall for her all over again. This breathtaking, unstoppable force of a woman who stormed into our lives, claimed her place, and hasn't stopped fighting since. Fighting with us, alongside us, and now for us.

"Swan," I press my lips against her cheek. Avery snaps out of her ravine and slides her fingers into mine. Bringing her knuckles up to meet my lips, I inhale her scent. "I love you so much." Avery sucks in a breath, parting her lips as if through all of the drama, she's simply forgotten how I felt.

"Oh, I love you too, Dax." Avery's head tilts to watch me kissing her hand, pressing her palm against my cheek. I will spend every day cherishing her, never letting her forget what we have. Anything to keep her looking at me like I'm her entire world. And knowing I get to share this feeling with my best friends, that there will always be someone to comfort her when I'm not quite enough, is a joy I couldn't comprehend until now. I just have to hold on tight enough to see us through this next storm. Only brighter skies can await on the other side, surely.

Leaning aside, I carefully move the stacks of books, creating a pathway to clear off the velvet sofa. Avery watches me, her eyes shadowed with exhaustion, but she doesn't protest. Once there's enough room, I slide onto the couch and gently tug her toward me. She comes willingly, curling into my chest with a sigh. Her hair smells faintly of lavender, and I rest my chin on top of her head, feeling her relax ever so slightly in my arms.

"How are you doing?" I ask softly. Avery snorts, the sound muffled against my chest. She shrugs, but I feel the tension in her shoulders. I'm not letting her off that easily. "No, seriously," I press, pulling back just enough to tilt her chin up and meet her eyes. My arm remains firmly around her, a cage of comfort she doesn't want to escape. "It's been a long time since you've been able to speak to a therapist. Talk to me."

Her features flicker with resistance, but after a long pause, she finally relents, her voice barely above a whisper.

"There's nothing to talk about anymore. I used to keep my pain private, much like how I used to hide myself away. I didn't want the world to see or know me. I just wanted to disappear." I run my hand up and down her back in soothing strokes, hoping to keep her grounded.

"What do you think you were hiding from?"

Avery's attention lingers on my bandage, a frown pulling at her mouth, but her answer is instantaneous.

"Love," she says to herself. "Heartbreak. I thought if I only relied on two people, the chances of getting hurt were much slimmer. They were meant to protect me from harm, and they both betrayed me in ways I didn't think were possible. The secrets and the scandals, and for what? Nixon is AWOL, and Cathy is... gone."

Her words carry a bitterness I've never heard from her before, and it strikes me how much she's still holding onto. It's the first time she's acknowledged any resentment toward Cathy, and the revelation sits heavy between us. I press my lips to her temple, lingering there as I let her speak, wanting her to get it all out in the open at last.

"I just wish she had told me something. Helped me to understand rather than let me piece it all together bit by bit, only to keep coming up short." Twisting her face into my T-shirt, I feel a trace of wetness seep through the fabric. I stroke her hair and hold her gently, my perfectly imperfect Swan. "There's an ache in my chest that won't go away. This tiny voice that keeps whispering that I can't save everyone."

"You can't," I agree immediately, tightening my hold on her. Blinking up at me with a flash of defiance, Avery looks ready to argue that she can indeed save everyone, despite her being the one to say it first. I smile at her stubbornness, picking at a loose thread on the college sweater she wears. "That's why you have us. All five of us."

Satisfied with that, Avery wriggles back into my hold, our limbs entwined. Resting my chin on her head again, she absently draws patterns on my chest, safely snuggled away from the rest of the world. It's just the two of us—no expectations, no masks, no need to fake smiles or force laughter. No pressure to be strong.

Beyond these walls, it's chaotic and demanding, but here, the quiet is absolute, broken only by the soothing rhythm of our synced breathing. My injured hand rests against her back, my other traveling beneath her sweater until I find the circular scars on her ribs. Avery doesn't react to my small strokes, as if she's at peace with me touching them now. As if she's accepted that they don't define her. Fredrick's actions don't define her.

"Do you regret it?" I ask finally, my mind unable to take the hint and slow down too.

"Regret what?" Avery tilts her head back, her breath skating over my jaw.

"Leaving the manor." She shakes her head, brushing a strand of hair out of her face.

"I could never regret you guys." My smile grows once more, but there's a flicker of doubt in my raised brow.

"Even Wyatt?" A dry laugh escapes her, a sweet and melodic sound cutting through the quiet.

"A week ago, I'd have said, 'Fuck Wyatt.'" She pauses, reaching up to trace the curve of my jaw with her thumb. "I mean, I totaled Hux's car with the sole intent of hurting him in any way possible. But yeah. Even Wyatt." Leaning forward, I press a tender kiss to her lips, letting it linger.

"I know he's not the easiest of people to understand, but deep, deep down, his heart means well." I say quietly, brushing my nose against hers. "He just shows it in ways that only seem to make sense to him."

"Tell me about it," Avery rolls her eyes, although there's a softness to her now. Every trace of anger and misplaced resentment between the two of them seems to have been resolved, thank fuck. We can finally all come together now; we can be a family again.

I kiss her again, deeper this time. My hand retracts from her side to curl around her neck, my tongue tracing her soft lips. She gives me all of her, opening and inviting me in further. My sweet Avery, clutching her hands in my T-shirt and tugging me impossibly closer. I grip her face, sinking my body lower so she can move to straddle me. My cock responds, twitching inside my jeans as if I didn't selfishly have her to myself all of last night.

It wasn't enough, nor do I doubt it ever will be. Avery doesn't realise how much I love her or how she enables me to be the rock she's slowly coming to rely on. It's an equal give and take. She boosts me so I can be here for her in any way she needs. Lowering my hand to her hips, I pull her down whilst rolling my hips sharply, stifling her gasp with my mouth.

"Guys!" a sharp shout breaks through our bubble. Hux rushes into view, not noticing how he kicks the stacks of books aside with his giant feet or stops me from dry humping Avery into an immediate climax. His brown eyes are wide and wild, seeming to see everything yet nothing at all. His chest is heaving, his fingers spread and hovering in mid-air. Avery sits bolt upright, accidentally rubbing against my shaft again. But none of that matters when Huxley remembers why he's disturbing us.

"He's awake."

AXEL

CHAPTER TWENTY

A flood of pain hits me, slamming my senses into overdrive. I want to gasp, but no sound passes my dry, cracked lips.

Why can't I move?

Shrouded in darkness, only the thump of my heartbeat in my ears tells me I'm not dead, not that I feel reassured. My body feels like I've been buried in concrete, every muscle too weak to push against the weight holding me down. My mind slipped through the fog to rouse a little while ago, but my eyelids are still too heavy to lift.

What the hell happened to me?

Using all my focus, I push every drop of my energy into twitching each of my fingers one by one. Satisfied my fingers are in working order, I slowly begin wiggling my toes back and forth to banish the pins and needles, sending tingles up my legs. A shudder rolls through my restricted spine, making me want to groan at the involuntary movement, but no sound passes my lips. Finally, after an eternity of lying in the pitch black of my own panic, I manage to crack my eyelids and blink a few times to focus.

A sea of stars greets me on the other side of my vision, glowing softly in a mix of pale yellow and green. There's something so familiar about the perfectly pointed shapes—something glaringly obvious lingering on the edge of my mind, but I can't quite grasp it. A solid weight beside me suddenly shifts, a hand slinking over my chest and heavy breath fanning my ear.

Fuck.

A scenario I've seen play out a thousand times before slams into me —a pained noise actually leaving me this time. A hand clasping my mouth, painted lips whispering to *'shh'* in my ear. A strong feminine fragrance clogs my throat, remnants of smoke and alcohol filling my nostrils as fingers brush across my exposed skin. Those glow-in-the-dark stars are my only anchor to reality, the only constant in this repetitive nightmare.

How am I back here? Did I ever even truly escape, or was it all a dream?

The figure clinging to my side sits upright, flicking on my space-themed night light to assess me. I will my body to move, but I'm stuck, glued to the mattress, and only able to scream in my mind. Soft hands touch my cheeks, the tears slipping from my eyes landing upon delicate fingers.

Please no, not again. I can't be here again.

My name is being said, but it might as well be miles away, battle cries of useless determination filling my ears as I stare at those damn stars. By the time I've counted the five points of each one, this should be over. Sitting upright, the darkened silhouette looms over me until I can no longer count, and I recoil until a sea of dark eyes and scruffy hair catches my attention.

Garrett.

The invisible binds holding me in place snap at the same time my chest bursts with relief, and I lurch upright to grab him. A shot of agony slices across my mid-section, pain blazing a trail through me until I'm slumped back and writhing in discomfort.

"Shit! Stay still, Axe. I'll be right back." Garrett's gone before I can beg him to stay, my outstretched hand desperately grabbing the air as agony of a different kind swallows me whole. He's barely left the room, and I'm already contemplating jumping up to chase him, not giving a shit about the repercussions.

The small unloved boy in me would do anything for a simple hug, and the broken man I am only wants it from him.

The pain in my side has lessened to an intense throbbing by the time he finally returns, flanked by a monster of a man in a white coat.

What the fuck is happening?

Garrett re-joins me in the bed and presses a kiss to my sweat-covered brow before pulling down the cover to expose me. Revealing me to this stranger. Suddenly, my worst fears take a turn, and I discover a new way for them to torture me. Garrett is tugging up the material covering my torso, presenting me like his prized whore. My eyes begin to swim, vulnerability sending tremors along my skin.

"It's okay, Axel. Trust me, it's going to be okay." I remain as still as possible, trusting his steady gaze. His hands stroke my arms as he makes an effort to block the man from my view. My body jerks as a second pair of hands skates over my ribs, my breathing hitching in suspense.

Count the stars. Each point, and then it'll be over.

Something sticky is peeled back from my ribs. A bandage maybe. It tears and tugs at my skin, bringing with it a searing pain. Spikes of fear course through my body like tremors, like harsh needles piercing my skin.

"He's panicking," the man says from a distance. My head is slow to follow the conversation, separating me from the room I refuse to be in. Not here, not with Garrett holding me down, not with the cool air brushing my exposed skin like long, spindly fingers. I inhale sharply, choking on the phantom scent of expensive perfume. "He's going to do himself some damage if he doesn't remain still."

"Axe, I need you to relax, okay?" Garrett pleads, but how can I? I don't know this man, but I know what happens in this bed. I know how the pain lingers long after the physical effects are done. How I'll have to relive it every night, with the new addition of Garrett pinning down my shoulders and sneering in my face. I have to stop this before it gets to that point. I can't let Garrett become one of the monsters I run from.

"I'm going to have to sedate him."

"No, please. I've only just gotten him back." Garrett links his fingers in mine, gripping my hand tightly every time I hiss or wince from whatever is being done to me. His eyesight doesn't flicker from mine the entire time, his undivided attention doing little to warm the coldness sweeping through my limbs. Vaguely, I feel myself shaking from head to toe, a layer of sweat seeping into the bedsheets beneath my back.

"He'll wake shortly. If he punctures his lung again, he'll have to go back to theatre."

I stare at Garrett. I beg him with my eyes, pleading with him to end this. To send this man away and wrap his arms around me, tell me I'm not actually back in this hellhole. But he doesn't do any of that. With a resigned nod, Garrett ducks his head aside, avoiding my watery gaze.

The sharp scratch of a needle is pushed into the crook of my free arm, a rush of cool liquid filling my veins, which has my muscles tensing. Almost immediately, I can feel the pull of drowsiness starting to drag me under, away from him. Droplets pool in the shell of my ear as tears stream down my face, my vision blurring in my desperation to stay in his warmth.

The pull of unconsciousness is merciless, dragging me back into the void I fought so hard to escape. My limbs feel like lead, but my mind flails, clawing to stay in the moment, to remain tethered to Garrett's voice and touch. His warmth is the only anchor keeping me from spiraling, and even that's slipping away with every shallow breath.

"I'll be right here, Axe," Garrett whispers, his voice cracking. "I'm not going anywhere." I try to hold onto those words, let them wrap around me like armor, but the drug is too strong, and soon, the glowing stars above me fade to black.

"-an abundance of krill attracts other visitors to the Peninsula in the summer. Antarctic Minke Whales."

Garrett's voice has filtered through the depths of my slumber several times before, but this is the first time I've been able to rouse enough to wonder what the fuck he's talking about. My senses are dulled as if I'm wrapped in thick cotton, but my ears prick just enough.

"They use their pointed heads and short dorsal fins to give them endurance-"

When I open my eyes again, the world is still blurry at the edges. The pain in my side is muted but persistent, a throbbing reminder that I'm alive. The stars on the ceiling glow faintly in the darkness, their soft light casting familiar shapes on the walls. For a moment, I wonder where I am.

Then the smell hits me. Dust, stale air, and the faint lingering trace of my mom's perfume. She's embedded into the walls, her shrewd gaze sweeping through every shadow of every room. It's like being punched in the gut. The memories I've spent years trying to bury come rushing back, suffocating me. This house, this room... it's the last place I ever wanted to be.

A low groan seeps from my achingly raw throat.

"Axel?" Garrett's voice cuts through the haze. I blink, my gaze shifting to find him reclined next to me on the bed, his expression etched with worry. Fading bruises line his throat, and his eyes are sunken. His hair is disheveled, his jaw shadowed with stubble, as if he hasn't left my side.

His hand cups my cheek, a relieved smile waiting for me when I manage to open my eyes. The room is a thousand times too bright, the permanent grogginess embedded into my skull magnifying tenfold. Breathing causes discomfort, so I lie perfectly still, trying not to move my limbs. Regardless, each inhale burns the back of my throat.

I want to speak, to tell him I'm okay, or at least lie convincingly enough to ease that pained look in his eyes, but all I manage is a rasping sound. Garrett leans forward, his hand warm and steady as it cups my cheek.

"Don't try to talk yet," he murmurs. "You've been through hell, Axe. Just... let me take care of you." He darts away, returning with a cup of water and straw, helping me to slowly sip. I pant around the straw, dropping my head back. Garrett says I've been through hell, and that's exactly how I feel.

The door creaks open, and my body tenses instinctively, the shadows in the hallway sending a chill down my spine. Huxley steps inside, his expression carefully neutral but his eyes sharp as they scan the room. Settling on me, he forces a small smile.

"Good morning, Sleeping Beauty," he says lightly, although I instinctively know it's not morning. "How are you feeling?" Hux eases onto the edge of the mattress and picks up my hand. A metallic weight trickles down my forearm; the compass bracelet I've been taking care of is still on my wrist.

"Like a sack of shit." I manage to grumble. Clearing my throat several times, I tip my head back to open up my throat. "Tell me I'm hallucinating and I'm not where I think I am."

Huxley's smile drops. Instead of answering me, he releases my hand and shifts to slowly lift me up by the shoulders. Garrett stuffs his pillow behind my back, and I sink back in my new elevated position to look around the room from my childhood.

Yep, I'm really here.

The midnight blue painted walls and solar system project I made in fifth grade hanging by astronaut-themed drawn curtains. My stomach rolls. In all of my nightmares, my focus was on the bed, on what I was subjected to. I'd forgotten how childish the decor was. The safe space of a young boy who felt anything but. Flicking off the TV sitting on the dresser, Garrett mutters under his breath.

"There was nothing I could do." Despite our company, he snuggles into my side, curling one of his long legs around mine. We're both wearing black lounge pants.

"Wher-" I clear my throat, "Where are the others?"

"I thought it would be best not to overwhelm you," Garrett rubs his face into my neck like a feline. "But they're all here, waiting to see you." They're all here. Tears prick my eyes, and I can't decide if it's from the comfort of knowing the Souls are nearby or the dread that they've walked into my waking nightmare. This house is a poison that taunts your veins and never truly lets you go.

Huxley, who was staring into the distance, working hard to stop his mouth from pressing into a tight line, suddenly stands, seeming to remember something. "I'll get some soup sent up." Huxley strides for the door, pulling it gently closed behind him. I shake my head weakly, the thought of food turning my stomach further, but it's too late. My grunts of protest become too much for my feeble body, leaving me immobile and breathless once again.

"It's going to be okay," Garrett breathes, his voice low. His hand finds mine, his grip strong and unwavering. "Whatever you need, Axe. I'm going to be right here."

Whatever I need. The words rush through my head, the tips of my ears starting to burn. What I need is to forget where I am. To be removed from the pain, distracted from the dull thud of panic within my chest. I need him.

Unashamed, I trail my index finger over Garrett's T-shirt, tracing the ridges of his abs underneath. His breath catches, but he doesn't stop me, and that small act of permission feels like an unspoken surrender. The warmth of his body seeps into me, grounding me in a way I desperately need. His gaze doesn't falter, locked onto mine, steady and intense. We've woken up beside each other countless times before, but this moment feels heavier, charged with something I can't name.

There's a shift in his expression, an almost imperceptible flicker in his eyes. His lips part, as if to speak, but the words dissolve before they can form. It's unlike him, this hesitation. Garrett always knows what to say, whether it's a joke, a taunt, or some line designed to deflect. Now, though, he's stripped bare, his usual armor gone. And I don't think he realizes just how exposed he is, how vulnerable he looks sitting there, watching me like I'm something fragile he's afraid to break.

A faint stirring of awareness pulls at me, the lingering fog in my head giving way to questions. What exactly happened to me? And more importantly, what's happened to Garrett? This intensity, this quiet between us, feels new. It's like there's a weight behind his gaze, layers I've never fully peeled back before.

The pain in my body dulls, eclipsed by the quiet electricity between us. To anyone else, Garrett is just a good-looking college guy. His dark hair catches streaks of gold in the right light, his eyes shift between fathomless and mischievous, and his smile can charm or cut depending on his mood. But that's not what I see.

I see the self-hatred living beneath his flesh. The way his jokes deflect, how his smile is a shield. He craves affection but convinces himself he doesn't deserve it. Someone who refuses to believe he deserves more than rough sex and empty promises.

My hand stills against his chest, resting over the steady thrum of his heartbeat. "Garrett," I whisper, my voice rough and tentative. It's not a question or a statement. It's a plea. For what, I'm not even sure. I just know at that moment I need something. His fingers twitch, brushing over my bare chest to still over my heart. He swallows hard, his Adam's apple bobbing.

"I love you so fucking much, Axe." He almost whimpers. Like an atomic bomb going off in my head, my ears ring, and I gasp. That's it. That's exactly what I needed.

Garrett's mouth crashes against me before I can say it back, all pretence of gentleness slipping away. It's a feral, desperate slanting of his lips over mine, hiding the slight tremor underneath. Garrett kisses me as if he won't survive without it, the hand on my heart clenching. I don't stop him, twisting my hand into his shirt as much as I can to drag him impossibly closer, despite the sharp ache in my side. The pain is secondary to the way Garrett pours himself into me like he's been holding it all back for too long.

Leaning over me, his hand presses a touch too hard on my sternum. A gasp is torn from my lips, interrupting our messy kiss. Garrett freezes instantly, relieving all pressure from my body. I keep my hand clenched in his T-shirt, not letting him go far. His forehead rests against mine as he pants, his warm breath mingling with mine.

"Fuck, I'm sorry," he murmurs, his voice hoarse. His thumb brushes over my cheek, wiping away a bead of sweat. "I shouldn't have—"

"Don't apologize," I rasp, interrupting him. My grip finally loosens on his shirt, my thumb smoothing over the fabric. "As soon as I'm better, I want you to do that for hours and hours."

"And I'm going to pull up a chair to watch," a soft voice cuts through us, alight with laughter. Just inside the door, with her hip popped and a tray in her hands, is Avery. "I thought we agreed to be gentle with him," she chastises Garrett, but there's no real venom in it.

"Avery," I breathe.

"Hey handsome." Her lips twitch, and she moves to set down the tray holding a steaming bowl of soup. Her golden hair rests over her shoulders, a logo on her sweater for Hollowbrook Academy. Hollowbrook? The name seems unfamiliar, but in my mind's eye, a domed building appears. Or perhaps it's a stadium, skidded with blood down the halls and a high-pitched scream escaping the locker room. Suddenly, it all comes flooding back.

CHAPTER TWENTY ONE

Eventually, Axel falls asleep in my arms. None of us were prepared for the sudden surge of panic he would have in response to seeing me. As if he was in a dreamy state, and I was the bucket of cold water dousing it. The drug that the doctor rushed in to give him has done its job, soothing Axel back into the slumber I'd only just got him back from. I understand the logic. Resting is needed to heal, but the episode has solidified what the doctor told us this morning. There is no quick fix here. Axel needs time, and we need to give it to him.

Hugging his head to my chest, I shift down into the pillows as a lone tear escapes my eye. Garrett shifts in my peripheral, returning from the bathroom.

"Peach," he frowns, but I wave him off.

"It's fine. I'm fine, honestly. You should get some sleep, Gare. You look like shit."

Garrett pauses in the doorway, his hand gripping the frame as he studies me. His face is etched with exhaustion. Dark circles under his eyes, his jaw tight, and his hair sticking up in every direction from where he's run his hands through it too many times. He doesn't move, though.

"Actually, if you're sure you're okay here," he breaks off, his eyes sliding back to the hallway. Whatever it is, Gare doesn't want to ask for it, nor should he have to.

"Garrett, go. I've got this." Garrett hesitates for a moment longer.

His lips press together like he wants to argue, but he finally nods, the tension in his shoulders sagging just a fraction.

"I'll be back soon," he promises, before stepping out into the hallway. As the door clicks softly behind him, the room feels impossibly still. The hum of the monitors fills the quiet, steady, and constant, a reminder of the fragile line Axel is walking. I glance down at him, his face peaceful in sleep, though the bruises marring his skin tell a much different story.

I adjust my hold on him, brushing my fingers gently over his head. His skin is damp with sweat, and I use the edge of the blanket to pat him dry, careful not to disturb him. Lower down the bed, his wrist glints where he's wearing my compass bracelet. A shuddering sigh rocks through my chest.

"You scared the hell out of me for a hot minute there, Ax," I whisper. I don't know if he can hear me, but I need to say the words anyway. I need to fill the silence. "You don't get to leave us, okay? You don't get to leave me."

Tears threaten to spill again, but I blink them back, focusing on the rhythm of his breathing instead. In and out. Slow and steady. It's enough to anchor me for the moment. The weight of the day starts pressing down harder, between the confessions Dax managed to draw out of me and how close I came to telling Axel how much I've missed him. I let my head fall back against the pillows.

The soft glow of the stars on Axel's ceiling catches my attention as I stroke my hands over his head, brushing my thumb along his cheek. The room feels heavy with memories of a once quiet sanctuary that was torn to shreds.

I can't tell how long I've laid there before the door clicks and cracks open. My arms tighten around Axel as if holding him close will somehow protect him from whatever is coming. A body steps inside, not seeking permission and not offering an explanation. The next minute, the cover is lifted, and a warm body curls in behind me.

"You're missing dinner," Wyatt mutters beside my ear. On cue, my stomach echoes with a hollow growl, and I feel the smugness radiate from him.

"I'm not hungry." Wyatt shifts closer, his arm sliding around my waist. The firmness of his chest presses into my back.

"You're a terrible liar, Angel, but I'll let it slide this time." he murmurs, his lips touching the patch of skin behind my ear. My focus remains on Axel, on the rise and fall of his chest and the faint crease still etched between his brows even in sleep. Wyatt speaks after a moment, his voice quieter, almost tentative. "You've been in here for hours. The students have packed up and piled into a row of minibuses, so it's much quieter now. We could sneak down and raid the fridge without being seen."

"It's unnerving when you're nice to me," I roll my eyes, and we both laugh softly.

"Well, you appear to have broken my mean streak. Now I don't know what to do with myself." This is true. Now that he's not scheming in private or deflecting any affection brought his way, Wyatt is left wide open. It's almost as if we get to rewrite his persona and fix all of the damage that he's been dealt. Or at least, he's finally open to letting us try.

Wyatt reaches out to stroke Axel's shoulder. His sigh is soft, his breath brushing against my neck. "You can't run on empty, and you won't do him any good if you burn out. Come have some food." I know he's right, but I still shake my head. After the way Axel reacted to me earlier, I need to know he's okay. That we're okay.

"I'll tap out when Garrett gets back."

Wyatt doesn't push any further. His fingers ghost my hair, tucking the loose strands behind my ear. "Alright. But you're staying with me tonight. No arguments." I smile despite myself. Wyatt's presence lulls me, the room falling into a fragile calm at long last. It's all too easy to slip into his comfort, remembering the way he held me in the tent. Even when I was pushing against him, fighting him every step of the way, he kept me safe. Actions speak louder than words, and Wyatt's actions scream everything he would never dare to voice. What he's afraid of saying.

The next time I open my eyes, the dim light filtering through the curtains reveals a shift in the room. Wyatt is gone, but we're not alone. Garrett rests on Axel's other side, his head resting lightly on Axel's chest, his posture protective yet tired. His dark eyes flicker to mine, and in the silence, the weight of guilt settles over his features like a shroud.

That's when I notice it. The deepening bruise mottling his cheekbone and the fresh, angry cut splitting his lower lip.

"Garrett," I whisper, careful not to disturb Axel, my voice cutting through the stillness like a blade. "What the fuck did you do?"

He doesn't flinch at the accusation, his lips pressing together. "Nothing that wasn't deserved." My stomach tightens. His tone is hollow, devoid of the bubbling emotion I'm so used to. Before my very eyes, it's as if Garrett is drifting away, slipping into the abyss. I push myself up, careful of Axel's limp form, and lean closer to Garrett.

"This isn't you," I insist softly but firmly. Garrett's jaw tightens, his gaze dropping to Axel's still face.

"Maybe it's who I should be," he mutters back. "Maybe if it was, Axel would never have gotten hurt in the first place back in Waversea." I can see the rabbit hole Garrett is diving down. His defense mechanism is humor, but it is also what makes him appear less like the tough guy. Less like the guy who could protect Axel from bigots. Perhaps he's going as far as thinking he shouldn't have fallen for Axel in the first place.

"No, Garrett. The Souls' dynamic relies on you being your cheeky self. You're our glue. I'm not saying you can't be in low spirits, but don't lose who you truly are. Who I fell in love with."

His head snaps up, dark eyes locking on mine with an intensity that sends a jolt straight to my chest. I see it there. The pain he's trying to bury, the doubt eating him alive. Slowly, I reach out, my hand brushing over the bruised skin of his cheek. My thumb moves in soft, rhythmic strokes, and he freezes under the touch, his breath hitching.

"Your jokes are trash, and let's be honest, your tattoos are shit, but I wouldn't change any part of you. You're hilarious and quirky and gorgeous and incredible."

Shifting away from my touch, Garrett shakes his head, refusing to listen to me. "Axel is the incredible one." I lean over and grab his cheek harder, causing him to hiss through his teeth. At this point, I think he needs to feel it. To realise he can't brush me off anymore.

"You're worthy of love, Gare. I freaking love you." His eyes widen, vulnerability flashing across his face like a lightning strike before it's buried under layers of fear and disbelief. But I hold on, refusing to let him retreat. "You're enough, Garrett," I whisper, my voice trembling now. "You've always been enough to me and to Axel."

Garrett's shoulders sag, a choked sound escaping his throat as he finally lets himself crumble. I lean forward, resting my forehead against his, our breaths mingling in the heavy silence. "We'll get through this," I promise. "Together."

For a moment, he doesn't respond, but then his hands come up to grip my wrists, grounding himself in the contact. It's not a full surrender, but it's a start. Between us, Axel hums slightly, his eyelids fluttering but not fully opening.

"Together," Axel whispers on a breathy exhale. I hold Garrett's stare, a matching smile creeping across our faces. We lean in together, pressing a kiss to each of Axel's temples.

"Welcome back," I smile. Waiting for Axel to rouse in his own time, I reach over to the table for his water. He shuffles against me to lift his head and sip through the straw. Just that small movement is enough for him to sink back down, exhausted once more. I chew on the inside of my cheek, worrying in silence again about the unknown length of his recovery. We could be here for months at this rate.

Searching for a distraction, I let my gaze wander to the posters lining the walls. Planets, galaxies, and spacecraft frozen in mid-flight. "I didn't know you were so into space, Axe."

His voice is hoarse, barely above a whisper, but there's a flicker of warmth in it. "My dad was low-key obsessed. He found the concept of space fascinating. We used to take trips together to watch the rockets launch at NASA. It's some of my favorite memories."

On his other side, Garrett shifts down beneath the covers to settle on Axel's chest again. "You've never told me that." There's genuine curiosity in his tone, and I reckon there are a lot of things Axel hasn't opened up about, too focused on the trauma he suffered to remember anything else.

"Did your... um, did Sharon go too?" I ask hesitantly. Axel shakes his head, his expression tightening ever so slightly.

"If it's not fashion or money, she's not interested." My nostrils flare in irritation, but this isn't news to me. I can see it in the way she carries herself and the way she speaks of Axel like an inconvenience. Axel finally blinks his hazel eyes wide open, awake at long last.

"Sharon never wanted kids, but my dad was twenty years her senior, and he told me he always wanted just one, perfect child." There's a bittersweet tilt to his lips that shows he was exactly that to his father. "When she refused to ruin her body for his selfish desires, they agreed to use a surrogate. Maybe that's why the maternal instinct never kicked in. All she cared about was the money."

I swallow hard, unsure how to respond. The image of his mother, distant and indifferent, doesn't fit with the man lying in front of me. The man who exudes quiet strength and has somehow kept his kindness intact despite it all.

"What did your father even see in her?" I ask, my voice tinged with frustration. "Surely he could have found someone else." Axel lets out a soft, humorless laugh.

"He wasn't a saint. I reckon he used her too. In our world, it's all about public image." I nod, knowing that all too well. It's exactly why Cathy went to such lengths to hide her affair with Fredrick. Why she used Wyatt as the scapegoat for her reputation. The weight of these revelations sits heavily between us, the unspoken complexities of Axel's upbringing clear in the dark lines of his face.

Reaching out, he takes my hand in his. Axel's eyes meet mine for a brief moment, steady and unwavering. Even now, horizontal and bandaged, he doesn't want to show weakness.

"I'm sure it hasn't been easy staying with me while Meg is out there somewhere. But it means the world that you did. I promise I will get better as quickly as I can. I'll do whatever it takes to get us back out there, searching for her."

"Meg's a tough bitch," I reply, echoing back what Wyatt told me. Who'd have thought Wyatt would become my voice of reason? "She will be giving one hell of a fight, and when we finally do find her, she'll beat my ass for putting myself in danger." I snort out a laugh. "Just focus on getting better. Now that you're awake, we can start looking for leads. That's what matters."

CHAPTER TWENTY TWO

"Garrett?" My name is called distantly. I mumble something incoherent and shift in my sleep. Axel's voice comes again, bleeding through the haze.

I jerk upright on my front, looking around the room wildly in panic. The dying sun is fading into hues of red and orange beyond the window, and as I adjust, my eyes settle on Axel. There's an amused hook to one of his eyebrows, those dazzling hazel eyes filled with mirth, and his lips slanted up into a smile. For a split second, I forget where we are. Who we are even. I'm just a guy being woken by a cute guy that causes my heart to flutter. Then, with the beeping of monitors increasing, reality hits.

"What's wrong? Do you need something?" My fingers impulsively twitch, drawing my attention to beneath the covers where my hand is wrapped around Axel's balls. He chuckles and nudges my shoulder.

"As much as I appreciate the massage, I really don't want to know what it feels like to have an erection with a catheter inserted." I shudder at just the thought, slowly retracting my hand.

"Sorry," I roll onto my back to stare at the ceiling. "I must have gotten carried away. It's been a long, *long* few weeks." Huffing, I force my eyes shut. *Great job, Garrett; he's barely lucid, and you're throwing your sex drive in his face.*

"I didn't mean like that, I just... there's been a lot of emotions to wade through and you know it's not my strongest trait—" Axel winces as he reaches over and pulls on my far shoulder, rolling me onto my side to face him. That same understanding smile is waiting to greet me, his handsome face far too accepting.

"You don't have to wait for me, you know. If you want to go and let Avery relieve you, it's okay. I totally get that you have needs." I'm already shaking my head.

"I will wait for you," I mutter stubbornly. I must fail at hiding the rare glimpse of vulnerability I can sense rising to the surface. Axel's brow furrows, his hand reaching up to cup my cheek.

"Gare. Everything is going to be fine now. I won't leave you again," he promises, but it's impossible to believe him. He doesn't know what's going to happen; none of us do. Doctor Marcus is due to give Axel a full checkover, but even then, what if he misses something? The smallest complication might send Axel straight back to the hospital. Clearing my throat, I nudge his hand from my face, quickly shutting down my stupid fucking emotions.

"You mind if I call on Avery to sit with you for a while?" Axel nods, sorrow dawning in his eyes as I shoot upright to leave the bed. Shoving my legs into a pair of blue tracksuit pants, I grab the matching hoodie from the arm of a nearby chair and leave the room, blood rushing through my ears too fast to hear Axel's protests.

The irony isn't lost on me. I've sat by his side day and night, refusing to let anyone else near him, praying for him to wake and listen to all of the ways I care about him. Now he's back, and I can't get away quick enough. Because now it's time to show up, to be the person I've been promising myself I can be for him. And what if I fall at the first hurdle? What if I just keep fucking up until there's no part of Axel left to save?

Rapping my knuckles hard on the next bedroom door along the hall, Avery answers, a stoic Wyatt at her back. His green eyes cut through me, assessing and judging like he always does. In direct contrast, Avery smiles and reaches for my head.

"You okay, Gare? Do you need something?" I shake my hand loose, taking a step back from the pity that pinches at her face. Yeah, I need everyone to stop being so fucking nice.

"Can you sit with Axel for me? I'm going to get the Doc."

"Is there something wrong with him?" Avery's large eyes widen even more, her feet already shuffling into the hallway. I give her a wide berth, pressing myself against the opposite wall.

"No," I sigh, withholding the rest of that sentence. *There's just something wrong with me.* "I just need some air." Air sounds a lot better than *space*. Nodding, Avery tucks her golden hair behind her ear and heads towards Axel's room. Her fluffy socks are silent on the carpet, her knock soft before she slips inside. Knowing he won't be alone lessens a sliver of the guilt building in my chest, but then Wyatt steps forward and continues to look me up and down.

"Is there something you want to say, Riot?" I clench my jaw. Unlike my usual, light tone, the nickname is hissed in mockery. Wyatt raises a singular brow but says nothing, pocketing his hands and watching me leave. I encounter the Doc in a large office he seems to have been given the run of. Currently, he's reclined on a chaise lounge with a book in his hands.

"Aren't you being paid to do something?" I kick the door with a harsh bang. He doesn't flinch, regarding me with poised interest. I suppose a doctor should be used to keeping his cool in heightened situations, but he seems a little too relaxed for my liking.

"It certainly isn't to take orders from you," he replies. Setting his book aside, Marcus plants his loafers on the floor, standing to be eye level with me. "You should ice that bruise." My eyes slide aside, ignoring both him and the pulsing ache that has taken root in my cheek.

Not my proudest moment, taking a hit when Axel was laid up in bed, but the other guy came off worse. Every student in the room was staring at me like some kind of God, and he happened to be the one who asked me how he could get some time alone with Axel to pick his brains. As if being molested has become something these weirdos strive for. My fist responded before my mouth could.

I guess I'm still glutton for punishment, the same way I was as a small boy who stubbornly waited for someone to care for him, despite the long-term effects it would cause. Before he woke, I was ready for Axel to be mine, ready to gut myself at his feet and let him piece me back together. I wanted to be exactly the kind of man he's been begging me to be all these years. But now that both he and Avery have confessed their love for me, it's become too real. Too fragile to handle with my reckless hands.

Remembering Marcus is still standing before me, his knitted sweater a shade of hunter green today, I roll my tongue over my teeth.

"Can you give Axel a once-over? Check his vitals and all that. Surely it's best we get him up and restore his strength as soon as possible." Marcus waits, staring evenly until I grunt. "*Please.*"

I exit the room, giving him the space to manoeuvre his hulking size through the doorway. Once satisfied, he heads for Axel's room while I sweep down the staircase, on the hunt for my next fight. Now that the students have left, I thought there would be no one left to cause conflict with. I thought wrong.

Turning the last corner before the kitchen, I barrel straight into Sharon. She collides with my chest, stumbling back on those ridiculously high heels with a startled *"oomph,"* clutching her Louis Vuitton bag like a shield. Her eyes dart to my crotch for a split second before snapping back to my face. I can feel my lip curling in a snarl, a guttural growl simmering in my chest like a panther advancing on its prey.

Slowly, a smile carves across my face, pulling painfully at the welt on my cheek. I've been waiting to catch her alone, and now I'm spiraling through hatred and self-doubt, it's the best possible moment.

I step forward, crowding her against the wall. My hands slam down on either side of her head, caging her in. Her eyes widen, the flicker of fear I've been dying to see flashing across her carefully composed features. I lean closer, my breath ghosting over her face as I let the rage sharpen my voice.

"I've been waiting years to confront you, Sharon. To make you pay for everything you've ever done to him."

From within the curtain of her straight, dark hair, Sharon's face twists into an infuriating smirk, but it doesn't hide the way her throat bobs when she swallows. "If Axel ever wanted the auctions to stop, all he had to do was ask."

The casual venom in her tone makes my hands curl into fists against the wall. Her manicured nail traces up the center of my chest, scraping along my jaw, sending a shiver of disgust rippling through me. My lungs burn with the effort of keeping myself steady, the words in my head screaming louder than ever.

He was fourteen. You were supposed to protect him, not exploit him.

Somehow, I manage to grab onto the last thread of self-control within my soul to speak somewhat eloquently.

"If Karma doesn't come for you one day soon, I'm going to flay you alive and roast you on a barbeque. Then I'll force feed you to every single one of all your pedophilic friends that have ever laid a hand on Axel."

A shudder ripples through her perfect, tailored pantsuit. The sight makes something primal in me stir, satisfaction clawing its way through my fury. I straighten, stepping back with the kind of smile that could haunt her nightmares, before turning toward the kitchen door. Sharon's voice, sharp and poised, stops me cold.

"You're worse for him than I ever was." The words hit me like a blow to the gut. I whirl around, the fire in my chest reigniting.

"The fuck did you just say?" Sharon's smug grin is back, her hand resting lazily on her hip like she owns the entire world.

"At least Axel always knew what I wanted from him. We had a transactional relationship." She tilts her head, her voice dripping with mockery. "You're dragging him along to prove something to yourself. He's a passing novelty to you. So tell me, who's the real abuser here?"

Before I can react, she spins on her heel, her ponytail whipping behind her. She strides away, her confidence slicing through the air like a knife. I stand frozen, my breath caught somewhere between wrath and disbelief. I can't move, can't think straight. Heat rushes to my cheeks, shame and rage battling for dominance.

How dare she?!

Red curtains my vision. I want to smash everything in close range and scream. To beat the living shit out of the closest possible person, feel their bones crack, and hear them beg for mercy until the beast within me is sated. Burn this whole mansion to the ground so that Axel can never be dragged back again.

But there's a darker desire worming its way to the forefront, one that is purely selfish. I want to be punished. I want to feel the retributions of what I've failed to do. Keeping Axel safe, keeping the Souls together, and protecting my heart from this constant ache of not being good enough. It's all too much to bear without an outlet. One that involves whatever pain it takes to root me back to reality.

The rage boils over, needing an outlet before I explode. My fist slams into the wall beside me, a burst of raw energy erupting from my knuckles. The impact reverberates up my arm—a sharp, jolting pain that should be enough to make me stop. But it's not. Not even close.

I hit the wall again, harder this time, my knuckles splitting against the painted surface. The sting is intoxicating, a brief distraction from the hurricane in my chest. Another punch, and then another. The drywall cracks under the pressure, but it isn't enough to drown out Sharon's voice still echoing in my head.

You're worse for him than I ever was. Who's the real abuser here?

The words sting deeper than any wound I could inflict on myself, but I keep going. Each punch is a release, a fleeting reprieve from the guilt eating me alive. I can't get the image of Axel limp and bleeding out of my head. He came to my aid and saved my damn life. I can't punish the asshole who hurt him, but I can punish myself.

Blood smears the wall as my breath comes in ragged gasps. My vision blurs, my body trembling as adrenaline surges through me.

"Stop," Wyatt suddenly growls, catching my fist in mid-air. I didn't even see him approach, too wrapped up in the straightjacket of my own mind.

"I don't want to stop," I grunt, trying to twist my hand free. "I want to hurt." Wyatt wrenches my arm backward. My other hand rises instinctively, but he moves faster, yanking me off balance with a forceful tug. My knees buckle, and I stumble, his arm hooking around my neck like a steel bar.

The fight bleeds out of me as he drags me away, each step disorienting. The coppery scent of blood clings to my skin, mixing with the dull ache spreading through my knuckles. I twist, trying to defy him in any way I can, but Wyatt doesn't let up, steering me down the hallway.

The next thing I know, we're in the gym. My back slams against a padded wall, Wyatt's arm finally releasing its hold. I stagger, catching myself with both hands on my thighs, chest heaving as I struggle to catch my breath.

"You don't want to hurt," he says, standing firm in front of me. I glare at the floor by his socked feet, my hands curling into fists again. The pain that cuts through my hands doesn't feel as sweet this time. Even so, my shoulders tighten, the impulse to lash out still clawing at me. "You just want someone to see that you're suffering, and instead of pretending everything's fine, you want them to tell you it's all your fault."

"Will you?" I risk a look up into his green eyes, sensing the spike of vulnerability within like a whip's lash. I'm struck by the lack of anger in Wyatt's features and stance, a lack of resentment in having to come and clear up my mess. Instead, Wyatt crosses his arms, his expression unreadable.

"No. This is Fredrick's fault, and Nixon's and Cathy's and every other fucker that has been playing God with our lives. We're stuck trying to clear up messes we didn't cause and somehow expected to mentally survive it." I look away, my jaw tightening. The gym feels too small, the walls pressing in around me.

"You can hit things if you want. Break your fucking hand, scream, and cry, but it's pointless. Because when you go back upstairs, Axel and Avery will still be there, waiting for you. Relying on you to show up." Wyatt sighs, releasing his arms to step forward. Next thing, his hands are on my shoulders, squeezing and releasing rhythmically to get my breathing to somewhat regulate. "It doesn't have to be scary. Trust me, I spent years believing it was."

I glance at him, the edge of his words piercing through the fog in my mind. I hate how broken I feel and sound, but I push through, desperate for the answers he's offering. "How did you get over it?" Wyatt smirks to himself, casting a glance over my shoulder.

"I didn't. But I've decided to stop running. I ran from Avery when she moved into the Manor, I ran from Cathy when I couldn't bear to play nice anymore. I've been running from you guys at every sign of attachment." His tone softens, and as he steps closer, I'm pulled into a willing hug from Wyatt Hughes. That's how I know I've gone too far.

"It's a shitty, lonely life, Gare, and it doesn't have to be. The people upstairs deserve better. They need a reason to smile and laugh, and live. It's our job to give it to them. So pick yourself up, think of a corny joke, and get back up there."

I open my mouth to argue, but Wyatt shoves my head into his neck. He's wearing his own orange hoodie for once, the mix of his and Avery's scents blending seamlessly. A rogue blond hair drapes over the hood.

"Don't do it for you, Garrett. Do it for them." He pulls back to put me at arm's length, his palms warm against my cheeks. His green eyes are more tender than I've ever seen them, his lips tilting into a small smile. "Go make them laugh."

I drag a shaky hand through my hair, my breathing slowing to an even pace. The scent of blood and failure is thick, clogging my throat, but I nod, the motion almost invisible. Wyatt releases me and takes a few measured steps back. This is what he does, offers the right words and then rebuilds the distance to see what I do. Giving comfort and then space, as if I might shatter at any moment. Maybe I will. But not now. Not tonight.

"Thanks," I mutter hoarsely, my voice rough like sandpaper. He doesn't respond, just jerks his head toward the door.

The hallway feels quieter than it should as I climb the stairs. My injured hand shakes, gliding along the banister, leaving behind the chaos I've caused downstairs. I hesitate at the top landing, swallowing the lump forming in my throat. *They're waiting for you.*

I step into Axel's room, the faint sound of laughter spilling out before I fully open the door. The sight steals what little resolve I had left. Dax is sprawled out on the floor, cards fanned out in his good hand, grinning like a kid. Avery sits cross-legged by Axel's bedside, her golden hair swaying as she pretends to consult Hux, who's leaning over her shoulder with exaggerated seriousness. Axel is propped up against a mound of pillows, the ghost of a smile tugging at his lips. His hazel eyes meet mine as soon as I step inside, warm despite the way I left him, and his smile grows just a little wider.

"There you are," he says, a little raspy, but his eyes are full of life for once. "Doc gave me the all-clear to start moving around and peeing for myself."

Dax looks up at me from his cards and snorts. "Should have heard him squeal when the catheter came out. I've heard newborn piglets make less noise." He jerks his head to the floor next to him with mock enthusiasm. "Come join us. I saved you a seat." I force a smirk, my chest tightening and loosening in the same breath.

"What's the game?"

"Blackjack," Avery chips in, her blue eyes sparkling as she glances at me. "Me and Hux are acting as the house, so you'll lose either way." For the first time in what feels like hours, I laugh. Not much, but enough to feel the edges of my anger dull. I settle down beside Dax, brushing my knee against his in silent gratitude, and pick up the cards they dealt me.

"Remind me of how to play," I nudge his shoulder. Looking between my two cards, Dax peers over and groans.

"Well, shit. You've already won." Lifting his bandaged hand, he uses the metal splint in between his flattened fingers to point to the cards in turn. "It's first or nearest to twenty-one wins. The ace counts as eleven and all face cards are tens. You've got one of each, so beginner's luck I guess."

I shrug happily, sneaking a peak over at Dax's hand. He's got six cards, all of lower value but collectively adding to a total more than twenty-one. He sighs and throws them down. "I got greedy and went bust. It's more fun when you bet with something." My eyes shoot directly to Avery, who is already shaking her head at me.

"Don't even think about it. I'm not about to play strip blackjack whilst Axel is too injured to get an erection." My bald-headed lover chokes on his breath, grumbling that he can get an erection just fine, while Hux takes in the cards and deals again. Glancing between my friends, my family, the weight in my chest starts to lift. The world outside still feels heavy, but here, in this room and surrounded by them, I can carry it. For tonight at least, I can show up.

CHAPTER TWENTY THREE

I walk into the kitchen, intent on locating some breakfast for Garrett and Axel, only to find the former sitting at the island with a huge stack of pancakes. Avery moves around the counters opposite, flour on her cheek and a splash of batter coating her apron. Hux is sitting beside him, a singular pancake on his plate that he's struggling through.

"Well, this is cozy," I raise a brow. All faces swing to me. "Any chance of some leftovers for our injured soldier upstairs?" Avery beams a smile that cuts straight through my morning haze, brightening my mood like a shot of espresso. I'm careful not to let it show on my face, though. If she knew the full effect she has on me, she'd be dangerous.

"I'm just starting Axel's and Dax's now. You want some?" she offers, pointing a spatula at me. I nod and move into the kitchen, feeling more at home than I have in months. It's the quiet, simple moments like this that I would have missed if I'd kept being a coward, if I'd kept running. I'm making an effort to appreciate the small joys while we still can.

I pat Hux on the shoulder as I pass, doing what little I can to reassure him his efforts aren't going unnoticed. I swear, after all this shit is over, I'm going to find him the best nutritionist and personal trainer, getting both his physical and mental states back to what they once were. Shuffling behind Garrett, I pause until Avery has turned back to her frying pan and lean into his side.

"How are you feeling this morning?" Garrett's head tilts, putting our mouths closer than I'm comfortable with, but I don't retract, letting him test the boundary I'm sure he would never cross. I hope.

"You shouldn't whisper in my ear like that, Riot. People might start to talk." It wasn't a real answer, but the glint of humor has returned to his dark eyes. That's more than was there yesterday.

I sit, instantly being handed a cup of coffee. Avery's blue eyes are glistening too, a look I can't quite understand etched into her beautiful face. She's flawless, without the need for make-up or her hair perfectly styled. Even now, the blonde strands are thrown into a messy braid, hanging over her shoulder. The striped, satin pajamas she's wearing are far too big to be hers.

"Have I missed something? Are there drugs in the pancakes?" I raise a brow, casting a glance down the island. I'm not comforted by the low chuckles that sound in response.

"Sharon left first thing for a business trip her husband arranged. She'll be gone until Friday." Huxley fills me in. I feel the instant relief that the others have clearly been basking in. That's one less problem to deal with for a couple of days.

Avery slides me a plate and returns to her frying pan, working on the next batch. Gare draws Hux into a conversation about weight training and how the pair will get back in the gym soon.

From the outside, I can see what's really happening, as Garrett takes Hux's fork and stabs it into a section of his singular pancake and then forces it into Huxley's hand. Hux is in the middle of discussing which protein powder brand would be best for bulking up, not noticing when he pops the pancake into his mouth and chews.

It continues like that, and when Avery asks Hux to reach another bag of flour out of the cupboard for her, Gare slides a pancake from his own plate onto Hux's now empty one.

Garrett giving up food is unheard of. I'm quickly drawn into the ease of it all. Like we're just a group of friends hanging out, not a bunch of people caught in the middle of a nightmare.

Movement in the door halts the conversation, Doctor Marcus appearing to join us. He's also been quick to make himself comfortable, moving across the space to refill the coffee machine with an air of confidence. Today, he's wearing a mustard yellow sweater, the collar of a shirt poking out at the neckline. Comfortable navy slacks cover his tall, thick legs. The life of a private physician seems to allow for a lot of personal time, apparently.

"Since you're all here, I'd be happy to provide an update on Axel, if you'd like." Marcus turns with a steaming mug in one hand and a protein bar he's located in the other. I lean on my forearms, nodding to continue. "He's doing well, all things considered. I've given him a round of antibiotics, although his pneumothorax has healed nicely—"

"Speak English, Doc," Garrett muffles around a mouthful of food. Marcus takes a sip of coffee first.

"His punctured lung is expanding the way it should, but Axel needs to take it slow. Ignoring the natural healing time of his broken ribs fixing back together, too much physical exertion can labor his breathing, risking another collapse. What we also don't want is to rush him, causing a part of his lung wall to stick together when healing. It could leave him with lifetime breathing issues. At best, he develops asthma; at worst, he's on an oxygen tank from the age of twenty-one."

"It's really that serious," Avery gasps, her eyes racing across the island counter as her mind whirls. The fleeting happiness from before fades away, and the fear for Axel takes over. She switches off the gas, the next plate of pancakes forgotten. Huxley calls out to her, beckoning her to come curl up in his lap. In my peripheral, Hux strokes her hair and kisses her temple, while Garrett continues to stuff his face. The sound of him chewing is enough to put me off my food.

"No rushing, got it," I huff. Rising from the stool, I scrape my pancakes onto Axel and Dax's stack. Removing a carton from the fridge, I pour them a glass of orange juice each and balance them in the crook of my arms whilst lifting the plate in my hand. A soft snort sounds behind me as I leave, Garrett's voice in my head, making a quip about being a domestic goddess.

I roll my eyes as I retrace my steps through the halls. It might not be real, and it won't last long, but a semblance of the gang we used to be is seeping through. How it was in the beginning, with Garrett's stupid jokes and everyone attending to a fragile Axel. Hux wasn't quite the headstrong jock back then, and Dax spent his days reading, escaping reality any chance he could get. When things were so much simpler.

Knocking on Axel's door, I open it and slip inside. Axel is fast asleep on a mound of cushions and seemingly alone. I look around, lowering the plate and glass onto his bedside table. Poking my head back into the hallway, I tilt my head this way and that until I pick up on it. Softly, a muffled voice can be heard if I strain my ears.

I follow the sound to a bedroom we don't use, crammed with dusty boxes and mismatched furniture. A mausoleum of memories with faded family photos and crumpled papers spilling from open cartons. Any light streaming through the tall windows is blocked out. Through a crack in the door, the stale air leaks out, heavy with neglect and dust, which causes my nose to twitch.

"Yes, yes I understand," Dax mutters. I catch a glimpse of his phone's light as he paces past the door, the device pressed firmly to his ear. He sighs, his voice weighted in a way I've never heard. "I'm sorry too. Thanks for calling." Hanging up his call, Dax swings the door open, his hand going direct to the back of his neck. He stops just short of barreling into my chest, a flash of guilt and then confusion passing through his tanned features.

"Were you snooping on me?"

"No," I narrow my eyes, deciding to half bend the truth. "I was coming to tell you that Avery made breakfast. Who was on the phone?"

Dax stiffens, his shoulders rising defensively as he uses his bandaged hand to cover the phone outline in his pocket. "Nobody important," he mutters, but his averted gaze and the faint tremor in his voice betray him. For Dax to be anything other than naively optimistic in every situation is enough to set my teeth on edge.

"Bullshit. Who was on the damn phone?" Dax shifts uncomfortably, his usually open and carefree demeanor replaced by a wall of quiet frustration.

"Leave it alone, Wyatt. You can't fix everything." He avoids my gaze like it burns. My nostrils flare.

"I can try."

"Not this time." His jaw works, and his good hand flexes at his side. Then he deflates, knowing I'm not going to back down and that I'll get the answer out of him eventually. Leaning back against the doorframe with a defeated sigh, Dax tilts his head upward, staring at the ceiling like it holds the answers he's looking for. "Just don't freak out, okay?" he starts, which does nothing to settle the unease creeping through my chest. "It was the Dean. I've lost my scholarship."

I clench my jaw, murder flashing in my green eyes.

"I'll call the Dean back right now. Get him to change his mind."

"It's not just him. The entire board voted. My unauthorized absences and lack of focus aren't in keeping with the Waversea ethics. It's a done deal, and you can't just throw money around to get your own way this time." Dax's lips purse, his words striking the cord he was aiming for. I puff out my chest and square chin.

"If it wasn't for my money, you'd have all been gone years ago."

Dax's mouth drops open. "I can't believe you just said that," he murmurs, but I don't take it back. There's very little in this world I can't use either my trust fund or Nixon's credit card to fix. But Dax sees that as cheating, and his moral compass won't permit it.

I've offered to pay for his entire degree multiple times, but he wouldn't let me. He wanted to earn it, hating to feel indebted to people. Even when we first met and he was wearing handouts from the donation bank, he would only let me buy him some new clothes if he could work off the balance. He mowed the lawn. Trimmed the hedges. Repainted the front porch. Pretty much renovated the entire frat house. I didn't even ask for half of it.

An image of Dax flares to life in my mind, sweating in the summer sun, covered in paint streaks and grime.Wyatt's smirk is fleeting, his nostrils flaring. He's worked so damn hard. He deserves his place at that school.

A few tense seconds pass between us, my stubbornness grating on his newfound resolve. Previously, Dax would have backed down and told me to do whatever I saw fit. Now, he's staring at me like a stranger who hasn't had his back for years.

Like I haven't taken them all on summer vacations to the Caribbean or flown Garrett to Paris just so he could eat an authentic baguette. Like I didn't pay for Axel to have the best trauma counseling for two years after coming to us or bought Dax's mom a stone memorial when I found out they weren't able to afford to give her a real funeral. That's who I am, and that's the only way I know how to love. Paying my way through life, keeping everyone housed, fed, and happy. It's all I have at my disposal.

Dax shakes his head, shoving against my shoulder to leave. I whip around, locking my hand around his arm.

"We're not done here."

"Why does it even matter to you so much?!" Dax twists his arm free and pushes my shoulder to force me to step back. I only move through the shock of Dax raising a hand to me at seeing him hold so much animosity toward me. "You've been holding me to this certain standard for years, like everything depends on me graduating, and I'm not going to lie, Wyatt, sometimes that pressure is crushing. Sometimes I just want to... be."

I grit my teeth, the words hitting harder than I expected. Dax has never told me this before, always going along with the rules I set, agreeing that it's what's best for him. Now he tells me I've been causing him stress. I swallow, pocketing my hands and rooting my gaze on the marble flooring beside his feet.

"Were you even going to tell me if I hadn't been in the right place at the right time?"

Dax shifts his weight, his voice tight. "What difference would it make? Our priorities lie elsewhere right now."

And that's the truth. We've all dropped everything to look after Avery. In truth, and through no fault of her own, once she entered the frat house, nothing except her seemed to matter anymore. We've let our studies slide, left our home without a second thought, and become versions of ourselves that we don't recognize, and I can't say I regret it. So as much as it pains me to watch Dax let all of his hard work go, as difficult as it is for me to just let it all slide, I do understand. He will figure it out, like he always does. I just hate that he has to.

"I'd best go eat. Avery will probably kill us both if we let those pancakes get cold." Dax hesitates, glancing back down the empty hallway.

"You go ahead. I just... need a minute." I nod, agreeing to give him the space to process. In a fashion, perhaps he needs the space to mourn his lost work and wasted time, to console himself that his future is no longer set out in an organized timeline, despite what he might have gained. Patting him on the shoulder, I pause at his side.

"Don't take too long. If Garrett finds a plate of pancakes by Axel's bedside, chances are there'll be none left." Dax huffs a laugh.

As I head back toward the kitchen, my mind churns, already calculating what needs to be done to keep him from falling through the cracks. Dax asked me why it even matters that he graduates, and the truth is, I respect Dax far too much to let him fall. He's smart and dedicated. He refuses to take handouts, earning his way through life, and when heartache arises, he doesn't run from it. He stays, embracing the pain and dealing with his issues before they consume him.

In short, Dax is the man I wish I could be.

AVERY

CHAPTER TWENTY FOUR

The days pass in a haze, each one blending into the next as we make use of every corner of the mansion. The gym has become the guys' second home, their grunts and thuds echoing through the halls as they push themselves harder with each session. Huxley stumbled upon an underground swimming pool the other day, and it's been our hidden retreat ever since. The library calls to me most often, though I've also wandered into the games room once or twice, letting the sound of Garrett and Dax's playful bickering pull me in.

At the start of the week, Axel could barely shuffle from his bed to the bathroom unaided, his movements slow and labored. Garrett flanked him on one side, his hands hovering protectively as Axel braced himself against the walls for stability. Each attempt drained him completely, leaving him to collapse into bed and sleep for hours until it was time to coax him up again to eat or try once more. It's becoming easier for him, his breathing isn't as labored, but his progress is still painstakingly slow.

I've made a home of sorts in one of the guest rooms, stacking my nightstand with books pilfered from the library. Lately, I've buried myself in studies about the stigma of depression and anxiety in men. Not that I think I could use any of the strategies without the guys noticing, but the knowledge comforts me. If I can understand even a fraction of what they're feeling, maybe I can help. Or at least not make things worse.

My nightly companion rotates. Whether there's an official timetable or they play scissors, paper, stone, I'd love to know. Either way, it seems there's an unspoken agreement that I only get one visitor per night, and unless I initiate otherwise, we stick to spooning.

As the week inches forward, Friday looms like a dark cloud on the horizon we're all too aware of but no one wants to mention. It's there, staring at me from the calendar on my phone, a reminder that we can't outrun what's coming. The students will return tomorrow afternoon, filling this house with noise and life, but with them comes the auction. The nightmare we've been trying to ignore will no longer be some distant threat. It will be real, pressing in around us.

Axel feels it too. His words are becoming fewer, and his silence stretches longer. He's retreating into himself, bracing for the inevitable. And tomorrow night, this house will be alive with the very horror he's been running from.

The butler has been keeping us updated with the few words he mutters here and there. Sharon, thankfully, will not be returning with her husband until late in the evening. Until the event is about to get underway. By then, we will have all retreated to the upper wing, our sanctuary away from prying eyes.

"Okay, break's over," Wyatt barks, clicking his fingers in front of my face. I blink up at him, lowering my phone, which has long since faded to black. I'd started with looking through photos of Meg but soon switched to the calendar app, counting the days since I've last seen her. I let her go on Christmas Eve, watching the car fade into the night, thinking she'd be safe. Believing that it was for the best. Wyatt clicks his fingers at me again, and I whack them aside, scowling.

"Alright, alright," I huff, standing from my crouching position by the mirrored wall. The harsh lights beam down on the space Wyatt has cleared in the middle of the gym. Stepping into the center, I stretch my back and roll my shoulders. "I'm here."

"Get into position," he demands. I roll my eyes and place my bare feet at opposing angles to one another, lifting my arms in a half circle in front of me.

"Anyone ever tell you how bossy you are?" I catch a quick glance to

Wyatt. He's across the far side, sitting on a weight bench with his own phone in his hand. His green eyes are unfazed.

"You said you needed to feel productive, and what better way than to keep up with your dancing? Dax has already lost his scholarship; I won't let you risk your future too."

I heard about the call and the subsequent argument. For half of last night, I had Wyatt pacing around the room, venting out loud about how all of Dax's hard work has been erased, then he tried to comfort himself with the fact that Dax could go back next year. The second half of the night, Wyatt spent it curled around me in bed, flinching in his sleep and murmuring that he needs to fix this. That he'll fix everything. Hence why I've let him convince me to come to the gym and get back to dancing.

Wyatt taps the play button on his phone, a melancholy melody leaking from the Bluetooth speakers around the room. I inhale deeply, raising onto my tiptoes the best I can without the support of my ballet slippers. The music bleeds through my veins, blocking out the guilt, sorrow, and regret, leaving only the stiffness of my muscles behind. I arch my arms gracefully overhead, transitioning into a soft plié. The mirrored wall reflects my silhouette as I slowly spin, lengthening through each limb.

The space feels different without the familiar hum of the studio and the polished floors beneath my feet, but I pour my emotions into every step. A pirouette flows into a sweeping arabesque, my leg extending behind me as my arms stretch toward an invisible horizon.

Wyatt's presence on the weight bench is something I'm both hyperaware of and determined to ignore. I move into a series of leaps across the cleared gym floor, but on the final one, my footing falters. The angle in which I land shifts my balance, my weight off kilter, and I stumble sideways. Before I can hit the ground, strong arms circle my waist, steadying me.

"Careful, Angel," Wyatt barks just as harshly, but his eyes are a different story. Filled with concern and relief, the intensity of his gaze makes my pulse race. Planting me back on my feet, Wyatt doesn't withdraw, his chest warm and solid inches from my face. I tilt my head upwards, my lips parting on instinct. A tremor rolls through my spine where his large hand delicately spans my lower back. The baggy tracksuit

I'm wearing does nothing to lessen the contact between us, my hands gliding up his chest to his neck. Wyatt leans in at the same time, his lips a whisper from kissing me.

"Fuck me," a voice sounds. "It's true then." My head whips aside, spotting a very pale Axel leaning against the doorframe. His entire body is shaking, and when he breathes, there's a small rattle that follows.

"Axel! What are you doing out of your room?" I gasp. Wyatt doesn't immediately release me, deciding to let Axel suffer under his glare for a moment.

"Why isn't Garrett with you?"

Beads of sweat pepper Axel's forehead, his eyes sunken and dark, but somehow he manages a smile. "The guys have been telling me you two are getting on. Some things need to be seen to be believed." Reaching out his arm, he beckons me to cross the room and tuck myself underneath. My presence is just for show, while Wyatt is the actual muscle on the other side.

Slowly, the three of us navigate towards one of the unused living areas. Once we've reached a white sofa, Wyatt sits with a cushion on his lap and lowers Axel until his head is resting upon it. I take the end with his feet, carefully lifting them to slide underneath.

The entire mansion is like a show home, everything pristine and beautiful, yet without a single trace of character. White sideboards hug the edges of the room, and a shaggy rug fills the center to take the cold edge off the marbled flooring. Exquisite vases and ornaments fill the surfaces on the coffee table, mantel, and windowsills, each one containing flecks of gold. I wonder if young Axel was allowed in here or if he was kept locked in his room.

"So, why are you really out of bed?" I ask, filling the silence as we all spiral into our own dark thoughts. Axel sighs, licking his cracked lips.

"I love Garrett," he starts. Wyatt gives me a strange look over Axel's head. "But he won't tell me what's going on. I need someone to be straight with me. Please."

"What would you like to know?" Wyatt responds instantly. Axel's chest deflates with relief, his head lolling slightly to the side.

"Everything. What actually happened to me? Why am I in this damn hellhole? Where did you two go, and why are you no longer trying to spite each other at every turn?" Nodding to himself as if recounting the questions he'd be saving, something dawns on Axel's face. He blinks his hazel eyes up at Wyatt. "Oh, and before we get into any of that, fuck you for your stupid note. I was in the frat house that night. You could have woke me up and explained what was happening before you disappeared."

"You would have tried to stop me. Just how Avery would have if I'd given her any time to fight back." Wyatt shrugs simply. As always, he doesn't care to explain himself or ask for forgiveness. Wyatt will die upon the hill that he always knows best, no matter how others feel about his choices.

"That's the most insane thing you've ever said," Axel blows out a ragged breath. His walk down the stairs unaided has affected him more than he cares to admit. Swallowing hard, Axel's brows pinch together tightly. "The guilt of losing Avery was tearing me up, you know. I blamed myself."

"It wasn't your fault, Axe." Wyatt cups Axel's head, absently brushing his thumb back and forth. It's as close to an apology Axel is going to get, and he knows it. Carefully tucking my legs up on the sofa, I hug Axel's socked feet close to my chest.

"Well, I can start you off with the info you want to know." I rub Axel's shins to get his attention back. His hazel eyes drift to my face, a silent plea there that I can't refuse. "Wyatt made love to me in this cute little B&B. Went on for hours, and then again in the morning. It made a change from his dick nudging my lower back in a sleeping bag." Both Axel and Wyatt's mouths drop open, although Axel quickly smiles. He nudges Wyatt's stomach with his head.

"Okay, I forgive you already. Tell me everything."

"Can we not?" Wyatt drags a hand down his face.

"Too late," I grin wide. It feels good to finally get this out in the open. To normalize it. Going all the way back, I explain to Axel what happened the night of Midnight Madness. The text from Fredrick, how I woke up tied up in Hux's SUV with a dog licking my face. The crash and subsequent three-day hike until we found out Axe was in the hospital. Wyatt listens for the most part, looking away at any mention of him being affectionate. The tips of his ears go red, but otherwise, he appears unaffected.

Axel, on the other hand, laps up every word that spills from my lips.

He pitches in every so often with *'it's about damn time'* and *'I bet you gave him hell'*, the tension in his jaw easing. Just for a short while, his pain and situation ebb away, until I get to the point of the story he's not going to like.

"Then Sharon showed up. The hospital called her to take you back into her custody. There was nothing we could do except come with you." Wyatt returns to the conversation then, his eyes meeting Axel's.

"And we will stay until you're strong enough to leave. There's no rush." My heart clenches, stilling my chest for a moment. Axel senses my shift, twisting his lips to look up at Wyatt.

"I get that you're not ready to run straight back into danger, but we all know there is a rush. We need to find Meg before it's too late." The tightness in my chest locks down, blocking air from entering my lungs. Meg's defiant face flashes before my eyes, shaking her head to tell me not to come, but she knows me better than that. I can't leave her there, and Axel agrees. "Surely there's something we can do while my ribs are healing. How did you get in contact with Fredrick before?"

Wyatt's jaw tightens, his muscles bunching as if he's physically holding back from jumping up and leaving. His hand flexes against the back of the sofa, and for a moment, I reckon he might storm out rather than continue the conversation. Then, with a heavy exhale, he rolls his neck, cracking it audibly.

"I... well, I have the phone number of an ex-con that works for him." The admission hangs in the air like a lifeline. I straighten, my heart thudding in my chest.

"You do? We could call it!" The words fall out before I can think them through, excitement and hope overtaking caution. Wyatt's head snaps toward me, his glare sharp enough to cut.

"And this is exactly why I didn't tell you," he growls, running a hand through his hair. "Your first instinct is always, *'how can I get myself killed the quickest?'*" My mouth falls open, but I can't deny that he's right.

"Okay, fine," I relent, tugging Axel's feet back into my chest, the weight steading on my legs. "But we could at least track it? Dax's cousin has done similar things for us before."

Wyatt pauses, his green eyes narrowing. He shifts his weight, his hand still resting on the back of his neck. Finally, he lets his arm drop and glances toward the window, the late afternoon light casting shadows across the room.

"Maybe," he admits grudgingly. "But we do it my way. No reckless stunts. We're already in over our heads, and I'm not losing anyone else."

I nod instantly. "We'll be careful," I promise. Wyatt doesn't respond immediately. Instead, he reverts back to stroking Axel's head, soothing the pair of them.

"Fine," he says. "I'll call Dax's cousin. But if this goes south, you stay out of it, Avery. Promise me." I nod, though we both know it's a promise I might not be able to keep. Axel sighs heavily, that tiny rattle still present each time he breathes. His hands come to rest over his stomach, where he toys nervously with his fingers.

"Since we're having difficult conversations," he glances at me from beneath hooded eyelids. "I've heard mutterings about an auction tomorrow night. What's the plan with that?"

"The plan is to stay the fuck out of the way," Wyatt snaps quickly. Axel's lips press into a thin line, his jaw tensing as he forces his eyes to mine instead of Wyatt's. His shoulders rise, then fall in a measured breath, clearly trying to keep his composure.

"I think you guys should go," he says quietly, his head turning to face away from us both. Wyatt jolts, just narrowly stopping himself from shooting upright from the sofa.

"Are you out of your damn mind? You want us to walk into your mother's circus of horrors like it's a fucking cocktail party? It's not happening." Axel doesn't flinch at the outburst, his calm almost unnerving.

"Axel..." I start gently, trying to deescalate the sudden rise in tension. We need to keep Axel relaxed, the doctor said so. "What do you think we could even accomplish by going?" Axel's hazel eyes flick to mine with a sharpness I rarely see in him anymore.

"The type of people who attend the auctions are beyond wealthy and have a lot of connections. They use the events to network as much as... other things. We're way out of our depth here. We could use as much help as we can get."

"Not by rubbing shoulders with those sick sons of bitches. We will make connections another way." Wyatt grunts, his expression fully shut down. A darkness falls over his green eyes, worlds away from the man in the gym who had his hands on my waist and his gaze on my mouth.

"What way? With what time? We can't just sit here and do nothing, even if Dax's cousin manages to get us an address. You just said yourself, we're in way over our heads, and we're not thugs, Wyatt. We don't go around killing people." A stab of anguish passes Axel's features, and for the first time, I see how haunted he is by what happened. I only know what Dax told me, but it seems Axel has another uphill battle to climb, and this one will test him far more than his physical recovery. Licking his cracked lips, Axel looks like he's barely holding it together. "We need help."

My chest tightens as I glance between the two of them. Wyatt twists to stare out of the window, resting his elbow on the sofa arm, effectively shutting up out. The pause is deafening, the weight on my chest crushing. Axel is spared the ticking of Wyatt's jaw from his upside-down angle, but I have a full, uncensored view.

"If Axel thinks it might be helpful," I start. Wyatt's head whips to me, fire burning in his eyes. I half shrug, hugging Axel's feet closer to my body. "I'm just saying we're a team, right? Everyone gets a say."

For a moment, the room falls silent, the weight of the conversation settling around us like a thick fog. Then Wyatt straightens his spine and rolls his neck. I can see his denial before he even speaks.

"You think Sharon is just going to let us waltz in there to snoop around?"

"She won't," Axel agrees, but the strain in his voice betrays him. "But I've heard... well, that she's taken a liking to Huxley..." Wyatt sucks in a sharp breath, pinching the bridge of his nose.

"Are you trying to kill me?"

Axel swallows hard, his Adam's apple bobbing as he starts grasping for reason.

"Sharon was too focused on appearances to risk causing a scene at her own event. The guests aren't all high-flying members of society. They are people who have a dirty secret to hide, and that gives us leverage. And not just on who's attending and who's bidding, but with what deals are being made in the back rooms. That's what people like Sharon do. They create alliances. We could use an alliance when we find Fredrick, someone unsavory to do what needs to be done."

I lean forward, reaching across the back of the sofa for Wyatt's hand. After a pause of hesitation, Wyatt stretches out and links our fingers. Between us, Axel stares at our hands like he's in shock.

"Axel has a point. As much as I hate the idea of going, we can't keep pretending this will all blow over if we ignore it. If Fredrick's making moves, we need to be prepared before he gets the upper hand."

Wyatt looks at me, his wild green eyes searching mine. He's torn, and I can feel the weight of his fear. Fear for me, for Axel, for all of us. Axel takes a shaky breath, his hands gripping the hem of his damp T-shirt. Sweat patches are increasing around his neckline, his body burning up with the strain.

"There's another reason as well. I know it's stupid. But...I kinda thought if you guys went, it would be like we're sharing the trauma. Like it might be a little bit less for me to carry on my own."

Wyatt runs a hand through his hair, muttering under his breath. Finally, he exhales sharply, looking down at Axel with reluctant acceptance. Axel nods, his relief palpable, although his skin is sheet white now. Wyatt notices it at the same time I do.

"Alright. Enough adventuring for today. Let's get you back upstairs before Garrett throws a fit." With a groan, Axel obliges, allowing us to slowly help him back onto his feet. I take his non-injured side, allowing his arm to drape over my shoulders heavily.

"Hey, I have an idea." I grin up at Axel as his face is pinched with pain. Wyatt is doing his best to shoulder his weight on the other side, but it's going to be a while before Axel is up and about properly. "How about a bath together? I can get Dax to read one of his new dark romances to us."

"Is it hot and spicy?" Axel peeks at me beneath his lashes. I snort and roll my eyes.

"Is there any other kind of dark romance?"

"You guys are weird," Wyatt huffs, but when I look over, he's trying to hide a small twitch of his lips. It's becoming much easier to read him these days, and I know now that, weird or not, Wyatt wouldn't want any of us to be any other way.

CHAPTER TWENTY FIVE

As Friday creeps closer, we do whatever we can to distract ourselves, to find small moments to disappear between the walls and pretend nothing else exists. My only reprieve from the guilt of hiding away is the thought that the auction could bring us closer to finding Meg. Currently, it's the only way to get some sort of answers, some sort of leverage. Axel has given us a way forward. Now we just need to swallow our pride and take it.

I believe that's why the next time Axel asks for help to bathe, we all appear in the bathroom. It's a huge space designed for indulgence, with dark marble floors, soft golden lighting, and a tub large enough to fit a small army. Or potentially, me and five Souls. The air is thick with steam, curling along the mirrors and clinging to our skin. Axel leans back against the edge of the tub, his broad chest rising and falling slowly, ribs wrapped in waterproof bandages. His head tips back, exposing the thick column of his throat.

I share a look with Garrett, giving him a small nod. There's no pretense as to why we all ended up here. We need a distraction as much as Axel does. I can only listen to Dax read sex scenes in his deep, sultry voice for so long. I'm desperately trying to remain focused on what's important, to put all other selfish desires aside, but when I'm stuck sitting around with nothing to do, the men around me are too enticing. And from the hunger in their eyes, they clearly feel the same.

Garrett moves, dropping to his knees beside the tub. Dipping a hand into the water, he teases his fingers through the bubbles, watching Axel stare at the ceiling. As with his baths before, Hux helped to ease him into the tub, letting the warmth lull him into a rare state of relaxation. But the longer Axel sits there, the more aware he becomes of the silence. Of the eyes on him. Slowly, he lifts his head.

We're all watching him. Me, perched on the edge of the tub. Huxley is leaning against the counter, his arms crossed. Dax is sitting on a stool nearby, his injured hand propped up, and a lazy, knowing smirk curling his lips. Wyatt stands off to the side, his hands loose at his sides, and his stance is wide. He's here for one simple reason. I asked him to be.

Axel stiffens, his brows knitting together. He knows this group too well. He knows we're up to something. "What? Why are you all looking at me like that?" Garrett's lips twitch, and he shrugs one shoulder.

"You just look so..." he tilts his head, his dark eyes sweeping over Axel's naked form. "Innocent." Axel scoffs, his cheeks flushing.

"I'm in a bath."

Garrett's fingers trail through the water to brush Axel's chest as he hums. "Exactly."

No one wants to act first, so I do. Standing, I move into the center of the room. Wyatt meets me halfway, his hands coming up to brush my waist. His thumbs skim along the hem of my sweater, lifting it inch by inch, the soft material gliding over my skin. A shiver follows, not from cold but from the way Axel's stare grows heavier, how his knuckles flex against the rim of the bathtub. Aside from a lace thong, I'm bare underneath.

"What is happening right now?" Axel's breath saws out of him, his hazel gaze flicking between us with uncertainty.

"We thought you might need a distraction." I tilt my head, watching him, watching the way his throat bobs. Axel exhales sharply, his muscles tensing beneath Garrett's taunting touch.

"I don't think—"

Garrett presses his wet fingers against Axel's mouth and smirks. "*Shhh.* Just sit back and enjoy." Axel barely processes the words before Wyatt's hands start to move on me again, raising to my breasts. He cups them together, presenting me to Axel before brushing his thumbs over my nipples. I sink my teeth into my bottom lip.

Dax makes a low, amused sound. "You guys are messing with him." But from the raspy urge to his voice, it sounds like we're messing with Dax too. I lean into Wyatt's chest, pushing my chest further into his pliant hands.

"Are we?" I murmur, eyes locked on Axel. It's so strange, like a dream in which Wyatt lets go of all of his reservations and publicly claims me. No more hiding behind closed doors or pretending the spark between us isn't real. It's out there now, in the open and laid bare for the rest of my men to see

Wyatt chuckles behind me, the heat of his breath teasing my neck. My skin prickles under the weight of the attention, under the way Axel stiffens, the way his gaze flickers from my collarbone to my ribs, to the teasing lace hugging my hips. Wyatt pinches my nipples hard, causing me to gasp, and a moment later, his mouth is on my neck.

Huxley, still leaning against the counter, remains silent. But his eyes are darker now, his fingers tapping idly against his bicep. His stare lingers on the way my body responds to Wyatt's touch, and I hold out my hand for him.

"No point just watching, Hux. My thong isn't going to fall off by itself." In two steps, Huxley has dropped his arms and dropped to his knees, stroking my legs and upper thigh. Everywhere his fingers touch, his lips follow—brushing over my clit through the lace before he leans forward and sucks the material into his mouth. His tongue is hot, sending a bolt of pleasure straight through me. Ever so slowly, he peels the thong to the ground and tosses it into the bathtub. I watch the black lace float amongst the bubbles, although as Hux pushes his face into my center and inhales deeply, I'm a goner.

Axel's mouth parts, but no words come out. He shifts again, the water sloshing slightly. Garrett moves to the back of the tub, his hands roaming over Axel's shoulders and neck, kissing his skin but not going any further. I watch through a haze of pleasure, my head dropping back against Wyatt's shoulder.

"Keep watching, Axe," Wyatt murmurs against my ear, his lips brushing that sensitive spot beneath it. His hands smooth over my hips, widening my stance for Huxley to slide his tongue over me. There's a contrast between his unhurried, almost lazy movements, and the way he sets my pulse racing. My nipples are pulled tight, aching for attention and Dax seems to know that instinctively.

Lips wrap around my nipple, and this time I release the groan that's been building within me. Wyatt's hands tighten on my hips, keeping me steady, while Huxley remains on his knees, his tongue dragging slow, deliberate strokes that make my legs tremble.

A deep exhale rakes from Axel's chest, and I force my heavy-lidded gaze to focus on him. He hasn't moved, his knuckles still flexed against the edge of the tub, gripping it as if it's the only thing keeping him grounded. Garrett's fingers idly trace along his shoulders, occasionally dipping into the water. Axel's chest rises and falls with uneven breaths, his eyes locked onto me, dark and filled with lust.

"Still with us, Axe?" Wyatt teases, his voice a rich hum of amusement and something darker. He's loving this too. The release of being open with his gang, of being honest about his intentions. Axel swallows hard, but he doesn't answer. He doesn't have to. The tension radiating from his body, the way his throat bobs, the way his jaw tics. He's fighting his desire, unsure of how to react, but still completely unable to look away.

A shiver rolls through me as Dax's teeth graze my nipple, the sensation sparking a fresh wave of heat in my stomach. His injured hand remains cradled to his chest, but his good one traces a slow path over the scars on my ribs. Huxley drags his mouth from my core to the inside of my thigh, pressing slow, open-mouthed kisses to the heated skin, each one deliberate, each one meant to make Axel squirm just a little more, before returning to my pussy. I can't take his slow torment anymore.

I brace a hand on Dax's shoulder, the other reaching back to tangle in Wyatt's hair. "I feel like Axel is getting bored," I joke, despite the heat bursting from his hazel eyes. Huxley's chuckle ripples through my core, mimicking the deep sound that rumbles from Wyatt's chest. He shifts behind me, his hand slipping up my stomach, fingers teasing just beneath my ribs.

"Then we must not be doing a good enough job."

Axel's fingers twitch against the rim of the tub, and for the first time since we started, his lips part. "You're all insane," he breathes, his voice thick with need. Garrett leans in, his mouth ghosting along the side of Axel's neck.

"It's okay to enjoy yourself, my love," he mutters, dragging his fingers through the water, trailing them up Axel's chest. "Let us do this for you." Axel releases a slow, shuddering breath, and he zeroes his gaze on me, watching every detail in perfect clarity.

"You guys are evil," Axel states, his jaw tight. Huxley pushes to stand, and lets out a soft hum.

"Only a little." The flush to Axel's cheeks is subsiding, his embarrassment waning as the water starts to move with more vigor. He's stroking himself beneath the bubbles. My view is blocked by Hux shedding his sweatpants and tossing them aside, his cock jutting thick and proud between us. I lick my lips but he slowly shakes his head.

"I don't need any more encouragement to cum quicker. Just looking at you all flushed like this gets me halfway there." Hux trails the red patches blossoming across my neck and chest. Settling his hands on my hips, he jerks me against his dick and leans in, just enough to feel his breath against my lips, but he doesn't close the space entirely. He waits, letting me chase him. The room is still, the air thick with anticipation, with something reckless and untamed crackling between all of us. I smirk just before I close the distance.

The moment our lips touch, it's electric. Hux releases a low moan against my mouth, his hand coming up, fingers threading into my hair, and gripping tight as if he can't help himself. The kiss is slow at first, all for show, but then something snaps inside him, and he's pulling me closer, tilting his head to deepen it. The taste of him is intoxicating, something spicy and heady flooding my senses.

His restraint slips and he lifts me to straddle his hips. I'm not sure who lines up Hux's cock with my entrance, but given that it's two hands, I'm presuming it's Wyatt. He holds Hux's shaft without reservation, gliding it into my soaking cunt in one smooth thrust. I tense, my toes curling and back going rigid. As soon as Hux is seated fully, I relax on a groan. He's so thick, so filling, and I've missed this.

The others are still there, watching, their presence a constant, charged hum in the back of my mind. Wyatt's fingers trace along my spine, soothing and possessive. Dax's lips ghost along my shoulder, whispering words of encouragement.

"You take him so well, Swan. I love watching you stretch over someone else's cock." The reaction I have to Dax's bold words is a lightning bolt of lust slamming through my core. Hux rocks within me, retracting and slamming back home. All the while, Garrett's hand rests on Axel's chest, their eyes trained on our display. This time, it's Wyatt who leans in to catch my ear beneath his teeth.

"Does he feel as good as I do, Angel? Or would you like Hux to have some assistance?" My mind reels, and although Huxley grunts, he doesn't reject the notion. Hux knows I belong to all of them, that they all have the right to pleasure me whenever they see fit. A finger slides through my ass cheeks and settles over my puckered hole. I arch back, encouraging Wyatt to continue exploring. To make me feel as euphoric as I know he can.

Hux creates a steady pace, sliding in and out of me with more measured control than I could muster. He coaxes moans from my lips, drawing my focus between his cock and Wyatt's mischievous finger. Wyatt lowers to spit over the curve of my ass, using his saliva to push his finger into my hole and work me into a frenzy. I feel myself contract, the edge of a blinding orgasm about to tear me in half.

"I...I," my voice fails me. Dax gently grabs my chin, twisting me to stare into his blue eyes.

"Use your words, Swan. Tell us what you want and we'll obey." I swallow, trying to wet my throat through my gasping. Hux doesn't relent his steady, harsh thrusts.

"I don't think Axel can see properly." Dax's answering grin is wicked, one I imprint in my brain. Releasing my chin from the grip of his good hand, he nudges Huxley's shoulder to turn and naturally, Wyatt follows. I find Wyatt's chest behind me again, giving me something to brace against when my body can't stay upright. All I can do is to be used, fucked and worshipped.

Garrett's grip tightens on Axel's shoulder, his breathing uneven. Axel's eyes are on fire, his pupils blown wide as he watches Huxley shatter me into a million pieces. My orgasm hits so hard and fast, I can't control the strangled sound that escapes my throat. All I know is, it's loud.

Huxley's hold on me is unrelenting, his strength the only thing keeping me tethered as the pleasure crashes through me, dragging me under like a riptide. My fingers claw at his shoulders, desperate to hold on as the world tilts on its axis. My body goes taut as I gasp and moan, and just as I'm about to come down, Hux breaks. He erupts inside of me, the repetitive throb of his shaft prolonging my rapture. His shoulders and chest shudder, his groan low in his throat.

Removing his finger from my back passage, Wyatt helps to ease me to the floor before both he and Hux step away to clean themselves up. I stand on shaky legs, cum dripping down my thighs as Dax takes over, standing behind me and winding an arm around my middle.

"Look at how much you affect us, Swan."

I force my heavy-lidded gaze to focus, to take in the scene unfolding before me. Axel's jaw is clenched so tight it could shatter, sweat pebbled over his forehead. He continues to stroke himself in the water, his hazel eyes dazed and cheeks tinged pink. Garrett's fingers dance absently over Axel's collarbone, like he's testing, teasing, waiting for the inevitable.

"Feel like giving a girl a hand, Gare?" I tilt a brow. His smile is devilish, but to everyone's surprise, Garrett shakes his head.

"Not this time, Peach. I'm not having sex again until Axel's ready." Axel jerks his head aside, his brow furrowed but he says nothing. I think he's past the point of comprehension. His every muscle coiled with tension, the warring need in his gaze enough to make my stomach tighten all over again. I feel Dax shrug against my back and he nudges me a few paces forward.

"Your loss, Gare." Lowering his arm to my thighs, Dax scoops two fingers through Hux's cum and pushes it back into me. I gasp, shock and something much darker churning in my core. He does it again and again, fighting a losing battle with gravity but no one cares. Even Hux and Wyatt have returned to watch, also stunned by Dax's brazen movements. Everyone's attention is on my body, the way I clench onto Dax's fingers each time and shudder when he retracts.

I'm a limbless wanton mess by the time he finishes, and his hand flattens on my upper back to bend me forward. Reaching out, I grasp the edge of the bathtub, my breath quickening as Dax shoves his lounge pants down and slams home into me from behind. I cry out, my breasts bouncing. Dax fucks me with reckless abandon. There's no taming him this evening, and I never want to ever again. This version of Dax is so different, so alive and free. So *bold*.

Wyatt doesn't stay away for long, planting himself on the edge of the bathtub still fully dressed in casual shorts and a T-shirt. I'm about to complain that Axel's missing out, but his groans fill the room a second later as he finishes himself into his bathwater.

Wyatt follows Dax's lead, gathering the cum on my thighs with his fingers, but instead of using it as lubricant, he jerks my jaw wide and pushes his fingers into my mouth. The telltale salty taste of Hux bursts across my tongue. I groan, sucking his digits clean whilst Dax propels me into another devastating climax.

Hux's silhouette appears through my star-speckled vision, his fingers vigorously rubbing my clit pushing me through one orgasm and straight into the next. My squeezing takes Dax down with me, and all the while, Wyatt continues to hand feed me cum. I don't pay attention to who lifts and lowers into the bath, only that my body has never felt so weightless. I lean against Axel's shoulder on his good side, trying to catch my breath. Garrett shifts to my side, dutifully smoothing my hair beneath the water.

"That was a stunning display, Peach." His dark eyes appraise me with something close to pride. I twist to peer up at Axel.

"Did you enjoy your show?" A small, lazy smile creeps over my face. Axel's brows are pinched and I know we've exerted him, but I also know he was going just as stir crazy in this house as us. Even more so. He needs a distraction, and more than that, he needs some good memories here. Ones that are created on his terms. Peeking his hazel eyes through heavy lids, Axel manages a slight shift of his lips.

"Same time tomorrow?"

CHAPTER TWENTY SIX

I cross the bedroom to peer out of the window, the soft thud of my sneakers against the carpet the only sound, despite five of us being huddled around Axel. The air is stifling, and our efforts to forget what's coming have failed. It's Friday. The day we've all been trying to prevent, despite the fact that it's been staring us in the face all week.

I glance at the astronaut clock on the wall, the second hand ticking far too loudly in the silence. Sharon's precious students will start filing in soon, their oblivious chatter filling the halls, completely unaware about our reservations for tonight's event.

The auction.

I rub the back of my neck, tension twisting its way up my spine. It's not just Axel who's on edge, though he wears it most visibly, retreating into himself more and more as the hours tick by. He won't even take an offered slip of water now. His skin is pasty and warm to the touch. Making himself ill won't be any good, but he won't listen to reason. Not until tomorrow morning when we all regroup and prove the auctions are survivable, I reckon.

Wyatt has been biting back his temper all morning, and even Avery has been uncharacteristically quiet. Not even the suggestion of baking or dancing will deter her from biting her nails and staring blankly into space.

"Are we really doing this?" Hux huffs from his spot, laying on his back at the end of Axel's bed. Garrett makes a noise in his throat, holding Axel's hand tightly to his chest. Avery is on Axel's other side, her head on his shoulder, although she's left enough space to not touch his tender ribs. Our self-proclaimed leader isn't present, preferring to be holed up in one of the unused rooms, stewing in his frustration alone. The guy isn't good at sitting still at the best of times, but he figured his nervous energy wouldn't help.

Leaning against the windowsill, I stare out at the driveway. The afternoon sun does nothing to lift my mood or lessen the ache in my chest. The minibuses will arrive soon, and with them, the start of the chaos. My fingers drum against the glass as my stomach churns. For all our planning and guessing, none of us really knows what tonight will bring.

A sudden flicker of movement catches my eye, pulling me from my spiraling thoughts. The gates at the other end of the long driveaway peel open, permitting entry to a singular car. My first instinct is that Sharon has returned, but I can't imagine her coming home in a standard yellow cab. I squint while leaning closer to the glass. The cab rolls up, its bright exterior glinting in the fading sunlight as it comes to a smooth stop just outside the main entrance. No less than a second later, a figure steps out from the rear door, stretching widely and rolling his neck.

A strange sense of déjà vu settles over me. As if my mind can't place the familiar man in this setting. He doesn't belong here. He belongs in my past, where he was at least a foot shorter and riddled with acne. But there's no mistaking the tall, wiry frame, the unruly curls, or the ever-present smirk that somehow manages to radiate confidence and mischief all at once. His face lifts to take in the mansion, his bone structure so similar to what I see in the mirror every day.

"What the hell?" I mutter, my voice low but sharp enough to draw the others' attention. Avery lifts her head, her brows furrowing as she follows my gaze. Garrett glances up too, his grip on Axel loosening.

"What's going on?" Avery asks, filled with concern.

"I'm not sure," I frown. "I'll be right back." My feet are already moving, carrying me out of the room and down the stairs two at a time. My pulse thunders in my ears, a creeping sense of unease prickling at the edge of my mind. *What is he doing here?*

By the time I reach the front door, he's standing there, hands stuffed casually in his pockets, like he hasn't just appeared out of seemingly nowhere. We're equal height now, his tanned skin a deeper shade than mine, and his eyes, although pale, are a muted gray rather than blue. His grin widens when he sees me, and for a moment, it's like we're kids again, sneaking out after curfew and covering for each other's reckless decisions.

"Cuz!" he calls out, laughing as if no time has passed. "You look like you've seen a ghost."

"Thiago," I breathe, my brows knitted tightly. Stepping aside to let him enter the lobby, he pushes a stack of lengthy garment bags into my hand. "What the hell are you doing here?"

"I invited him." Wyatt walks up behind me. His stewing seems to have paid off because he looks like the image of calm and collected now. Outstretching a hand, Thiago takes it, and I'm still left with all the questions.

"And you asked him to pick up your dry cleaning too?" I ask, readjusting the heavy weight over one arm. My comment goes unanswered.

"Wyatt, I take it," Thiago nods, shaking his hand firmly. "Thanks for flying me out. Life was getting rather boring since Dax stopped keeping in touch." My cousin winks and nudges my shoulder, following Wyatt through the lobby as if it's his own mansion.

I trail behind them, still trying to wrap my head around what's happening. Thiago moves through the house with the same effortless confidence he's always had, like he belongs here, like this sprawling estate isn't the most absurd backdrop for his sudden reappearance in my life. Wyatt walks ahead, gesturing to the different wings of the house. Downstairs is a sweeping tour, with the pair quickly climbing the staircase. I think they're going to see Axel, but they turn right at the top and head in the other direction.

"What's going on here? You've brought my cousin into this?" I hiss under my breath, nudging Wyatt's shoulder. My words are clipped, but he doesn't flinch. He never does.

"Don't blame me. Avery batted her big eyes, and guess what? She got her own way." Shrugging me off, I follow him into the musty old bedroom I wandered into the other day. Except it looks nothing like the darkened, dusty space stuffed with stacked boxes and one man's forgotten past.

Apparently Wyatt hasn't been pacing all day but rather creating some secret hideout that my cousin is about to move into.

Gone are the towering boxes that once blocked the sun, their contents now neatly stacked against one wall or relocated entirely. A wide desk sits in their place, positioned beneath the tall windows to make use of the natural light. The air smells faintly of lemon-scented cleaner, though the faint musk of the room's previous state lingers underneath.

The mismatched furniture now forms a cohesive, albeit eccentric, setup. A worn leather chair sits at the desk, its cracked surface giving it a rugged charm. To the side, a narrow bookshelf holds a mix of technical manuals, old novels, and a few potted succulents. A futon, stripped of its dust and draped in a dark gray blanket, occupies one corner, doubling as a bed. Wyatt must have raided every corner of the house.

"Where did you get all of this?" I gesture to the dual monitors humming softly on its surface, accompanied by a sleek laptop and an array of cables snaking toward a power strip. Wyatt turns his head to hide his smirk.

"Sharon's office."

Thiago whistles low, stepping past me to take it all in. "You did all this for me? I'm touched," he quips, running a hand along the desk's polished surface.

"Don't flatter yourself," Wyatt retorts, leaning against the doorframe with his arms crossed. "You've got the information I need you to look into. Make yourself at home. I'll have the butler bring some food up." Before he leaves, he relieves me of the garment bags, telling me to circle back to Axel's room around sunset. Thiago swivels in the desk chair, testing it out, a grin tugging at his lips.

"Not got much to say, Cuz? Couldn't shut you up as a boy." I look him over, settling on the afro sprouting from his head.

"You need a haircut. You look like Sideshow Bob." His laugh is unfiltered, a raw joyous sound that I had forgotten was so infectious. His eyes drop to my bandages and splint.

"And you look like you've been jerking off too hard." I use my good hand to flip him off. Slapping his knee, Thiago returns to twisting the chair in full circles, soaking in the view like a man who isn't tied down. Someone who's free to enjoy whatever life throws at him, which currently is our latest drama.

It feels like forever ago since we've spent time together in person. The last time being before my mom passed, actually. Being my aunt's son and growing up in a rough part of town like we did, we spent every day after school and every weekend terrorizing the locals. That was before my mom got sick, and although she refused to stop pulling doubles at the hospital, I decided to stay home every chance I got. To be one less problem she'd need to deal with.

Thiago finally spins to face the monitors, already cracking his knuckles in preparation. "Well, this is all exciting and everything, Daxy boy. Now, tell me what the hell we're really dealing with here."

I lean against the desk, the unease in my chest only growing. I relay what I can, bundling Avery's adoption and Cathy's death, Fredrick's kidnapping of Meg, Axel's injury, and our current predicament in this mansion, the auction happening tonight, all into one clusterfuck of a tale. Thiago listens intently, threading his fingers over his stomach, and when I'm finished, he lets out a low, long whistle.

"So that girl you had me track down for you a few months ago," Thiago taps his thumbs together, "she's your girlfriend, and she's here right now, cuddled up in bed with someone else?" I reach over to shove his chair into another spin, dislodging the growing grin on his face.

"It's not like that, man. Story time is over, let's dive into what Wyatt's asked you to do before he comes back to check that we're not fucking around."

"He does seem like quite the ballbuster," Thiago agrees. "He called me yesterday morning, telling me to pack and get on his private jet. The dry cleaning was already on board with directions to bring it with me, and he'd pay me extra." A disbelieving chuckle escapes him, his knee twitching up and down.

"You could have said no if you had other plans."

"Dude, it was a *private jet*," Thiago's grey eyes blow wide. I raise a brow, used to his deflecting nature. The grin on his face slips, and he sits forward to put his elbows on the desk. "Truth is, timing couldn't have been better."

I toy with a groove in the wooden desk, avoiding Thiago's gaze. I still don't like that Wyatt went behind my back with this, snapping his fingers and commanding people around. As nice as it is to reconnect with family, he's brought my cousin into a situation we can't predict or control. Not to mention Thiago's knack to get himself into dangerous situations, even without Wyatt's help. Surely there's something better out there for him, something safer?

"You could always get a real job," I say, wincing at the way it sounds. Thiago looks at me knowingly with his eyelids half-mast. It's not the first time we've had this argument.

"Not one that pays like this. The work might be few and far in between, but I've learnt to be careful in the meantime. Besides, hacking is all I'm really good at. You know that." I swallow past a lump of guilt in my throat.

Thiago is a high school dropout, letting his ADHD and dyslexia get the best of him. He can hyperfocus on a screen and digit code for hours, but give him a notepad and pen and he's a goner. Although it's never been said out loud, we started to drift apart from that point onwards. I was the one who got out, who made the grades to go to a private college. He's the one who stayed behind to care for my aunt until she was killed in a gas station robbery gone wrong. Now he's just stuck there without any motivation to leave.

Thiago claps me on the bicep, breaking through my thoughts. His grin has returned in full effect. "Move out of the way, Cuz. I've got work to do." He switches on the monitors and pushes in a USB drive, his fingers flying over the keys.

A knock sounds a moment later, the butler delivering the promised food beneath a silver cloche. I thank him, taking the plate over to the desk and unveiling a towering club sandwich with fries. Thiago's excitement is visible, his eyes hungrily eating the food before he's managed to shove it into his mouth. Between tapping keys and grabbing for more fries, he becomes consumed by his task, muttering to himself here and there. I drop onto the futon, covering my eyes with my hand.

By the time voices filter in from the front lawn, we've got nowhere. My throat tightens as if a hand circles my nape, compressing my windpipe. The minibuses have arrived, and we're quickly running out of daylight. I'd hoped amidst the stress of living through tonight's auction, I would have at least been able to give Avery some good news. A lead that she's desperate for.

"Don't you have somewhere else to be?" Thiago asks. He's pulled a baseball cap out of his bag to wear backwards, although it fits awkwardly over his afro. Ironically, he's rolling a pen between his fingers, although he won't be using it. "Your stress levels are impacting my productivity."

"I haven't even said anything," I grumble, pushing up from the futon. He chuckles to himself, not even bothering to cast a glance over his shoulder.

"Exactly. Worst hacking companion ever. Go on back to your girl so I can put my headphones in and concentrate better. Your energy is throwing me off."

"Fair enough," I agree. Striding past, I quickly smack the cap off his head and make it out of the door before the pen collides with the other side of the wood. I find myself smirking, feeling a little lighter than before. It may not be my ideal family reunion, but seeing Thiago has reminded me we're not as alone as I'd thought.

Heading towards Axel's room, I mentally shift gears. There's still so much to prepare for, but for the first time all day, I feel like I can breathe. Whatever happens tonight, we'll do it because Axel asked us to, and we'll face it together.

HUXLEY

CHAPTER TWENTY SEVEN

I return from the bathroom, a towel slung low on my hips. Avery walks in a moment after in a matching towel, the plush pebble gray material hugging her naked body. Her hair is piled onto her head, although the tendrils that have fallen loose are beginning to curl from our recent shower.

I was thankful when Garrett kicked us all out of Axel's room to let him sleep, relieving us from sitting with our thoughts, and Avery was only too happy when I suggested a distraction. AKA, I ate her cunt on the bathroom counter until she screamed and bent her over in the shower until we both came hard.

Avery's chosen bedroom is empty, although a suit has been draped across the bed covers. The fit looks tailored, and the sheen of the jacket appears expensive—exactly Wyatt's taste. Beside it, a beautiful dress in navy satin is perfectly laid out, not a single crease in sight. The straps are strings of diamonds, following a low dipping neckline to a sapphire-colored gem at the bottom of the V. Mesh panels have been cut out of the sides to give a hint of skin underneath.

I bristle at the sight. I don't want anyone, especially Sharon's friends, to see any part of Avery. But alas, I'm not the puppet master. Just the puppet.

"Never fails to surprise, does he?" Avery smirks, running the silky material through her fingers. I grunt, opening the suit jacket to find my underwear has also been selected and carefully folded on the white shirt.

"Just a fucking creep, I reckon." The sound of Avery's laughter soothes my irritation, not just at Wyatt's micromanagement but the situation as a whole. I have no interest in dancing along to Sharon's tune, but tonight's appearance isn't my choice, and apparently Wyatt is granting wishes like a freaking genie these days. I just wish he wouldn't dress me up like livestock for it, given Sharon's prior interest in me.

Dropping my towel, I reach for the boxers, sensing Avery's eyes roaming over every inch of my skin. I shudder at her hungry gaze, despite only just having her all to myself for a change. Somehow, even when I'm not my muscliest or best self, Avery looks at me as if I'm the man of her dreams. Sometimes it's nice to think I didn't always have to share those dreams with four other men.

Silently walking across the thick sheepskin rug on her tiptoes, she leans into me, bracing her open palms on my chest. I allow her to walk me back a few steps until the wall leaves me nowhere else to go. The towel wrapped around her falls away, pooling at our feet, the warm press of her breasts nestled against me.

"Were you not satisfied with my performance in the shower? I've only ever had five-star reviews before," I raise a brow. Avery twists her lips, looking at the ceiling in thought.

"Hmmm, there might be one or two things I'd like to bring up with your complaints department," she rolls her tongue over her teeth. I bite back my grin, hoisting her up and spinning us in one smooth move to trap her against the wall.

"You weren't complaining whilst your grip on my hair was tugging me closer, suffocating me with that beautiful pussy of yours," I growl into her ear, "or when I was slamming into you, my balls slapping against your clit." A shudder rolls through Avery's spine. Although my cock is quickly growing between us, I shift my hold to cradle rather than crush her, my thumb brushing her nape.

Her fingers graze the circular scar by my collarbone, the steady beat of my heart thumping beneath her hand. Strong and dominant, powered by the protective need to keep her safe. We hold eye contact for a moment, our breaths mingling until my eyes flutter closed and I close the distance between our lips.

Avery's mouth moves against mine slowly, a slow reprise to our feverish desire in the bathroom. She pushes my wet hair back from my face, grabbing my jaw and opening me up to her. Our tongues clash halfway, coiling around one another's until we're left breathless. If there's one thing I'm sure of in this fucked-up world, it's that I'll never get enough of Avery's taste. Of the way she makes me want to be the best version of myself, just to lay down at her feet and hope she deems me worthy. I can't help but stare, tracing her features with my eyes and bathing in the feel of her soft skin and delicious curves.

"What are you thinking?" Avery tilts her head to one side. I grin now, putting aside all other trepidation to focus on what's real and what's right in front of me.

"How lucky I am."

Avery snorts, wrinkling her nose up. "I don't think you're lucky given the harm and disaster I've brought into your life. You should be running as far away from me as possible."

"Yet I'm right here, looking into your beautiful eyes and thinking, it's totally worth it." I can tell Avery doesn't fully believe that, but some things just take time. She'll see the truth in my actions and in the ways I will always protect her.

Settling Avery onto the floor, I murmur that we should probably get ready before Wyatt comes to check on us. I dress quickly, the extra-slim fit shirt barely fitting over my broad shoulders. I'm not in the finest shape, but still, the fit appears intentional. The slacks are also far too skinny, as proven by Avery's unladylike snort when I turn to reveal my accentuated bubble butt.

"What the fuck?" I strain against the material, getting the impression I would burst through if I twisted too far. Given the tailored fit, there is only one possible reason Wyatt's left me this suit. To dangle me in front of Sharon and fuck knows who else as man candy. "No way, nope. Not doing it." I start yanking the material off vigorously. Buttons fly and seams rip as I sneer, naked once again, as I rummage in the drawers for some dark jeans and a white polo.

"She's not going to be happy," Avery singsongs. This only spurs me on as I ruffle my hair into a shaggy mess.

I turn to help her pull the dress over her head, letting the material cascade down her body. It fits like a glove, the floor-length skirt flaring out when she spins side to side. A pair of glittering, silver heels are waiting at the foot of the bed. I bend onto one knee, kissing each of her feet before sliding them into the six-inch heels. Avery's eyes glimmer like aquamarine diamonds, and her smile is far more reassuring than I'm sure she feels. I leave her to sit at the vanity, pulling her hair free of its tie. Like golden, silky magic, it flows down her back in soft curls. Stunning, effortless, just like her.

One item remains on the bed, a heart-shaped sapphire necklace that will bring out her eyes perfectly. Internally, I both curse and thank Wyatt for being so overbearing. I approach Avery while she's applying her lip balm, and I drape the piece around her neck, fastening it before pulling her hair through the loop. Her gaze catches mine in the mirror, a weak smile waiting to be reciprocated.

"Well, at least we look the part," she half shrugs. I take her hand, leading her to the door and then beyond, refusing to talk myself out of tonight anymore than I already have. Axel thinks it could be beneficial, and he wants us to experience this for his sake. It's the least we can do after the sacrifices he's made.

Wyatt and Dax are waiting for us, leaning over the banister to watch the lobby underneath. Their suits, unlike mine, give the right amount of trim fit and modesty. In turn, they acknowledge Avery burrowing her way between them. Dax with a kiss on the cheek and Wyatt with a fiery glare up and down her body. He might as well strip her naked and gape at her, it would have been less intrusive. I join Dax's side, resting my forearms on the banister too. If anyone has an opinion about my polo shirt and jeans, it goes unsaid.

The students downstairs are a far cry from the relaxed yobs we met last week. They form two lines, standing shoulder to shoulder in the finest suits and dresses, their hair either slicked back or in perfect chiffon buns. Each one has a thin, red strap and a small label around their wrist. Impeccably dressed up like little dolls. At the forefront, braced by the entrance, are Sharon and a man with his hand pressed against her lower back. Mr. Barrett is making a rare appearance, it would seem.

Alongside the chime of a grandfather clock, the doorbell chimes at exactly six. From then on, the main entrance remains open to the flocks of wealthy guests arriving, the driveway a constant hum of engines. Many arrive in limos, which promptly leave, whether to save space or the presumption that a ride back home isn't needed tonight; I'm guessing the latter.

Each guest is quickly swept up in the arm of a student, their movements mechanical and trained. It's like watching a performance, but there's no applause waiting at the end of this act, just something darker. Then, they're ushered through the right archway to the side of the mansion that remains unused. I suppose its use just became apparent.

Top Knot is the last to take his chosen, a man with a salt-and-pepper beard and a predatory smile that makes my stomach churn. He's a regular, it seems, holding his hand out for a waitress to rush forward with a full whiskey glass. Dax shifts beside me, his jaw tense, blue eyes glinting under the chandelier light. He doesn't say anything, but his knuckles whiten as he grips the banister. Top Knot and the man laugh about something, striding away out of sight. Only then does Sharon turn and lift her chin to us, her polished smile all charm and cruelty.

"It's rude to linger," she calls. "If you're joining us, then you'd best do so now. We don't permit late entries." Wyatt's shoulders straighten, his posture tight enough to snap, but he begins to descend the stairs. Dax holds Avery's waist, and I take up the rear, pushing my hands into my pockets to save them curling into fists. Uncomfortable doesn't even begin to cover it.

"I thought I made the rules clear," Sharon snips, looking over us all disapprovingly. "You're not to be present for these events." The man standing tall by her side steps a little closer and smoothly rubs her back.

"Now, now, dear. A few extra guests won't hurt." I instantly don't like him.

I would put him in his fifties, well kept with a head of thick blond hair. A few inches shorter than me, it is clear that he keeps his body in shape through his designer blue suit. Most evident is his imposing presence, an unnerving calm that fills me with unease. In fact, after assessing Avery rather closely, he smiles. Both Wyatt and I have the good sense to step in front of Avery, blocking her from his view. A common occurrence in this house, it seems.

"I thought you didn't attend these events," Wyatt grits out, his jaw clenched tight. Mr. Barrett remains unfazed while his wife stares daggers.

"I thought I should be present, as there are *others* in the house. We wouldn't want anything to go wrong now, would we?" He eyes us each carefully, trying to figure us out. "Let me introduce myself, Richard Barrett."

The pasty man puffs out his chest arrogantly, not intimidated in the least by the three guys that are all easily a foot taller and glowering at him like he's pissed in their milk.

Holding out his hand, no one takes it, and Richard finds this all the more amusing. A tall body suddenly appears from behind us to slap away the offensive limb with a snarl. His dark, shaggy hair flicks forward into his eyes, his shoulders rising and falling with the weight of his breathing.

I catch Wyatt's confused eye, also wondering what part of *'stay with Axel'* Garrett couldn't seem to understand. It appears he's picked up my suit from the bedroom floor, the ripped shirt hanging open over a white vest, the suit jacket and slacks pulled on in haste and not quite straight. He doesn't care. He's here to prove a point.

"Didn't feel like another millionaire on his deathbed then, Sharon?" Garrett hisses. "I heard Husband number two had only just wheezed out his vows before he croaked."

"And such a shame it was." Sharon holds a hand to her heart, as if she has one. "But Victor believed in the cause, and he'll be sleeping peacefully that his money has turned what was a singular experience into a whole enterprise." She signals towards the ballroom, where the sound of exaggerated laughter booms around the entire manor.

I don't look away from her pinched face. *A singular experience.* As in, one Axel against a room filled with thirsty, greedy women. My stomach churns, her wickedness knowing no bounds.

"You really are vile," I repeat from the morning she called me down to the spa. Sharon's pale eyes flash to mine, her painted lips twisting into a smile. She thinks she's winning, and I suppose as long as she's pulling all the strings, she is.

"They don't seem to mind," she gestures to a few students passing to retrieve trays of champagne flutes and head straight back. "Imagine drowning in student loans until presented with the chance to not only survive but to live a life you'd never dreamed of. They're well paid, making invaluable connections and gaining experiences the ordinary can't even imagine, all for the small cost of surrendering their bodies once a week. I've done it myself for years. Trust me, it pays to be promiscuous."

I think we all look away in disgust at the same time, staring at various spots on the floor. Garrett goes one step further and spits at her open-toed heels.

"It's a brothel, no matter how you sugar coat it."

"Agree to disagree. Everyone here is of consensual age and by choice. They're free to leave whenever they wish, as are you," Sharon adds, as if we're here by choice. The sick feeling in my stomach has increased during this interaction, with the taste of bile lingering in my throat.

None of this ended with Axel leaving. It only snowballed into something much bigger than any of us. Sharon's morals are one thing, but the hum of activity in the room down the hall is her validation. All of those people are swelling her ego, proving that she can control whatever she sees fit under this roof. I know the others are thinking it too, but we're getting Axel out of here as soon as he's able to be moved.

The clock chimes again, another hour passing. Richard slips his hand around Sharon's waist and pulls her into his side possessively. Together, the pair stride away, not bothering to look back. We're trailing just behind anyway. Garrett steps into Wyatt's side, giving him a slight shove with his shoulder and casting a glance back at Avery. Or rather, Avery's cleavage.

"What were you thinking, dressing her up like that?"

Wyatt grunts but doesn't indulge him. "What the hell are you doing down here? Someone needs to stay with Axel." Another round of shoulder shoving happens, and I debate splitting them up, but I'm the fortunate one who has Avery's arm linked in mine.

"He's asleep, and his door is locked." Garrett waves a key in the air before returning it to his breast pocket. "You shouldn't be flaunting Avery around in front of these predators."

"She's a big girl," I hear Wyatt's eye roll. "And a beautiful one. You should be self-assured that it doesn't matter who's looking at her, as long as she's looking at you." Beside me, Avery's eyes are as wide as saucers, and when Wyatt peeks over his shoulder at her to wink, she stops walking completely. "Or maybe she'll be looking at me." Dax crashes into our backs, hissing at the jolt of his damaged fingers.

Did he just make a joke? Wyatt the serious? Wyatt the runner from all problems and happiness? Whatever character he's slipped into, he maintains it as I encourage Avery to step into the ballroom. Running the length of this wing, the wooden dance floor is surrounded by lavish chairs and set tables, tall candelabras glimmering on each. Velvet curtains in the richest shade of plum are drawn over a row of windows. Gold flourishes line the ceiling and surround the chandelier hanging in the center.

We enter the room as a tight unit, ready to play out this charade and get back to our rooms as quickly as possible. Behind us, the butler closes the doors in turn with a loud bang. Many eyes turn our way, but Top Knot's are the ones that stick out to me the most. He quickly excuses himself from the older man's company and bounds over. The smile on his face is Joker-worthy as he clasps me on the shoulder like old friends.

"Huxley! You made it. Thank fuck it's Friday, am I right?" He winks before letting those eyes wander. I resist blocking Avery from his view, just about. Wyatt is right, naturally people will look. She's stunning, but we can't swaddle her forever. Although the possessive part of me struggles to stand down, my arm tensing into a steely grip around hers.

"Evening, Taylor," Avery bats her lashes. At least this brings his attention back up from her breasts. Disregarding the other guys looming over us, Top Knot looks back to me with his wicked smile still in place.

"You know, you should join us on stage tonight. It's a hell of a thrill." My mouth gapes open, the notion spiking just a fierce response within me. I'm temporarily dumbfounded by it. Before I can conjure the words without exploding, his name is called from across the room, and he salutes us goodbye, disappearing back into the crowd. His top-knot appears every so often, and soon enough I realize who called for him.

Sharon ascends a temporary stage, her tight dress restricting her movement. Top-Knot and Richard follow just behind, remaining one step down like her loyal lapdogs. Once in front of the microphone, she clinks her glass lightly, calling for silence. The giggles and murmurs subside almost instantly, replaced by a tense quiet hinged on the side of anticipation.

Apparently, it's showtime.

AVERY

"Good evening, everyone," Sharon smiles at her enthralled audience from her raised podium. My stomach twists painfully, my heart hammering so hard that I'm sure it's visible through the thin straps of this dress. I have no idea what game Wyatt is playing, dressing us up and parading us around when the idea was to lay low, but I can't spare it any thought now. Not when I'm about to witness a live reenactment of Axel's trauma taking place in front of me.

"Welcome to what is due to be another splendid evening. A small bit of housekeeping for the newbies, and then we can jump straight into the main event. The auction." A round of cheers and raised glasses fills the room, tempering down as Sharon lifts her hand. "As you will have noticed, each one of our Lots has a number stripped to their wrist. This figure is the early buyout fee if you should wish to secure your partner for the evening, although I must say, bidding is half the fun," Sharon winks, accompanied by another round of agreement. "I do hope you have all had the chance to mingle, because I'm going to now ask the Lots to leave the room to prepare.

"We have an exciting development this evening." I swallow harshly while dread turns my stomach to stone. A few of the keen-eyed guests cast sly glances our way, sensing that we're new here. Luckily, Sharon reaches for Taylor's hand and beckons him onto the stage.

"Tonight, our beautiful Taylor here is available for silent bids only.

If you'd like to try your chances, please find the pens and paper at the back of the room, where you can slip your bid into the box provided. The highest bid at the end of the night will be the winner." Taylor's eyes create a beeline to the man he was hanging on the arm of and gives a challenging raise of his brow. Sharon allows him to leave, joining his fellow friends on the dance floor.

"As always, transfers need to be settled in the drawing room before you are able to claim your prize. For early buyouts, please come see me now. Otherwise, take your seats, and happy bidding."

With this, the students wave fluttery fingers and some even blow kisses before departing through a door at the back of the room. Taylor is last, his head poking out of the crowd to search for Huxley. When their eyes connect, Taylor gestures to the back room with a questioning raised brow. Huxley stiffens, his clenched arm crushing mine, and he curses *'fuck no'* under his breath.

The guests choose their seats, a few waitresses smoothly filtering in to make sure a champagne glass is in every hand. Bidding paddles are casually placed on the tables, like this is just another Friday night dinner party. The polished chandeliers overhead cast sharp light across their faces, illuminating their predatory expressions. The atmosphere is suffocating, each breath of air heavy with the sickly sweet scent of expensive perfume.

Huxley's arm is still locked with mine, and I can feel the tremble in his muscles even as he tries to hold himself together. I glance sideways at him, his face pale and his jaw set tight. He refuses to look at me, his gaze glued to the stage where Taylor had disappeared moments before. I don't know what's beyond that door, and I don't want to know.

Wyatt steps closer to us, his presence a source of both comfort and frustration. He nudges Huxley's other side, forcing us to move towards a lonely table in the back corner. Overcast in shadow, this table seems to be reserved for spectating only, which no one tonight seems interested in. They're all muttering excitedly between themselves, hungry for their piece of flesh.

As I choose my seat, Hux tucks me in, and Dax takes my side. His phone buzzes faintly in his pocket before he slides it out to check the screen. He doesn't say anything, but his shoulders tense, and the way his thumb hovers over the screen tells me the message isn't good. Before

Hux can settle on my other side, Garrett slides in, his hand hot and firm on my thigh.

"The time has come," Sharon's voice cuts through the murmurs as she moves to the edge of the podium, taking the microphone with her, "to see your first Lot. Please show a warm welcome back to Trixie." Mostly the gentlemen start to cheer, but a few women whoop too, the energy in the room turning electric. The back door opens, and my breath catches in my throat.

Trixie exits, striding confidently in black kitten heels and nothing else. Completely naked and holding a pair of handcuffs, she catwalks across the ballroom floor, putting on a brilliant show of self-assurance whilst swinging the metal loop around her finger for it to catch the light. Her perfectly rehearsed smile stays in place, her shoulders squared to push out her chest. She has a phenomenal figure, pert breasts, and slim legs. It's no wonder a handful of paddles shoot into the air.

I gape, blinking through the shock yet unable to look away until Trixie has retreated to stand center stage. Once there, Trixie clasps her hands in front of her, pressing her boobs together, widens her stance slightly, and lowers her head in submission.

She stays like that, listening to Sharon calling out the bids like an auctioneer and shouting *'sold'* to a portly woman with vibrant orange curls near the front. Trixie looks up, smiles at her temporary owner, and makes her way over. I lose sight of Trixie's head, so I shift into Dax's space to see she's dropped to her knees by the chair and remains there for the rest of the evening.

Then it happens again. This time it's Zara, a blonde who has a braid resting over each shoulder and a teddy bear in her hands. She's much more lively, skipping along the dancefloor, letting everything bounce. When she comes near enough, I catch a glimpse of bold freckles over her nose and cheeks that must be artificial. She follows the same routine, clasping her teddy bear and bowing her head in submission on stage, before going to kneel by the man who has purchased her.

One after the other, the students reenter the room. All butt naked with a prop of some description, all embracing the crowd's attention on their exposed skin. Cards shoot into the air, the guests practically salivating over the human beings paraded before them. The numbers climb higher and higher, absurd figures being thrown around. With each Lot, Sharon's enthusiasm grows. She's laughing and joking. At one point, she smacks the ass of a naked guy when he passes. It's a circus, and she's the ringleader.

I'm not sure at what point I faze out, my mind taking a path of its own. When the next student exits the back room, all I see is Axel. My sweet, innocent Axel being gawked and pawed at. The smart, loving man I know reduced to being livestock, all for the benefit of the woman cackling on the edge of the stage. My hands grip the fabric of my dress as I fight the urge to turn away, but I force myself to watch. I owe it to him to bear witness to what he has been subjected to. I'm plagued by the images of what Axel might have endured, what parts of himself he sacrificed, and I can't stop the tears that spill down my cheeks.

"Peach?" a voice whispers in my ear. The hand on my thigh squeezes, trying to ground me, but I reject the comfort. I need to watch and experience every depraved moment. I need this to reignite the fire in my soul that I let fizzle out. Everyone who parades themselves naked around the room becomes Axel to me. One woman grabs her prize, shoves two slender fingers into his mouth, and when he gags, the whole table around them hollers.

My heart shatters.

"Peach," Garrett twists my chair, breaking my trance on the room. I can't fully make out his dark, bottomless eyes in our shaded corner, but I can tell they're boring right through mine. "Come back to me." Both of his palms settle on my thighs, kneading me gently. It takes valiant effort to remember to speak, to think, or to breathe. A sob lodges in my throat.

"I can't... I just," the words fumble out. Beyond Garrett's shoulder, both Wyatt and Huxley are looking over in concern, but neither approaches, giving Garrett the space to console me. He licks his lips, nodding slightly.

"I'm not going to tell you it's okay, 'cause that's a fucking lie. None of this is okay, and I know what you're thinking. If it helps, it wasn't exactly like this for him."

Garrett's words are like a stone tossed into a deep, still pond, rippling through the images in my mind. My vision, blurry with tears, clings to Garrett's silhouette, his broad frame blocking me from the madness happening all around us. His hands press firmly against my thighs, kneading gently, pulling me out of the swirling darkness and anchoring me to him.

My brain wants to resist. As though it doesn't want to come back. It doesn't want to leave the haunted images behind because that would be like leaving young Axel behind. Leaving him to suffer alone and endlessly. My hands tremble, and I twist the fabric painfully between my fingers. Every sound in the room, Sharon's gleeful commentary, the cheering, the vile cacophony of laughter. It all rings like a bell in my skull, impossible to drown out.

Garrett leans closer, forcing me to breathe in his freshly showered scent, the tickle of his hair gracing my forehead. I inhale his exhale, twinged with mint. "Look at me," he says. My chest heaves as I fight for air, my ribs expanding painfully against the tightness that binds them. I shake my head, unable to obey.

His hands slide from my thighs to my forearms, prying my fingers away from the crumpled fabric of my dress. Garrett's tattooed fingers are warm as he threads them through mine, grounding me in their steady grip. Slowly, he lifts my hands, his touch firm but patient, like he's coaxing a bird back into its nest.

"Peach," he murmurs again, the nickname soft and familiar, tugging at something deep inside me. "I know it's hard, but you're here with us. Not back there. Stay here."

The tears don't stop, but they shift. They're no longer hot streaks of pain but cool drops of release. I blink hard, and Garrett comes into sharper focus. I can make out the strands of his messy hair, the barely visible hint of stubble along his jaw, and the lazy open collar of Hux's ripped shirt.

I glance over his shoulder again, drawn to the emerald green behind him like a moth to a flame. Wyatt watches closely, his expression heavy with concern. Huxley is beside him, arms crossed so tightly over his chest that his knuckles are turning white. His eyes are fixed on my face, taking each tear trailing down my cheeks as a personal heartache. I hate how vulnerable I must look. Weak and fragile and broken.

"Focus on me," Garrett urges, moving to hold my nape like he's physically holding me in the present. "Count the missing buttons on my shirt if you have to. Hell, count the tattoos on my neck and tell me how shit they are. I know you like doing that." His lips quirk into the smallest smile, and despite everything, a faint laugh bubbles up from my chest. It's weak and fleeting, but it's there, and it feels like breaking through the surface of deep water after holding my breath for too long.

I let my eyes travel across his open shirt, his chest firm beneath a white tank top. The jacket has a subtle sheen under the dim light. I focus on the rhythm of his thumbs as they sweep over my skin and the way his presence seems to fill the space around us like a shield. The noise of the room dulls, fading into a low hum at the edges of my awareness. I'm not fully present yet, but I'm closer than I was.

"I'm so angry," I whisper, the words spilling out before I can stop them. My eyes dart toward Sharon, still cackling like the queen of this spectacle. Garrett grunts in agreement, his grip on my neck tightening just slightly, just enough to draw my attention back to him.

"I've felt that anger for years," he says. "But we didn't create this hellhole. We didn't put Axel here. We're not responsible for their sickness," his eyes dart around and quickly come back. His own breath saws in and out, the hand on my nape shaking with the restraint to hold himself together. Garrett is going through the exact same turmoil as I am, although probably in much more vivid detail.

"But there's a flipside too. We get to heal him. We get to build him back up to be even stronger than before and to show him what real love is. Thanks to you."

"I haven't done anything," I instantly shake my head. Garrett hisses through his teeth, his hand slipping from my neck to my cheek, giving me a rough shake.

"You've done everything," he growls almost angrily, releasing my hand to smack his chest directly over his heart. "You've unlocked me."

There are no more pretty words, and they're not needed. Garrett's omission breaks something loose inside me. I press my forehead against his shoulder, letting his essence seep into me. He wraps his arms around me, holding me close, and for the first time since this nightmare began, I feel like I can breathe again.

The sound of bidding rises, the auction continuing without pause. But it feels distant now, like a bad dream fading in the light of morning. Garrett releases my shoulders but doesn't let go, his steady presence a lifeline as I begin to piece myself back together. Wyatt and Huxley have relaxed somewhat, though their postures most likely won't relax until we're back upstairs in a cuddle puddle.

Steadily coming back to the table, I glance to Dax, who has been frozen until now. He breaks his stillness to glance at his phone clutched tightly in his hand when buzzes again. Wyatt catches the slight purse of his lips.

"What is it?" Wyatt presses his forearms onto the table and whispers harshly. Dax shrugs him off.

"We'll discuss it later."

Garret groans, pressing himself into my sight and casually hanging his arm over my shoulder.

"Please, for the love of fuck, can we discuss it now? I'm struggling to remain in my seat."

"It's Thiago," Dax sighs. "The number Wyatt gave him was a dead end, already disabled, and any previous data on it was encrypted." Dax's phone buzzes again, and he glances down, his lips pressing into a thin line. This time, he leans into the table and lowers his voice. "So instead, he's found a hidden security system in this room, and he's working through the true identities of those present, trying to give us something to work with."

My eyes flick around the corners of the room, spotting the tiny red lights hidden within the gold edging. I never would have noticed, and I wonder if the attendees are aware.

Opening an image, Dax turns his screen slowly for the rest of us to see, the glow briefly illuminating each of our grim faces. A gentleman with a thick moustache in the same shade as his light brown comb over, standing tall and proud as he accepts some award. He's wearing a stiff black jacket, yellow stripes on the cuffs, and a checked tie. His badge identifies him as Warren Briggs, Chief of Police.

I suck in a breath at the same time Garrett's arm around my shoulder tightens.

"That's the man Taylor was talking to," Wyatt mutters.

"He's yet to bid on anyone," Huxley adds very observantly. All of our heads whip to the man in question, sitting off to the side and slowly sipping champagne. He doesn't jeer or holler; he doesn't draw any attention to himself. Hux clicks his tongue. "I bet he's waiting for the silent auction of Top-Knot."

This is what Axel wanted. For us to make valuable connections and push forward with searching for Meg. That's the ultimate goal here, to bring my twin home safe. It's what we're all fighting for. Wyatt swallows, his mind jumping into overdrive with possible scenarios. I see it in the ticking of his jaw, the pop of his knuckles against his palm. But whatever plan he might come up with is cut short, as Huxley apparently makes the decision for us.

"I'll go."

"Go... where?" Dax frowns, and Hux jerks his head towards Warren.

"There's an empty seat next to him. I'll go... I don't know, mingle?" He half shrugs, already pushing his seat back. Garrett releases me to sit forward and hold out a hand.

"Wait. You want to mingle with someone who came here to peg a man with the same body shape and hair length as you? What are you going to do, crawl into his lap and call him Daddy?"

Huxley pales slightly, but he doesn't look any less adamant. "I suppose. I'm his type, and we need a way in. I could do some digging, get something we can blackmail him with." Garrett erupts in a bout of hysterics, earning a few glances from around the room. He can't contain himself, the entire notion is ridiculous to him.

Wyatt tells Garrett to settle down before turning back to Hux. Shaking his head, he curses beneath his breath. "You can't just rush into this. We need to discuss—"

"There's no point having a plan if we miss our shot," Huxley growls back. "What if he only comes once a month, or a few times a year? How long are we going to attend these sick-fests with the hopes of implementing a well-thought-out plan?" Huxley's nails dig into his palm, his chest rising and falling rapidly. He looks like he's on the verge of bolting, his body vibrating with barely contained rage. Rage aimed at Warren, the performance taking place on stage, and us for shooting down his suggestion.

Steeling himself, he pushes to his feet and rounds the back of the table. His fingers brush my back on the way passed, and my trace snaps. I shoot up in my heels, spinning to grab Huxley's polo and pull him into me.

"So we're whoring ourselves out now?" I enter the conversation, previously dumbstruck by what I'm hearing. "Shall I strip down and jump up on stage? Maybe someone will spill all their secrets to me while I straddle them.”

Hux’s chocolate eyes darken, his nostrils flaring. He doesn’t like that idea, so he apparently knows exactly how I feel. I know what he’s thinking. He wants to get answers so we can get closer to finding Meg. But I made a vow to not let us become fractured along the way, to allow them to sacrifice themselves for my mission. My hand finds Huxley’s, squeezing it tightly. “We can find another way.”

But Hux pulls his hand away, his gaze shifting back to the man sitting oblivious a few meters away. His shoulders straighten, and he forces a calm expression onto his face.

“Wyatt isn’t the only one prepared to lose you if it means saving you.”

My chest tightens. The very idea of Huxley having to interact with this man and pretend to be interested makes me want to scream. He shouldn’t have to do this. He shouldn’t have to sacrifice his dignity. *Hypocritical, I know.* If Warren liked women, I would already be in his lap, flirting my way towards asking for a favor. But Huxley has been through so much, his confidence is barely hanging on by a thread. The damage of trading his soul for my cause could be irreparable.

That must be what drives the anger to explode within me. The injustice of it all screaming louder in my head than Sharon’s following cackle.

“Well, maybe my love for you is too selfish for heroics, but I’m not prepared to lose you. Not one little bit.” I try to storm away, but I don’t make it very far. I can’t leave the room, can’t bring myself not to watch. At the back of the dining room, I press my back aside the wall and fold my arms. Wyatt comes to stand by my side, his expression hardening into something unreadable. Hux bridges the gap between himself and the man, and with every step, my heart aches more.

This isn’t right. None of it is right or fair, and a faint voice tells me we’re playing into Sharon’s hand.

Warren’s profile reveals itself as he turns his head and greets his new companion. My stomach twists with renewed unease as I notice the way his gaze lingers a little too long and the way his lips curl into a faint, greedy smile. His expensive suit stretches slightly as he offers out his hand, his eyes locked on Huxley. After a moment of hesitation, Hux accepts it and sits in the vacant seat.

The rest of the auction fades into the background as the two of them engage in conversation. I can't hear what's being said, but Warren's body language is relaxed. Huxley, on the other hand, is visibly tense, though he's doing his best to hide it.

Wyatt steps closer to me, his hand brushing against mine in a subtle gesture of support. I glance at him, and for a moment, I see the cracks in his carefully constructed facade. He hates this just as much as I do, but he knows it's necessary. He knows it needed to be done, even if he'd never have asked Hux to do it.

AVERY

CHAPTER TWENTY NINE

My fist connects with Huxley's forearm, pain splintering across my knuckles.

"Fuck," I growl, bending low to throw my shoulder into his abs. I manage to push him a step backward before he twists sideways, so I stumble forward. Catching myself before my face becomes best friends with the floor, I swing out my leg and groan as our shins crash together. "Stop just defending and actually *do* something," I glare at him, hopping on my good leg and holding the other to my body.

I would be the first to admit, after last night, it was a terrible idea to agree to a sparring session with Huxley. But that's exactly why he's asked. He knows I need to vent, and he's offering himself up like some sacrificial lamb anyway. I'm furious. So much so that the little sleep I did manage to get was filled with horrible dreams of Hux on a stage being pawed at whilst Axel was forced to watch. We were supposed to be aiding his recovery, not sinking him further into it.

Seeking his own brand of punishment, Huxley's not even trying to retaliate. He just keeps blocking and deflecting at every turn.

"Maybe we should take five?" He offers sheepishly, helping me to hop over to the wall. I slouch back and rub the latest addition to the mass of bruises and bumps beneath my leggings.

"I can't rest. I need to be ready." For what, who knows, but it keeps me from feeling restless. *Useless.*

Slumping down next to me, Huxley faces the gym. Unlike me, his blond hair isn't slick with sweat, and his muscles don't seem to be burning. Instead, he hunches over his knees, the sports shorts he borrowed slipping down his thighs. I look away, refusing to be distracted by his increasing muscle.

"Burning yourself out won't do any good either. We can break for lunch." Damn, if Huxley is proposing to eat, I must be overdoing it. My eyes slide past his head to see the sun almost drifting directly overhead; not that time has any concept to me anymore.

"Not yet. Let's go again." Huxley reluctantly moves to stand with me, returning to the spot we cleared in the center of the room. The machines and benches have been pushed again in favor of the cushioned mats we've laid across the floor.

Squaring his shoulders, Huxley gets back into position. His soft brown eyes meet mine, steady and accepting, as if he's doing me a favor by letting me vent on him. That quiet composure would usually be a comfort, but today, it grates on me. I need to feel the weight of resistance, the sharpness of struggle, and he's giving me nothing but indifference.

"Ready?" he asks, his voice as even as his stance.

I withhold my response, bouncing on the balls of my feet. My hands come up, fists tight despite the ache in my knuckles. Darting forward, I fake a left jab before twisting my body to aim a right hook at his ribs. He blocks it effortlessly, his forearm meeting mine with a dull thud. The impact sends a shockwave through my arm, but I grit my teeth and push harder, trying to force him off balance.

Huxley doesn't budge. Instead, he shifts his weight, his foot sliding behind mine in a way that sends me stumbling back onto the mat. I land on my ass with a grunt, my pride bruised more than my body.

"You're not focusing," he says, his lips pinched as he holds out a hand to pull me up. I smack his hand away. I think the opposite is true. I'm focusing too much, trying to bury everything else except the need to feel and cause physical pain. At least I know Huxley can take it if he'd just let me get one punch in.

"If you're not going to take this seriously, what's the point?"

Hux's stubbled jaw tenses and a flicker of something—maybe

annoyance or concern—crosses his face before vanishing. "You're mad at the wrong person." I chew on the inside of my cheek and look away.

"Am I?" I grit my teeth. "Because I'm pretty sure I'm mad at you." Hux looks away, redness twinging his cheeks. He knows I'm lying. I know I'm lying, but I need to do something to scrub the images from last night from my brain. Hux talked to Warren late into the evening, letting the man tentatively stroke his arm and hair. As predicted, Warren did win the silent bid and left with Taylor, but Hux got what he wanted. The promise to return next week.

That's not all I'm mad at. I'm angry at Sharon, the college kids who are encouraging her sick friends to attend these auctions, and the amount of people to let this all happen to Axel in the first place without feeling the need to step in on his behalf. But currently, Huxley's little scheme is sitting at the top of that shit heap. Getting to my feet, I ignore Hux's pitiful look when my aching arms rise again.

"You're fighting yourself more than you're fighting me," he states, moving into a stance that mirrors mine. I take a deep breath, the adrenaline coursing through me, making it hard to think and hard to breathe. Huxley doesn't move first, giving me space but watching me closely, his presence infuriating and grounding all at once.

This time, when I lunge, he doesn't just deflect. He counters, stepping into my space and sweeping my legs out from under me in one swift motion. I hit the mat hard, the breath knocked from my lungs. Before I can fully recover, his hand is there again, offering to help me up. I take it, the heat of his palm grounding me as I rise to my feet.

"Better," he exhales slowly. "But you're still telegraphing your moves." I'm barely upright when he moves again, faster than I anticipate, his arm darting out to grab my wrist. I twist instinctively, trying to break free, but his grip is firm. Throwing an elbow into his ribs instead, there's a soft *'oomph'* of shock that leaves his lips as I wheel around, slamming my palms into his chest to put some distance between us.

Hux uses this as a chance to shed his black tank top, baring his firm chest and tensed abs. Tossing the material aside, he's coming at me again, his eyes glinting with the challenge. *Finally*, I think, just before he swoops me up with his shoulder. I'm thrown onto my back with his weight crashing on top, causing the air to whoosh from my lungs sharply.

I wriggle, not letting him grab my wrists like he's trying to, and throw punches into his side in quick succession. Somehow managing to shift my knees between the cage of our bodies, I use all of my strength to push him aside and roll away quickly. Scrambling to my feet, his hand catches my ankle and drags me back down.

"You're not fighting fair," I grunt after slamming into the mat on my front. Kicking out wildly, Huxley drags me backward whilst climbing up the length of my body. His hand rounds my throat in warning, not squeezing as he traps me beneath him.

"You think anyone who gets close to us is going to fight fair?" Huxley breathes against my ear, ruffling my loose hair. I clench my jaw, uselessly struggling beneath him. "Does anyone in this twisted world give a shit about what's fair anymore?" His chest is heaving against mine, barely concealed restraint twisting his voice into something unrecognizable. Pushing himself upright, Hux downs a bottle of water and grabs his tank top from the floor. "We're done for today."

I shift into a seated position, huffing and seething. Sweat coats my skin, and my thoughts consume me. Hux is right to call it quits now before someone, most likely me, gets hurt, but the brat in me just can't leave it alone. Where I should be thankful he is giving me an outlet, I'm furious with myself about just how weak I am. How complacent I've become, hiding behind the Souls and letting them take the consequences. The rounded scar on Hux's collarbone glares at me like an accusation.

I wanted to believe I wasn't the naive, pampered princess who was once locked away in Hughes Manor. That I'm not the girl who dances for fun or lines up my highlighters in rainbow order. The reality isn't comforting.

Holding out his arm to escort me to lunch, Hux raises an expectant brow. I wish I could concede. I wish walking out of that door didn't seem like yet another failure to add to my ever-growing list. But he doesn't understand that I don't need saving. I need support. I need to improve and push myself to uncomfortable limits. My nightmares have become reality, and nothing I do is helping anyone. At least this, maybe, hopefully, can help to prepare me.

Stand up, fists raised, stance widened. I huff a strand of hair out of my face, the rest of it having fallen free of its bun, the hairband hanging loosely on the end. "Again," I say, my voice steadier this time.

"Swan," Hux pinches the bridge of his nose.

"I said, again." A chest pressed against my back, large hands landing on my hip and holding me still before I can strike again.

"Hux, Axel is asking for a bath, and Garrett would like your help," Wyatt states, the warmth of his hands seeping into me. "I'll take over here." His hands tighten, refusing to let me move. I find I'm not trying to. Wyatt will fight with me. He'll brawl and anger me until something productive happens. He won't let me off easy.

Looking between the two of us, Huxley exhales loudly before he leaves. The winged angel splayed across his entire back shifts as he walks, the flex of the muscle beneath causes her wings to flutter. Guilt tries to surface, but I push it down, saving it for later. Suddenly, I'm alone with Wyatt, and the air is crackling with a different kind of tension. One where compassion doesn't belong.

Wyatt steps around me, his green eyes flicking over my flushed face, the loose strands of hair sticking to my temple. I'm just glad he can't see the bruises starting to bloom on my shins. Setting my jaw, I tilt my head up to meet his face.

"Come on then. Fists up." A slow, dangerous smirk spreads across his face.

"Oh, Avery, you don't want to fight." Wyatt chuckles to himself, his voice low and taunting. Scoffing, I throw my head back and stare at the ceiling. Great, another guy to tell me what I want.

"I assure you, *I do*." Gripping my chin, Wyatt slowly shakes his head. His smirk falls away as his hands roam, smoothing my hair back off of my face.

"I get that you're frustrated. I don't like our current living situation any more than you do, but hurting Huxley isn't going to make you feel any better."

"It might," I shrug. Wyatt's eyes narrow, seeing through me in an instant. Extracting myself from his touch, I throw my hands up, slapping them down hard on my thighs. "How could he do that? After everything he knows Axel has been through." It all comes bubbling out. The true reason behind my anger. The betrayal I've been holding onto since last night's dinner. Wyatt closes the gap I've made, refusing to let me run from this.

"It's because of everything Axel has been through that he's stepping up. He's saving Axel from being subjected to any form of it ever again." His body towers over mine, heat radiating from him like a furnace. His face inches from mine. "We will find a way out of this. We always do." His voice is low, almost gentle, but his eyes are anything but. They burn with frustration, with desire, with something I can't quite name.

"So if you're not going to fight me, why are you here?" I glare, my body pulled taut with the raging emotions that I can't let consume me. Wyatt's small smile returns, his eyes dropping to my lips.

"Because I'm going to fuck you instead."

CHAPTER THIRTY

I move swiftly, grabbing Avery's wrist and spinning her around. Her back slams against my chest, bringing the fight in her surging to the surface. She's all fire, thrashing against me, her wild energy crackling in the air. I feel her pulse hammering under my grip on her wrists, her soft curves colliding with my hard lines. She's resisting, but I can see through it. The way her body responds, the way her breaths hitch.

"You don't want to fight, Angel," I repeat beside her ear. "You want to feel justified in your anger. Spoiler alert, you're not."

Her body stiffens as I snake an arm around her waist, hauling her backward with me. She thrashes harder, but it's no use. Her heat, her scent, her rage. It all fuels me, sharpening the edge of my control until it's a thin, taut thread.

Avery's lost sight of what matters, what's real. Just because she is pissed at Huxley doesn't mean she gets to punish him. It's not our place to judge our chosen family, which is why I tend to walk away and let them figure out their mistakes for themselves. Then afterward, I swoop in and fix the fuckups they've made along the way.

Reaching the mirrored wall, I spin and press against the glass, the cold shock biting her skin through her thin T-shirt.

"Let me go," she snarls, although her voice lacks conviction. I let the corner of my mouth curl into a smirk as I lean in, my breath brushing her lips.

"Not until you've come hard enough to see stars," I mutter against her neck, punctuating the words with sloppy kisses. "And when you can barely stand, I'm going to march your spanked ass upstairs to apologize to Huxley."

Stopping at the point where her neck meets her shoulder, I let my teeth graze at her soft skin, tasting the salt of her sweat. I savor the shudder that ripples through her as I bite down, just enough to leave a mark.

She tenses, defiance flashing in her dark eyes when I meet them. I can see her guilt buried beneath the layers of anger and stubborn pride, and I seize on it. My thumb brushes the corner of her jaw, tilting her face so she can't look away.

"We're all doing our best here," I say softer now. "You were too hard on him. Don't you agree, Angel?" She doesn't immediately answer, too wrapped up in the way my fingers trail downwards, ghosting the fabric pulled tight over her breasts. Her body shudders beneath me, every nerve alight with anticipation. Finally, she nods.

"Good girl," I rasp before crushing my mouth to hers.

Avery instantly falls victim to our fierce clash of teeth and tongue, of pent-up anger and raw, unfiltered desire. Never in my wildest dreams did I think I'd be able to both calm and infuriate her like this, have her like putty in my hands. Gripping her hair, my body presses her harder against the wall. In return, she fists my T-shirt, yanking me closer and not letting go.

"Wyatt," she gasps against my mouth, but it's not a protest. It's a plea. She's finally surrendering. I growl low in my throat, gripping her hips to lift her. Those long, toned legs automatically wrap around my waist as I stride toward the weight bench. Lowering her down, I follow, my body caging hers, my lips never leaving hers.

Deft fingers sink into my hair, tugging sharply to open my mouth wider. Then her tongue is sweeping inside with the same possessive hunger I feel. I adjust her on the bench, ensuring she feels every inch of my cock pressing against her core. There's no denying our connection anymore, and there's no use being coy about craving it. Avery has let me in, and it's only fair that I do the same for her.

"Look at you," I murmur, pulling back just enough to meet her gaze. Her eyes are heavy-lidded, her lips swollen and parted, her chest rising and falling in frantic rhythm. "So desperate and willing." I let my thumb brush the underside of her sports bra, teasing her and watching her shudder. "If I'd known I was doing you such a service, I wouldn't have let you beat on Huxley for so long."

Her glare is weak at best, out of habit rather than heat, but I don't give her a chance to retort. My hands slide beneath her shirt, her skin hot and smooth under my palms. Her back arches, pressing her tighter against me, and I drink in the sound she makes, a desperate little gasp that goes straight to my cock.

I dip my head, dragging my teeth along her neck, pausing to suck and bite until those hands in my hair are tugging harder. She moans over and over, each one spurring me on, driving me deeper into the haze of this need that demands to be fulfilled. Now that I've started to learn Avery's body, I can't stop. I can't take back the scratch marks imprinted in my back or unhear the way she cries my name when she clenches around me. There's no going back.

I lift my face from her neck, swallowing to get a handle on myself. Focus Wyatt. Lesson first, reward after. Withdrawing my mouth, hands, and body from Avery, she blinks up through her haze, the image of wanton desire. I wish I could freeze-frame her like this, chest heaving and reaching for me. Gripping her thighs, I spin her around, steadying her with a flat back on the center of her back.

Avery gasps when I tug down her panties and leggings, leaving them coiled around her knees. She's in prime position, bent over and bared to me. I inhale her sweet scent, my mouth going dry. My hands roam over her hips and ass, gripping and kneading, occasionally skating my fingertips over her cunt.

"I can't believe I resisted this for so long," I mutter to myself, letting my hunger bleed into every stroke, every squeeze. She's stunning when she's being submissive.

"Yeah, you truly deserve a medal," Avery grunts, and I swear I can hear her eyes roll. My cock twitches. Scratch that, she's irresistible when she's being a fucking brat.

The sharp sting of my palm meeting her ass is immediate, and the yelp she lets out is music to my ears. I deliver another spank, this one harder and faster. Her shocked cry is infused with a moan, doing unknown things to me. Being with her, pleasuring her, short-circuits my brain. She wipes anyone who came before from existence, erases the rest of the world, and leaves me reeling. It's just us and the feel of my palm soothing her reddened skin. When my fingers dip back towards her center, my brows shoot up, and I bite down on my free fist to hold back a groan.

"Soaking wet for me already?" I taunt, my voice thick with satisfaction as I tease my fingers through her slick heat, circling her clit with slow, deliberate movements. Her hips rise instinctively to meet my touch, a silent plea for more, and the way her body responds so openly makes a tremor run through me.

"I'm always wet for you, Wyatt," Avery breathes, igniting something primal inside me. I wanted to resist, to make this last, but her soft moans filling the gym give my fingers a life of their own.

Pushing inside of her, I become enthralled by her tightness all over again. My free hand braces on her thigh, holding her wide open for me as I thrust deeper, curling my fingers to hit that perfect spot. Her back arches, her hands clutching at the bench, nails biting into the leather. She's pure fire in my hands, and I can feel her unraveling with every movement.

Her soft, broken moans reverberate throughout the empty gym, filling the space and wrapping around me. I cannot resist her, especially when she's like this.

"Fuck it." I pull my fingers back, earning a whimper of protest, until I sink down and thrust my tongue into her. A muffled groan escapes me at her irresistible taste. The sound is raw, feral, and she answers with a moan that leaves me undone. I grip her cheeks wide, spreading her for me. Swirling my tongue, I drag the wetness out of her, the taste both intoxicating and addictive.

Avery cries out. Holding her steady, my tongue flicks and circles, teasing her clit before diving back into her heat. Her thighs tremble around my head.

"Wyatt, please. I—" she mumbles. "I want you to fuck me." I laugh against her cunt; the vibration causes her to shudder again. I glance across the room, catching sight of her in the mirror. Her flushed face, her eyes rolled back, her lips parted in ecstasy. The sight is enough to make me ache, and I press my tongue harder against her, determined to drive her higher.

She starts to tighten around my tongue and the fingers that have rejoined the party, slowly fucking her into the abyss. Her hips are bucking, and suddenly, she's coming undone around me. Even then, I don't stop. I devour her, piece by piece. Tear her apart with pleasure until her cries echo through the gym, and I feel her release flood over me, her body quaking.

I rise, wiping my mouth with the back of my hand, my chest heaving as I watch her. She looks utterly wrecked, her hair wild, her lips swollen, her eyes glazed over with satisfaction.

"Look at you," I murmur, rounding her side to lean in and brush my lips against hers, letting her taste herself on me. "Completely ruined for anyone else." Through her glassy stare and her pinkened lips, Avery slowly comes back to herself. A slow, small smile carves across her face.

"Garrett does it better." A shock of laughter bursts out of me. Damn her, but her insolence just serves to make my dick that much harder.

Gripping her jaw, I drag her from the bench whilst tugging at my shorts. Freeing myself, Avery's eyes widen greedily, but I jerk her up to face me at the last second.

"No teeth," I growl just before I feed her my cock.

CHAPTER THIRTY ONE

The water glistens like molten glass, only broken by the steady rhythm of Huxley's arms slicing through the surface. Stroke after stroke, he moves with precision, his body cutting through the pool as though he's trying to outrun something invisible. Something I implanted into his head. He's been at this for a while. Long enough that his muscles must be screaming, but he doesn't stop. He doesn't even pause. The water surges around him, each lap more determined than the last.

I watch from the shadowed edge, my arms wrapped tightly around myself, my nails digging into my sleeves. I did this to him. Filled him with shame because I couldn't face my own fear. I ran from it, hid from it beneath layers of misdirected anger. The images of last night are still burned into my mind. The auction, the Lots, the way Sharon laughed and paraded them like trophies. And Huxley becoming entangled in it.

I squeeze my arms tighter around myself. I came to the underground pool room in search for him, needing to offer the apology that Wyatt rightly instructed me to give. But the longer Hux swims, the more I feel like I'm intruding. Maybe it would be better to wait until later, once he's worked through his thoughts, but I can't leave. Not after the way I yelled at him, the way I let my anger take over when all he was trying to do was help.

Hux reaches the end of the pool, flips effortlessly, and pushes off the wall for another lap. His body is a blur of motion, his muscles taut under the sheen of water. Every movement is deliberate and controlled, yet I see the cracks. The desperation in the way he powers forward, the way his strokes become just a fraction less fluid as exhaustion creeps in.

He's running himself into the ground.

Kicking off my sneakers, I pull down my leggings and tug the sweater over my head. Wyatt's cum is still seeping out of me, soaking through my knickers. I leave them and my sports bra in place and slowly step into the pool as if Hux might suddenly sense my presence. He remains oblivious as I descend the side steps, lowering myself to sit in the warm water and draw my knees up to my chest. Huxley doesn't notice. He's too consumed by whatever storm is raging inside him, too focused on the next stroke, the next lap. The water laps gently against my shoulders, my chin resting on my knees.

Huxley was right to find solace down here. There's a peacefulness within the whitewashed walls, a simplicity that helps to forget about the mansion upstairs. Fluorescent bulbs make up for the lack of windows, chlorine, and cleaning products tainting the air. Alongside one wall, there's a wooden bench, a few towel hooks, and that's it. One door permits entry via a staircase just beyond, another remains tightly closed and presumably locked.

Water ripples around my body in a small wave, the clash on movement recentering my focus. At the far end of the pool, Hux dips beneath the water to spin and push himself off the wall to lap back towards me. His movements are slower now and less refined. He's slapping the water rather than gliding through it, an obvious tension in his shoulders. He begins to falter ever so slightly, his body giving out, but his mind refuses to stop.

"Hux?" I finally say, my voice barely louder than a whisper, swallowed up by the soft echo of water against tile. I try again, louder this time. "Huxley?" He hesitates mid-stroke, his head turning toward the sound of my voice. Our eyes connect, and everything I wanted to say goes straight out of my head.

For a moment, he just treads water, his chest heaving as he takes me in. Droplets cling to his hair and his eyelashes before they slide down his face like tiny rivers. He doesn't say anything, working hard to regulate his breathing to an even pace. I hug my knees tighter, searching for the resolve I came in here with. After what feels like forever, Hux swims over me, his strokes lazier now, until he's close enough to sit on the ledge beside me.

Pressing my lips together, I watch the water shifting around us. My cheeks feel hot, my ears prickling under the weight of his stare. I know I'm in the wrong and that I need to apologize, but saying sorry doesn't feel like enough. Hux nudges closer, bumping my shoulder.

"This is a new look I haven't seen on you before. What is it?" He leans forward, cocking his head and studying me. The blush on my cheeks turns to an inferno.

"I'm... embarrassed." I scrunch my eyes shut. Suddenly, large hands spin my legs, dislodging my arms banded around them. I fall clumsily against Huxley's front, forced to look up at his smug expression.

"What are you embarrassed about, Swan?"

I toy with my tongue between my teeth before speaking quietly.

"That Wyatt had to reprimand me."

Huxley's entire face lights up, a smile breaking free and his eyebrows rising.

"Embarrassed?" he chuckles to himself. "That sounds mortifying." I laugh too, relieved to have the rigid atmosphere burst wide open. I finally feel like I can breathe again, straightening my spine and squaring my shoulders. Offering his hand, Hux waits for me to accept it before pulling me into the safety of his body. His chin is on my head, his biceps caging me in. "Take me through what's happening in that beautiful mind of yours."

"That I love you." Hux's arms tense, his entire body going stiff beneath me as he inhales sharply. It isn't the apology he was expecting, but it's the truth, so I keep going with that. "I know it's unfair to hold you each to a different standard, and if Garrett had offered himself up last night, I wouldn't have been so angry. Actually, I probably would have expected it, and I'd have rolled my eyes and cursed him out in the morning." I wriggle free to look into Hux's patient brown eyes.

"But with you, you've worked so hard to build yourself back up after the shooting. Both physically and mentally, and when you offered yourself up last night... I wasn't upset. I was terrified. I saw you at Warren's table, offering yourself up like it didn't matter, like you didn't matter, and it... it broke something in me. The lengths you'll go to protect me and to save Meg," I shake my head, my throat tightening.

"I'm terrified that I'm going to lose you again in the process. Every way that I picture us getting out of this situation, I lose someone. And instead of dealing with that, I lashed out at you. I made you feel guilty when you were just trying to protect me. I'm truly sorry."

Hux's expression shifts, a flicker of pain crossing his face before he looks away, his gaze dropping to the water.

"I wasn't only trying to protect you," he says quietly. "I was trying to do something, anything, because I felt so fucking useless just sitting there while Sharon paraded those kids around like cattle. The whole game she's playing, the money she's making, and they're all encouraging her. Every single person in that room. I'd kinda hoped by attending the auction, we'd see a way to shut it down for Axel's sanity. So that he can finally move on. But it was apparent there's no stopping her, and that was eating me alive."

The raw honesty in his voice cuts through me like a knife, and I reach up to push his wet hair back from his sharp jawline.

"You're not useless, Hux," I say, staring into his eyes so he might actually hear me. "You've never been useless. You've always been the one who holds the Souls together without them even realizing it. Wyatt might be the leader, but you silently protect them all. And now, you're doing it for me and Meg too."

"You shouldn't put me on a pedestal, Swan. I'm just... me," he exhales sharply, dragging a hand through his wet hair. I raise a brow and tilt my lips. Exactly. He's just Huxley, and that's all anyone needs him to be. "I just wanted to make it stop. All of it. I thought if I put myself out there, maybe I could get some sort of win for us. I'd sacrifice anything for you."

His sentiment strikes my heart, smashing through my reserves. I'm not going to be able to explain to Hux just how incredible he is today, not when I've spent the morning bringing him down. I hate myself for that, but he's still here. Right here in front of me, so I start with pushing up and touching my lips to his.

Huxley lets out a quiet breath, his shoulders relaxing for the first time since I walked in. He holds me like I'm delicate, his mouth slanting across mine. He tastes like chlorine, a metallic hint twinged with salt. The water around us stills, the strain easing with it. The knot in my chest loosens just a little, and I pull back with a faint smile.

"I love you," I say again, making sure he sees and hears my sincerity this time. His chocolate brown gaze flicks between my eyes, searching for something. Reassurance, maybe. I brush my thumbs over his cheeks, feeling the weight of his head push against my palms. His lips part, ready to return the sentiment.

"Cannonball!" A yell slices through the quiet, reverberating off the tiled walls.

"Garrett, don't you dare—" Hux shouts. But it's already too late. Garrett has launched himself into the air, tucked into a ball. Hux throws up a futile arm, but the impact sends a massive wave crashing toward us, soaking my hair, face, and even the dry steps behind me. I gasp, sputtering as I wipe water from my eyes, my laughter bubbling up despite myself.

"Now that's how you make an entrance!" Garrett cheers triumphantly, grinning like a mischievous child as he shakes water out of his messy, dark hair like a wet dog. A black T-shirt clings to his broad chest, and his boxers fluorescent neon green flash beneath the surface.

"For the record," Dax says smoothly as he steps into the pool area, settling on the step behind me, "I did try to convince him to wait until you two were done with your moment."

Despite Hux's arms wrapped around my waist, Dax casually kneads my shoulders, one more firmly than the other. I gasp, twisting to see that both of his hands are on me rather than just one. "Doc Marcus approved me for no more bandages. I just have to be careful." He gives me a small wiggle of his fingers. I can't help my beaming smile at the relief that one of our issues has finally worked itself out.

Oblivious to the joy Dax and I are currently sharing, Garrett hollers across the pool. "Freezing my nuts off on the stairs while these two eye-fuck each other? Not my idea of a Saturday night!" He dips beneath the water, the outline of his silhouette gracefully gliding through the water to resurface at the base of the stairs. His dark eyes dazzle with mischief.

"You're insufferable," Hux mutters, although his annoyance is tainted by a trickle of humor. Like me, he's probably thinking it's nice to have the old Garrett back for a little while, although Hux would never admit to such a thing. Garrett kneels on the lowest step for his shoulders to leave the water and plants a hand on his chest.

"Me?! You guys are the ones who didn't invite us to your pool party.

I found Dax moping around the kitchen, eating peanut butter straight out of the jar."

"That was you," Dax deadpans. "I was doing recon with Thiago on the other party guests."

"Exactly. We all needed a break," Garrett flips onto his back and floats, spreading his arms wide like a starfish. Dax's tentative hands leave my shoulders to pull my soaking hair back and tie it in a ponytail for me.

"Wait," I frown, "who's with Axel?" Garrett rolls his head my way, only one ear out of the water.

"Wyatt's on the graveyard shift." Garrett drawls lazily, waving a hand back and forth in the air. I gasp, looking to Dax for clarity.

"Axel's asleep, and yeah, Wyatt's with him." The tremor in my chest settles, but I twist back, sharply splashing water at Garrett with as much force as I can muster. The wave hits him square in the face, but he only laughs harder, spitting water like a fountain.

"Don't call it that!" I narrow my eyes. Given just how serious Axel's injuries were, I won't be accepting death jokes anytime soon. Garrett doesn't care either way, his grin splitting all the way across his face.

"Or what, Peach?" Garrett flips onto his stomach and paddles toward me like a crocodile stalking its prey. I let him do his taunting until he's close enough that I launch myself out of Huxley's hold and shove Garrett's head beneath the water. I hold him there for only a second, knowing I don't have the strength to beat him, but I do have the agility to escape.

Pushing through the water, I propel myself by sheer force to reach the other side of the pool. If I can just reach the side, I'll shoot up onto the edge and be gone before Garrett's even recovered. But I don't make it more than a foot away from him.

Hands grab my ankles, dragging me backward. I twist my body to fight against it, kicking wildly within the water. Garrett's grip is relentless, but I manage to wriggle free for a moment, only to be caught again, his laughter vibrating through the water as he drags me closer.

Breaching the surface, I only manage to gasp a singular breath down before Garrett's back on me, his arms around my middle. He drags me to the bottom, taking every rogue elbow and missed kick. Spinning me around, he winds his legs around my waist and grabs my face in his hands. A few precious air bubbles leak from my lips just before his mouth crashes against mine. I still, no longer fighting but finding myself kissing back. Although I won't last much longer without air.

Wrenching back, I tap Garrett's shoulder insistently and point to the surface. His dark eyes flick upwards, his hair floating around him like a black halo. He uses his grip on my face to drag me back to him. His mouth covers mine, and as Garrett brings his hands forward to squeeze my cheeks, he breathes into my parted lips. I inhale him all the way into my lungs, and his satisfied smile is everything. Without the jokes and the stress of the world above, I feel like I'm seeing Garrett's true self, and it's surprisingly calming.

Unwrapping his legs from my waist and replacing them with his arms, Garrett kicks off the floor and propels us to the surface. I come up sputtering, my hair plastered to my face, but Garrett is already retreating, his arms slicing through the water as he swims away as if nothing happened. Or perhaps he has another prey in mind now.

Garrett turns his attention to Huxley, who is already launching himself at Garrett like a torpedo, knocking them both under. Garrett resurfaces almost instantly, but before he can retaliate, a cascade of water smacks him square in the face. One that came from Dax's stronger hand. The pool explodes into chaos.

I use the distraction to dart away, but apparently, I'm not safe from anyone. Dax is already on the move, closing in with a mischievous grin. Before I can make it to the edge, he uses his good arm to collect water and send it crashing towards me. I retaliate, cupping water in my hands and flinging it back at him. Totally pointless, considering we're all soaking and flinging ourselves around the pool in our underwear, but we dissolve into laughter regardless. Water and curses fly all around whilst Hux and Garrett are busy trying to drown each other, and Dax descends on me.

"I thought you were supposed to be taking it easy!" I yell, still splashing regardless. Dax chuckles.

"I am," he confirms by only using his stronger hand to splash and keeping the other one firmly beneath the water. I relax and let the smile grow once more.

For a fraction of time, there are no worries, no whispers of the outside world. I indulge in the chaos, reveling in it. Eventually, Dax leans against the side of the pool, having exhausted himself. Garrett swims to the edge, planting his hands firmly on the tile to hoist himself out of the water. The movement is so effortless. Water drips from him, pooling at his feet as he quickly wraps his top half in a towel.

"Okay, I admit that was long overdue." Dax chuckles softly.

"I aim to please," Garrett quips, using two fingers to give Dax a salute.

Huxley mutters something that sounds suspiciously like *'aim for silence instead'* before splashing Garrett one last time, setting off a ripple of laughter that echoes through the pool room. Gare offers Dax his hand and hoists him out of the water, helping to pin a towel around Dax's waist. It's a simple gesture, and yet my heart is fit to explode from the sentiment. These wonderful boys have been looking after each other long before they started looking after me.

Before I can head out too, Huxley catches my waist. It's all too easy to move me in the water, gliding me wherever his large hands see fit. Right now, it's against his expansive chest. His smile softens, and he leans in close enough to murmur in my ear.

"I love you too, Swan," he answers finally, barely more than a whisper but full of quiet certainty. I press my forehead to his, letting the world shrink down to just the two of us, the gentle sway of the water around us mirroring the steady rhythm of my heart.

My eyes sting, and at long last, the tears that well up in them are for a good reason. Because this introverted girl who was scared to let anyone in will never be alone again. I have a team of men ready to fight and die for me, to do whatever it takes to bring my twin home. This is what love feels like. It's messy and imperfect, yet so achingly beautiful that I wouldn't have it any other way.

CHAPTER THIRTY TWO

I should've known Thiago couldn't be trusted with an audience. I left Avery alone in the library for not even twenty minutes, grabbing us some snacks from the kitchen. In one aspect, we have the run of the mansion around Sharon's many outings, whether it be business meetings or shopping trips she's using to occupy her time. I suspect if it weren't for our presence, she'd be home more often. Garrett and Wyatt cross my path, heading to the gym for another round of sparring. Hux is currently helping Axel with some gentle physio under the watchful eye of Dr. Marcus.

Tray in one hand, I stumble back through the library doors, drawn in by Avery's laughter. Such a sweet, pure sound that I didn't realize I'd been missing until it filtered through the hallways. She's exactly where I left her, curled up on the library's velvet sofa, her legs tucked under her. The book she was previously reading is now on her thigh, forgotten about in favor of giggling at whatever story my dear cousin is currently butchering. Her eyes light up even more when she sees me, not even trying to hide her amusement.

"Speak of the devil," Thiago sniggers, lounging in an oversized armchair across from Avery, arms spread wide like a king telling war stories. "Were your ears burning? I was just telling your girl about that summer we decided to start our own side hustle."

"Welcome back," Avery grins mischievously, patting the cushion beside her. I place the tray on the low coffee table, smacking Thiago's hand away when he tries to reach for a churro. The set-up of dunking chocolate and caramel seems much less romantic with my cousin leering over it. I cautiously sit, reclining back with a sinking feeling in my chest. Of all the things I wanted Avery to know about me, none of them will include whatever Thiago must be recounting.

"Apparently, you fancied yourself as quite the entrepreneur." Avery bobs her eyebrows. She curls into me on instinct, pushing her sock-clad feet beneath my thigh. I force a smile, swallowing past the lump in my throat. Trust Avery to put a spin on everything to put me in a positive light. My memory is more jaded by a pair of hungry children who scammed people to help put food on the table. Like me, Thiago was the man of his household, even at the ripe age of eleven.

"We were con artists. Although geniuses might be a more appropriate description." Thiago chuckles, remembering our past much more favorably.

"Well, come on then, someone needs to spill." Avery looks between the two of us, but her stare lingers on me for a beat longer. I let out a weighted sigh, tracing absent circles on the inside of Avery's wrist. I remind myself to get her bracelet back from Axel at some point.

"We'd steal empty spray bottles from the convenience store, fill them with tap water, slap a label on them that said holy water, and sell them outside the church." Avery's mouth drops open as she stares at me wide-eyed.

"No."

"Oh yes," Thiago grins. Suddenly, she's laughing again, a breathless sound that rattles through her whole frame. "Dax, that's so bad." Despite her accusation, her body is warm and soft where she leans against me, squeezing my knee with little touches of acceptance. My past isn't something I bring up often since there are not many happy memories to reflect on, and in her own small way, Avery is reassuring me that her opinion won't change.

"We were providing a service," I argue, letting a smirk shine through. "People were desperate for that holy water." Thiago snorts.

"They wanted to bless their homes, not to spray their furniture with whatever came out of the gas station tap." Avery gasps and tilts her head, delight sparkling in her blue eyes.

"How did you not get caught?"

Thiago leans forward, elbows on his knees, as he sneaks a churro after all. "Oh, we did. One of the older ladies caught on when her home started smelling like a sewer. She tried to kill us with her cane." I pinch the bridge of my nose, my cheeks burning.

"She nearly took my arm off, and her tiny dog held a grudge. Chased us every time we walked past."

"I never understood how that damn chihuahua managed to escape that fence every single time." Thiago takes a bite of his food. Reaching down, he lifts the leg of his jeans to reveal the tiny scars peppering his ankles. "That yappy little demon needs holy water more than anything. How come it never seemed to bite you?" It's my turn to grunt this time.

"I was faster."

Thiago chuckles, shaking his head. "Didn't stop your screaming, though. The dog was barking, you were screaming, and I swear, the whole neighborhood was watching." Avery loses it, her head dropping back on the sofa. She grips my arm as she laughs, a full-bodied sound I can't help but mimic. It was stupid of me to think anything Avery heard in this room would matter. She loves me for who I am now, not the toerag I once was. Her words are broken, heaved out between her hysterics.

"I cannot picture you two menaces running from an angry old lady and her dog."

"Her demon," Thiago corrects, holding up his index finger. Avery shakes her head and wipes at her eyes, still giggling. My cousin's pale eyes are alight with amusement, reveling in the way Avery is responding to his stories. Another feeling that is neither distress nor humor arises, that lump in my throat subsiding.

"Oh, there's plenty more where that came from, Querida." Thiago smirks at me, knowing exactly what he's doing. I narrow my eyes, my jaw tensing. "There was the time we headed to the docks and offered to wash the boats for cheap."

"That's enough of that," I interject, sitting forward. Avery's legs are dislodged, and she's forced to straighten, but I'm too focused on removing the tray from Thiago's reach. "Don't you have some work to be doing?"

"Aww, don't be a grouch, Dax," Avery pouts, her hands on my

shoulders. "I could listen to this all day." I give her a side glance, assessing her wicked smile. I know she could, and that's the problem.

"I'd rather you were kissing me all day," I return her grin. She seems to like that idea, and Thiago huffs, just like I knew he would.

"Fine, be boring love birds. I'll just go back to my hole," Thiago stands. I feel a small pang of guilt until he snatches the tray from my hands. "And I'm taking this with me." I let him go, deciding to pull him up for his shit-stirring later. As he slips between the polished mahogany shelves towering around us, seemingly going back to looking for whatever book brought him in here, I turn into Avery's waiting hug.

Her arms slide around my neck as I sink into her embrace, my fragile fingers pressing into the small of her back. They throb slightly but I don't retract them, too wrapped up in finally being about to hold my girl properly again. Avery is still warm with laughter, her breath light against my jaw as she tilts her head up, blue eyes bright and searching. I don't hesitate. I cup her cheek, letting my thumb trace the soft curve of her cheek before leaning in, brushing my lips over hers in a slow, deliberate kiss. Avery sighs against my mouth, her fingers threading through my hair as she angles herself closer, her chest pressing against mine.

The library around us fades, the scent of aged books and the scuffing of Thiago's sneakers melting away. I inhale Avery's vanilla scent, drawing her deep into my lungs and further into my heart. I crave these moments when we're alone, when she gets to be solely mine.

Her hands slip lower, gripping the fabric of my shirt like she never wants to let go either, and I groan against her mouth, pulling her onto my lap. She moves easily, her thighs framing mine, her weight settling onto me. The velvet of the sofa is soft beneath us, but it's nothing compared to the silk of her skin as my palm skims up her spine, drawing shivers in its wake. I press a trail of kisses along her jaw, down the column of her throat, relishing the way she tilts her head back to give me more.

"I've always loved you," I murmur as my lips brush over her pulse. "Even before I knew you."

"I'm all yours, Dax," Avery sighs against me. Our mouths collide again and again, the speed of my pulse increasing. I could have Avery like this forever and never tire of her lips, her body or her mind. She's beautiful in every possible way.

Pushing against my chest so I'm forced to lie back and look up at her, Avery tilts her brow over her large, curious eyes. "What does querida mean?" My hands clench on her waist automatically, a sudden pain shooting up my fingers but I manage to ignore it.

"Something my cousin shouldn't be calling you." I raise my hips to grind against her, tightening my hold. Avery doesn't miss the move, my jealousy reigniting something in her blue gaze. Her smile is full of trouble, disappearing as she leans in to lick a path across my throat.

"You don't call me pet names in Portuguese," she nibbles my earlobe. A choked sound escapes my lips, punctuated by my hips snapping again to push my hardening cock against her center.

"Are you complaining?" I turn my head, capturing her lips bruisingly this time. Where I usually provide gentle strokes, my hands grip Avery's thighs in a demanding hold, dragging her along my length. She meets each roll of my hips, rubbing my shaft through my sweatpants, creating a weeping mess in my boxers. Tremors roll down my arms as I hold back, reminding myself that I'm not this type of man for her. She has enough egotistical assholes to deal with.

Pulling back, I breathe a few times, forcing myself to fill the heated silence. "Thi and his mom came to the US much later, so she only spoke Portuguese with him at home. I was born here, and my mom wanted me to be more Westernized. She was worried about me fitting in, so we made an effort to always speak in English."

Avery nods, and although I know she was only teasing, she looks at me with fresh eyes. I let her explore my face with her gaze and her hands, happy to give her the time to work through whatever is going on in her beautiful mind. Perhaps Thiago has given her a new opinion of me, but she's still here. Still smiling at me as if I'm special.

"What are you thinking?" I ask, trailing my fingers over her thighs. Avery chews on her lip, contemplating her answer.

"You've never needed anything from me."

"I need many things from you, Swan. And you provide them all." I reply instantly. Reaching up, I curl a hand around her nape, and she melts into my touch. There's a small shake of her head, dislodging the hair from behind her ears.

"No, not like the others. You haven't needed help to heal with anything." I smile at this. It's in Avery's nature to help people, to feel the need to fix them. Tugging her closer, I let our breath mingle and lips toy with each other.

"I made peace with my demons a long time ago. I know who I am and what I have to give you. It's not money or muscle, but I'm pretty sure it's something you crave. Love and care, my complete understanding and attention."

"That's all I want," Avery breathes. Our mouths crash together, a merging of passion and promise. Since the day I met Avery, I've never faltered in my feelings or needed clarity. She's the epitome of everything my mom raised me to look for in a partner, and who she helped to prepare me for.

Avery's tongue skates over mine as a sharp knock sounds at the open door. We both look aside, although I'm half expecting Thiago to be there, creating a diversion before he ducks out. Instead, the elderly butler is standing in his usual black and white uniform, his eyes strictly on the bookshelves ahead.

"Your presence is required in the dining hall this evening. Dinner will be served at seven sharp. Formal dress is compulsory."

Avery exhales harshly against my lips, her fingers still tangled in my hair as she pulls back just enough to glance at the butler. I sense she's about to say something unsavory, but she doesn't get the chance. The butler turns on his heel, his expression unreadable as he leaves.

Avery shifts in my lap, trailing her hands down my arms before she sighs. "Guess we will have to revisit this later." I nod, rubbing circles over her hip before reluctantly letting her slide off me. Our bodies are a far cry from the languid state we were just in, our spines and shoulders stiff. I smooth a hand around Avery's waist, keeping her close as we storm into the hallway, colliding with a pair of very sweaty figures.

Wyatt and Garrett are scowling, their jaws set and their shirts damp with sweat. Wyatt is stretching his shoulder, his green eyes sharpening when they land on Avery before flicking to me. Garrett, as always, is the first to speak.

"The only thing that would lighten my mood right now is finding out the butler walked in on the two of you fucking over the fairy fiction." He slings an arm over Avery's shoulders. She rolls her eyes but doesn't shake him off.

"Sharon doesn't have a section specifically for fairy porn," I mutter, mostly to myself.

Wyatt's gaze flickers between us before he exhales, rubbing his knuckles over his jaw. "We're being bossed around for dinners now?"

"We're not doing anything until we've spoken to Axel," Avery grits out. Those recent smiles are nowhere to be seen, tension holding her painfully rigid.

Wyatt nods, and the four of us move through the sprawling hallways of the mansion, a heavy silence pressing in. When we reach Axel's door, I knock once before pushing it open. Inside, Axel is perched on the edge of his bed, stretching his arm in slow, measured movements under Huxley's watchful eye. The Doc isn't present anymore, but the room smells faintly of antiseptic and a trace of his cologne. Axel glances up, a furrow forming between his brows.

"What's wrong?"

"The butler called for a formal dinner tonight," Avery explains. "Has anything been said to you?" Axel and Huxley shake their heads, but Wyatt strides forward, his sharp eyes catching something on the bedside table. Sitting neatly beside the lamp is a thick envelope embossed with a dark wax seal. After giving Hux a curious look and receiving a shrug in response, Wyatt reaches for it cautiously. He slides a card out, quickly scanning the words on its surface. A sigh deflates his chest, his eyes lifting to the ceiling.

"This isn't from Sharon," he growls. I cross the room in time with Garrett and Avery, leaning forward to read the name scrawled across the bottom in an elegant, practiced hand. Richard Barrett. Gare snorts, swiping the card from Wyatt's hand.

"What a cockwaffle. As if we're going to attend a dinner hosted by the she-devil's husband. Did he really think—"

"I'm going," Axel says all of a sudden. The atmosphere in the room turns glacial, as if any breath harsh enough could shatter it. We're all staring at Axel, our eyes bugging out of our heads, but he's not looking. His focus is on his feet, his fingers flexing and unflexing against his thighs like he's trying to bring himself back to the room.

"Axe," Wyatt starts, voice low with warning.

"I'm going," Axel repeats, firmer this time. He finally looks up, his haunted, hazel eyes stern and resolute. "If Richard wants to see us, there's a reason. I want to hear what it is." Avery shakes her head, folding her arms.

"You don't owe him anything."

"I know," Axel nods. "But I want to see this through anyway. I don't expect you to understand."

"Well, that's good news," Garrett scoffs sarcastically, tossing the card onto the bed like it's tainted. "Because I really don't."

I open my mouth to tell Axel this is a terrible idea. But I see the way his hands won't stay still, how his jaw clenches like he's bracing himself for the inevitable blowback. He's thought about this. He knows how we'll react. And he still stands firm.

For a moment, only silence follows. The weight of Axel's decision settles over us like a thick, suffocating fog. Everything we've been on high alert for, everything we've wanted to protect him from, could be undone in this one evening. But Axel has so many demons within these walls, and I promised to do whatever I can to alleviate his struggle of being here. I have to trust he has his reasons without needing an explanation. Exhaling sharply, I rake a hand through my overgrown hair as I nod.

"If you want to go, Axe, then we go," I say simply. Avery's lips press into a thin line, Wyatt clenches his jaw, and Hux stares out the window, but no one argues. And maybe that's the most significant sign of all. Even though none of us understand Axe's choice, we still won't let him face it alone.

AXEL

"You really don't have to do this," Garrett tells me for the seventh time. I wince, pulling a white shirt over my shoulder and tugging the material across my chest.

"So you've said," I grumble. When I struggle to both hold the shirt closed and fasten the buttons, Gare steps in and lightly smacks my hands away.

"Then why are you?" He huffs, buttoning my shirt to the bottom. Then, he bends to help me step into my slacks and pulls them up my legs, fastening the clasp a little too roughly. I slowly lower onto the bed, feeling the energy already draining out of me.

"Can I ask you a question first?" I hang my shaven head, working on getting my breath back. "Why have you never gone to visit your parents?" Gare's dress shoes, which were pacing before me, come to a sudden halt. When he speaks, his voice holds no familiarity. Only pain and loathing.

"They don't deserve any effort on my part. They failed me. It's my job to survive them, not to console them."

"And if they were right here, continuing their lives like you were just a minor inconvenience?" I query. It's different for Garrett; his parents are serving time for neglect. They're actually being punished. From my standpoint, Sharon is being encouraged. I lick my cracked lips, continuing to stare at the untied laces of his shoes.

"You wouldn't want to look them in the eye and finally tell them how you felt? I've dreamt for years what I might say to Sharon if I got the chance, how I might be able to put the past behind me at long last."

"And if it only brings everything back up, undoing all of our hard work. What then?"

"Garrett, the things I was subjected to in this house, in this room, they aren't going away. No matter the distance. I'm not getting over it." Gare exhales sharply through his nose, kneeling before me. His fingers curl into fists on my thighs, and I watch the way his jaw tightens, the way his lips press into a thin line like he's fighting against something that can't be put into words. I've rarely seen him so conflicted, a storm of fury swirling in his bottomless eyes.

"I don't want to turn this around on me, Axe. I know this is your trauma to bear. But I'm the one that holds you sobbing at night, who lets you fuck me when you need something else to focus on. I've taken you to counseling, and there was that semester we tried art therapy together." Garrett looks away to clear his throat.

Usually, he'd make a quip about us sneaking into the art cupboard when the therapist was distracted by others to paint a piece of art all over my face with his cum. Not today, though. Today, Garrett appears solemn, and my chest aches from the sight.

"On occasion, handling your pain has been so much, I've needed to step away and drink myself unconscious, sometimes to fall into bed with the nearest person just to get away from it. I'm not that selfish asshole anymore, and I'll always be here for you, but it's not... it's not just you who feels the effects of your nightmares."

"I didn't realize I was affecting you so much," I frown, leaning away from him. I get a direct shot of pain up my side, and Gare rocks forward, gripping my thighs tighter.

"No, no. That's not what I'm saying. Can't you see that I've always loved you? I've always cared, so much that it kills me to see you hurting. I will do whatever it takes to keep you safe. I just want to make sure this is what you want." There's an edge to his voice. A plea disguised as frustration.

I let out a breath, tilting my head back. This room smells the same. Looks the same. Feels the same as when I was a boy. Spending every day here has started to soothe something in me. It's the one place I never would have returned to willingly, but maybe it's where I needed to be.

To remember the times I studied at my desk, made my paper mache solar system, and played my gaming console for hours. Those times when my dad would bring home a new Lego set and we'd spend all weekend building huge, complicated spaceships. I now recognize that he was avoiding Sharon too, so it made sense for us to avoid her together.

Being here has given me the time to rewrite the suffering.

Reaching out for Garrett, my fingers push through his messy hair, smoothing it away from his dark eyes. "Please see this through with me. Let me face the monster that haunts me. Since we're here anyway, I feel like I need to at least try."

Garrett watches me for a long moment, then scoffs under his breath. "If Richard so much as looks at you wrong, I'm putting his head through the table."

"I'd be disappointed if you didn't," I smirk. The ghost of a smile tugs at his lips too, but he doesn't respond any further. He just reaches for my tie, looping the silk around my collar with ease, his fingers lingering against my nape for half a second longer than necessary. His eyes flicker to my lips, indecision warring between his brows. I know what he's thinking. He could probably distract me by sucking my cock, just like he did in art therapy, but he doesn't try it.

Instead, Gare dresses me dutifully until Avery pokes her head around the door and announces the time. Ten minutes to seven, as preplanned to arrive just as the food is coming in and leave soon after. I leave the two of them to finish getting ready, waving off their concerns as I slowly make my way down the hallway.

The Souls mean well, but their help is becoming suffocating, and it's doing the opposite of what they intend. I need to build up my own strength instead of always relying on others, even if I stay close to the wall for extra support. My ribs throb, tugging with each step. I could handle my exterior aching, but the sharp burn of my chest anytime I move too much is debilitating. It's as if my own lungs are trying to starve me of oxygen, no matter how steadily I breathe.

Evans, the butler who's worked in this house since my father hired him decades ago, is waiting for us at the bottom of the staircase. Dax, Wyatt, and Huxley are already by his side, wearing the same suits they're using to attend the auctions. A sad smile pulls at my lips, thankful that they are following through with yet another one of my requests without the same inquisition that Garrett gave me.

Each one has taken their own passive aggressive stance against the dress code, though. Hux has used his tie to fix his hair back in a scruffy ponytail, Wyatt's shirt is only buttoned to above his navel, revealing the large dragon tattooed on his front, and Dax's sleeves are rolled up to the elbow, his jacket tucked through the crux of his elbow.

Wyatt meets me halfway up the stairs, carefully looping his arm around my waist. I lean into him, not realizing how hard I was gripping the banister. A few droplets of sweat have broken free across my forehead, but I make it to the bottom mostly unscathed.

"Come on, let's get this shitshow over with." I prompt, pushing forward to lead the way. Evans hurries to my side, unable to shake his role despite my lack of acknowledgment towards him. I haven't spoken a word to him since my mother started using me for her personal gain, and he decided his loyalty to me or my father didn't mean enough to do anything about it.

Dress shoes click loudly on the gleaming marble floor as we stroll to the left side of the mansion, every wall pristinely white with no homely additions in sight. No artwork, portraits, or photos. No evidence a complete family once lived here. Just a series of closed wooden doors that match the network of beams crisscrossing overhead and a cold emptiness that will always exist.

Evans rushes forward as we near a double doorway, rounded black iron doorknobs matching swirling decorations covering the timber. The dining room is usually reserved for clients and guests of high importance. He pushes the doors open one at a time, permitting us entry to a scene I've imagined a million times but never truly believed I'd see again.

Sharon sits at the end of the table, her posture perfect and a glass of red wine delicately cradled between her manicured fingers. Her painted lips are split into a wide smile, leering against her husband and laughing at some secret joke between the two. I welcome her distraction, allowing me to take in the scene without her immediate attention. A long mahogany table adorned with crystal glasses and silverware gleams under the chandelier's glow. The air is thick with the scent of something rich and savory, but it does nothing to curb the nausea rolling through my stomach.

Finding support in the Soul's steady eyes, I lower into a rigid dining chair with slow, careful movements. My ribs protest, but the discomfort is nothing compared to the weight pressing on my chest. I run a hand over my shirt, smoothing out imaginary creases. My palms are already damp.

Sharon laughs again, tilting her head in a telltale way that tells me she's been drinking since mid-afternoon at least. Still, her brown hair is swept into an elegant twist, her face as poised as ever. For a brief, foolish second, I think she won't address me at all. That she'll pretend I don't exist, the way she always has.

Then, her assessing gaze lifts and lands on me. There's no shock. No softening. No guilt. Just a slow, knowing smile.

"Axel." Her voice is as smooth as the silk napkins folded before each plate, concealing the hidden edge of sarcasm I know her to use. "I didn't think I'd see the day you finally came home." I notice Wyatt stiffening in the seat opposite me. Dax is by his side, offering his silent support with a hard, icy stare at Sharon. But she has yet to take her eyes off me.

"We both know I wouldn't be here if there was any other choice, and this isn't a home. It's a hellhole," I grit out. Sharon sighs dreamily and rolls her eyes.

"He did always have a flair for dramatics," she leans into her husband's side, grinning once again.

"Did someone say dramatics?" Garrett chooses that moment to enter the room, Avery on his arm. They separate to float towards the two seats either side of me as if they were attending any other casual dinner party. Garrett plants a kiss on my cheek, a playful gleam in his dark eyes. I see then that he's wearing his entire suit backwards. Avery has buttoned his shirt up his spine and knotted his tie high into the collar at his nape. I snort a laugh, which quickly becomes a hiss, knowing that reverse stitching of his pants can't be comfortable. But he's doing it anyway.

Avery looks like the Queen of Minxes this evening. Her dress is basically a slip of negligée. Black lace cups her rounded breasts perfectly, the flowing skirt reaching the top of her thighs. Paired with towering heels, she's twisted her long, golden hair up and secured it with a large claw clip. All eyes at the table feast on her hungrily, Sharon no doubt seeing dollar signs, whereas her husband is openly leering. For that reason only, I move the conversation along swiftly.

"Richard, is it?" I raise a brow. The man in question snaps his jaw shut and straightens, tugging on the cuffs at his wrists.

"Indeed. Thank you for attending this evening, Axel. I've heard so much about you." I purse my lips together, but it's Garrett who leans his elbows on the table and tilts his head dreamily.

"So this is a bonding session rather than a dinner? I do hope there will still be food." Richard ignores him, his beady eyes trained on me.

"I merely wanted to meet you, since the opportunity has presented itself. Although it's apparent you don't go anywhere without your entourage." Richard gives the other guests a sweeping glance around the table. "But that's understandable. It is best we all become acquainted properly, given that we'll be living together for a while."

"Not if I can help it," Wyatt growls low. Noticing Richard's confused glance, Wyatt straightens and clasps his hands before him. "I will ensure Axel is out of here as soon as he is able to return home."

"You mean that little academy of yours?" Sharon's lip curls, clutching her wine glass and swaying drunkenly. "A waste of time if you ask me."

"Luckily, no one asked you." Huxley's nostrils flare.

Avery flicks out a napkin and covers her thighs with it. "And you don't need to know the whereabouts. Axel's home is wherever we are." I bite back a smile at everyone's readiness to defend me. Even Dax, who is known for sitting back and assessing, is watching me closely, searching for any sign that I might crumble before the starters are served.

The waiters enter right on cue, half of which place the plates, and the others carry trays with flutes of champagne bubbling gently. It isn't lost on me how there are no females amongst them, whether for Sharon's or Richard's benefit; I can't be sure. Garrett immediately reaches over to remove the champagne glass that's placed in front of me, catching the retreating waiter to request an orange juice since I can't drink on my meds.

After giving him a quiet thanks, Gare's hand slides onto my thigh as I push the scallops around the plate, not interested in enjoying any part of this evening. Even if the scallops and roasted celeriac smell and taste divine, they are bitter like ash on my tongue, and my stomach is twisted tightly. Sharon waits for me to take a tentative bit before deciding to speak to me directly.

"Since you are here, it would be a good time to tell you that Richard has a niece who is very—"

"I don't give a fuck," I interrupt around my food, staring her dead in the eye. It's comically predictable that she would try to set me up with someone right in front of the others. All strategy and no class. Sharon pouts her red lips as if that would change my demeanor.

"Her name is Sasha. She's studying aerospace engineering and already has an apprenticeship waiting at NASA when she completes her degree." Although that does sound pretty cool for this *Sasha*, she is associated with the devil incarnate, and I'm a taken man. "Maybe you should accompany her to the annual Caudwell Gala next month?"

"Even if I was going to attend some stupid gala, where I'm sure you'll be in attendance, my preferred date would have a little more packaging between his legs." I reach over to slip my hand into the backward collar around Garrett's neck and pull him close to rub noses with me. Cocking his eyebrow, he stares at me expectantly until I've realized my mistake, and a laugh escapes my lips. "Sorry, a lot more packaging."

"Come now, Axel. Stop being ridiculous. I want grandkids while I'm still young enough to enjoy them." Releasing his collar, my eyes remain glued to Garrett's face, the strength passing through his hand on my thigh the only reason I'm still in my seat.

"Valuable goods, you mean?" Garret scoffs, rolling his eyes. Avery sucks in a breath, and the men opposite are all sitting stiffly, their food mostly untouched.

"There's no need for that, Gary," Richard chimes in. Garrett's eyes shift to a spot beyond my head, his expression turning murderous, and I fight to hide my smirk. This should be interesting.

"Call me Gary again," Garrett shoves a scallop into his mouth and then points the fork across the table, "and I will yank your small intestine out of your mouth, rip your large intestine out of your ass, and use you as a human skipping rope."

A full-bellied laugh leaves my throat, the first one in forever, which quickly creates a stitch in my side. But I don't care. The scallop between

Garrett's teeth bursts, juice seeping down his chin while he continues to glare with unbridled fury. Richard flicks his mortified eyes to Sharon, who tells him to pretend Garrett is not in the room. That's fine by me; pretend he's not here while I lean over and drag the pad of my tongue over the salty juice from his chin to his lips. Garrett swallows loudly, his tongue sticking out to tangle with mine.

"Oh, for all of our sakes, Axel, stop that!" Sharon shrieks. "I'm fully aware of what you're doing and that it is all for my benefit. Well, it won't work!" Cutlery clashing loudly against her bowl mixes with her exasperated sigh. I keep my eyes on Garrett's dark ones, our breaths mingling as I reply.

"What am I trying to do?"

"The same as always. Acting out, showing off. Whatever it takes to anger me." I turn my head to see her shoot out of her seat, and Richard places a hand on her arm, trying to calm her with quiet words. Moron. Opening my mouth, Avery throws her napkin down on her plate of untouched food.

"Why on earth would he give a shit what you think? You broke him in so many unfixable ways, used him for your personal gain, no matter the cost to his sanity. Axel is rebuilding his life. You're just pissed your cash mule has left you far behind."

I remain frozen, despite the pride swelling in my chest. The air goes taut, their eyes remaining locked in a stare-down until Richard somehow manages to coax Sharon back into her seat. Avery sits also, reaching out for my hand on instinct. Everyone is watching, trying to anticipate Sharon's next move, which is impossible. She reaches for her wine glass, downs the remaining, and starts to laugh bitterly.

"You always were such a spoiled little shit, Axel."

"Spoilt?!" I nearly choke on my own breath. "How do you figure that one in that fucked-up head of yours?" Richard gives me a warning glare, but it is obvious he has no real power here, not when Sharon is on the warpath for blood.

"You got all of your father's money," she hisses.

And there it is. The real crux of our fractured relationship. The reason why Sharon felt justified pimping me out when she discovered my father's money was all tied up into my trust fund, prepaid college fees, and a yearly allowance that is handled by an external account she wasn't aware of. I mean, what did she expect?

"Hmmm, I suppose you're right. And guess what? I gave it all away." Sharon's face turns to a shade of beetroot, the same crazed look in her eyes as the night she'd found me freshly shaven and finally free. If I had thought writing those checks to abused children's charities had helped to alleviate some of my grief, it's nothing compared to how watching my self-proclaimed mother's internal seizure is healing old wounds in my battered soul.

The waiters return at that moment with our main courses balanced on the palms of their right hands. Minuscule versions of duck confit are placed in front of each of us, but Sharon is too busy twitching and seething to notice. Spearing a teeny tiny carrot on my fork, I notice Garrett glaring at his food as if it will magically transform into a pizza. Across the table, Huxley fails to suppress a yawn behind his hand, and Dax follows suit. Wyatt looks like he's on the verge of snapping, the veins pulled tight in his neck.

Guilt swamps me that my brothers and Avery have been dragged to my childhood home alongside me, but at the same time, I wouldn't survive staying here on my own. If boredom doesn't kill me first, my nightmares sure will.

To his credit, Richard clears his throat and tries to diffuse the tension cracking around the table, although he only makes it worse. "Look, I know there is some... history here, but while staying at this house, you will treat and talk to your mother respectfully."

Garrett's grip tightens on my thigh, more likely to restrain himself from flying into a rage, but I pat him gently in a silent command to stand down. I've got this one.

"She is no mother of mine. I feel more bonded to the surrogate who carried me, and I don't even know her name." Richard isn't satisfied with my response and takes it upon himself to act like a father figure I don't need.

"Now listen here, your mother has been through a lot in her previous marriages. She's had to work hard to support herself and keep this house afloat after you left. Her methods may be unsavory at times," he winces at her sharp glare, "but she is an incredibly resilient woman. And I'll have you know—"

By now, I've tuned out completely. My hand on Garrett's turns into a tight fist, which he returns. My pulse kicks up a notch at the sheer audacity of some stranger sitting in my dad's house and telling me how incredible the woman who whored me out for it is. My blood, sweat, and tears quite literally went into keeping her here. My stomach rolls again, and I shove the plate away sharply.

Since the Shadowed Souls welcomed me into their group, I've tried to leave my desire for physical aggression behind. There was a short period of time where anyone who looked at me too long would meet the end of my fist, my actions driven by misplaced anger. I haven't felt the need to lash out like that in a long time, until tonight.

Tonight, I'd happily bust my stitches to launch myself across this table and choke out the conceited son-of-a-bitch still lecturing me about Sharon's resilience. Visions of each and every way I could hurt Richard are soothing my twisted soul. I could pummel him with my fists, smash a vase over his head, and strangle him with the curtain tie. The list goes on.

Sure, he would be taking the brunt of my anger on Sharon's behalf, because I don't hit women, even if they are psychotic bitches. It would serve a fleeting purpose. To prove I'm not the vulnerable kid I used to be, but I can't even bring myself to do that. Instead, I remember the wasted tears and the nights spent screaming. The panic attacks and the voices in my head that tell me I'll never be enough.

Sharon has tried to break me down, and for the past few years, I believe she has succeeded. But instead of lashing out, I exhale through my parted lips and release Garrett's clenched fist. I roll my shoulders, feeling lighter than I have in years. I decide right here and now to cut the ties, severing her manipulation once and for all. She can't affect me anymore.

Our untouched plates are cleared, and I use the table to push myself upright. I've done what I needed to do, quickly getting the clarity I wanted. Sharon won't be phased by harsh words or insults. Nothing I say or do will penetrate her sense of entitlement. The only way to get under Sharon's skin is by taking away what she really cares about. Her money and popularity.

That's why she hates me. I ruined her precious reputation when I refused to be her pretty, angelic boy and transformed myself into a menacing skinhead that bites back. I was no longer *marketable*, and I intend to stay that way.

"You can't leave yet. Dinner has only just begun," Sharon instantly chastises me. I'm sure there's plenty more she'd like to say, plenty more slander she's ready to fire at me like bullets to my psyche, but my meds are beginning to wear off, and my abdomen is starting to ache. I've found closure in the place I knew it always was, with those sitting around the table who represent my true family.

The tightness of her lips and twitch in her left eye all betray just how annoyed she is, and I bathe in that small victory for one more moment. Her outer shell is tougher than ice, but once it cracks, it shatters.

"It's my house. I can do what I like." My reply sends a further flare of anger through her brown eyes, her mouth opening and closing a few times like a fish out of water. Another fun clause of my father's will; the mansion becomes mine when I turn twenty-one later this year, and I won't waste a second putting it up for sale. There are too many memories in these walls that need to be forgotten. "Besides, I've got an entire feast right here."

I stroke the length of Garrett's throat with my finger, tipping his chin up to be captivated by his smile. Finishing his drink, he rises and links his fingers through mine. Turning towards the door, a sea of blue catches my attention. Offering my free hand out to Avery, she blinks a few times before accepting, a knowing smile lifting her lips as I gently tug her to her feet.

"You too, Swan. You're my dessert."

AVERY

Despite his obvious discomfort, Axel pulls Garrett and me into a darkened room with an iron-tight grip on our fingers. The musty, familiar scent of aged paper and ink wraps around me like a cloak, mingling with the faintest hint of wood smoke from the dormant fireplace. Moonlight filters through the arched window, casting silvery patterns across the room, illuminating the black leather sofa and matching armchairs. The space is perfectly secluded from the power plays and cruel intentions lingering outside.

Holding the straps on my heels, I step onto the circular sheepskin rug, its soft fibers curling around my toes, grounding me in the moment. Axel releases our hands and flicks on a tall lamp, its glow pooling around him as he sinks into one of the armchairs whilst clutching his side.

"No offense, Axe, but you don't really seem to be ready for... that." I point to the hauntedly handsome man standing beside me. Garrett's hair flicks forward, shielding the intensity of his black eyes. There's no way he could be gentle enough, especially not after the tensions of the evening and the simple fact that it's been far too long since either of them have been intimate.

"Oh, I'm not joining in, physically," Axel smiles. As best as he's able, he leans back in the armchair and steeples his fingers almost casually over his stomach. I throw a look to Garrett, who's standing rigidly straight beside me with a determined clench to his jaw.

"I want to wait," he states. My brows shoot up. "I want you to be involved."

"Well, I'm right here, and I promise you, I'm very much involved. Some might even use the term 'in charge'." A tremor of surprise ignites within me. Garrett tilts his head, keeping his posture stiff. Flickers of lust and uncertainty pass across his half-lit face. "Now, both of you, strip."

Heat floods my cheeks, and I catch my bottom lip between my teeth, feeling a thrill of excitement coil in my stomach. After so many weeks of him being too injured to take control, Axel's dominating presence is intoxicating. I can't deny him.

Slowly, I reach up, sliding one strap of my dress down my shoulder, then the other, never breaking eye contact with him. Garrett hesitates a beat longer before yanking his tie loose. The fabric of my dress pools at my feet, leaving me in nothing but my lace thong. My fingers hook under the delicate waistband, and I slide it down my thighs, stepping out of it and kicking it aside. Beside me, Garrett shrugs off his slacks and boxers, his movements rough and jerky.

"All of it, Garrett," Axel demands. My eyes flicker to the shirt still clinging to Garrett's shoulders, fully buttoned to his crotch. He swallows hard, his Adam's apple scraping the collar. There's a slight tremble to his hands, other than that, he appears unaffected. Although I know better.

I lean in and whisper, "I promise I won't look," but Axel has other plans.

"You will look, Swan. You'll kiss and lick, and touch him all over until he can't take it anymore. I want to hear him beg me for permission to fuck you." My thighs clench together on instinct. I've never known Axel to push like this before, but I'm not mad either. There's very few people in this world who can tell Garrett what to do, and sometimes a harsh nudge is needed. "Garrett. This is what I want. Take it off."

A tense beat passes where I'm unsure if Garrett will refuse and storm out. Suddenly, he's pulling his shirt over his head, buttons scattering across the floor in his haste. The rise and fall of his firm chest is labored, but I can't resist peeking. Under the layers of illustrations and artwork, Garrett's abdomen flexes, and fuck, he's beautiful. Without an ounce of fat on him, every muscle is well defined and taut. My mouth goes dry, remembering Axel's earlier promise.

We stand there, bared and vulnerable under Axel's unrelenting gaze, the weight of his attention making my skin prickle with awareness. My nipples pebble, pulling into peaks that ache to be touched.

"Kiss her," Axel orders, his thumb brushing slowly over his bottom lip. The edge of his command makes my knees weaken.

Garrett doesn't hesitate this time. He turns and pulls me into his arms, his mouth crashing down on mine. His tongue sweeps into my mouth as I gasp, hungrily devouring me until I'm weak and breathless. This is exactly how I knew it would be—exactly why Axel is putting himself on the sidelines. Garrett can toss me around, use, and fuck me any way he likes, and I'll keep coming back for more.

Digging his fingers into my arms, Gare's solid erection is already nudging at my abdomen. Molten heat sets me on fire with need. My hands clutch at his shoulders, nails digging into his skin as a moan escapes me, the heat of his body searing against mine. I arch into him, desperate to get closer. Behind us, Axel's sharp intake of breath punctuates the charged silence.

"Is she wet for us?" he asks. Garrett's hand immediately slides down to my ass and dips into my center. We both groan into each other's mouths at the feel of how wet I am, Garrett's long digit easily pushing inside of me. I nibble on his bottom lip and trail kisses down his neck as he pumps his finger in and out, adding a second for good measure.

"Soaking," Garrett's voice is strained, his muscles bunched beneath my fingertips. "What's next?" He asks with clear desperation in his voice.

"Put your hands behind your back and keep them there while Avery does whatever she wants with you." I can hear the smile in Axel's tone as Garrett's fingers are still inside of me. He doesn't immediately let go, his nails digging into my hip and his chest heaving beneath my lips. When I'm sure he's about to refuse and bend me over like a rag doll, he removes his hands so quickly that I gasp at the sudden loss of contact.

Clasping his hands behind him, Garrett's stares upwards, trembling with desire and something else. Fear, possibly. I cut a glance to Axel, who's still smirking, and gestures for me to begin my assault. Until he's begging for permission to fuck me.

I don't go slow, nor do I hold back. Firstly, I trail my teeth along the sharp line of his collarbone, reveling in the way his body tightens beneath me. His chest continues to move rapidly, the uneven rhythm betraying his struggle to stay still. I press open-mouthed kisses across the tattoos covering of his chest, letting my tongue follow the curve of his skin as I map the contours of him for the first time.

When I reach his nipple, I run the flat of my tongue over it in a slow, deliberate motion. His sharp hiss slices through the air, his arms trembling to stay locked behind his back, desperate to maintain control. I feel the tension in him, the unspoken battle between wanting to push me away and surrendering to my touch.

Instead of pulling back, I double down, repeating the motion with more pressure, circling the sensitive bud until his breath catches. I glance up at Garrett, and his face is a canvas of contradictions. Jaw clenched tight, eyes squeezed shut, but a faint flush creeping up his neck, betraying how much he feels this. His vulnerability makes my chest ache, but I don't stop. I move to the other side, my mouth latching onto the second bud. This time, I add a soft bite, just enough to draw a sharp inhale from him.

"You're so beautiful," I whisper against his skin, low enough for only him to hear. He trembles under my lips, his resolve fraying at the edges, and I know I'm pushing him to his limit. But I've waited so long to touch him like this, to make him feel how much I adore every part of him, even the parts he tries so hard to hide.

When I feel his control is about to snap, I shift lower. Carving a path through his valley of abs with my mouth, I drop to my knees on the soft rug. His cock is painfully hard and pulsing right in front of my face. I blow on the most sensitive part of his dick, causing his shaft to jolt further.

"Stop," Garrett grinds out through his teeth, but his body says otherwise. A bead of precum gathers on his tip, which I lick away in one, clean motion.

"Why? I'm having far too much fun." Starting from his ankles, I slowly scrape my fingernails up his calves, along the inside of his thighs, and ghost his balls with the barest of touches. His frustration is clear by his growling, but I'm having way too much fun to stop. Painting featherlight circles across his groin with my fingers, I lean forward as if I'm going to take him in my mouth, but I stop short and smile up at him wickedly.

A feral growl escapes Garrett's throat as his hands dart out, tangling in my hair with a commanding grip that leaves no room for hesitation. Before I can prepare, he thrusts his cock deep into my throat, the suddenness stealing the air from my lungs. His hold is bruising, forcing me to stay in place as he sets a punishing rhythm. Each thrust is relentless, his smooth head gliding over my tongue, filling and owning me completely.

I clutch at his thighs for balance, nails biting into his skin as I try to keep up with the pace he's set. Garrett's raw hunger is palpable, his true sexual nature finally breaking free. Desperate to match his energy, I let my hands roam, sliding one beneath him to scratch lightly at his balls. He shudders above me, a sharp inhale signaling his approval, and his grip on my hair tightens just enough to toe the line between pleasure and pain.

Then, just as quickly as it started, Garrett releases me and pulls me to my feet as if I weigh nothing. His fingers curl around the back of my neck, firmly guiding me toward Axel's chair. I can imagine the fury in his dark eyes, my mind kicking into overdrive. Perhaps I pushed him too far.

Garrett pushes me down onto my knees once more, the plush rug soft beneath me. Lifting my wrists, he places my hands on either side of the armchair, effectively caging Axel in.

"You want to test my restraint, Axe?" Garrett's bites out, his voice dripping with challenge. "Let's see how good yours is."

The head of his cock grazes my entrance, teasing me with my own wetness. One hand snakes around my body, his palm finding my clit and pressing firmly, sending jolts of pleasure through me. The other curls around my neck, tilting my head up until my gaze locks with Axel's. The intensity in Axel's eyes is magnetic, his jaw tight, his pupils blown wide as he watches me squirm beneath him.

In one fluid motion, Garrett slams into me, all the way to the hilt. A cry escapes my lips, the stretch and fullness overwhelming in the best way. Garrett's breath is hot against my ear as he thrusts, his deft fingers traveling lower to hold me open to his harsh thrusts.

Axel has released his own dick from his pants, his fisted hand slowly pumping up and down his shaft as he watches our every move. Although it's not like before, the three of us are connected in this moment, our pleasure and ragged breaths mingling in the air.

My cries echo around the room as Garrett builds up a vigorous rhythm, each thrust hitting my G-spot. His fingers tighten around my neck, purely animalistic noises sounding behind me, but Axel is the opposite. Calm, composed. Legs spread wide, casually stroking the impressive length of his cock, his eyes churning at the scene being played out for him. On his wrist, my compass bracelet slips free of his cuff and glints in the light. My eyes flick down, my tongue poking out to moisten my lips. I want him, although I know he's not ready.

Smirking down at me, Axel runs the knuckles of his free hand across my nipple, and I arch my back in response, desperate to be closer to him. Every drag of his fingers sends sparks flying throughout my body, my toes curled and fists clenched. Abandoning his dick, he gives my breasts his full attention, rolling my nipples between his thumb and forefinger with the occasional sharp pinch. I try to lean into his touch, but Garrett has me locked in place, pounding relentlessly and filling me completely.

An orgasm rips through me like a tidal wave, delicious destruction tearing me apart on a silent scream. Garrett's hand shifts towards my mouth, and I bite down hard on the fleshly part between his thumb and forefinger, riding out the intense waves with muffled moans. My walls are gripping Garrett's shaft so tightly, he's momentarily forced to slow while I bathe in the euphoric feeling, riding out every last wave until it's subsided. My limbs are suddenly weighed down, tingling from head to toe. If Garrett wasn't holding me, I'd have melted into a blissful puddle on the floor and refused to get back up again.

Axel's eyes haven't wandered from mine, returning to smooth his hand up and down on his dick. I shift my hands from the edge of the seat, drifting across the leather to rest on his thighs. Garrett tries to yank me backwards until Axel warns him off, a silent conversation passing between the two, which I'm too distracted to concentrate on with Axel's cock straining for my attention.

"Gently," Garrett whispers into my ear, almost threateningly. He keeps his pace slow and steady, curling my braid around his hand to keep control as I lean forward to take all of Axel into my mouth. His velvet softness eases across my tongue as I carefully pull back, licking every drop of saltiness as I go. Axel leans all the way back in his seat, groaning and urging me to continue by cupping my jaw. Every so often, his hips tilt upward slightly, allowing me to take him deeper. Garrett grinds within me, a sensual shift in our usual dynamic where not just one person is in control but two.

Keeping my pace even, I take Axel between my lips again and again, swirling my tongue around his tip each time. Gripping his base tightly in my hand, I pump alongside my steady sucking until the desperation in his groans calls for more. Hollowing my cheeks and occasionally scraping my teeth along his length, I take him all the way into my throat just as he explodes on a curse. Warm, salty cum spills into my mouth, and I swallow as I go. Garrett holds me in place by my hair, forcing me to take everything Axel wants to give, not that I would have moved anyway.

The second I pull myself free from Axel's release, Garrett picks up his punishing rhythm again. His arms wind around me like a cobra pinning its prey in place, driving into me at such a speed I can barely catch my breath. Each slam of his body against my ass feels like a spank, his movements erratic as if he wants to teach me some sort of lesson. Each thrust drives me closer to the edge, pushing me further into the raw, unrestrained desire we've been missing. Axel tracks all of it, his cheeks pinkened and his cock twitching despite himself.

When Garrett's mouth finds my neck, he bites down sharply. I cry out in protest a second before another orgasm rips through my body. Stars burst behind my eyelids, my inner walls fluttering. Still, he doesn't relent, using me to vent all of his pent-up sexual frustration. My nails rip into the arms of the chair, Garrett's shouts joining mine as his cock swells and pulses within me.

Finally freeing me from his hold as he chases his release, I slump forward onto Axel's thigh. I'm definitely going to ache in the morning. Garrett grinds against me one last time, prolonging his pleasure before leaning his weight over my back. His fingers interlink with Axel's, the three of us absorbing the last few moments before our troubles return with a vengeance.

"Sorry if I went a little too hard there, Peach. It's been a while."

"Oh, did you?" I tease, wriggling my ass back against him. "I was actually wondering when you were going to start." There's a sharp tug on my hair and a bemused laugh from Axel. It feels good to be laughing together again, to be connected, and to feel alive in general. I'm slowly but surely getting my boys back.

Garrett lifts his weight from me, his arm around my middle as he leans aside for his discarded boxers. Tentatively, he holds the material between us before pulling his cock out, cleaning me up without much regard for himself. Using this distraction, I quickly grab his shirt and slip it over my shoulders. Before Garrett can protest, my arms are in the sleeves, and Axel is helping me to button it all the way down to graze my thighs. Garrett narrows his eyes, a small smile playing about his lips.

"You know I'm not against wearing your dress back to our room."

"I know, but at some point, you need to stop hiding." I twist my head back to him and wave a vague hand towards his chest. "I mean, it's selfish, really. Hiding all of those artist's hard work." Garrett huffs a laugh, his arms twitching as if he wants to cover himself from my view. But ultimately, they remain by his sides.

"I thought you thought my tattoos were shit," he comments dryly. I shrug, a smirk cemented on my face.

"Depends how much of a dick you're being on any given day." Axel nudges me to help him stand, and then peels off his own shirt to give to Garrett. The bandage on his side is stained dark maroon in the center, evidence that we pushed him too hard. That I went too far. "Oh, Axe," I raise a hand to his ribs. He's quick to catch it and raise my knuckles to his lips, pressing a kiss there.

"Totally worth it," he murmurs. Garrett is beneath his arm in the next second, dressed in the shirt and slacks, helping to walk Axel towards the door.

"I'll go get Doctor Marcus," I announce, but I only make it a step out into the hallway when Garrett's free arm winds around my waist.

"Dressed in my shirt with my cum dripping down your thighs?" He laughs darkly. "Take Axel back to bed and wait for me there. I'm not wasting free lube like that." Passing Axel's arm over to hook across my shoulders, Garrett bounds down the hallway and disappears in the direction of Marcus' office. Axel gives me a knowing look, his eyebrow raised.

"You know now he's had a taste of sex again, he's going to be insatiable."

"Oh God," I chuckle under my breath. "What have we done?"

GARRETT

The day after that tedious dinner, although the after-party was sensational, I decided we'd all been separate for long enough. It took a herculean effort from the five of us who don't sleep for nineteen hours a day and two full days to finish the job, but at long last, I have my wish. One huge bed. Or rather, three double beds pushed together in Axel's childhood bedroom. At one point, I curled up with Axel just to watch a shirtless Hux, Dax, and Wyatt get sweaty using power tools. Avery joined us soon after.

And sleep came blissfully after that, until tonight, of course. Axel's limbs are wrapped around my body, holding me in place by sheer force. Avery is stretched along the length of his back like a cat, but the rest of the elongated bed is empty. I stare at the ceiling while Axel taps his fingers impatiently on my shoulder, and Avery sighs every now and then.

None of us can pretend the auction isn't happening downstairs, and while I've been ordered to hang back, Avery is staying away by choice. She couldn't put herself through it again, not when Hux is planning to make his big move on Warren Briggs tonight. Across the wall, the clock ticks louder and louder, like a worm burrowing into my thoughts and eating me out like I'm an apple. Fuck that rapey worm.

Careful not to jerk Axel too quickly, I unpeel his arms and legs from the cocoon he's created around my body. He tries to cling tighter, but luckily for me in this instance, he's too weak. "Gare," Axel growls with more force than I expected. "Don't."

But I'm already moving, shaking his grip off as gently as I can. The clock continues to tick, mocking me. I swing my legs off the bed and plant my feet firmly on the floor.

"I'm going." Axel's hand reaches for me, but I'm quicker. I'm across the room, rifling through the drawers to find something to wear. Anything to work off the nervous energy threatening to explode out of me.

"Garrett," Axel repeats firmly, his voice causing the hairs on the back of my neck to stand up. I pause, my hands pressed on the wooden surface. It reminds me of how he played the Dom for Avery and me, and I shiver at the memory. But then I remember the woman who caused him so much pain is downstairs, living her best freaking life, and the anger boils up again. Hux is down there playing his role, while I'm being told to sit and stay, teetering on the verge of a psychotic break.

Turning back, I throw my arms wide, my voice pitched unnaturally high. "I'm not an apple!" And with that, I go back to the drawers while Axel pinches the bridge of his nose. I finally tug out a pair of clean boxers, Dax's, I reckon, when a soft hand touches my back. I spin around, looking down at Avery's large, beautiful eyes. "I know what you're going to say," I sigh, balling Dax's boxers into my fists. "But I can't just sit here. We're supposed to be a team. We've always been a team."

I implore her to see my reason, but I know it's useless. In about ten seconds, she'll smile sweetly and tug me back towards the bed, where I'll be stuck in my own head all night. Her hand glides across my body, sliding over my covered abs and chest. I inhale sharply, still not used to being touched there, but it's not as torturous as it was before. Closing my eyes, Avery's cheek scrapes mine, her lips by my ear.

"Wear something outrageous. And I'm coming with you." My eyes fly open and my head jerks back to see an evil smirk appear on her usually angelic face. I splutter a response, choking on a manic laugh until Avery presses her fingers to my lips. "You are not an apple. And I can't lie here like a lemon all night either."

"You could never be a lemon. You're a peach," I snort, amusing myself. Avery's eyes twinkle with mischief, and I decide right then and there, she's spent far too much time with me. Avery giggles against my chest while Axel groans from the bed.

"You two are going to make matters worse," he sighs but has already deflated back into the pillows, knowing it's useless. I nod in earnest. That's exactly the point. We're going to make things so much worse—for Sharon.

When the dresser proves to hold nothing suitable, Avery has the idea to sneak into the student's quarters while they're preoccupied downstairs. I've never seen her so rebellious, sneaking around on those silent ballerina feet, using the student's wardrobes like her own thrift shop.

I only hesitate for a moment when she asks me to take off my T-shirt, pulling the material over my scruffy hair and keeping my eyeline above her head. She dresses me like a gothic ken doll, skintight pants, and combat boots. The belt buckle uses diamonds to spell out the word 'SLUT', and the leather jacket hangs heavy on my shoulders, only leaving a sliver of my body visible through the mesh top she's picked out. Avery completes the look with black nail polish on my fingers. I'm busy blowing them dry as she changes, her body briefly and gloriously naked in some girl's room until she's dressed similarly to me.

Her hair is tossed up in a messy ponytail, her bright red lips the only color amongst her black catsuit and thick eyeliner. She steals a pair of chunky heels to rival my height, and I hold out my arm.

"Ready?"

"Let's go fuck some shit up," Avery nods. My wrinkled little heart swells.

"God, I've never loved you more." I sweep her into a hurried, passionate kiss, smearing said lipstick, before sweeping her out of the room and down the staircase.

The noise emanating from the ballroom is a powerful mix of enthusiastic chatter and bitchy whispers. Butler Bill, as I've taken to calling him in my head, is just closing the main doors as we appear. He glowers, but holds off long enough for us to slip inside, punctuated by the bang on the wood at our backs. The smartly dressed students take no notice, too focused on bidders who are eager to feel the goods before the auction starts. Good, we're not too late.

Being head and shoulders above everyone else, I'm able to see the set of French doors at the rear are open this evening, leading out onto an equally as packed terrace. Busier than last week, I wonder what the special occasion is.

From out of the crowd, Sharon steps onto the podium, no sign of her lapdog this evening. Not a hair is out of place, tightly tied back in a slick ponytail with the deep shade of red on her lips matching her tight bodycon dress. A spotlight shines down on her brightly as she starts the same spiel to welcome everyone and outlining the rules. She has the full attention of guests in the finest suits and cocktail dresses, the students, the staff, and across the far side, the Souls.

Dressed in their own suits and shiny black shoes, they blend in perfectly. Wyatt and Dax stand by the window, sipping champagne. Hux is a few feet in front, accompanied by Warren Briggs.

"Stick with me," I mutter into Avery's ear. Linking our fingers, I guide her along the edge of the ballroom, exiting via a patio door at the back. Each table holds a bucket, presumably for ice and champagne, a glass bowl of salty snacks, and a large parasol, fitted with an electric heater to beat down on those sitting underneath. Avery and I settle into a table near the back, finding blankets have been provided. How thoughtful.

After reciting her speech, Sharon asks the students to leave via the back door and for the guests to get comfortable. The salty snacks currently have my full attention until Avery's nails are embedded into my hand. "Ouch!"

"Look," Avery hisses, still refusing to withdraw her talons. I follow her eyeline to watch Hux, in his posh penguin suit with his hair gelled back like Wyatt's, striding beside Taylor to exit through the back door. My stomach plummets, the snack falling free from my fingers.

"Holy shit," I breathe.

"What the hell is he doing?!"

I pat Avery's hand, twisting her body into mine much like I did last week. "Trust him, Peach," I whisper into her ear. "He's a big boy."

"I know. And they are all about to know it too." Jerking her chin out, I also see the group of ladies and a few men, hungrily following Hux with their eyes and licking their lips. I smile, winding an arm around her shoulders.

"You're cute when you're jealous. Do you ever get jealous about me?" Avery rolls her eyes and gives my side a little shove. Once all of the guests are seated, the waitresses come around with the champagne bottles and bidding paddles. I take one of each for show.

The first Lot is called out, a heavily freckled guy of medium build with bright auburn hair. He struts the length of the ballroom before detouring around the patio and finally finishing on the stage, his dick swinging between his meaty thighs the entire time. A small group of ladies to our right corner to giggle and bounce with anticipation. Sharon presents him as Nolan the artist, given that he's twirling a paintbrush around in his fingers, and suggests the bidding starts at fifteen thousand dollars. A plump woman in front of me gets ready to shoot her hand into the air.

"Hey Aves," I call out loud enough for anyone nearby to hear. "Wasn't Nolan the one who gave crabs to a whole group last week?" Avery's eyes flash to me, but she doesn't miss a beat, tapping her chin in thought.

"Oh no. I heard they were fleas he got from the cat. That guy sure loves licking pussies."

The women around us balk and gasp, a few quickly rushing away to filter the rumor through the crowd. Avery and I try not to fall apart laughing, our composing slipping as our shoulders shake. Bringing a hand up to cover my mouth, I clear my throat and opt to drink some champagne instead.

Sharon calls again for the bids to start, her face dropping as no response comes. She appears absolutely horrified, looking around the room in confusion. Shooing Freckle Face from the stage, she flaps her hand for the next girl to jump into the spotlight. A blonde with purple tints in the ends of her long curls bounces onto the dance floor, her chest hugely fake and her waist teeny tiny. Introduced as Vicky, she pushes her tits together whilst I lean back to put my feet up on a nearby chair.

"Vagina wider than the Grand Canyon, that one. I tried to fuck her once; it was like throwing a sausage down an alley." I call loudly. Not surprisingly, a flow of hushed whispers passes from one end of the crowd to the other, and no bids are entered. Sharon stomps across the stage on her black heels, dismissing Vicky with a harsh whisper.

Next, a brunette rushes into the ballroom. She's quite pretty, an eyebrow cocked over her doe eyes as she nibbles on her bottom lip suggestively. Floral tattoos follow a line from her shoulder, down her ribs and hips, and all the way to her ankle.

"Let's start Felicity off at ten thousand, shall we? She's rather wild and enjoys sharing partners with a group." Sharon's voice rolls through the speakers dotted around the patio.

"Don't forget how she passes out every time she cums, without fail. We had to call for an ambulance last time!" Avery basically shouts this time. Murmurs and questionable glances are passed around, and no one bids on poor Felicity either. She runs off stage, holding her face in her hands, but I can't bring myself to feel bad. I'm too busy having the time of my life by ripping away the only thing Sharon cares about. Money.

"Moving on," the plastic shrew continues. "A few of you might recognize Karen—"

"Oh, not Chlamydia Karen!" I yell. "My dick has been itching for months!"

"Whoever that is needs to report to me at once," Sharon glares through the French doors. It quickly becomes apparent that she can't see much past the spotlight gleaming overhead. "There have never been any complaints with my Lots, and they are all tested for sexual diseases on a weekly basis." There's a defiant tick in Sharon's jaw, but still no one raises their hand to bid. Silence falls over the ballroom and gardens, only the sound of crickets filling the empty void around us. She huffs and moves on.

"Well, Daniel here—"

"Cries when he cums!" Avery cups her mouth to shout. Holding a hand up against the glare, Sharon squints out into the crowd and demands whoever is ruining her auction to come forward. I shrug down in my seat, dragging Avery down with me until our noses are level with the table. Many of the guests around us are shifting uncomfortably, the wooden knock of their paddles being put down. Most of the Lots seem to have understood tonight isn't happening for them and stopped bothering to come out, except for one.

Taylor, aka Top Knot, steps onto the stage confidently, widening his stance and crossing his arms in a dare for anyone to challenge his reputation. His cock is thick, hanging freely, and even I strain for a better look. I'm only human after all. It's no wonder plenty of guests around us sigh dramatically, clearly familiar with him, and Sharon smirks knowingly.

"Ahh, Taylor. Now here is a young man no one can dispute against. He has a perfect track record for satisfaction, always goes the extra mile, and is especially well-equipped, if I do say so myself. Since it's been a slow evening, we will start the bidding at fifty thousand dollars."

Every head of those sitting around us spins around sharply, waiting for approval to bid. So many pairs of eyes are pleading to be given the all-clear, but it's not me that responds to their questioning stares.

"Oh yeah, sure. Best night of my life," Avery calls out, much to the delight of every woman around us. Their shoulders sag, and they share relieved smiles. A few paddles start to rise. "Until he went on top for sixty-nine without telling me about his rectal condition. I've never been able to get the smell of shit out of my nose."

An uproar of cries and gagging gives us the perfect cover to duck out. Slipping the rest of the way to the floor, we crawl beneath the tables and jump a low wall. The grassy bank beyond slopes, sending us skidding towards the pavement at the bottom. I manage to catch Avery before she breaks her ankle, stomping to a stop with my chunky combat boots.

From there, we casually stroll around the edge of the mansion, enjoying a little bit of quality time together. Every time Avery glances at me, we fall into hysterics again, drowned out by the sounds of screeching tires and the blaring of car horns. Guests seem to be in a rush to leave now that the party is over. Hand in hand, we enter the main entrance just as Sharon steps into our way.

"You little shits," her lip peels back in disgust as she assesses my outfit. "I told you to stay out of the way. You must think you're so funny." I shrug and nod. That's exactly what I think.

"Life's all shits and giggles until someone giggles and shits," I agree. Avery snorts loudly. Deciding to ignore me, Sharon pushes her way through us, trying to control the amount of people leaving with her fake smile back in place.

"Please, please come back inside. This is all a misunderstanding, I assure you." We leave her to it, gliding back towards the ballroom to complete one big circuit. Annoyingly, there are still plenty of guests present, those who were sitting inside the ballroom being too far away to hear our warnings. Through the center, a pair of green eyes carve out a path towards me.

"Oh, hey, Riot. What did we miss?" I ask as he approaches, Dax trailing just behind. His glare is deadly, although it bounces off me like water rolling off a duck's back.

"Don't try that bullshit with me. You nearly messed everything up for Hux." Wyatt's head tilts aside, guiding my attention to where Hux is currently hand-feeding Warren a grape, his suit very much still intact. I force another shrug, despite Avery's hand going tense in mine.

"Sorry about that. As much as I'd love to see Huxley do a naked parade around a ballroom, Avery here wasn't feeling as generous." Wyatt's lips press into a thin line, his sharp green eyes darting between Avery and me. I know that look. Controlled fury. It's the same look he gets before a game and, evidently, mostly every time he looks at me.

"Hux has been stressing about tonight all week, and you almost blew it because you can't sit still for five minutes." Wyatt exhales through his nose, his patience clearly running on fumes.

"*Almost.*" I counter, flashing him my most disarming smile. "But I didn't. And look, our boy's still in one piece and fully clothed. Mission accomplished, right?"

Before Wyatt can retort, Dax places a firm hand on his shoulder, his calm energy tempering the storm brewing in Wyatt's chest. "Let it go," Dax mutters. "It's done now. We need to focus." Just then, his pocket starts to vibrate, and he steps away to answer the call. Wyatt visibly reins himself in. His attention shifts to Avery, and his glare softens a fraction.

"I hope you know what you're doing," Wyatt finally says, his words aimed at both of us but are clearly meant for her. Without waiting for a response, he turns on his heel and disappears into the crowd, Dax trailing after him like a silent shadow.

The tension lingers in the air, thick and suffocating, as Avery exhales shakily beside me. Her grip on my hand loosens, and I glance over to find her staring at Huxley, her eyes swimming with concern.

Hux has moved to stand by the far wall, Warren leaning casually against it, gesturing animatedly with his whiskey glass. Huxley looks composed, nodding along at the right times. But we know him too well. The slight tightness in his jaw, the way his hand clenches and unclenches at his side, the tiny cracks in his façade are all too apparent to me and Avery.

And then it happens. Warren tilts his head toward the exit, his lips curving into a predatory smile. Hux doesn't hesitate. He pushes off the wall, his movements fluid as he leads Warren toward the hallway, away from the crowded ballroom.

As they pass, Hux's brown gaze flickers to Avery. It's brief, just a split second, but the weight of it is enough to make her freeze. His face is unreadable, but his eyes tell a different story. There's a bleakness to them, a silent acknowledgment of the risk he's taking. Avery swallows hard, her fingers twitching in my hand. I don't need to look at her to know she's holding back tears. And for once, I don't have a joke or a quip to fill the silence.

Huxley walks off with Warren, his shoulders squared, his steps steady. But the farther away he gets, the heavier Avery leans against me. I wait a few minutes, ensuring no one is watching before I spin her into my arms and hold her tight whilst she cries into my shoulder.

"I've got you, Peach. Everything is going to be okay," I promise without any reason to justify it. I seriously hope Huxley has thought long and hard about the lengths he'll go to for whatever information he's seeking, because some dark corners of our minds are impossible to come back from.

AVERY

CHAPTER THIRTY SIX

The ballroom hums with low-murmured conversations, clinking glasses, and the occasional burst of laughter. The chandeliers dim, casting a gentle golden light as music begins to play through the hidden speakers. Slow, sensual tones, no doubt meant to encourage dances of the same nature. Sharon may not be here, but she's still managing to manipulate the evening.

Those still with companions couple up and take to the center of the dancefloor, and it becomes apparent that over half of the Lots are left out. They line the walls, scowls etched into their faces as they glare at Garrett and me. The man on my arm puffs out his chest, the leather jacket separating ever-so-slightly to hint at the tattoos beneath his mesh top. A part of me blossoms with pride, this being the closest he's ever come to showing off the muscled body he hides. But that part is sadly overshadowed, my mind remaining elsewhere.

For the hundredth time in five minutes, I glance back at the open double doors. Whatever is happening, Huxley is still firmly out of my reach, and I don't think I will rest until he's back with me.

Wyatt notices, of course. He's been watching me closely since we rejoined him and Dax by the window. His sharp, green gaze is rooted on my face, but he says nothing. Dax is pretending he's not checking me out, but the PVC catsuit on my body fits like a second skin. My cleavage is scandalously exposed, and a sliver of misery cuts through me as I think how much Meg would have approved.

I twist to look out the window, although nothing greets me but darkness. *Breathe, Aves*, I hear Meg's voice in my head. You're getting close. It won't be much longer. I wish my mind's tricks worked, but they do the opposite. The chasm between myself and my twin has never felt so vast. And Garrett being Garrett, he's decided the best way to keep me from spiraling is to keep my hands full. Literally.

"Here," he says, shoving another flute of champagne into my hand. "Drink." I arch a brow at him, lips pursed, but he only grins, plucking a tiny canapé from a passing tray and pressing it to my lips. It smells like truffles and something expensive I can't quite place. "And eat. We can't have you drinking on an empty stomach."

I sigh but let him push it into my mouth, chewing absently. The rich, buttery taste barely registers. He's already turned back, relieving the waitress of her tray and telling her to *'jog on'*. This time, he feeds me something wrapped in prosciutto, and I take it without argument. It's easier than telling him I don't have much of an appetite when my stomach is a twisting mess of nerves.

"Good girl," Garrett whispers, but his usual flirtation lacks heat. He's distracting me the only way he knows how. Wyatt nudges Garrett with his elbow, muttering into his own champagne flute.

"That's my line."

My gaze drifts to the double doors again, hoping I can will Hux into walking through them. Instead, a man walks past, following the hallway towards the gardens. My brow twitches, but I can't decide why. A moment later, he's back, clearly lost, and this time, he pauses for a second to peer inside and then quickly strides away again. Something about him feels familiar, although the champagne is making my brain sluggish. I feel like I should recognize him, but not in this setting. He just feels wrong.

A touch at my wrist makes me flinch, the glass flute dropping from my hand to smash at my heels.

"Fuck, Peach," Garrett gasps, his hand on my wrist tightening. He drags me a step to the side, still balancing his tray in his other hand, and lets Wyatt scrape the glass aside with his dress shoe. Dax steps into me, his blue eyes glistening with concern.

"Is everything okay?" Dax tilts his head, careful not to crowd me. My chest is heaving slightly, panic rising, although I don't know why. Convincing myself I'm being an idiot and that I am in fact just a bit tipsy, I nod.

"I'm fine, I just thought I saw... I don't know, he looked a bit like—"

Dax's phone starts to buzz loudly from inside his jacket pocket. He frowns, excusing himself before stepping away to take the call. Wyatt's nostrils flare as he rejoins us, the air growing thick around us. I feel it, Wyatt feels it, and Garrett seemingly does not. He pops another canapé in his mouth, chewing thoughtfully as he glances down at my heels.

"You know if the whole ballet thing doesn't work out, have you thought about becoming a foot model? There's a whole market out there for cute dainty feet pics."

Wyatt looks to the ceiling for patience. I'm sure his response would have involved the market of sweaty old men with foot fetishes. Mine would have been a sarcastic comment about a ballerina's feet being the least 'cute', given the blisters and sores I sport after grueling training sessions.

But neither of us gets to voice them.

"Thiago's seen something," Dax returns to whisper harshly. "We need to go."

"Go... to go where?" My eyes widen. He could have said leave the ballroom, return to Axel, and retire to bed. But he didn't. He just said 'go', in a decisive tone I don't hear from Dax often. Dread seizes my spine, my entire body running cold in an instant. Dax turns to Wyatt, leaning in to keep his voice quiet.

"Plan D," he mutters. Wyatt's eyes flash, then return to their steady coolness. He nods and removes the platter from Garrett's hand with unnerving calm. Placing it down, his hand then touches my lower back, and he smoothly urges me out of the ballroom.

"Wyatt, what—"

"Trust me," he interjects. Dax and Garrett, who is suddenly back in bodyguard mode, flank us as we turn out of the ballroom. Our steps are unhurried, a false pretense of the terror grappling inside my chest. I thought we'd go straight back to Axel, but instead, we veer right and step into an empty billiard room along the hallway. The door is pressed closed with a click, and suddenly, Wyatt rounds me, his hands clasping my upper arms.

"Do not fight me on this," he says sternly, but where I previously would have taken his tone as hatred, I now know it to be fear. Wyatt is scared, and that's enough to make me nod along.

"Please, just tell me whatever it is," I beg. Wyatt releases my arms, pulling me into a brief yet firm hug, his lips pressing against my forehead.

Oh, fuck. This is bad.

"Thiago caught something on the ballroom security feed just now," Dax steps forward, his face ashen. "A face he didn't recognize, so he ran it through his software."

"And who is it?" Garrett folds his arms, the leather jacket squeaking in protest. Dax rolls the words around his mouth before parting his lips to speak.

"Thiago said it's Avery's dad. He's here in the mansion."

My pulse spikes. Fredrick is here. As if he can preempt the direction of my thoughts, Wyatt steps into my eyeline again, blocking out everything except his green eyes.

"Don't even think about it," he growls. Two other bodies cage me in, which is all that keeps me from crumbling to my feet. "Fredrick won't come alone. We can't risk sitting here for his men to storm the mansion. I'll find Huxley, and we will search for Fredrick together. Gare, help Avery to get Axel ready for moving."

"We could take one of the minibuses," Dax adds thoughtfully. "There will be enough space for everyone, and the seats will recline for Axel to lie down. I'll convince the doctor to pack up and come with us." Even Garrett seems in agreement, and as the silence settles like a weighted blanket on my shoulders, I realize they're waiting for me to speak. Licking my lips, my throat is suddenly dry, my limbs numb.

"I have to see him," I whisper, already anticipating their response. Wyatt growls, Dax almost whimpers, and Garrett curses, but at least the three of them step back to give me some room to breathe. I notice too late how I've walked into their trap, an empty room with a closed door. They knew I'd try to run. So, instead, I try to find Wyatt's soft spot for me. "He has Meg. This could be my only chance to get him to give her back."

"At what cost?" Wyatt hisses, knowing the answer. At any cost. He's shaking his head, but Dax steps into my side, running a hand over his face.

"We're losing time. Gare, get Axel ready. I'll grab the Doc and Thiago, and we'll be right there. Wyatt, take Avery with you." Wyatt glares venomously, but Dax doesn't back down, his fingers linking with mine. "She will do this whether you permit it or not. At least if you agree, you'll be there to protect her." Blinking up at Dax, my eyes fill with tears that I refuse to let fall. He kisses my cheek, his lips remaining against my skin.

"Be safe, Swan. Come back to me." He releases my hand and sweeps out of the room without waiting for a response. Garrett's jaw is tight, but he leaves too, not hanging around to make a big declaration. I breathe shallowly, facing Wyatt. I know he'd rather I hid in the background, that I was some sweet little submissive he can cage to keep safe, but this is my fight.

"We can't run from this," I say stoically, shoving down all of my own fears to placate his. I've known for a while that the time is coming to face Fredrick, and I'm as ready as I'll ever be. Wyatt sighs, striding towards the door.

"Can't you ever do as you're told?"

"If that's what you wanted, you should have picked a different girl to fall in love with." I turn on my heels, watching his back tense up. There's a powerful shift of muscle beneath his shirt, as if he's struggling to reign back a monster living within his skin. Bracing a hand on the door, Wyatt glances back at me, his hair flicking forward.

"I really had no choice in the matter."

I suck in a harsh breath, and he leaves. Rushing to remain by his side, we slow as we enter the main lobby. Nothing appears out of place, students flirting with the few patrons they have left or each other. After an unsuccessful night, some have chosen to find solace in each other, making out by the grandfather clock or straddling on the stairs.

Wyatt bypasses the staircase leading to Axel's wing. I glance up, nibbling on my bottom lip in an effort to calm myself. Dax and Gare will have that side covered, and nothing bad will happen to Axel.

We pass the frat-style living area, games room, and kitchen, taking the set of stairs across the other side of the mansion. This is where the other guests rooms are, and presumably where Hux will be entertaining Warren. I shudder at the thought, but urgency pushes me forward. We don't need Hux to seduce the chief of police anymore; Fredrick is right here.

Wyatt is a man on a mission, his face set like stone. He whips open each door, revealing the room beyond. Most are empty, some occupied, to which he receives a round of harsh cursing. Wyatt does care, striding onto the next while I mutter apologies and close the doors again after a good look that Hux isn't present. Some images will never be scrubbed from my brain after tonight.

Somewhere along the way, I find my hand in his. I'm not sure who initiated it, a mutual desire for comfort and a way for him to drag me along. We're nearing the end of the hallway, another set of stairs apparent in a left alcove. These ones aren't as wide, but just as grand. Cast iron railings and marble flooring, the smudge of a dirty man's footprint on the bottom step. I share an apprehensive look with Wyatt.

Suddenly, a door bangs open beside us. I stifle a scream as a very disheveled, pale Huxley stands there, his chest heaving. His blond waves are wild from having fingers combed through them, his pupils blown wide, and his shirt open. His pants are firmly buttoned.

"I got it," Hux breathes, his voice not quite his own. I reach for him instinctively, but his focus is on Wyatt. The leader who sent him on a mission, and now he's ready to report back. Producing a wrinkled piece of paper, the edge torn hastily at an angle, there's an address scribbled on it. "Fredrick's place. It's a witness protection hub, which is why Thiago couldn't find it. The bastard is pretending he's scared of the other inmates, all the while he's working with them." Wyatt takes the paper from Hux and pats his arm, his head hanging slightly.

"The bastard is here. Thiago caught him on the ballroom cam." I didn't think Hux could turn paler, but he manages it. I use the moment's distraction to peek beyond Hux's frame and into the room. The bedsheets are a ruffled mess, but only because Warren Briggs is lying on the covers. There's a red mark blooming along his cheekbone, like he's been hit.

"Did you beat him up?" I gasp.

"Well, I wasn't going to fuck him?!" Hux says incredulously. "I just needed to get him upstairs to knock him out so I could access his phone. The trickiest bit was prying his eyes open for his face ID.”

“I thought the plan was to drug his whiskey?” Wyatt raises a brow. I pinch the bridge of my nose. Of course, he was in on this.

“It wasn’t working quick enough. He almost got his tongue in my mouth.” Hux shrugs and steps into the hallway, closing the door to block my view. Wyatt exhales sharply, his fists clenched at his side. But before he can say whatever’s brewing in that dangerous head of his, a new sound cuts through the air. A violent one from the floor above us, as if something has been smashed.

Wyatt and Hux both freeze, but only for a split second before they’re running up the stairs to our left. I have to race to catch up, half hearing a whispered growl from Huxley asking why I’m here. I push aside my exasperation, focusing on the hammering of my heart trying to leap out of my chest.

At first glance, the third-floor hallway appears empty, but then we hear raised, angry voices seeping through the crack in the door at the end.

“Sharon’s bedroom,” Huxley says grimly. I don’t want to know how he knows that. Wyatt doesn’t hesitate. His long legs eat up the distance, his body thrumming with lethal tension. Huxley is a step behind him, his expression unreadable, while I push forward, ignoring the instinct screaming at me to slow down. For us all to not run into this, fists first.

Wyatt throws the door wide, but our presence goes unnoticed. The room is as lavish as I’d expect from Sharon. Deep red drapes, a four-poster bed with gold trim, a vanity cluttered with expensive perfume bottles. Through a set of stained glass doors, figures jerk and shout from the balcony.

The display is jaded by the colored glass, but we creep forward, catching Sharon’s slender form holding her own against a man towering over her. His back is to us, but he’s tall, broad, and dressed in a dark suit that fits just a little too stiffly. His fingers are wrapped tight around her wrist.

“Let go, you bastard!” she snarls, twisting violently. Something gleams between them, caught in a game of tug-of-war. I squint to see what it is—the flash of metal catching the moonlight. Whatever it is,

Sharon grits her teeth, digging her heels into the floor as she struggles to twist it free.

"Give me the drive," her attacker jerks her closer, his voice dangerously low. Wyatt stiffens in my peripheral.

"Go to hell," Sharon hisses back, wrenching herself sideways. I can see what's coming, like a scene from a movie that has me stepping into Huxley's side and my hand curling around his bicep.

"You first," a low growl sounds, and he shoves her chest, ripping the flash drive free at the last moment. Sharon's eyes go wide, her body pitching backward. For a split second, she flails, trying to grasp onto something, anything. Then she's gone. Her scream echoes, shrill and raw, before it cuts off with a sickening thud far below.

A breath of stillness follows, horrified and thick. My fingers start to tremble against Huxley's shirt fabric, his body twisting to draw me in. Tilting his head to my ear, he simply breathes. In, out. A simple command to mimic the rise and fall of his chest beneath my cheek. Wyatt's hand touches my back, stroking absentmindedly.

I don't care for Sharon, but to see and hear a life taken right in front of me is jarring.

The balcony door is pushed open, the shadow of the tall man stepping through. He stops in his tracks at the sight of us. Wyatt's hand on my back tightens, and my blood runs cold. That distant memory I couldn't unlock in the ballroom slams into me. A tailored suit, dark brown with a crisp white shirt. He's older, his hair more salt than pepper, and there's a stiffness to the way he holds himself. A rigidness and a sneer I've rarely seen.

For a moment, there's only stunned silence. It's not Fredrick. Not my real father, but my adoptive one.

"Nixon?"

CHAPTER THIRTY SEVEN

Nixon stands before me, the same as he ever was. Tall, composed, and wearing a suit that probably costs more than a semester at Waversea. His tie is loose around his aging neck, his sleeves rolled up, as if this was just another business deal gone sour. His face, sharp and unreadable, betrays nothing. No remorse. No surprise. Not even satisfaction.

As if he didn't just shove a woman off a fucking balcony. As if he's just the resigned, unloving bastard who raised me to a standard I could never reach.

My mouth feels dry, my chest tight. I can't decide what to focus on. The blood pounding in my skull, the way Avery's fingers twitch like she's fighting the urge to grab me, or the quiet calm on my once-father's face.

For the first time in my life, I don't know how to react. Sharon's scream rings in my ears, cutting through the roaring in my head. Axel's words from before replay in my mind. We're not murderers. And that's never been so apparent to me. I don't know if I can really do whatever it takes to keep Avery safe, like I've been promising. The thought terrifies me.

"I hope you're fucking happy," Nixon growls, holding the flash drive in the air. He's yet to address the fact that Avery is standing right beside me.

Unable to respond straight away, I just stare at the drive,

dumbfounded. My body is frozen in a way it hasn't been since I was a kid staring up at this same man, waiting for a term of endearment that won't come. He's never loved me, and it's never been as apparent as the way his face contorts into a scowl right now.

I feel Avery at my side, her breath shallow. Huxley is stock-still, his eyes unreadable as he watches Nixon like he's assessing another predator. I should move. I should do something, but all I can do is stare. Because Nixon isn't supposed to be here. Not at this auction. Not in this house. Not in this world I thought I built apart from him.

And yet, here he is.

Then, finally, Nixon huffs and pushes the drive into his pocket. He tugs his sleeves back down, fixes his cufflinks, and straightens his tie. It's so fucking normal, so routine, that a sharp, bitter laugh bubbles up in my throat. It doesn't make it past my lips. Instead, I hear my own voice, hoarse and disbelieving.

"What the fuck are you doing here?"

Nixon exhales sharply, as if I'm the one being unreasonable. "Cleaning up your mess, as per usual." He tilts his head, studying me. "Do you even know how stupid you've been?"

I can't breathe. My ribs feel like they're caving in. A lifetime of memories surge forward, slamming into me like a freight train. The years of disappointment, the belittling I thought I'd come to terms with. Apparently, I haven't. I've only buried them deep, deep down.

Nixon wasn't abusive physically. Just withdrawn, cold, and hateful. It's no wonder I didn't understand what love was until Avery showed me.

"I believe you owe us an explanation," Avery says with an air of composure, and the sound brings reality crashing back into focus. Sharon is dead. There's a body lying in the courtyard and a house full of students beneath our feet. Someone is going to notice her soon. Straightening, I mimic the way Avery is facing Nixon, her shoulders back and chin raised. My respect for her shoots off the scale. Nixon looks at Avery at last, his pale eyes remaining hard.

"Sharon Barrett is a snake of a woman who exploits anyone she can," Nixon grits out. No one attempts to tell him that Sharon isn't anything anymore. "She didn't leave me much choice when she reached out to blackmail me with a video of..." Nixon swallows, looking into a far corner. "You two."

Avery draws in a sharp breath at the same time my stomach plummets. If Sharon has cameras in the ballroom, she must have had them all over the mansion, including the gym. This is why Nixon is being so cold with Avery, too.

"I thought I could trust you to protect her, Wyatt," Nixon continues. "You're her brother." His disappointment is palpable, but I'm used to it. Used to this same argument.

"No, I'm not. I've been telling you for years. She is not my sister."

"The world thinks differently," Nixon snaps. Hux takes a microstep in front of Avery on instinct. If I wasn't on high alert, refusing to show weakness, I'd thank him. Nixon rolls his neck, straightening even further to put us at the same height. "What would have happened if this footage got out to the press?"

"Your reputation would blow up in flames?" I suggest with a shrug.

"You'd both be arrested," Nixon glares at me. "On paper, you are adoptive siblings. The circumstances don't matter."

I scoff at the injustice of it all. Avery and I have practically been strangers for years, regardless of my forged birth certificate and her false adoption back to her real mother. I've never lived with her until a few months ago, when Nixon moved her into Waversea.

But there's no time to argue back and forth. If we don't leave soon, we could be arrested for another crime entirely.

I turn to Avery and Hux, ignoring Nixon's presence behind me.

"We need to get out of here. Axel should already be in the minibus, and we have Fredrick's address," I say urgently, cutting through the haze of unaddressed shock lingering in the room. Nixon tries to interrupt, contesting going to Fredrick's house, but I don't give a fuck what he thinks. I'm here trying to fix the mess he's been creating for years.

Instead, I grab Avery's hands and implore her to only look at me.

"Richard is going to pin this on us, especially if he knows about the camera footage. If we're sitting in a police cell, who will protect Axel? Who's going to save Meg?"

Her breath hitches. There it is. That sharp clarity slicing through the fog, pulling her back to me. Avery doesn't hesitate when it comes to the people she loves.

She nods once. That's all I need. Our bodies press together. Hux ushering us along with hurried movements. We push toward the door, the urgency in our steps mirroring the panic crackling in the air. But just as we cross the threshold, Avery jerks to a stop. I tug her forward, but she resists, her entire body going rigid. Turning, she holds her hand out to Nixon.

"The flash drive," she demands. Her tone is laced with ice, any affection she felt towards Nixon is now a distant memory. He's failed in so many ways, but threatening to separate us has sealed the deal. When he refuses, I step closer to her back, a solid show of support.

"Give it to her."

There's a flicker in Nixon's expression. It puts me on edge, this version of him that sees straight through me, peeling back every layer until there's nothing left to hide. He knows exactly what I want with Avery. He always has. It was foolish to think I could send so many love letters to the manor without someone else reading them. I just don't know how long he's been aware.

It's why he pulled me from Rachel's house and took me to the safe house. Why he trusted me to protect her above all others. Ironic, since he was the one who pushed me away from her in the first place. But none of that matters. There's no going back now. I'm staking my claim, and nothing, not even Nixon, is going to stand in my way.

His lips curl into something resembling a sneer as he steps forward and pushes the flash drive into Avery's hand, his eyes locked on me with a deadly promise. "When you get both of the girls killed," he says smoothly, voice dripping with cold certainty, "I'm coming for you."

Avery presses back against my chest, either testing my resolve or to provide relief. It doesn't matter; I'm good. I've been building up to facing Nixon my entire life. Unflinching, I hold his steady gaze.

"And when both of them are safe, I'm exposing you for the fraud you are." It's not worth mentioning anything about Sharon lying dead in the courtyard. I don't care for her death, and on a base level, whether Nixon only came here to get the blackmail footage or to protect Avery, it's one less thing to worry about. Not that I'll be thanking him anytime soon. Instead, I tilt my head, my eyes narrowing.

"There's not enough room in this world for both of us." A smirk twitches at the corner of my lips as I step back, guiding Avery with me. "Don't get too comfortable, Nixon."

We race through the mansion's empty hallways and slow to a casual stroll when anyone passes. I'm on high alert, listening out for the moment someone discovers Sharon, and the longer that passes, the more I'm wondering why it hasn't happened yet.

The night air is thick with tension as we push through the last set of doors and step onto the mansion's long driveway. Gravel crunches beneath our hurried footsteps, the distant murmur of the remaining guests inside a stark contrast to the storm brewing beneath my skin. I'm driven by a need to protect those I love, blocking out all other noise.

The minibus is parked just beyond the stone fountain, its headlights slicing through the darkness. The side door is already open, Garrett leaning against it like he's been keeping watch, arms crossed over his chest. Beside him, Thiago fidgets, adjusting the strap of his laptop bag.

"I wiped all of my traces; no one will know I was there." Thiago says as soon as he sees me, his tone clipped. His sharp, pale eyes flick to Avery. I don't know what he's seeing through her stern exterior, but it's something long enough to linger until she's ducked into the minibus.

I follow, taking a quick headcount. Dax is up front in the passenger seat, his legs sprawled wide, and his phone in hand. Axel is stretched out across the back seat, propped up by a makeshift barricade of duffel bags and pillows, his eyes closed but his breathing even. The only person who looks as pissed off as I feel is Dr. Marcus, perched on the seat in front of Axel, arms folded and jaw tight. His hair is slightly disheveled, and his gaze tracks me like I'm the one responsible for ruining his night.

"I do not appreciate being bossed around. I need to speak to my employer about this." I pat Garrett's shoulder, jerking my head to get in whilst stewing on an answer for the Doc. There's no way I can announce his employer is dead, so I settle on a different truth.

"Axel is your patient." I snap, yanking the door closed behind me. "You work for him, and you go where he goes." The doctor exhales through his nose, fingers tapping against his bicep.

"Moving Axel right now isn't ideal. He's stable, but travel could set him back." I grit my teeth, dragging a hand through my hair. When I initially decided we needed to leave, it was with the threat of Fredrick hanging over us. Now, there's a twisted tale of blackmail and murder waiting in that mansion, and we do not have the time to sit around and wait for the cops to come and interrogate us.

"Not moving him is worse," I say bluntly. Dr. Marcus doesn't argue; he just sighs and leans back against the seat, muttering under his breath.

"Alright," Huxley says, sliding into the driver's seat and gripping the wheel like he's ready to punch the gas. "What's the plan?"

I drop into the seat beside Avery, yanking the tiny piece of paper from my pocket. Handing it to Thiago, I tell him to search for available hangers to which we can get Huxley's jet chartered. Thiago nods, already pulling out his laptop, but before he can type a damn thing, the doctor jerks upright in his seat, like I just suggested throwing Axel out mid-flight.

"Absolutely not."

I turn to level him with a glare, already too wired for an argument. "We'll go slow. Take it at Axel's pace."

"No," Doc Marcus snaps, his tone cutting through the tense air. "Axel physically can't fly for at least three weeks, and only then after an x-ray shows his pneumothorax is fully healed. It's too risky otherwise, and all of his progress could be undone."

Axel groans just then, his hands covering his ears, most likely getting a headache from being manhandled out of his room and shoved into a compact minibus. Garrett rushes to his side, skidding onto the floor between the seats and out of view.

Beside me, Avery reaches up and places her hand on my chest. "Wyatt, we can't sit here any longer," she whispers. I don't have time to react, to even think, before Huxley interrupts again.

"Where am I going here, Wyatt?" he calls urgently, fingers drumming impatiently against the steering wheel and his eyes piercing mine through the rearview mirror. I press my knuckles against my brow, forcing myself to stay calm. Everyone is counting on me not to crack, not to fail. For the first time, we have a location for Meg, and she's waiting to be rescued, but Axel's not going anywhere fast.

"Drive for a while," I order, jaw tight. "Thiago, find a motel where no one would think to look for us. We can plan together in the morning."

No one argues, knowing we don't have a better option right now. However, my harsh tone causes Avery to retreat because she knows I'm being forced to choose between Axel and Meg once again. I drape my arm over the back of her seat and pull her into me, needing to feel her warmth through the bitter cold seeping into my bones.

The engine rumbles to life, and as we pull away from the mansion, I glance over my shoulder one last time. Somewhere in that house, Nixon is watching. Somewhere out there, Fredrick Walters is waiting. And I have no fucking idea what's going to happen next.

CHAPTER THIRTY EIGHT

The motel room smells like stale cigarettes and cheap disinfectant, but it does the job. The receptionist was blind, accepted cash, and didn't take a name. A flickering neon sign outside the window casts an eerie red glow against the walls, pulsing like a heartbeat.

I sit on the edge of the lumpy mattress, my hands clasped between my knees, trying to ignore how my fingers won't stop trembling. The adrenaline is fading, leaving behind a strange hollowness in its wake. Behind me, on another of the four beds, Doc Marcus hovers over Axel, fussing over his bandages, while Garrett sits on a chair at his side.

We had one stop, in which Marcus jumped off the bus to relieve himself by the side of the road, and Wyatt could quickly tell the others about Sharon's demise and the reasons why. Surprisingly, he didn't leave anything out, and unsurprisingly, Garrett's two responses were, *'Thank fuck the bitch is dead,'* and, *'Can I get a copy of that tape?'* Axel is yet to say anything.

Across the room, Wyatt is muttering to Hux, their heads bowed in low conversation, while Dax hangs over Thiago, his laptop humming softly on the desk. Wyatt's shoulders are rigid, anxiety coiling through his frame. He hasn't stopped moving since we got here. Pacing, planning, and unraveling whatever temper is making it impossible for him to relax. After the way he held me on the minibus, his thumb constantly stroking my skin and his foot bouncing against mine, I should say something to help. Do something to help. But my own thoughts are a tangled mess.

Fredrick's address is lying on the table for all to see. A tangible, dangerous connection to the twin I've been yearning for. Every second I can see it, I can imagine the torture I could be saving her from, using my childhood as reference. The only reason I'm not halfway out the door already is because Wyatt is watching me like he expects me to bolt at any second.

And honestly? He's not wrong.

Thiago suddenly scrubs a hand over his face, breaking the silence. "That's me for the night. I can't even see the screen anymore," he closes his laptop and moves to stand. Wyatt quickly puts a hand on his shoulder, pushing him back into the seat.

"No one's sleeping," Wyatt barks a little too loudly. He pinches the bridge of his nose, his exhaustion apparent, but he won't give in. The need to get us out of the state, as far away from the crime scene, is pushing him to be snappy. The fact it coincides with getting one step closer to Meg puts extra pressure on him to pull this off. "We don't have time."

"We don't have a choice," Garrett cuts in, rolling his eyes. He's yet to change out of his leathers, and I reckon he's feeling the look. I, for one, couldn't wait to get out of that catsuit, changing in the minibus with Wyatt glaring daggers at Thiago and Marcus to keep their eyes averted.

I nod, straightening my back and rolling my stiff shoulders out.

"He's right. We're running on fumes, and if we're walking into Fredrick's house like this, we might as well shoot ourselves in the foot first." Wyatt looks like he wants to argue, but even he knows it's the truth.

"Fine," he grits out, looking at his phone for the time until daylight. "Three hours. Then we regroup here."

A collective exhale filters through the room. No one truly relaxes, but it's something. Thiago and Marcus pack up their equipment, heading for the rooms we booked out next door. Wyatt has one too, under the pretense that he'll also be staying elsewhere. Since the whole sibling blackmail thing, which is currently burning a hole in my pocket, Wyatt is being extra cautious about how our relationship appears to the outside world. He doesn't trust anyone outside of the Souls and me anymore.

Once again, Axel tells Garrett to change clothes. Gare's dark eyes flash down to the mesh top beneath his jacket, a pinch of uncertainty flashing over his face. I catch the white-knuckled grip Garrett has on the lapels and suddenly realize the problem. He doesn't want to take it off in front of the others. Picking up a random duffle bag since they were packed in a rush and everyone's clothes are mixed together, I head toward the bathroom, ordering Gare to come with.

The lock is flimsy, but it holds as I shut Garrett inside. "Strip," I tell him, my attention already on the bag at my feet. I rifle through, picking out some flannel pajama pants and a white tee, and in the background, I hear clothes hitting the floor. I'm careful to keep Garrett out of my eyeline, using the mirror at an angle so his reflection is hidden as I hold the clothes out. He takes them.

My reflection in the mirror is a stranger. Wide, haunted eyes, my shoulders tight and lips pressed tightly. I can forget about wrangling my hair into submission, my ponytail matted around the hair tie. When I don't hear any sounds, I peek over my shoulder to see Garrett's outline. He's standing, facing me, completely naked, and stroking his cock.

"What are you doing?" I turn fully now, keeping my eyes on his. He tenses at his chest being on display but doesn't shy away. Instead, his smirk is lazy, his fingers continuing to glide up and down his length. I must admit, the black nail polish on his tattooed hands is doing something for me.

"Oh," Garrett pretends to be caught out. "You told me to strip and then bent over in front of me. I thought that was an invitation." I lean back and grip the basin. We only have three hours until the stress starts all over again, the unknown forcing me to be both petrified and reckless. When no immediate answer comes, a voice calls from inside the room.

"Is he getting a blowjob right now?!" Axel calls.

"These walls are paper thin, you know," Wyatt growls a moment later. I grin before I catch myself. I shouldn't be able to smile or enjoy myself when I know Meg can't do the same. But then I think about the five men who are all emotionally leaning on me and who need something to keep going. Especially since it's my war that they are fighting.

Picking up the white T-shirt from where Garrett discarded it on the railing, I urge him to put it on before I unlock and swing the door open.

"If I'm not supposed to suck it, what do you want me to do about that?" I point to Garrett's cock, standing thick and proud for all to see. This is one area that Garrett isn't self-conscious about, and for a good reason.

"You can suck it, Swan," Huxley nods, much to Garrett's dick's excitement. "I just think we're past closed doors at this point." A simmer of uncharted territory ripples through the six of us. Without Garrett being completely overbearing and forcing us all to push these boundaries, I find all eyes on me, an equal amount of intrigue and caution awaiting my next move. All the while, I'm thinking, '*We have three freaking hours, and I'm exhausted*', so I decide to compromise.

"I only have the energy to make one of you come. Are you all in agreement that Garrett is the receiver?" The man in question makes a giddy little noise, like he might explode if we don't get an answer soon. Dax takes pity on him first.

"It would be rude to deny him now."

"Well, if I must," Garrett sighs dramatically, swanning across the room to sit against Axel's headboard with him. His grin is huge, as if he's been waiting years for this exact scenario. I shake my head to myself, following him to the small double bed. His and Axel's long limbs take up the entire length, not leaving much room for me to crawl between his legs. Chairs clatter as the three other spectators drag the metal along the length of the room to settle at the foot of the bed.

"You won't get much of a view back there," I frown over my shoulder. Wyatt snorts.

"It's the only view I want." Like every time Wyatt compliments me, my heart flips over itself. I pause, deciding they might as well get a proper show if that's the case. Stepping back off the bed, I wriggle out of my pajamas and climb on, the mattress springs squeaking loudly. As I bend forward, a round of appreciative groans echoes around the thin walls.

Garrett's cock is still hard against his stomach, and there's a part of me that enjoys the power at this moment. It's intoxicating. The way his breath stutters when I drag my nails lightly up his thighs, the way his muscles tense in anticipation. How Axel's hazel eyes drink in every movement between the two of us, his own pants starting to become tented.

I shift, settling between Garrett's tattooed legs, and let my lips brush the sensitive skin along his hip. He inhales sharply. I glance up at him, amused at how quickly his teasing confidence wavers under my touch. I'm just enjoying how his jaw is locked shut for once. I let my tongue flick against the head of his cock, moving slowly to work my way down his shaft, moistening as I go. He's silky smooth against my tongue, the lightest taste of salty precum gliding across the roof of my mouth.

Taking him deeper, my own arousal flares beneath the surface. I feel myself growing wetter, the cool air brushing against my cunt. Knowing they're watching and that they can see everything drives my desire to a new high. I'm drunk on it, rolling my hips in mid-air and putting more gusto into the blowjob than possibly ever before.

A hand brushes a few fallen strands of hair from my face, and I blink up to see Axel stroking my face. He feels my cheek hollow, his hand doing an exploration of its own to feel Garrett's cock bobbing in and out of my throat. When Garrett's eyes open to watch, they're blown wide with lust, his cheeks twinged pink and his hands fisting in the sheets.

"Careful, Gare. You don't want to finish straight away. That would be embarrassing," I smirk against his shaft. Laughter rumbles from Garrett's chest.

"I'll come after you, Peach." On cue, hands caress my ass, fingers skimming over my wetness. I didn't hear anyone move, but when I try to look back, Axel keeps his hold on my face.

"No one told you to stop," he grins. With his encouragement, I take Garrett back into my mouth, distracted this time by the sensations running up the back of my thighs. My asscheeks are pried apart, the cold air hitting me more directly. Fingers roll over my clit and my hips in too many places to only belong to one person.

I can't stop the moan that vibrates around Garrett's shaft when fingers trace through my wetness, dipping closer to my center with unbearable slowness. The sensation sends a shiver up my spine, my entire body responding to their touch, my knees digging into the cheap motel bedding as I try to focus on the weight of Garrett in my mouth.

Garrett curses above me, his hips jerking slightly. I smirk around him, taking him deeper until he's nudging the back of my throat, swallowing around his length just to hear the sharp breath he sucks in. A second set of fingers joins the first, spreading me open and teasing the slick entrance of my cunt.

"Fuck," I whimper, the sound muffled around Garrett's cock, my thighs trembling. I hear a chuckle from behind me, warm hands gripping my hips, steadying me.

"You like this, Swan." Huxley's voice is low and smooth. It's not posed as a question because he already knows the answer. He can feel how my body is responding as my arousal coats his fingers. Axel hums from where he still cradles my cheek, brushing his thumb just under my eye, his touch gentle in contrast to the intensity coiling between my legs.

"She loves having all of our attention. Don't you, sweetheart?" I nod around Garrett, my answer too muffled. I hollow my cheeks again, drawing a groan from Garrett, and the praise only fuels me. His hands grip my hair, his restraint slipping.

Huxley chuckles, and suddenly, I feel the press of a finger as someone pushes inside me. A gasp leaves me, my body jolting, and Garrett groans as the movement pulls against his cock.

"Keep going," Axel reminds me, his thumb dragging across my bottom lip, smearing saliva and precum in its wake. The finger inside me curls, stretching me deliberately as another joins, then quickly a third. I buck and groan, my eyes falling closed. I'm vaguely aware that Axel's hold on my chin and Garrett's grip on my hair are keeping my head bopping up and down, but my entire focus is on my own pleasure.

A slow drag, a quickened pace, a twisting motion. A disjointed rhythm I can't predict. I'm pulled in all directions, my hips tilted upward. I can't get enough, but I can't relax into it either. Each thrust catches me off guard, my moans growing louder around Garrett, my movements more sluggish. As my brain is trying to envision who is fingering me so expertly, yet unpredictably, I suddenly go still as the perfect image slams into place.

It's all three of them. Hux, Dax, and Wyatt standing shoulder to shoulder, pumping into me with individual pace and skill. Realizing I've stalled on Garrett's dick, a sharp spank is delivered to my ass.

"Be good for us, Angel," Wyatt warns. The nickname makes my stomach twist with heat, a needy whimper escaping as I take Garrett even deeper, eager to chase the praise, to feel him unravel under my touch, just like they're doing to me. Someone presses against that sensitive spot as if I've given them a map of how to find it, and I know I'm about to break.

My skin feels tight under the weight of their attention, my body temperature soaring. I'm too hot, too sensitive to the fingers fucking my cunt. The feel of Garrett's cock pulsing on my tongue, the stretch of fingers inside me, the way Axel is watching me like I'm the most mesmerizing thing he's ever seen. All I know is that I'm drowning in them—in their touch, their voices, their control. And even though I know I'm a goner, I refuse to go down alone.

I let my tongue swirl around the tip of his cock before sinking down again, swallowing him as deep as I can. "Holy shit, Peach. You do that so well." Garrett's head thumps against the headboard, his body tightening beneath the white tee. I'm right there with him. When the first spurt of warm cum floods my mouth, my body retaliates.

I'm hit with a shockwave of pleasure so intense it steals the air from my lungs. My thighs quake, my body tightening around the fingers buried deep inside me as my orgasm slams into me. A cry rips from my throat, muffled around Garrett's cock as I tremble, my muscles locking, fire scorching through my veins.

"Fuck, she's squeezing us," Hux groans, another hand smoothing down the curve of my spine. "So goddamn tight." Their pace doesn't falter as they drag out every pulse, every shuddering aftershock. Axel strokes my cheek and jaw, murmuring praise to Garrett and me. The latter pumps into me, and I swallow greedily, taking everything Garrett has to offer. For all of us, this was a distraction, and we succeeded.

Once the tremors subside, I finally drop into the nearest vacant bed, exhaustion claiming me almost instantly. My legs are moved, the cover drawn back, and a body slips in behind me. I'd guess Huxley from the tickle of his long hair and the firmness of his muscled chest.

A scraping sound brings the next bed closer, and through cracked eyelids, I watch Wyatt strip down to his boxers and lie in front of me. I force myself to wake, wanting to memorize his expression. Devoid of sternness, he stares at me so openly that I must remind myself it hasn't always been this easy. To lie together and simply be.

Dax must be the one to turn off the light and plunge us into darkness, save for the red motel sign outside. Still, Wyatt watches me closely until I can no longer stay awake. I jerkily reach out, placing my hand on his chest just before I slip under, his warmth anchoring me to the shitty motel room that I wouldn't change for the world. Because that's where my men are, and that's where we will finally be able to bring Meg when she's saved.

Those eyes follow me into my dreams. A green Siren, neither guiding me home nor drawing me into danger. It's as if my mind can't decipher that last lingering look. The need to memorize my face, the silent apology I was too tired to acknowledge. Subconsciously, I seem to know something isn't quite right.

For that reason, when I wake many, many hours later to find a folded piece of paper on my pillow, I'm not even surprised. I'm more disappointed when I sit up to see Axel sobbing into Huxley's neck and Dax standing by the window, picking at his lip, because Garrett has decided to leave us behind too.

CHAPTER THIRTY NINE

My Dearest Avery,

You've probably already figured out that I never intended to take you with me. That the promises I made to you were false, and that I knew any chance of a future for us was a myth. We are victims. Brought together by fate and torn apart by circumstance. I take the blame for pushing you away yet pulling you close. For holding you to a standard that I wasn't able to match. Among it all, something is blaring clear. We never stood a chance.

Through the years, I've penned hundreds of these letters, written thousands of words never meant to reach your eyes. But none of them matter more than the paper you now hold in your hands. I owe you so many apologies, and it's long overdue that you received them.

I'm sorry for loving you. None of this would have happened if I hadn't. I could have stayed at the manor all these years; I could have been a protector and a companion to you. I could have spoken with Cathy more, understood her secrets, and prevented her death. I could have reasoned with Nixon on how best to keep both you and Meg safe. If it hadn't been for avoiding these feelings I have never dealt with, everything would have been so much easier.

I'm sorry for all of the shit I've put you through, for the friendships I've severed, and for putting Meg at risk. It's no consolation, but at least in the very end, I did try to put things right. I needed a plan that didn't involve you putting yourself in danger. I had to know that you were strong enough to hold the Souls together. I've spent my time with each one of them, ensuring they are the best versions of themselves for you, just like you wanted. It's the least you deserve after a life of neglect and heartache.

Lastly, I'm sorry for failing you this one last time. I looked into your big, beautiful eyes, knowing this is how it was always going to end. Whatever short time we had, I am a better man for it. I've learned not to hide from affection, not to shy away from the difficult feelings I'd usually suppress. I now understand the difference between love and sacrifice.

And I know I've lost all hopes of you loving me back.

Although I have no right to ask, and I know you will not listen, I beg you not to follow me. Stay with the Souls, give them the love they need. Take my place as their leader. You will do a much better job than I ever did. People depend on you now. Being reckless with your life will have an irreparable impact on everyone around you. There are many things in life that they can survive, but losing you is not one of them.

I will love you forever, so much that it hurts. I will hold you and the fragments of our relationship I allowed myself to enjoy in my heart. And I will do whatever it takes to bring Meg back to you. Consider it my parting gift.

Always yours,
Mr. XO.

CHAPTER FORTY

"So it's been you this entire time?" Garrett openly gapes at me from the seat opposite. He leans forward, elbows propped on the table, his dark eyes flicking between mine like he's trying to pry open my skull and read whatever's inside. "You've been the one sending her cards and letters and chocolates and flowers and gifts. Since she was like, what, eleven?"

I sigh, regretting writing Avery that damn letter whilst Garrett was hanging around, wanting to go before Axel woke up. Now he knows everything I've spent years trying to keep guarded.

The jet lurches forward, engines roaring as it races down the tarmac, pressing me back into the plush leather seat. The force of acceleration hums through my bones, a steady climb pulling us higher and higher, until the ground falls away beneath us. I divert my gaze to the window, the hanger shrinking into a patchwork of gray and green. I wince at the pressure popping my ears, but Garrett remains unaffected, sitting back with a smirk.

"Damn, Riot. You went about this all wrong. I thought you didn't know you loved her, and I needed to help coax it out of you." It's my turn to scoff, giving my dickhead best friend an incredulous look.

"And how have you helped with that in the slightest?" I drawl, and he ignores me, lost in his own little world.

"But if you'd told me you were head-over-heels in love with her, well shit... I might not have pursued her so hard." Gare whistles, reaching for the minibar despite it being eight in the morning. I shake my head, a disbelieving smile creeping through.

"You're a fucking liar. You'd have strung her up in my bedroom and forced me to watch you pleasure her day after day."

"Now there's a thought," Garrett trails off, his dark eyes turning black as he sips from a mini bottle of whiskey. I kick his shin beneath the table, although I'm also mad at myself for putting that image out there. I can't stop seeing it each time I blink.

"Doesn't matter," Garrett's eyebrows raise, a wistful look passing over his features. "She'll never fuck you now. All that bullshit you fed her about being a team and sticking together? You should know not to make promises you can't keep."

I sigh, hating that he's right. It's a lesson I was once so disciplined in, and another barricade Avery smashed straight through. It's like when she's with me, curled up in my arms and staring at me like the entire world is ours for the taking; anything will bubble from my lips. I'll tell her exactly what she wants to hear, that I'll bring Meg back, and that I'll carve a way for us to be together. I'd bring the freaking world to her feet. And once she steps away, the weight comes crashing down when I realize I can't do any of those things.

"She'll never forgive you either, you know?" I add in as a last minute snide comment, although it's a beat too late. Garrett leans back with a cocky stretch, kicking his feet up onto the empty seat beside him. Garrett doesn't care to reprimand himself. He doesn't tell himself he's not worthy of their love or stand down to let others step in. He's a bulldozer, demolishing the social norm and putting himself directly in the center of the chaos. He takes love he doesn't deserve and never feels bad about it, unlike most people who strive to feel justified in accepting someone's affections.

My jaw clenches the longer I look at him.

"Yeah, she will," he grins like the Cheshire Cat, sipping his tiny whiskey bottle and winking. "No one can stay mad at me."

And I know he's right, the charming bastard. Even Axel, who will give him hell, will come around eventually. They always do.

Night is due to fall any moment as we enter the quiet suburb. I've been behind the driver's seat of a rental Ferrari GT all day, with Garrett munching on stolen airplane snacks, drinking his body weight in orange juice, and pissing in the empty bottles. The glucose sugars have kickstarted his energy levels, his body physically vibrating in the passenger seat.

Around two hours ago, the radio was turned up to deafening, and it's yet to go back down, while Gare pounds his head back and forth and screams lyrics at the side of my face.

"I really hate you sometimes," I mutter under my breath. Although I am grateful for the company. Garrett is doing a fantastic job at distracting me from thoughts of Avery and how she's probably cursing my name right now.

Halfway through Teenage Dirtbag, I flick off the radio and ease the car to a crawl, staring through the passenger window as we roll up to the address we've been searching for. There's nothing sinister about it from the outside, but I know better than to let my guard down. I've dealt with Fredrick before, and to him, appearances are everything.

The sun is slipping below the rooftops, bleeding streaks of burnt orange and violet across the pointed rooftop. Shadows stretch across the pavement as I ease the Ferrari to a stop, the low hum of the engine purring through the chilled air. Garrett is still oblivious to the tension gripping my spine, drumming out a final beat against the dashboard with his sticky fingers.

"At least let me finish the song before reality hits," he whines, slumping back dramatically. I send him a flat look.

"We're about to break into a house, not headline Coachella."

Garrett pouts, then leans forward, peering through the windshield. "Doesn't look like a kidnappy kind of place." And that's the problem. It doesn't. The house is clean-cut and prim, the kind of place with a well-manicured lawn and a porch light that flickers invitingly. No bars on the windows, no rusted-out vehicles in the driveway. It's almost... painfully normal. No one passing would know what mess is hiding behind this pretty façade or that there is a girl trapped inside.

As if a switch has been flipped in his head, Garrett reaches back into the back seat for the metal pipe, his face hardening. He exhales, cracks his knuckles, and climbs out of the car. I do the same, my fingers tightening around the crowbar I brought as we move toward the house.

The front door is locked, but Garrett solves that with a well-placed kick just below the handle. It splinters open, swinging inward with a dull groan. I smack his arm before he enters, mouthing, *'what the hell.'* We'd agreed I would take the lead, and in my mind, we'd check the perimeter first. Gather some intel before we burst in. Garrett obviously had other ideas.

Stepping inside, the air hits me first. Stale and thick, tinged with something sharp beneath the lingering scent of wood polish and stale cologne. I scan the room. It's eerily still like no one has been here for weeks. But there are signs of life. Cigarette butts overflowing in the tray by the leather couch, an empty drinking glass on the coffee table, discarded men's shoes just inside the door.

When we're not immediately confronted, I ease the door closed as much as it will allow and follow Garrett onward. Floorboards creak beneath our shoes, parts of the house shifting with our presence. But there are no screams, no pleas for help like I'd envisioned. When we cross the threshold into the dining room, I see why.

The dining table is knocked over, shards of porcelain from a broken plate scattered across the floor. A chair is lying on its side, one leg snapped clean off. A deep scuff in the wooden flooring leads toward the hallway, like someone was dragged. Garrett stills, his hyper demeanor long gone.

"Fuck," he breathes. I swallow down the rising panic.

"Check the rooms."

We move quickly now, methodically checking every darkened space with our metal weapons raised. The kitchen is empty. The fridge hums, but the power in the rest of the house feels empty. The skid marks stop in the hallway, leaving no further trace.

Upstairs, the bedrooms appear undisturbed. Shopping bags of new clothes and toiletries lay untouched, the curtains pulled back, and bedspreads made neatly. All except for one. A pink monstrosity covered in unicorn posters and a vanity against a glimmering feature wall. The mirror is smashed, the floral sheets are twisted, pillows thrown across the floor, and in the dim light, I spot a single drop of blood on the carpet. Bending down to inspect it, the crimson glistens. It's fresh.

Garrett crouches beside me, running his finger along the seam of his pursed lips. "Would he really be stupid enough to bring Meg to his own safe house?" I rub my eyes, my rattled sigh doing nothing to alleviate the strain in my chest.

"Something weird has happened here, for sure. But whatever it is, we're too late. Meg's not here."

"So where the hell do we go now?" Garrett stands, cracking his neck as he peers out of the window, the heavy weight of the pipe thumping against his thigh. The answer isn't in the house.

We search every inch, but there's no sign of her. Just a collection of fragmented evidence, whispers of a struggle, but nothing leading us to Meg herself. I'm ready to slam my fist through the wall when Garrett suddenly spins and grips my arm. Despite my arguments, he tugs me to my feet, down the stairs, and out of the back door at the rear of the kitchen.

At the far end of the backyard, there's a garage, only big enough for one car. Its door hangs open and swings with a quiet creak against the crisp night. The scent hits me from a few feet away—a thick and metallic potency that is unmistakable.

Blood.

Without wasting any time, I use my crowbar to hold the door open and step inside. A body sprawls beneath the hanging light, the bulb swaying slightly, casting flickering silhouettes across the stained concrete. Fredrick Walters is on his back, eyes glassy, mouth slightly open as if caught mid-protest, with a singular bullet hole through his head. A dark pool has spread beneath him, seeping into the floor's cracks.

"Shit," Garrett mutters, nudging his lifeless arm with his foot.

My stomach churns. Not because he's dead. I couldn't care less about the bastard, but because this means we have no leverage. No leads. Meg is still missing, and the one man who might've known where she was is currently bleeding out beneath us. Any hopes of returning to

Avery as the hero she's always trying to make me out to be just vanished. I rake a hand through my hair, gripping tight at my scalp.

"We're fucked."

"Yeah." Garrett exhales slowly. "Unless Meg did this. Maybe she's managed to escape and gave the bastard what he deserved." I chew on my inner cheek. Optimism has never been my strength, and somehow, I can't picture Meg being familiar with shooting through someone's skull at point-blank range. There's a slim chance I'm mistaken, but this screams the work of a professional.

"I really hope you're right, Gare, but I can't afford to hang around here and dig around any longer. Being present at two murders within the same week doesn't bode well for me. We can talk theories on the way back to the jet." Nodding, Garrett attempts to kick this body one last time, but I catch his shin with the crowbar, shaking my head. Fredrick is dead. We can finally put him behind us and have one less threat against Avery to worry about.

Just as we're about to turn away, a shrill noise cuts through the silence. So loud that I flinch and wave the crowbar around, expecting an immediate attack. Instead, the noise repeats, drawing my gaze down to Fredrick's body.

A phone shines through the pocket of a vintage, knitted cardigan, vibrating in time with the ringtone. I pause long enough to notice his corduroy trousers and checked slippers, an unsettling and nauseous feeling sweeping over me. The man lying before us is a far cry from the crazed mafia leader I met previously. Something doesn't quite add up.

Garrett half shrugs and starts to reach out for the phone when I grab his shoulder to stop him. "What?" he frowns, and I can't help my eye roll. Locating a cloth on a nearby workbench, I slip the device out without leaving any fingerprints and use my knuckle to answer the call. The number is blocked.

"You're late," a voice grunts. I hold the phone steady, my mind racing with how to best handle this and coming up completely empty. I figure I'll let the man talk to himself until a moment arises that I can take advantage of, but as usual, I'm always one step behind. "You were supposed to be here ten minutes ago, Wyatt Hughes."

Garrett stiffens beside me, and my grip on the phone tightens, my heart slamming into my ribs. I press my lips together, controlling my breathing before forcing an air of authority.

"I wasn't aware I had a front-row seat to Fredrick's death, or I would have made sure I was on time," I reply steadily, playing the devil's advocate until I know who I'm dealing with. A loaded chuckle follows.

"His death wasn't part of the plan, but in your absence, he began asking questions. Going back on his word. My hand was forced."

"I was under the impression that Fredrick pulled his own strings." Another laugh, this one booming and bitter. I cut a sharp glance to Garrett, who's wringing his hands around the pipe, his knuckles going white. Trepidation worms its way through my psyche, leaving a dull ache behind.

"Everyone has a boss. Even the group of delinquent kids who have been playing gangster, believing they could walk in here and retrieve their friend with what... a pipe and a crowbar?" I shoot a glance around the garage, spotting nothing out of the ordinary.

Toolboxes and a workbench, a few saws, and spanners hanging on iron hooks. It's evident a car hasn't been stored in here for a long time, as I only now notice heavy chains linked through metal loops on the floor. It's more of a budget torture room, and something I'm sure wasn't included in the original plans for the safe house. This is a recent addition.

Turning back toward the house, my heartbeat thudding in my ears. In the kitchen window, a black silhouette stands behind the blind, his hand raised to his ear. I flick my gaze to a gate in the fence, one that will give us an escape without passing back through the house. I use the crowbar to hook Garrett's wrist and slowly start tugging him out of the garage and back into the night.

"Where is Meg?" I demand now, done with these games. We've been outsmarted, and we need to get out of here. Another dry chuckle echoes through the loud speaker.

"You can have the bitch for the right price." My feet freeze in place, and Garrett bumps into my side. So this is a ransom? Could it really be that easy? I barely manage to withhold the laughter that wants to bubble out of me. At long last, this is something I can do. I'm not so helpless after all. "Keep this phone with you. I'll text with a time and place."

"I'll be there," I say with certainty, nodding to the silhouette as if he can see him. His breath saws through the receiver.

"Not you. After the bullshit I've been put through, I'll only be dealing with Avery Hughes directly from here on out. Any sign of your little gang or the cops, and the girl dies instantly."

"See, that's where we're going to have a problem—" The line goes dead. Garrett swears under his breath, rubbing his nape as his eyes stare endlessly at the ground.

"Well. That's not great," he mutters unhelpfully.

"No, it fucking isn't." I tug Gare the rest of the way to the gate, taking our escape while it's being permitted. I briefly pause by the car, vaguely wondering if it's been tampered with, but the device in my hand is my insurance. A dead man's phone, which has made me a messenger between this unknown foe and Avery. At least I have several hours of traveling ahead of me to decide exactly what message I'm going to deliver.

AVERY

CHAPTER FORTY ONE

"Ironic, isn't it?" Axel rasps, propped up beside me against the headboard. I raise a brow lazily. "The woman who was supposed to be my mom is dead and I've never felt more free, whilst trapped in this shithole room and crying over a dickmunch who left us behind." He huffs a laugh but there's no humor in it. I merely nod, looking around the peeling wallpaper with a fresh wave of disgust.

I was hoping, with time, the motel room might appear more sufficient in the daylight or that we'd grow accustomed to the stench of mold creeping into the walls. I was wrong on both counts. Either way, we don't leave, and not only because we have nowhere to go.

Axel's sobbing has done a number on his lungs, as Dr. Marcus informed us during yesterday morning's check-in. Just before he left for good, declaring his disgust at his new surroundings, the Doc put Axel on strict bed rest, which involves cuddling into me while Dax reads us fanfics from his phone—anything to distract us from those who are missing.

Huxley has been stomping in and out, apparently 'running errands.' He located food, the greasiest pizza I've ever seen or tasted, leered over Thiago's laptop for hours whilst intimidating the man using it, and ran a few laps around the motel at various times of the day. He says he's getting a lay of the land and checking for anyone suspicious, but I reckon he doesn't know what to do with his pent-up frustration. I feel the same, but another body milling around won't help.

At lunchtime, a pair of uniformed officers pounded on the door. My heart dropped to my feet, the fear that Wyatt and Garrett weren't coming back slicing through me, but they only wanted to talk about Sharon. Huxley's SUV, which has now been impounded, had been left at the mansion, and somehow they'd tracked us here. Richard spun a lovely tale of Sharon's hospitality, looking after her only son in his time of need whilst we terrorized their staff and took over their home. Meanwhile, Axel had to pretend that her death was news to him, and we were subjected to their questions. Our surroundings are incredibly suspicious, but they left within an hour, threatening to be in touch.

Another exhausting day of restless emotion as our lies and secrets catch up with us. Night falls, and Axel nestles down, his head resting on my chest. I stroke his shaved head, becoming lulled by the gentle sound of his breathing. While he was awake, I felt the need to suppress everything I was feeling. Pushing it all down until I wasn't even sure what it was. Hate, fury, regret.

Now that he's asleep, I could let it rise to the surface and actually deal with it all. But that sounds exhausting, so I just lie here, stroking his head and focusing on those in this room. Those who need me not to crumble. Dax passes by to kiss my cheek and whispers in my ear that he's going to attempt a shower. I manage a weak smile, and the mattress at my feet dips where Hux takes over as watchdog.

"There's room up here, you know," I mutter down the bed. Hux glances over his shoulder, peering at where the beds have been pushed together, and shakes his head.

"I'm waiting for Thiago to return. I gave him a dinner break around three hours ago."

"He's allowed a rest, Hux. This isn't his fight." I get a grunt in response.

Still stroking Axel's head, I close my eyes, allowing myself to go somewhere else in my mind. At first, the darkness behind my eyelids was just that—darkness. But then, it deepens, taking form as I put all my strength into picturing a beach, a smooth rolling of waves against the shore, and my boys sunbathing in a line of gorgeous bodies. It's a sweet image, yet so far away from our current state.

Somewhere beyond the haze, I know Huxley is still sitting at the foot of the bed, rigid and restless. I can picture him exactly as he is, leaning forward, elbows on his knees, fingers pressed together like he's about to pray but doesn't believe in anything enough to bother. The glow of Thiago's laptop screen is long gone, and with it the occasional clack of keys. The only thing left is the sound of Axel's breathing and the creaky sighs of the old motel walls settling around us.

It should feel safe. Instead, it feels like the calm before a storm. I let the feeling wash over me, let my thoughts sink into something soft, somewhere in the space between sleep and waking. It reminds me of when I was little, when I'd press my face into my pillow and pretend the world didn't exist for just a few minutes longer. Back then, I was always waiting for something. Waiting to be wanted. Waiting to be safe.

Now, I'm waiting for Wyatt and Garrett. I wish I could feel hopeful, that they're going to find Meg and finally bring her home to me, but everything feels wrong. Once again, Wyatt has led a crusade to fight my battles for me, whilst I sit around imagining the worst. A cold prickle crawls up my spine. The distant hum of Dax's shower fades, replaced by a rhythmic sound muffled like footsteps on carpet.

A moment later, a damp and delightfully naked Dax rolls into my side. His fingers paint patterns around my arm, mouth pressed against my cheek. He doesn't leave an inch of space between us, and I wouldn't have it any other way. The longer I spend with Dax, the more clingy I'm becoming. The infatuation between us isn't lessening; it's entwining into something frantic and unhealthy, yet I love it. I lean into his chest, breathing in the smell of cheap shower gel and something uniquely him.

"Dax," I twist my head to breathe in his ear. For one moment, I crave some privacy for my confession. "You can't ever leave me behind." My voice cracks, the admission bursting open the dam I'd shut down over my emotions. Dax dislodges Axel's head, gently shifting him onto my shoulder so that he can drape himself over my body.

"I wouldn't even consider it," he replies breathily. The tears I've been holding back start to fall, silent at first but they won't be wrangled into submission. Huge wracking sobs burn my throat, and I know that my jerking is hurting Axel but I can't stop. My lungs won't expand, my chest clamping down on itself. Axel's arm wraps around my middle tightly whilst Dax holds my face, our foreheads touching. He doesn't let an inch of space between us, absorbing my misery as his own. Hux still doesn't move up the bed, but a hand wraps around my ankle.

Suddenly, a knock raps on the door and the dip in the mattress is gone, Huxley rushing forward to whip it open. He's already cursing out Thiago when he cuts himself off and grows strangely silent. I wipe my cheeks and eyes harshly, irritated with myself for holding everything in for so long, only to burst open like that.

Pushing up onto my elbows, I slowly adjust to the dim light as Garrett steps in first. He moves like he owns the place, like he always does, like the entire world is his to bend and break as he pleases. But I feel like by now, I know him better than that. He's masking something.

Wyatt follows close behind. His jaw is tight, and his green eyes are sharp in a way that makes my breath catch. He looks wired, his expression completely closed off, and his shoulders stiff. I try not to jolt Axel, but he wakes anyway, groaning as he pushes himself up to sit. I support him as best I can, moving us to lean against the headboard with his arm pressed into mine.

"You fuckers," Hux slams the door closed. He stands in front of it, his arms crossed as if Wyatt and Garrett might change their minds and run back out of it. Dax shimmies off the bed, shedding the towel around his waist and dragging on some sweatpants.

"I didn't think you'd be back so soon," Dax mutters, not as harshly. Perhaps he is too relieved to see them back safe to stare murderously like Huxley is. Completely oblivious, Garrett peels off his jacket and tosses it onto the chair by the window. He moves to the bathroom, leaning over the small sink in the corner to wash his hands with a little too much force. In my peripheral, Wyatt steps towards the bed, raking a hand through his hair.

"Angel," Wyatt speaks directly to me. I scoff, avoiding his eyes. "Can we talk?"

"I don't know, can we? Or do you want to write it down in another letter?" I snap back. I finally look at him, and as I knew it would, all of the anger I've been holding onto rushes to the surface. He was expecting my reaction, his head slightly bowed. His T-shirt is crumpled and sweaty, a smudge of something dark across his front.

"I deserved that," he unclenches his fists at his sides. "But I really think it would be best if we stepped outside." My narrowed eyes bore a hole in his face, and Hux widens his stance in front of the door. Wyatt isn't taking me anywhere.

"Whatever it is, just say it, Wyatt," Axel grounds out. His hand rests against his chest, pressing down to keep his breathing even. My fingers tangle in the fabric of his T-shirt, an attempt to ground us both.

"Fredrick is dead," Garrett announces, striding back in with a small hand towel drying his hands. He lets out a humorless laugh and tosses it against the wall. "Someone put a bullet in his head before we even got there."

I freeze, forgetting how to react. *Dead.* The man who ruined my childhood, haunted my dreams and then returned to do it all over again. The monster I had to survive twice. *Dead.* I've wished to hear those words so many times, wanting to close the door on my past and no longer let it bleed into my future. I return my gaze to Wyatt, watching his throat bob as he swallows.

"And Meg?" I ask tentatively. I know the answer because she's not here. They didn't bring her back, but I need the confirmation.

"We searched everywhere," Wyatt sighs. "There was no sign of her beyond the mess of a struggle."

Silence spreads like a stain across the room. The air feels thick, pressing down on my chest like Axel's, making it harder to breathe. My fingers tighten in his T-shirt, but I barely feel the fabric beneath my grip. Fredrick has left this world with answers I will never retrieve, snatching my closure in one final act of cruelty. My heartbeat pulses in my ears, louder than the creak of the motel walls, louder than the sharp exhale Wyatt lets out.

I was hoping Wyatt's dramatic exit was for a reason. That his written apology was a placeholder for the real one, in which he marched Meg through the door and said, '*ta da*". I don't blame him directly. If she wasn't there, then there was nothing he could do. But I can't help the betrayal that cuts me so deeply as if Wyatt himself has deceived me.

My mouth feels dry, as if I've swallowed dust. I want to ask a hundred questions. Who else was there? How bad was the struggle? Was there blood? But I can't seem to form the words.

I glance at Garrett, at the set of his jaw, the way his nostrils flare slightly as he leans against the wall with the forced casualness he wears like armor. He won't meet my eyes, and that tells me enough. It was bad.

Huxley speaks first, a prolonged growl from the front of the room.

"And you just left?!" The veins in his arms clench, tracing lines across his forearms. Garrett lifts his head, his expression blank.

"No, Hux. We stayed and had a fucking tea party with his corpse."

"*Asshole*," Huxley spits, that nervous energy coming back. Flinging his arms down, Hux spins and throws the door open, declaring he's going to find Thiago. I feel bad for the Brazilian who's about to be on the receiving end of his frustration, and apparently, so does his cousin. Dax exhales, raking a hand through his damp curls.

"I'd better make sure Hux's fists only fly at the walls," he grumbles and exits a moment later. Wyatt doesn't move at all. He watches me closely, his eyes dark and his jaw locked so tight, I half expect his teeth to shatter.

"I would really like a moment alone with you if you don't mind," Wyatt tries to ask me again. I resolutely look to the ceiling, huffing through my nose. A rejection is on my tongue when Axel nudges my arm, his voice a low croak.

"Go. I need to say a few choice words to Garrett anyway." Axel's breathing is ragged, his whole body shaking with unspent rage, but after a beat, he lets go. His hand drops to his side, his shoulders heaving in an effort to stay calm. I don't feel comfortable leaving him, but Wyatt takes his cue to hold out his hand. I wriggle forward and accept it with a rough squeeze meant to hurt, but I know it won't even phase him.

"You'd better grovel properly," I glare at Garrett. A devilish smirk crosses his face that he has no business letting loose.

"I'll be on my knees and begging for forgiveness, Peach." I roll my eyes but let Wyatt accompany me into the night air. It's a fresh balm after a day cooped up and hardly moving. I'm guided along the motel building, passing door after door and turning at the end corner. The streetlamp doesn't quite reach this patch of grass, a bush creating a dead end. Once we're out of sight, I wrench my hand out of Wyatt's and spin on him.

"What? What could you possibly have to say to me?" He steps into my space, and I shove at his chest. Wyatt continues to advance, effectively backing me into a corner. My shove might as well be a whisper against the steeliness of his chest. Sharp breaths slice through the thick air between us, and even though I can't see them, I can feel his eyes are on me. Wild, burning green, containing everything he felt unable to say in front of an audience.

He should be apologizing, telling me that he meant to take me with him to Fredrick's house, but he has a valid reason for leaving me behind. Instead, he moves faster than I expect, closing the distance between us with one step. One movement, one decision, and then his hands are on me.

His fingers dig into my jaw, tipping my face up, and before I can snarl another word, his mouth crashes down on mine. He steals my kiss, his thumbs prying my mouth open and his tongue sweeping inside. Wyatt avoids my teeth as I try to bite back, his lips crushing against mine without permission.

It's not soft. It's not an apology. It's raw and desperate, but I won't let him take my forgiveness so easily this time. I'm done with showing Wyatt mercy.

I shove at him again, harder this time. My fists find his shoulders and rain down blows, but he doesn't move. He simply tightens his grip on my face and pins me against the brick wall. I'm forced to feel him, to taste his anger, his regret, and his obsession. My nails bite into his arms, dragging deep enough to sting. For a moment, it almost works. His breath stutters over my face, his lips parted, but he still doesn't let me go. I hit him again, trying to twist myself free.

"You don't get to do this, Wyatt," I half-heartedly snarl. My words lose their edge coming from bruised lips. His forehead presses against mine, his fingers trembling where they cup my jaw and shift to my hair and nape.

"I have to," he murmurs roughly. "You won't listen to me otherwise."

A sharp laugh rips out of me, the shift of my chest momentarily dislodging his. I try to step aside because Wyatt still has me where he wants me, and one carefully placed leg blocks my exit. There's no space to move, so I settle for speaking my mind instead.

"You think this is how you get me to listen? By trapping me against a wall in the dark because you're too much of a coward to talk to me with others around?" Wyatt stiffens. His jaw clenches so tightly I hear his teeth grind together. "What was it you couldn't face, your boys thinking you'd gone soft? Or was it apologizing in general?"

"I love you," he says like a gunshot to the dark. I go still. We've danced around the knowledge of how Wyatt feels for a while now, but he's yet to say those three words out loud. He doesn't give me time to recover, process, or react. His hands slide down my arms, wrapping around my wrists and trapping them between us.

"I love you, Angel. I've loved you since I was too young to know what it meant. I loved you even when I hated myself for it." His voice drops to a hoarse whisper. "I loved you even when I hurt you." His honesty slams into me, a juxtaposition of responses filtering through my mind. My throat tightens, and the part of my brain that cares for Wyatt fires back up. His lips touch my cheek, dragging a slow path to my ear.

"That's what I couldn't say in front of the others. Not... not for the first time at least, but it's all I've been thinking since I left your bed two nights ago." A shudder passes between Wyatt's shoulder blades, almost as if he's fighting with himself to keep going. To force out the confessions he never thought he'd admit.

"And yeah, I may be a coward, but I also know apologizing is useless. Because I can't promise I won't leave again. You've known this for a while now that I'll do whatever it takes to keep you safe, Angel. If that means walking away, I'll walk. If that means becoming a monster, I'll become one." Returning his mouth to hover over mine, Wyatt ghosts my lips with a tender touch. "But I will never stop loving you."

I shake my head, weakly trying to break away, but he doesn't let me. His fingers tighten around my wrists, his grip firm but not cruel. My heart wars with my mind, my emotions and logic clashing. For my own sanity, I can't keep letting Wyatt make decisions on my behalf, keeping me in the dark, and then offering me snippets of his love in return. But at the same time, I can't change him. Wyatt has built up his defenses for a reason. He struggles to trust and finds it impossible to admit his feelings. This is why, when I tried to maintain my protests, they sound more like a whimper.

"You don't get to say that and expect me to accept it."

"I don't expect you to accept it," he says. "I expect you to fight me every step of the way." And then he kisses me again, slower this time but just as passionate. A gentle coaxing of my lips, a light teasing of my tongue. As if he's trying to brand himself into my skin. As if he knows I'll hate him every time he makes snap judgments for me. And maybe I will, but I kiss him back anyway.

DAX

CHAPTER FORTY TWO

Somehow, by the grace of a calming tone and a dash of good sense, I convince everyone to pile into the minibus and head to an empty diner down the road. The neon sign outside flashes that the establishment is open twenty-four hours, but judging by the grimace of the lone employee behind the counter, it is not.

The seven of us enter, announced by the ring of a bell over the door, and instantly descend to a long, rectangular table. My cousin opens his laptop, his fingers flying over the keys to bring up news reports that have begun popping up all over the internet. Avery sits beside him, quietly entranced, as I order six coffees and a chocolate milkshake. If looks could kill, the middle-aged man in a pinstripe uniform and apron would have just flayed me on the spot.

I glance over at the table, witnessing the dynamic as an outsider. Garrett paws at Axel, stroking his neck and shoulder, sitting flush to his side whilst Axel remains stoic, his jaw clenched. Hux is drumming his fingers on the table and glaring at Wyatt, who is distracted by the phone in his hand. He gave us a quick rundown about the ransom request in the minibus, but that conversation isn't as done as he probably hopes it is.

At least we're out of the dank motel rooms. A change of scenery and an injection of caffeine will do wonders for us all. Some of us are running on minimal sleep and empty stomachs. I become this evening's waiter, handing out steaming mugs two at a time. I'd attempt to carry them all on a tray, but I still don't trust my fingers to hold up under the strain.

Placing Huxley's down in front of him, he snatches it aside, spilling the boiling liquid over the table and his hand, although he isn't phased. He's too busy being pissed at the side of Wyatt's head while I grab some napkins and clean up around him.

"There's no use holding a grudge," I mutter in Hux's ear. "He's not even aware that you're mad."

"Then maybe I should tell him," Hux grips the table's edge. He is about to stand, but I quickly plant my hand on his shoulder.

"Another time." I give him a lingering look until he grunts and nods. Where I'm just happy that the boys are back safe, even though they didn't storm in like the heroes they were hoping to be, Huxley has picked a personal vendetta with Wyatt for not taking him along, too.

I found him outside, kicking the vending machine just after we'd realized Wyatt was missing, ranting that he's a much better choice. That he is far more level-headed and tough, that he's been really trying to eat and bulk up for this exact reason. I can't quite decide if Hux is livid that Wyatt deemed him unfit to go or that Garrett was chosen above him.

Leaving Hux to settle, I take my coffee and Avery's milkshake from where they've been left on the counter and sit on her other side. She doesn't look over, too engrossed in the laptop, but her hand reaches out seeking mine. I lean over her shoulder, peering at the multiple windows littering the screen.

Each one mimics another, a small tweak to the news headlines and camera angle of the house. It's an ordinary, quaint house on a nice street, with a white picket fence and porch. All of this is illuminated by red and blue flashing lights and surrounded by police tape. The photo in the top left corner of the screen shows the ENTs wheeling out a black body bag.

"Police were called following a reported disturbance and found the body of a man suspected to be convicted felon, Fredrick Walters. No one else was discovered at the property, although there are signs of a struggle and hair belonging to an unidentified female.'

I stare at the words on the screen, the glow of the laptop casting harsh shadows across Avery's face. She's deathly still, but when I glance down at our joined hands, I notice the slight tremor in her fingers and how she grips me tighter, like I'm the only thing keeping her grounded.

A droplet of water splashes against my coffee-colored skin. Another tear slips down her cheek, silent and slow, catching the light for half a second before disappearing beneath her chin. She doesn't sniffle. Doesn't make a sound. She just stares, as if the words might rearrange themselves into something softer, something that doesn't mean what they clearly do.

Meg was there. We were too late. My chest tightens as another tear falls. I don't think she even realizes it's happening.

"Aves." I whisper her name, barely more than a breath, but she doesn't respond. Her lips are parted, her shoulders curled in. She's not present anymore; she's lost in the depths of everything she's been holding in. Everything she's been so desperately trying to hold together for both our sakes and her own.

I reach out and close the laptop. Her breath hitches, the light abruptly cuts off, and the words are gone. But she still doesn't move.

"Hey Swan. I forgot my sweetener. Come with me?" I try again. She nods now, hiding her face behind the curtain of her hair as we stand. I take her hand, gently tugging her past empty booths and sticky tables. She follows, silent and pliant like she doesn't have the energy to resist.

By a self-service counter, I pull her into my arms and rest my chin on her head. She instantly sags, her body succumbing to the tears she was desperately trying to hold back. If the others have noticed, they leave us to ourselves. We're ghosts in the background of their exhaustion, their fraying tempers, and their forgotten coffees.

Avery's hands slip beneath my shirt to hold my waist, craving skin-to-skin contact. A barely-there sound escapes her lips. Half a sob, half a breath. I rub slow, soothing circles into her back, letting her cry, letting her break. Muttering low words, I promise to never let go. It's the only thing I can say with my whole heart, and I know I won't fail her.

In a very short space of time, it's become glaringly apparent that Avery is the love of my life. The woman I was meant to find, the reason that all of my life experiences have made me who I am today. I was so ready to slip into this role, even before I knew her. I was ready to love and give a part of myself to someone else, and she appeared right on cue. She's my soulmate.

It's in the way my chest tightens when she hurts, the way my world shifts to orbit hers without question. She is mine, in whatever form she comes in. Fire and fury, softness and sorrow. If she needs me as a friend, I will stand beside her. If she needs me as a soldier, I will fight for her. And if she ever lets me love her the way I want to, the way I ache to, then I will never, never let her go. That's the easiest promise I've ever made.

After a short while, shorter than I expected, Avery's breath shudders, and she straightens. A hardness falls over her features, and right before my eyes, she builds herself back up, brick by brick. I almost tell her she doesn't need to be strong, that I can carry her for a while longer, but she's not putting on a front for me. She's doing it for herself, to protect her heart from the pain.

"We're back to square one," Avery hiccups, her face tight and wet. "I-I just want her back. I need to know what's happening to her."

"I know, Swan."

"It's been weeks, Dax," Avery's brows flicker into a scowl. She wipes it away just as quickly, but I stroke my thumb over her cheek. She's mad, and that's understandable. We're all mad, but we handle ourselves in different ways. To me, shouting and punching things won't change the facts. Blaming each other won't help us to work together. So I sit back and assess, stepping in for emotional support when needed. And right now, Avery needs reassurance.

"We'll keep looking for as long as it takes." Her watery blue eyes shoot up to mine. My entire world is held within their ocean depths, and although I wish I could offer her more, I refuse to lie. I can't promise that we'll find Meg. I can't tell her everything will be okay. I just hold her steady until her shaking slows and her breathing evens out.

I'm in awe of her resolve. Time after time, Avery refuses to break. She inspires me to do the same—to be the man she needs and that the others can't quite manage to be through no fault of their own. We all bring something different to the table, and I'm okay with that. Avery deserves it all.

"Guys, the text has come in," Wyatt calls across the diner. Avery's feet are moving before I've had a chance to let her go, leaving me stumbling on air. I follow the blonde flash, planting myself back in the chair where my mug still sits. Rather than take my side, Avery rounds the table and crawls into Huxley's lap. His brows raise, the grinding of his jaw taking a break. She grabs at his arms, drawing them around herself like a suit of armor, and nods to Wyatt.

"Harbor Bridge Casino, Friday at seven. Avery comes alone." Wyatt reads out loud, tossing the phone across the table to prove that's all the text says. Axel runs a hand over his shaved head, and Garrett at his side goes still. I watch Avery closely, but she doesn't give anything away. She's resigned to the fact that we have five days to wait. Five days to plan and prepare. Five days to argue about the fact Avery is absolutely *not* going anywhere alone.

My cousin, who happens to be the only one who actually drank his coffee and is on full alert, cracks his fingers loudly.

"I'll get on tracking the number and pulling everything I can on the sender. The casino will have blueprints and a surveillance system we can use. Give me a day or two and I'll have everything—" Thi is cut off by the scraping of Wyatt's chair. It pierces the air like the slice of a blade, cutting through the growing tension.

"Where are you going?" Huxley demands, his face nestled against Avery's. Wyatt waves his hand through the air, disregarding us all in one swoop.

"I haven't slept in days, and we won't solve anything else tonight. I'm going to bed." And one by one, we concede to do the same, starting to leave the diner. I pause at the door while the rest of the Souls assist Axel into the minibus to peer back at Thiago.

"You coming?" I ask, seeing that he hasn't moved from his seat. He has, however, reached across to grab the rest of the mugs and drag them closer to himself. He snorts, opening his laptop back up.

"Are you kidding? I've got a new project, a twenty-four-hour diner, and Wyatt's credit card details. Come pick me up in five days." I shake my head, not doubting my cousin's excitement for a second. He enjoys nothing more than getting his teeth into his coding. The more illegal, the better.

I climb back into the minibus, settling beside an already-asleep Wyatt, his head lolled back against the seat. Now he's been given a small window of reprieve; it's allowed him to settle at last. Avery is in a cuddle puddle with Axel and Garrett, the latter clinging on from the outside like an unwanted koala. Huxley drives us out of the parking lot, and I give a small wave to the Brazilian who has relocated into a booth, a fresh mug in hand and a relaxed smile on his face.

Well, at least Thiago is happy.

AVERY

CHAPTER FORTY THREE

Seven o'clock at the Harbor Bridge Casino.

A sign hangs above the door, displaying a bridge logo to match its name. The lavish interior is visible through a set of gold-handled glass doors flanked by security guards. I hesitate for a moment before pushing through, my fingers slipping against the cool metal. As soon as I step inside, the scent of expensive cologne, stale smoke, and alcohol overwhelms me. The room is a dazzling assault of light and sound.

The ceiling is littered with shiny domes across its hand-painted expanse, cameras hidden within, so I can't see the way they face. Crystal chandeliers illuminate the sea of bodies moving between glossy poker tables and flashing slot machines. The rhythmic clatter of chips being stacked and shuffled lies just beneath the hum of conversation, occasionally interrupted by the triumphant cheers or disappointed groans of gamblers.

Thankfully, Wyatt didn't force us to stay in the motel all week but moved us to a lavish hotel a few blocks away. Aside from allowing Axel to recover in a bed that wasn't more metal spring than foam, it gave Thiago a better chance at running his surveillance, sending the boys to circle the casino on various rotations and stake out the place.

Dax headed out this afternoon to acquire me an outfit that would blend in with the casino patrons and afford me a quick getaway should I need it. The jumpsuit is burgundy red, cinched at the waist by a thick belt that hides a wire in the lining. My shoes are flat and lace up in a similar color.

I move forward carefully, my gaze flickering over the people gathered around the nearest roulette table. A woman in a backless red dress laughs, draping herself over a man too focused on his dwindling pile of chips to acknowledge her. His blond waves dance across his shoulders as his chocolate-brown eyes peek back to look at me. I quickly duck my head.

To my left, a group posing as businessmen in tailored suits sip whiskey, discussing stock trades as if they're not mere college students playing a role. Everyone's in place, at the ready, in case this all goes to shit. Axel has stayed back with Thiago, watching through the cameras and listening through the mic.

Under the guise of their protection, I manage to turn away from the Souls, the warmth of their stares creeping up the back of my neck. Everything about this place reeks of indulgence, of high stakes and desperation wrapped in a thin veil of elegance. I grip Fredrick's phone tighter in my hand, scanning the crowd. I don't know who I'm looking for or where I'm supposed to go.

There are too many eyes here. Some disinterested, some greedy, some watchful. I pass a craps table, my ears catching the dealer's smooth voice calling the play. I force myself to walk deeper into the casino, keeping my head high and my stride steady even though my heart is thrumming against my ribs.

Guards keep their distance from the patrons, their black outfits blinking between the machines as we travel through the center aisle toward a set of opaque double doors at the other end. This section of the casino is weirdly muted, with only the tinks and clanks of machine levers being pulled or buttons being tapped. No one speaks, merely hunching forward to pull their turn and then leaning back on a huff in quick succession. Ahh, this is where those who are down on their luck and filled with despair come.

Distracted by a balding man who curses and slaps the machine, I feel a presence pass behind my back. Before I can react, a hand clamps around my wrist, a man I'm unfamiliar with guiding me through the crowd. I don't resist him, allowing myself to be pulled along whilst casting quick glances up to his face. He's thick-necked and tattooed with a scar that disappears into his black hairline. Within his black suit, he carries the weight that makes people move out of his way. He gives me a look, assessing, before jerking his head to a door at the back of the casino.

"This way," he says, his voice rough like gravel.

"Who am I meeting?" I ask, not receiving an answer. For all I know, this is the man who's now pulling the strings I'm caught up in. He doesn't answer. Just grips my wrist a little tighter and keeps moving. I weave through the maze of tables and past a bar where a bartender watches us with mild curiosity. I could make a scene, but that isn't the plan. I need answers, and if Meg is here, right here in this very building, then I have to go with him.

He leads me past the main floor, through a set of heavy doors marked *'Private'*. The instant we step through, the noise of the casino dulls, muffled by thick walls and expensive carpets. The hallway is dimly lit, lined with doors that I don't want to know the purpose of.

"Is Meg here?" I demand. Again, no answer. Just a low grunt as he stops in front of a door at the end of the hall. He opens it, and I'm ushered inside. The room is nothing like I expected. No hostage tied to a chair. No ransom exchange in progress. Instead, a blackjack table dominates the space, its felt surface pristine beneath the glow of a hanging pendant light. Nine chairs surround it, and only one is occupied for now.

A dealer stands behind the table, shuffling a deck with practiced ease. He's an older man, dressed sharply in a black vest and tie, his face unreadable. Along the far wall, three more men linger. They certainly look the type to have been Fredrick's men, their necks marked with prison numbers and their faces molted with similar scars to the man who retrieved me. Standing in smart suits with their hands clasped behind their backs, each one has a pistol tucked into their waistbands. A shiver of unease trickles down my spine.

I'm nudged forward by a hand between my shoulder blades. "Take a seat." I resist at first, turning back with more defiance than a girl who is grossly outnumbered should.

"I came here for Meg. Name your price, and the cash will be delivered in minutes." I announce, somehow managing to keep the quiver out of my voice. Wyatt has been working on obtaining money for a few days, unsure of how much we'd need but wanting to make sure there is a sizable amount ready. The task has renewed his sense of purpose, and for once, I think I might have actually seen hope flare in his green eyes.

The man chuckles tauntingly, his hard face splitting into a grin that doesn't look natural.

"I said there was a price, but I didn't mention money." My gut plummets, but at least I've learned something. He is the man from the phone. This time when I'm forced towards the seat, I take it since my legs are about to give out anyway. If I pretend really hard, I can almost convince myself that this is a dream. A trick of fantasy where I get to play a role and leave unscathed. That's the only way I'm managing not to break into pieces.

Four chairs sit to my left and three to my right. My stomach tightens at the prospect of who might be joining me, or will it all be ex-cons who believe I owe them something? I glance at the dealer as he continues to shuffle his pack of cards ominously, and then to the men along the wall, taking it all in. Every detail, every possible exit, which concludes at the closed door at my back and another beyond the dealer. At some point, I will need to relay this all back into the mic at my waist, giving Thiago everything he needs to tip off the police.

The longer I'm made to wait for someone to make a move, for anyone to say *something*, the more my leg twitches, bouncing up and down.

"Who are we waiting for?" I ask no one in particular, and it falls on deaf ears. I'm subjected to watching the dealer flicking cards hand to hand, doing tricks with his experienced fingers that draw me into a trance. It's easier to focus on him than the men leering over me. A lone woman in a lion's den. They could do whatever they want to me, and there's nothing I could do to stop it.

Was it stupid to come into this room alone? Definitely. Did I have a choice if I'm to put this all behind me and save my twin finally? Not at all.

If the positions were switched, Meg would be here, head raised and a string of curses flying from her lips. She'd sacrifice herself without a second thought, and that's without having a group of men who love her endlessly just beyond the door. At Thiago's code word, they'll storm the room and save me. I have to force my lungs to expand, reminding myself that I'm not truly alone. I have an out; I just hope they can get here quickly enough if the time arises.

I become more wound up, tightening myself into a knot so that when the door behind me bursts open, I flinch at the intrusion. Twisting, I'm temporarily stunned at the mass of bodies pushing their way inside, invading the room and stealing all of the air in my vicinity. Men are shoved into the chairs all around me, black fabric bags whipped off their heads, but I already know what I'll find. A pair of green eyes find mine across the table, a note of apology held within them. A sinking feeling threatens to drown me as I look around, one by one, my men coming into focus.

"This wasn't the deal," I blurt out, stuttering over myself. "You said just me." A booming chuckle sounds from behind, the man that brought me in gripping the back of my chair and jerking me back roughly.

"That's exactly right. I said just you, and look who we found." One last henchman shoulders his way into the room, gripping the hood so tightly around his captive's head that it's a wonder if he can even breathe. A shaky hand hovers over his ribs as he shuffles in, his lower half still in flannel pajamas.

"Apologizes for the delay," a new lacky says to who I assume is his boss. "We had to retrieve this one from the hotel." He whips the hood from Axel's head, and I briefly close my eyes. *No.* Our only saving grace is that, since they've clearly been tracking us while we were tracking them, they don't appear to know about Thiago. He's not one of our gang and hasn't been with us since the beginning.

My fingers seek their way to the belt at my waist, needing to feel the trace of the wire. Needing that reassurance, or else I'll succumb to the panic attack rising within me.

Shoving my chair back beneath the table, the thug's mouth lingers by my ear. "You didn't follow the rules, so neither will I." Then he's gone, pacing around the table, strong and smug.

I sit there, back straight, and reassess our situation. From my left, Huxley, Dax, and Wyatt are forcibly held in place by the men who brought them in. On my right, Axel and Garrett hang their heads forward, resigned. The two empty chairs at the end of the row haunt me.

"I suppose an introduction is in order," the scarred man continues. He rolls his neck, seeming all too pleased with himself. "I'm Harrison, and I'm the man you'll be dealing with from now on."

"What happened to Fredrick?" I ask, my position in the center giving me the confidence to be our spokesperson. I was all geared up to get these answers anyway. Harrison rolls his thumb over the chunky gold rings on his thick fingers.

"He grew soft." I hold his sharp gaze, waiting for him to continue, but he doesn't seem inclined to offer anything without being prompted.

"So you've taken it upon yourself to take over his grudges? We haven't done anything to you." Under the table, Wyatt nudges my knee in a warning. The man holding his shoulders sees the shift in movement and yanks Wyatt back into the chair, hissing to be still. Harrison appears amused by the scene.

"Fredrick grew soft," Harrison repeats like a mantra, justifying to himself why he put a bullet through Fredrick's skull, "but he wasn't stupid. Imagine a scrawny addict who came into a jail, no connections or leverage. A man so weak, he needs to empower himself by picking on little kids. Yet somehow, he managed to work his way through the ranks without ever lifting a hand. By convincing those stronger than him to do his dirty work. He was good with his mouth, and he gave himself some sort of importance."

The henchmen in the room grunt their agreement, grave looks passing their faces. They clearly agree, looking to Harrison as their new superior. He thrives under attention, and I note that him overthrowing Fredrick was only a matter of time. Harrison is too much of an alpha to be ordered around, and he's too involved in his story to realize that we don't really give a shit.

"We all bought into it—this scheme that would sate our inner monsters. We'd have all the money we could think of when we robbed the Hughes of their wealth, and after that, all members of the family were ours to do whatever we pleased. The only person off limits was precious Avery. I must say, I can see the appeal."

His dark gaze roams over my body, leaving me feeling naked despite the covering of my jumpsuit. I fight against covering myself, pretending

I'm not intimidated. Around me, all of my men are painfully rigid. Harrison makes a scene of licking his lips and continues speaking, a gritty edge to his voice now.

"Fredrick promised us blood. I've spent years becoming invested in his vendetta, listening to how we're going to implode your perfect little family," Harrison cuts a look to Wyatt. "And once we're released, a group of insolent college kids have us running around the country like fucking idiots. Of all the times we could strike, and Fredrick told us to hold off. He didn't want revenge, not really. He wanted a second chance, and that's not what I signed up for."

"You signed up for money. I have duffle bags of it ready to go; all you need to do is say the word." Wyatt juts out his chin. The veins in his neck are taut, his fingers clenched around the seat beneath him. He's trying to draw the attention away from me, taking over as the leader he was born to be.

"Do you?" Harrison grins. Axel makes a choked sound in the back of his throat and with it, drains Wyatt of his resolve. My teeth clamp down on my tongue in an effort to hold back my groan. They retrieved Axel from the hotel where he was guarding the money. Those duffle bags and our leverage are long gone.

"He's got the money. Now he's out for blood," Garrett mutters, his head still hanging forward. Dark hair flicks forward to cover his eyes, dread leaving his limbs limp. Harrison clasps his hands, a sharp sound sending a ripple of winces through us.

Without waiting for an answer, Harrison unsheathes an old-style revolver from his waistband and places it on the table, facing Wyatt. "Shall we get on with it, then?"

HUXLEY

"What's the game?" I ask, entering myself into the conversation. Wyatt glares, but I ignore him. I can't sit here helpless, just another bystander while he and Avery act like this isn't all of our fight. We've all been in this from the start, dragged into their family drama through association.

Harrison grins, reveling in the power we're giving him. He spins the gun in smooth circles on the felt table and then snatches it up, clicking the chamber open and showing us all the shining bullet sitting inside one of the six compartments. Once satisfied he's played his part, he flicks it shut and grins.

"A take on Russian roulette. I'm sure you all know how to play blackjack." He drawls, clearly uncaring either way. We all shoot a look around the table, all too familiar with this game. Or so we thought. "Too bad if not. The winner of each round gets to elect who takes the shot. When the bullet has found its host, the rest of you can walk free."

"And if we don't comply?" Wyatt asks, his jaw tight. Harrison rolls his eyes dramatically, the scar fading into his hair and catching the dim light.

"Then you all die. But it's much less fun and far more clean up."

I open my mouth, demanding the girls are left out of this, but Avery is quicker.

"We want to see her first." Harrison's attention on her is long enough to be considered uncomfortable, trying to glean an answer to a question only he knows. Then, with a sinister grin, he turns to his men lined along the wall and speaks with an amused drawl.

"Bring them in."

Two men disappear through a door at the back of the room. A stilted silence falls over us, Avery's eyes cemented on that door with all her hopes pinned on whoever returns. She's been waiting so long, only to be let down repeatedly.

My breath is hindered, my heartbeat pounding a brutal rhythm against my ribs. It's in my nature to step up, to put myself in the firing line for my men. But from my position on the side, I'm merely a bystander, unable to reach Avery and Axel should they need protecting. Instead, I can just grip my thighs, forcing my sweaty hands to stop shaking. Seconds later, the men return, dragging her between them. *Meg*.

My stomach lurches, and suddenly, Avery is moving, shooting up from her chair. Wyatt is the one who catches her before one of the suited henchmen does, the man at his back allowing him to ease Avery back into her seat forcibly. He mutters in her ear harsh words that could save her life. We need to be rational here and wait out Harrison's game if we all want to leave afterward, Meg included.

The men don't linger, heading out back as soon as Meg is placed in the chair at my side, and fuck, she looks awful. Her hair is tangled, hanging in loose brown waves over her shoulders. Her rags look like they used to be a pair of leggings and a sports top, but there are more slices in the fabric than closed seams. Her skin holds hundreds of minor lacerations through those gaps, all recent. Like a tiny switchblade has nicked her over and over, a slow and tedious torture.

Dark circles carve shadows beneath her hollow eyes, and her skin is ghostly pale. The once-bright, defiant girl I knew is gone, replaced by something brittle, something worn down to the bone. She doesn't meet anyone's gaze.

When the door opens again, I hardly pay attention until Wyatt's sharp gasp lifts my head. A man is being carried in and dragged around the back of all of us, his suit torn, dirty, and disheveled. Nixon is slumped in the chair beside Axel, his lip split and bloodied, bruises forming like ink blots along his cheekbone. His hands rest limply on his lap, although there's tension in his shoulders and a flicker of rage beneath his exhausted expression. He's hurt, but not broken.

Harrison leans back against the far wall with a contented sigh, pleased with the setup he's created. In one fell swoop, he managed to get all of the people Fredrick was chasing in the same room. He nods at the dealer to begin the game, who pulls out a chair and sits opposite us all. The cards are dealt, landing smooth and crisp in front of me: Dax, Wyatt, Avery, Garrett, and Axel. The two newcomers are spared from playing, but I doubt the courtesy will be extended regarding the punishments for losing. Avery's eyes flick to Meg once more, her attention unsettled. It's killing her to be so close but not to be able to hug her twin. What's worse is that Meg won't even look at her.

For both Meg's and Avery's sake, I have to focus. I have to win.

A nine is placed before Wyatt, an ace for Dax, and a ten of spades for me. The cards in front of Avery, Garrett, and Axel remain just out of my sight. The dealer places another ace in front of himself with a smirk. The tension is thick, interrupted by the faint wheezing coming out of Nixon's bloodied lips. The jack of diamonds placed in front of Dax names him the winner of the round. He looks Harrison in the eye as the ex-con twirls the revolver in his hand, inhaling deeply.

"You," Dax states coldly. Harrison expects as much, flipping the gun around and bracing it against his temple. He doesn't hesitate to pull the trigger, a dull click leaving him smirking. He drops the weapon back on the table, far enough out of our reach but close enough to be threatening. We go again, fresh cards being slid our way.

The dealer's voice cuts through the air, naming totals and flipping cards. My mind is a blur of numbers and panic, of strategy and dread. The house wins the next round, meaning Harrison has won. His grin splits wide enough to reveal a few golden teeth. The gun is snatched up in his hand in the next second. He raises it and points it directly at Avery.

The Souls at the table, myself included, try to rise, all shouting that we'll take the shot instead. The goons behind each of our chairs use brutal force to get us back under control, and through it all, Avery sits still and straight, her eyes fluttering closed. The trigger is pulled, a click reverberating through the room. The silence that follows is deafening.

My pulse roars in my ears, and a brutal drumbeat hits my skull. Somehow, I find myself back in my seat.

After that, we all reach for our cards with trembling fingers, jarred by the casualness of this madman. Fredrick was a psychopath in his own right, but it became evident in the end that he wouldn't hurt Avery. He had many chances but left her alone towards the end, shifting his focus elsewhere. Despite never meeting him, I genuinely believe that had the occasion come, we could have reasoned with Fredrick and bargained for her life.

Harrison is far more dangerous. He has no reason to be here other than a sense of being owed something in return for the years he's wasted at Fredrick's side. Currently, he's invested in what cards are being artfully flung around, determining our fate. His fingers twist the revolver round and round in circles against the felt tabletop. I try not to look down the end of the barrel each time it flicks past me, all too familiar with the devastation that follows a tug of the trigger. The circular scar on my collarbone, which hasn't been a nuisance in the longest time, suddenly throbs.

A four of hearts is dealt to Dax next and a seven to me. I keep my poker face solid, not betraying the rising panic for Dax's hand. I know he isn't a blackjack fan, but we've played enough over the years for him to make a rational decision. The dealer lays a face-down card next to his five and leans forward on the table, linking his fingers beneath his chin. For a seemingly irrelevant employee from the casino, he's enjoying this a little too much. I wonder how much he's being paid.

"I'll stick," I say first, looking over to Dax with raised brows. Come on, you've got this. There's still hope.

"Hit me," he breathes, a quiver in his tiny voice that has Wyatt tensing. Picking the top card from the deck, the shining silver bridge logo stamped across that too, the dealer slowly leans forward and turns it at the last moment to reveal the ten of spades. *Bust.* Harrison watches over it all with interest; his lips curved into a wicked smile that has my teeth grinding together, the urge to leap across the table and strangle the bastard overwhelming. But men as powerful as him always have a second in command, briefed and ready to step into his vacant spot and continue his work just as he's done with Fredrick.

As the dealer flips over his last card, all my breath leaves my body. I win. "You," I repeat Dax's choice. Another quick click of the trigger leaves Harrison beaming. We're down to three more chances. Playing on is agony; the weight of the cards in my hand starts to feel like lead.

I'm out quickly in this round, left to watch the other make bold or stupid choices to stick or hit. While Garrett is chewing on his inner cheek, prolonging his choice, I glance at Meg. She is staring at the floor, her face blank, her shoulders curled inward. Like she's already made peace with whatever fate is waiting for her. I refuse to accept that.

Shifting my shoe forward, I nudge her bare foot. She doesn't respond, having retreated into her own mind, protecting herself from the anarchy happening around her. I suppose if she can't hear or see us, she won't feel the same distress that Avery obviously does. I hear Wyatt mutter her name, bringing my attention back to the game.

"Avery, it's your turn," Wyatt tries again. She barely hears him. She can't tear her eyes away from her twin. Wyatt touches her knee, trying his best to bring her focus back to the table, and it's permitted this time. Swallowing hard, Avery's empty eyes glance over the cards in her hand. She sticks despite only having a total sum of six. Her mind can't carry on, pretending that someone's life in this room isn't hanging in the balance.

As the others gamble too highly without reward, Wyatt sits across from the dealer; his focus zeroed in on the next card being flipped. The dealer leers as if he has a personal feud here, his lip curling when he goes bust. Wyatt exhales, his green eyes settling on Harrison's face. For the first time, I see something shift in Harrison's expression. Annoyance. He knows he's running out of chances to walk out of here.

Lifting the revolver, Harrison rolls his neck and lifts it to his temple as Wyatt speaks, his voice flat and emotionless.

"Nixon."

A collective inhale shakes the room. Nixon stiffens beside Axel, his battered body still having enough strength to react. His bruised jaw tightens, and his hands clench into fists on his lap. He should have seen this coming. We all should have.

The tension is suffocating, pressing down on my chest like an iron weight. I know Wyatt hates his father, or adoptive father, I suppose, but to choose to end his life over an ex-convict who is threatening our girl? There's no one I couldn't forgive at this moment, just to ensure Avery's safety. The blonde has twisted in her seat to watch Wyatt closely, but the string of pleading for mercy doesn't come. She doesn't say anything in favor of the man who admittedly loved and cherished her the way a father should for the last eleven years. The realest father she's known.

My eyes flick between the revolver, Wyatt's rigid expression, and Harrison's surprised grin. Harrison lets out a low chuckle, the sound slithering up my spine.

"Bold choice," he muses, rolling his wrist to point the end of the barrel toward Nixon's slumped head. Nixon exhales slowly. He doesn't beg. Doesn't even flinch. Avery's hands grip the edge of the table, her knuckles white. Wyatt keeps his gaze locked on Nixon, unreadable and unmoving. Harrison leans forward slightly, his lips curling, his eyes gleaming with something far worse than amusement.

Then he pulls the trigger, and the gun fires. A crack rips through the silence. Deafening and absolute.

Nixon slumps forward, his body lurching before it's caught by Axel, who surges up despite the bruises along his ribs. Blood spatters across the table, over the deck of cards still in play, over the green felt that is meant for wagers and cheap entertainment. Not this.

Avery screams, her hands flying to cover her ears. I doubt she thought it would actually fire; the injustice of it all splattered crimson across the far wall. The round had the bullet primed; the bullet was meant for Harrison.

Whether by the gunfire or Avery's scream, Meg flinches so violently, her chair scrapes backward. A ragged sound tears from her throat as her body jerks to life, no longer trapped in whatever hollow place she's been buried in. She gasps, chest heaving, eyes wild. They are so much like Avery's but duller, clouded. For the first time, she looks at her twin sister. Locking their gaze, the screaming stops, their chests heaving with so much that needs to be said, but there's no time.

The thud of the revolver is dropped on the table, its dull metal catching the light. I don't know where to look or what to do. Now that the shot has been fired, we can leave, right? But the rough hands of the ex-cons behind our seats wouldn't suggest that is the case.

Despite the nauseating scent of gunpowder still clinging to the air, I struggle to put the facts together. Struggle to come to terms with how fast Nixon went from being here, alive and breathing one second, and gone the next. It was so quick, so final. I glance at Meg again, instinctively reaching for her panicked, shivering body. My hand is swiftly hit with the butt of a gun, which is then turned and pressed against my head.

"Don't fucking move," my personal goon spits. "We're not done here." I freeze in place. My entire being starts and ends where the circular barrel is pushing at my temple, memories of the bullet slicing through my shoulder. Except this time, if the gun is shot, I wouldn't even feel it. I'd be like Nixon, here and then gone. Alive and then not, in a split second, leaving Avery and my brothers behind. A singular thought rounds my mind on a continuous loop. *I'm not ready to die.*

Harrison watches us all, his mouth tilted at an angle. Opening the chamber of his revolver, he puts a fresh bullet in and spins before snapping it closed.

"We go again," he announces coldly. Terror filters through me, and I manage to scowl at Wyatt. The hollering picks up again, my brothers yelling to call Harrison a cheat or complain that it's unfair. As if any of it's fair, as if Harrison was ever going to stick to his own rules. We should have killed him when we had the chance, but now I'm the one with a heavy metal weight pressing against my head. Dully, I come to comprehend that there weren't any rules to begin with. Whether by Harrison or one of the men working for him, we would never leave once we entered this room.

CHAPTER FORTY FIVE

My pulse thunders in my ears, my breathing echoing like an empty rattle in my chest. I should be fighting for control like the others, but I can't bring myself to clear the daze coating my vision. It's like the room is spinning in slow motion, Meg's haunted blue eyes blinking at me through the chaos. Huxley is frozen in place, a gun at his temple.

Dax is trying to hold Wyatt back, as my stepbrother grapples to stay standing despite the multiple goons trying to push him back into his seat. I don't see the taser drawn until it's shoved into Wyatt's side, forcing him into submission. The zapping jolts through my senses, and Wyatt's arm hit me on the way down, a heavy thud against my arm and the chair groaning beneath his bulky weight.

Beside me, Garrett is cradling a blood-smattered Axel, protecting him as much as he's able with his arms wrapped around Axel's shuddering shoulders. Clearly, the body staring blankly at him is having a huge psychological effect on Axel's mind.

I can't bring myself to look at Nixon. I can't even consider what the blank look in his eyes means. For all of his misgivings, he was my parent. My last living parent. I swallow, forcing the thoughts back, knowing I'll need to deal with some things later. If there even is a later.

Harrison catches my eye, his smile menacing as he orders the dealer to set up a fresh game. The first card is tossed across the table, landing face-up in front of me, and just as I resign myself to this never-ending hell, the lights flicker.

At first, the bulb blinks, plunging us into bouts of darkness and then flashing bright again. A chill grips me in its claws, a voice in my head telling me not to be stupid. Not to risk the family I have left. The flickering casts jagged shadows across the card table, making every movement feel disjointed, like a stuttering film reel that's skipping frames. I force my eyes away from the dead body, from Axel's traumatized expression, from the twisted smirk curling at Harrison's lips. I set my sights back on Meg, and in the next bout of darkness, I move.

Wyatt groans beside me, his body twitching from the aftershocks of the taser. He feels the brush of my leg shift against him and tries to push himself towards me. Luckily, like the other men in the room, he's too slow. The light flashes on, catching me nearing the wall. I half debate tackling the man holding Hux hostage, but in a split decision, I know I can't risk it. Two more steps, plunged into darkness again, and I'm throwing myself in Meg's unexpecting arms before the next blackout.

Meg stiffens as my weight crashes into her, her arms frozen at her sides as if she doesn't know what to do with me. My fingers clutch at the tattered fabric of her top, desperate and clawing, grounding myself in the little warmth she has.

She smells different. Gone is the floral shampoo I remember, replaced by sweat, blood, and fear. She feels different. There was no familiarity or returning hug or grasping desperation to get closer to me like I imagined. But beneath it all, buried under months of pain, she's still my twin and my best friend. I need to get her out of here.

The lights flash back on, and she jerks away as if she's been burned. Unfortunately, I'm not the only one who was in a rush to reach her. Harrison's laughter cuts through the space between us, his hand grasping her by the hair. Meg's body slips away from me, her raspy scream beside my ear. I grapple blindly, wrapping my hands around her arm and moving to stay with her. Vaguely, I hear shouting and banging against the other door, just a minute too late.

"Police! Everyone inside, come out with your hands up!"

Someone unfriendly comes up from behind, rough hands grabbing at my arms and shoving me forward. I refuse to let go of Meg as we're pushed and pulled in the same direction, leaving the roar of commotion behind. A strangled noise rips from my throat as I fight, twisting and struggling, my flat shoes dragging against the carpet as I'm hauled through the side door.

The lights in the room flicker back on, stabilizing at last. I wrench my head to look back past the suited man trying to block my view. Wyatt fights the effects of the taser, scrambling forward into Dax, but another sharp zap sends him crumbling again. It doesn't stop him from snarling my name, outstretching a hand.

Dax curses, stuck beneath Wyatt's weight. Huxley looks at me longingly, but his body remains taut, forced still by the cold steel pressing against his skull. I catch a final glance of Garrett whispering something into Axel's ear, hopefully consoling him whilst embracing his shaking body. The door slams closed, cutting me off from those who hold my heart. Instant panic for their safety flares, but I can't go back and change my decision.

Clinging onto Meg's arm, we're dragged down a short passage and thrust into the night. A car is waiting; its rear door has already popped open, and we're thrown inside. Harrison drops into the passenger seat, his henchman skidding over the hood to jump into the driver's seat and peel us into the busy main road.

The car swerves sharply as the driver cuts through the traffic, putting distance between us and the casino. The city lights blur outside the window, streaking past in a mess of neon through the windows. I barely feel the jolt of the ride. My fingers are still locked around Meg's arm, where we've been thrust into the back seat, but she doesn't move. She doesn't even flinch.

"Meg," I whisper, my voice shaking. I shake her arm, trying to anchor her, but she's never seemed more distant. Her eyes are cast aside, her hair matted. I release my grip, not knowing where or how to touch her. I settle on taking her hands and holding them between us. "Hey, I'm right here. It's just us."

Meg blinks a few times, slowly returning to the present. What has happened to her that she can zone out so easily that she doesn't care what happens to her body? Meg pulls back her hands and twists, curling in on herself without looking at me. I can only watch, stunned, as her body presses against the door like she wants to disappear into the metal. Her breathing is shallow, and her head is tilted slightly downward.

I glance toward the front seat, where Harrison is relaxed, his elbow propped against the window, fingers tapping idly against the doorframe. In his other hand is the revolver that churns my stomach. I feel sick just looking at it, not having the time to think of Nixon. To mourn the man I know, regardless of who or what he was to others. Harrison mutters quick instructions to his right-hand man, and although he isn't looking at us, I feel his attention lingering. We don't have much time.

I shift, twisting toward Meg. I try to soften my voice, to keep it steady even as my own panic claws at my throat. "Meg, please. Say something." She still doesn't acknowledge me. Her blue eyes, those same sharp, knowing eyes that always used to catch mine with a teasing smirk or an exasperated roll, are hollow. A ghost of the girl I knew.

Tears sting the backs of my eyes, but I swallow them down. I can't cry, nor can I allow the frustration in me to bubble over. I could scream until my lungs burned at the injustice of it all. I've finally got her back, have her here to hold, and it's like she's not here at all. Swallowing hard, I press my hand over hers, gripping her cold fingers.

"I know you're scared. I am too. But we're gonna figure this out, okay? We're getting out of this." I promise quietly, hoping that if I can at least bolster her, I will feel a sense of renewed confidence myself. The smallest twitch in her fingers beats against mine, and a rush of hope floods my system. It's something. Encouraged, I keep going, my voice growing more anxious.

"The boys will come for us. They won't stop. You know that, right? They're probably already tearing that place apart, trying to get to us." Her lips part slightly, but no sound comes out. I don't want to overwhelm her, but I also know I can't do anything to help us without her being at least semi-responsive. I lean closer, wrapping my arms around her body, and this time, I'm not met with the same stiffness.

"You're not alone anymore, Meg. I'm here now. I won't let anything happen to you." Finally, her head moves just a fraction, barely a shift in posture, but it's enough. Enough for me to see the silent tears trailing down her cheeks. Something inside me breaks. She's crying, but the murkiness in her eyes is not relief. It's not hope. It's resignation.

"No," I whisper, shaking my head. "Don't do that. Don't give up."

A sob catches in my throat, but I don't let it out. "I need you, Meg. I've been trying to find you. I never gave up on you. Please don't give up on me." I plead, my voice cracking. My breath stutters as I drop my forehead against her shoulder, and my body trembles. We've come so far, but it suddenly feels like we've made no progress at all. "It can't end like this."

The car speeds us into oblivion, but I can't consider anything beyond this back seat right now. Then, so quietly I almost miss it, Meg finally speaks.

"It's already over." Meg's voice is broken. Detached. Like she truly believes there's nothing left worth living for. Not even me. She turns her head and blinks at me, and with an ache in my chest, I realize she's already slipped too far. She's already bracing for the worst.

The car jerks as we take a sudden turn, and Harrison hums in amusement. "You might want to save your breath, sweetheart," he muses, still not looking back at us. "No sense in trying to fix something that's already shattered."

I want to scream. I want to claw at him, to shake Meg, and to fight until my body gives out. But all I can do is tighten my grip and pray that I can still reach her before it's too late. That the Souls will find us somehow, someway. I must be strong enough to carry the both of us.

It's as if there's been a personality shift, from the version of Meg that used to console and tell me nothing was unbeatable, to the introvert I used to be, hiding from this world. Hiding from ever feeling hopeless again, but I'm not completely hopeless now. I know there's something worth living for. I know someone will save us.

CHAPTER FORTY SIX

I barely register the voice over the ringing in my ears. My limp form is pressed against Dax, my breathing shallow and uneven. The pounding grows more insistent, rattling the door on its hinges. A second later, the distinct crack of the door splintering cuts through us all.

A swat team swarms the room, a plastic barricade shoving the suited man against the walls. The goon holding Huxley at gunpoint makes a run for the rear door and is shot in the back without hesitation.

The Souls sit stock still in our seats, clearly distinguishing between the assailants and the victims. It doesn't lessen how roughly we're yanked from our seats and patted down, but without resisting, we're escorted out without the need for handcuffs. At our backs, a few more shots are fired, and with each one, my eye twitches.

The casino is a ghost town, having been completely evacuated beneath the clamor of slot machines. Stripped of life, its gaudy neon lights flicker weakly against the suffocating quiet. The scent of stale smoke and spilled liquor lingers in the air, mingling with the metallic tang of blood that won't leave my nose. Half-finished drinks sit abandoned on tables, their condensation pooling onto velvet tabletops.

My legs feel like dead weight as I stagger forward, barely held upright by the grip of the agent guiding me toward the exit. Dax is tugged beside me, his eyes darting around and trying to get my attention. But I don't care about any of it. I don't care about the barking orders of the SWAT team; I don't care that Nixon's body is lying on a games table, I don't care what's going to happen to us. All I care about is Avery and Meg's safety. Whether I beat myself up about misplacing that deadly bullet or not depends on what happens in the next ten minutes.

As my senses come back to me, the effects of the taser wear off, and a dull roar builds in my head. Louder than the ringing, louder than the shouting, drowning out everything else. I yank myself free of the agent's hold, stumbling forward ungracefully. A heavy hand clamps onto my shoulder, wrenching me back.

"Stand down!" I throw my weight against them, my chest heaving.

"Wait, there's... we need to help my—" I cut myself off. What am I supposed to call her? My girlfriend? My adoptive sister that I like to choke and sink my cock into?

Wrenching myself free for a second time, I spin and hold my hands up, staring down the barrel of yet another gun. The agent regards me with caution. "Two girls have been taken hostage by an ex-con called Harrison. They might still be here."

The agent's scowl doesn't shift as he shoves me back into line, forcing me out of the main entrance and toward the flashing lights of the waiting police cruisers. "A vehicle was reported speeding away from the building during our raid. We have cars searching the area."

His uncaring tone belittles the words that slam into me like a freight train. I suck in a breath that doesn't feel like enough, my knees nearly giving out beneath me. They got away.

The others are herded outside, their faces grim and their bodies stiff with the same tension overriding my bones. Garrett is supporting Axel, flanked by officers on either side. Huxley moves like a ghost, his usual sharpness dulled, his expression muted. We're crowded in the parking lot, much less monitored than those who actually had guns on their person.

Someone is talking to me, one of the officers maybe, but their words barely penetrate the buzzing in my skull. My fingers twitch at my sides. Every nerve in my body is screaming to move, to do something, and to tear through the city with my bare hands until I find her.

But instead, I'm stuck here, standing in the center of a crime scene, corralled like a fucking bystander while men with badges pretend they have control of the situation. The static of several walkie-talkie buzzes, a brief report coming in that the car they were searching for has gotten away.

We're out of time. Then, past the flashing red and blue, past the rows of uniforms and the cordoned-off entrance, like a freaking angel, I see Thiago. He's standing just beyond the yellow crime scene tape, his pale eyes scanning the parking lot until they lock onto mine. The moment our gazes connect, he lifts a hand and waves me over casually, like this isn't life or death, like I'm not already teetering on the fucking edge. I don't think. I just move.

Before I can take two steps forward, a hand clamps around my bicep, yanking me back. "Where do you think you're going?" The officer barks, his grip tightening on my shirt like he expects me to start running. I turn sharply, my teeth grinding.

"I can help find the girls." He chuckles and shoves me back into Dax and Hux.

"You need to stay here until we've sorted everything out." He says dismissively. "Leave the searching to the professionals." He strides away before hearing my snort, putting his younger colleague in charge of watching over the five of us. Rage flares in my chest, but I force it down because wasting time arguing will only keep me here longer. Turning to our new overseer, I speak slowly, keeping my temper in check.

"You don't understand. I can track them." His brow furrows, suspicion flashing in his eyes.

"And how exactly do you plan on doing that?" I exhale sharply, my patience wearing thin.

"Look, I have a confession that I shouldn't be telling a cop, but if it saves their lives, then so be it." The Souls move in, gathering around with their ears pricked.

"What is it?" Dax raises a brow, and at my slight hesitation, Garrett sighs dramatically.

"Spit it out, Riot. Nothing you do shocks us anymore." I scrub a hand over my face. Might as well get this over with.

"Avery has a tracking chip in her." A thick silence follows until Garrett lets out a low whistle, shaking his head with the kind of exasperation that tells me somewhere between he's impressed and mortified.

"Well, fuck me. You do still have that shockability factor."

"Whereabouts?" Dax asks, keeping his composure. Axel's head is hanging forward, quietly absorbing the conversation around him.

"In her neck."

Huxley completely loses his composure, choking on an outraged laugh, his features with disbelief and fury.

"You tagged our girl?!"

"I did it when I drugged and took her," I admit, my voice flat as I let the truth settle. "While she was unconscious in the back of Hux's car." The cop glares, but to his credit, he doesn't pull out his notepad and start taking notes. He listens, hopefully understanding my involvement is secondary to the current situation. He can take me to the station when Avery and Meg are safe with the Souls.

Huxley runs a hand down his face and then turns on his heel, walking a short distance away like he needs space to process. Axel's jaw ticks. There's no shock in Gare's expression anymore, just a reluctant acceptance that, yeah, I did something this fucked up.

"Fucking hell," Dax mutters under his breath, shoving his hands into his pockets and staring off into the distance.

"Explain," Axel suddenly demands. I sigh, impatience flaring despite myself. Of course, Axe wants to know all of the facts before deciding how he feels about it.

"When Fredrick told me he was going to take Meg, I wasn't foolish enough to think he'd suddenly leave Avery alone." I force my voice to stay level, my gaze shifting between them all. "So, on the way back to the house, I stopped off at the dorms. There were rumors about a kid in bio-chem acquiring sedation drugs and other unsavory items. I paid him a visit, bought his entire stock, and disposed of everything except for one sedative syringe and a tracking chip tagger."

Axel exhales through his nose, nostrils flaring slightly, but otherwise remains silent. His hands curl into fists at his sides. Dax is still watching me carefully, his expression unreadable, while Garrett just shakes his head like he can't decide whether to strangle me or thank me.

"I thought it would be best to be prepared," I continue, quieter now. "I just didn't think I'd have to use it on her that very night."

A thick silence follows. I wait for the shouting to start—maybe a punch in the face—but Hux doesn't return to deliver it. Axel exhales a long, slow breath that does nothing to ease the tension in his frame.

Then, finally, Garrett breaks it, dragging a hand through his hair with a dry laugh.

"We are going to have a serious talk about boundaries later," Dax crosses his arms. I meet his gaze, a scowl deepening at the corners of my mouth.

"You'll be thanking me when it saves her life."

No one else speaks. We don't have time to argue about morality or ethics. Right now, the only thing that matters is that we have a way to find Avery. The cop considers his options, casting a glance at his superior. When he looks me over, he seems to have come to a decision.

"Do you have a way to follow the tracker?"

I nod, gesturing for Thiago to approach. He slips beneath the tape and manages to avoid being seen until the throng of our bodies covers him.

"Tell me you have a signal," I demand, my pulse roaring in my ears. Thiago's eye roll doesn't fit the setting. Placing his laptop on the hood of a police car, he opens it to reveal the map he already has loaded. Of course, Thiago already knew about the chip in Avery's neck since I told him earlier in the week as insurance. He wasn't phased in the slightest, but clearly, he doesn't have the high expectations of me that his cousin does. Tilting the screen towards me, I nearly collapse in relief when I see the blinking dot on the map.

"She's moving fast," Thiago murmurs, tracking the signal as it weaves through the city streets. There's a beat of silence, hesitation flickering across the officer's face, his gaze bouncing between the glowing screen and the rigid set of my jaw, as if debating whether or not to trust me.

His stalling presses in on all of us. Every second wasted is another mile between us and Avery, another stretch of road leading her further out of our reach. My hands turn to fists at my sides, itching to force the officer to move, to let me go, to do something other than stand here and waste time. Dax leans in beside me, his shoulders squared, his own tolerance wearing thin.

"What the fuck are you waiting for? You have a location," he juts his chin towards the officer. I've never heard Dax speak so aggressively to anyone, let alone someone who could have him locked up for it. Garrett, still clutching at Axel like he's the only thing keeping him upright, mutters something under his breath, too quiet for me to catch, but whatever it is makes Axel's lips purse underneath the dried blood splatter covering his face.

Huxley finally rejoins us, his breathing heavy, his hands shoved through his hair in a way that leaves a mess of unruly waves, but I barely glance at him. I know exactly what he's thinking and feeling—the same thing we all are. Rage. Helplessness. That deep, gnawing fear clawing up our throats like poison, threatening to drown us in the possibilities of what could be happening to Avery and Meg right now.

The officer clears his throat, his gaze locking onto me with something between skepticism and reluctant understanding. "This is completely unethical and could hinder the investigation when it goes to court," he relays as if reminding himself of the consequences of his next decision.

"I don't give a fuck about any of that. You have the lives of two young women in your hands. What are you going to do about it?" I tilt my head. Challenging a cop who hasn't entirely made up his mind probably isn't the best decision. His mouth twitches into a fragment of a frown. He doesn't like this. Doesn't like me. But I don't give a fuck about his moral code. I care about getting Avery back.

Thiago makes an impatient noise, tapping a finger against the laptop. "They're heading south, fast. They'll be out of the city limits if we wait much longer." I don't hear anything after that, not really—just the sound of my pulse pounding. I approach his shiny uniform, ignoring the way another agent shifts, clearly ready to intervene.

"They're in danger. Right now. While we're standing here, they're being taken further away, and God knows what kind of situation they are in. I need you to take action, or believe me, I will do something stupid myself. Either way, I won't stand here and let them disappear for good."

A muscle jumps in his jaw. He knows I'm right. He fucking knows. A decision is made between the straightening of his shoulders and the authoritative stance he adopts. With a heavy sigh, the officer finally nods.

"Fine. I'll gather a few cars and personally take you two," he says, looking pointedly at Thiago and me. The rest of you will be taken to the station for questioning." The Souls appear reluctant but agree. *This is the best shot we've got right now.*

As promised, the officer heads off to collect a few others, announcing that we will do a drive-around based on his hunch. That's fine with me. Holding his laptop carefully, Thiago follows me into the back seat of the nearest police cruiser. I have a few precious seconds to turn a sharp glare on him.

"What the fuck took you so long to tip off the police? We had a plan," I grit through my clenched jaw. Thiago, to his credit, doesn't even flinch.

"I only had three minutes, tops, to climb into the vents with my laptop when I saw the thugs storming the hotel to take Axel, and Avery's mic stopped transmitting as soon as she stepped in that back room. I was completely blind on the ground and trying to gauge when you needed backup whilst hiding for my life."

Thiago puffs out his cheeks at the inconvenience of it all. I have to remind myself he's here as a favor to Dax, not because he has a dog in this fight. Forcing my jaw to unlock, trying to stay positive, I reach across him to close the door. Huxley catches it before I get the chance.

"I swear to fuck, Wyatt," he growls, his blond waves falling forward around his narrowed eyes. "If you don't bring her back to me alive, I'll end you. You've made too many mistakes at her expense." His voice is low, barely restrained, with the kind of quiet rage that promises violence if pushed just an inch further. I level him with an unflinching stare while Thiago cowers between us.

"If I can't bring her back safe, I'm not coming back at all."

And Hux knows from the seriousness radiating from my posture that I don't mean I'll be going on fucking vacation. It's taken me a long time to come around, but I know now that there's no me without Avery. There's no believing in heaven without my Angel.

Avery landed in my life like an atomic bomb, destroying my existence as I knew it and leaving a fresh slate in its place. Now all I need is to get to her so I can start to rebuild a world she can be free in. All her fears and reservations about me will vanish when she realizes I don't want to cage her. I want to encourage her to do whatever her heart desires. To live and love and cry and laugh, and I want to be there every step of the way. I'm done putting any distance between us. I'm done watching from the side lines.

The young officer eases Hux back by his shoulders, slamming the door closed with a thud of finality. Dropping into the driver's seat, protected from us by a mesh grate, he twists the key in the ignition, the engine rumbling to life beneath us as red and blue lights flicker across the interior. His hands tighten around the steering wheel as he radios in our transport, his voice clipped and professional, but something flickers beneath it. Hesitation, maybe, or the weight of knowing he's putting his credibility on the line for our sakes.

"Tell me where to go," he twists his head to call back. Thiago is straight on it, using his illegal hacking skills to chase the signal and read out the current location. We've got a lot of ground to make up, and I pray that Avery can hang on. The car pulls forward, rolling toward the main road through the mass of flashing lights and uniformed bodies swarming the parking lot. Instead of watching my Souls fade into the background, I press my knuckles against my temples, squeezing my eyes shut for half a second.

Unexpectedly, a hand rubs my shoulder, and when I peer up, Thiago isn't looking at me, but he doesn't withdraw his hand. I frown for a moment, then nod, thankful for his show of comfort. This man doesn't know me, and he certainly doesn't owe me anything. Yet I believe he can sense the lengths I'd go to and that I mean well in the depths of my damaged heart.

Mimicking his small smirk, because it seems like the right thing to do, I sit straighter, ready to face the world once again. For the first time since we entered the casino, something inside me clicks into place. Harrison thinks he's won. Thinks he's gotten away. But he's wrong. Because no matter where he runs or where he hides, I will find him. And I will burn his entire fucking world to the ground to get to my girl.

AVERY

CHAPTER FORTY SEVEN

The car lurches as the driver takes a hard right, tires shrieking against the asphalt, sending me careening into Meg's side. She barely reacts, her body still as loose and limp as when I stopped begging her to reply to me, her head knocking against the window with a dull thud. The seatbelt is the only thing keeping her upright, and even then, she looks like a ghost of herself, drained and hollow, staring blankly at nothing.

Vaguely, I feel the car slow, and my heart picks up a notch at the thought of arriving at a destination. However, we just blend into traffic, becoming lost amongst the masses. I swallow against the lump in my throat, my pulse hammering in my ears. Every instinct in my body screams at me to do something, to move, to fight, but my options are running thinner by the second.

I shift carefully, assessing the back seat without drawing Harrison's attention. He appears far too relaxed in the passenger seat, his fingers tapping idly against his knee. He's watching the road ahead, seemingly at ease, but I don't miss the sharp flick of his eyes toward the rearview mirror, checking on us every few seconds.

Aside from the seat belts, which are impossible to break without a tool, I have nothing but the damp warmth of Meg's arm pressed against mine. A cold rush of night air filters in through a cracked window after Harrison declared he couldn't handle Meg's smell. I don't even notice, my mind firing on so many other levels that my senses appear dulled.

Behind the wheel, his henchman is focused, hunched over the steering wheel like he's desperate to push the car faster. The traffic lights ahead flash red, and for a breathless moment, I wonder if he'll run straight through. He doesn't, coming to a hesitant and brief stop. Peering through the window, I try to catch someone's attention and fail when realizing the glass is blacked out. Then I try the door handle to no avail, and a click sounds beside my ear.

"Don't even think about it," Harrison growls, the gun pushed against my head. I let my hand drop away, retreating into my seat. He grins, twisting back in his seat, the gun settling back on his lap. The light turns green, and we glide forward in unison with the cars all around. Lost to the masses, no one suspects us. No sirens. No flashing lights. The city keeps moving, completely oblivious. I squeeze my eyes shut, slowly breathing through my nose.

Okay. *Okay.* I need a plan. Angling my body towards Meg, I keep my voice barely above a whisper. "Meg." No response. I nudge her with my shoulder, my fingers curling against her palm. "Meg, you with me?"

Her lashes flutter, but she doesn't turn to look at me. Instead, she blinks sluggishly, her mouth parting like she wants to say something, but the words don't come. My stomach twists. I don't know what they did to her before arriving at the casino, but I can guess, and every possibility makes me want to rip someone's throat out. It's evident the longer she remains unresponsive to me, that she's under the influence of something. I try again.

"Meg, I need you to stay awake. We'll get out of this, but I need you with me, okay?" A flicker of awareness crosses her face, but it's gone just as quickly, swallowed up by whatever fog they've forced her into. Harrison chuckles under his breath, shaking his head at the entertainment I'm apparently providing him. I clench my jaw, refusing to stop trying. Meg, the real version of her, wouldn't give up if it was me.

The city blurs past in streaks of yellow street lights and fluorescent storefronts. The hum of the tires against the road fills the silence, but it doesn't drown out the rapid pounding of my pulse or the shallow wheeze of Meg's breathing beside me.

She's slipping further away with each second, her head lolling against the window, eyelids fluttering. I don't know if it's from exhaustion, drugs, or shock, but I do know that if I simply sit here and hope the Souls save us, it'll be too late. I need to act now.

I continue my search. My fingers stretch out without moving my body far, feeling for anything I can use, but the car is sleek, expensive, and clutter-free. No stray pen, loose wires, or discarded wrappers with sharp edges. Then, my wrist grazes against something rough. My breath catches, but I'm careful to keep my face passive when Harrison flicks his eyes to the rearview mirror. He looks away, and I continue my exploration.

Just below the seat belt buckle, where the leather seat meets the center console, the thin edge of a plastic peeks out, looped and forgotten. I cast a quick glance at Meg's wrists, noting the thin indents marring her pale skin. The exact type one would receive from being bound by a zip tie. Whether the one poking my finger is from her old binds or intended for a new one, it's now wedged in the crack between the seats. A stroke of luck, a miracle in the form of hardened plastic, and I nearly let out a hysterical laugh.

Keeping my movements small, I angle my body just enough to pretend I'm not reaching for it, my fingers straining. The zip tie is stiff, resisting as I try to work it free without drawing attention. My arms ache from being kept so rigid, my wrists screaming from the unnatural angle, but finally, after a few torturous seconds, the tie gives, slipping loose into my palm. I curl my fingers around it, tucking it behind my back to keep it hidden.

Now comes the hard part. I swallow, shifting just enough to push my weight against Meg, making it look like I'm just adjusting in the seat. I don't expect a reaction from her, but she makes a faint, broken sound with a slight movement, barely more than a breath. Harrison looks at us in the mirror, eyes sharp with amusement.

"Aww, how touching," he croons, his voice dripping with mock sympathy. "Worried about your sister, sweetheart?"

I meet his gaze head-on, my grip tightening around the plastic. The driver cuts into another lane, heading directly for the merging of the freeway. I'm running out of time. There's too much distance between us and anyone who might be trying to follow. As soon as we hit the freeway, it will be speeding and lane-hopping directly out of the state. We'll be as good as lost. It's now or never.

"Not as much as you should be worried about me," I manage to smirk without my voice breaking. Harrison's smirk falters, confusion flickering for a split second before I move. I lunge forward, arms lurching over the seat, the zip tie stretched between my fists. Harrison doesn't have time to register what's happening before I loop it over his head and pull.

His body jerks violently, a strangled gasp bursting from his throat as the plastic cuts into his skin. He thrashes, fingers clawing at his neck, but I hold on, bracing my knees against the seat for leverage, teeth gritted as I pour every ounce of strength into tightening the restraint around his throat. His gun clatters to the floor, slipping from his grip as his hands scramble uselessly at the zip tie, nails scraping against plastic.

The driver shouts, swerving the car hard enough to send my body whipping sideways, but I don't let go. Thanks to Wyatt, this isn't my first rodeo, and I know exactly how to derail a car I don't want to be in.

Harrison chokes, a garbled sound ripping from his throat as his face darkens, his limbs flailing wildly. The driver is yelling, trying to reach for him while still gripping the wheel, but the car is veering dangerously now, the tires screeching as we careen toward the curb. Suddenly a bone-crushing force slams into my face.

Stars explode in my vision as pain shatters through my skull, my grip instantly loosening. My head snaps back, the taste of blood filling my mouth as the driver's elbow connects solidly with my cheekbone. The world tilts, everything swimming in and out of focus, and before I can recover, the car jerks to a violent stop.

The force flings me forward, my forehead smacking into the back of the headrest with a sickening thud. The zip tie slips from my fingers completely, and Harrison gasps, sucking in ragged, desperate breaths as he claws at his throat. I try to blink away the black spots dancing in my vision, my mind sluggish, dazed. Stupidly, despite the agony flaring through my face, all I can think is, *'That was so badass. I bet Meg is impressed'*.

But Meg isn't much of anything. She doesn't react, and she doesn't cushion my fall or stop Harrison from reaching back to grab a handful of my hair. Wrenching my head back towards him, Harrison's furious, red-faced snarl fills my spinning vision.

"You little bitch," he wheezes, his voice raw, his eyes murderous. His fingers tighten in my hair, yanking hard enough to make my scalp burn. "You're gonna fucking pay for that." I let out a slow, fragile breath, blood dripping from my lip onto my chin. But I don't look away.

It's surprising how many thoughts can fly through a mind in less than a moment. How someone can reflect on their life, their choices, and how they ended up here. I was the girl who was so afraid of being hurt again, both physically and emotionally, that I refused to leave the home I was fortunate to be welcomed into. At Wyatt's expense, but I didn't know that at the time. I was so scared of love I hid from it, unaware of how much my heart craved affection. Then I met my Souls.

They were instantly drawn to me because they believed it was their job to protect me. I've often thought men are more affected by fairy tales than women, boosting their noble intentions and giving them a false sense of purpose always to be the savior, even when the damsel is more than capable of saving herself. Would prefer to, in fact.

I didn't need saving; I needed liberating. And here I am. The new Avery is the girl who knows what she's worth and what she can face. I'm a woman without limits because I have love to bolster me. And ultimately, if my bravery is for nothing, I have men to mourn me. I've made my mark on this world rather than hide from it. And I stuck to my promise to save Meg.

So even through the haze of pain, even as my head pulses with the force of the impact, I hold Harrison's gaze, my lips curling into the faintest, bloodstained smirk. "Then hurry up and do it." Harrison's grip on my hair tightens for a fraction of a second, his fingers like iron claws against my scalp before something in the rear windscreen spooks him.

He abruptly lets go, shoving me backward with enough force that I slam against the door, my already battered body jolting from the impact. My ears ring, not grasping the sharp bark of orders being shouted from outside. The sudden blaze of red and blue lights floods the inside of the car, painting everything in frenzied flashes of color. The wail of sirens pierces the night, cutting through the static hum in my skull and dragging me back into the present.

"Shit," the driver hisses, his head snapping toward Harrison, his hand already yanking a gun from the waistband of his jeans. "They took the backroads and made a beeline for us. How the hell did they know where we were?" Two pairs of accusing eyes cut to me in the mirror, but I can't even bring myself to shrug.

Harrison swipes a hand over his raw, reddened throat, his breath still rasping as he bends forward to locate his dropped revolver. Twisting in his seat, he glares down at me, fury radiating from him in waves. For an endless moment where my heart forgets to beat, I'm sure he's going to turn the gun on me, his fingers twitching around the grip, but then...

Bang. Bang. Bang.

Gunfire erupts outside, bullets slamming into the car's frame, shattering the passenger-side window. Glass rains down in jagged shards, and I drop down, instincts taking over as I scramble down into the footwell, reaching blindly for Meg. She doesn't resist as I haul her against me, curling my body over hers, shielding her from the chaos unfolding all around. Her breath is brittle, her entire frame trembling beneath my grip, and fear coils sharp and tight in my stomach.

The car jerks suddenly, the doors bursting open as Harrison and the driver run for it. They fire wildly over their shoulders, the deafening cracks of their guns mixing with the return fire from officers, but neither of them hesitates. I glimpse Harrison's silhouette vanishing between two parked cars, the driver hot on his heels. As soon as the chase is taken away from the vehicle, it's surrounded by uniformed figures.

Heavy boots thud against asphalt. The clatter of weapons being raised. My fingers tighten around Meg, my heart slamming against my ribs as I force myself not to flinch at the aggressive yells of *"Hands where we can see them!"* and *"Stay down!"*

Somewhere through the madness, through the storm of flashing lights and weapons trained in our direction, Wyatt's voice cuts a path directly to my ears. He yells my name, a rough and desperate sound that twists my insides into knots. That singular word, that raw rasp, imprints itself in my skull.

I lift my head just as the car door is wrenched open, my eyes immediately locking onto his. He's standing there, his expression a violent tornado of emotions, his jaw tight, his wild green eyes searching every inch of me like he's trying to memorize me, to assess every injury, every bruise, and every breath I take, in one single glance.

And then he's crouching beside the car, his hands reaching for me. I clasp his shaking fingers as they brush over my bloodied face and my tangled hair. The throbbing of my cheek intensifies at his gentle touch; his chest is rising and falling rapidly. His entire body vibrates with barely restrained anger. He exhales sharply. "Angel."

That's all he says. And it's enough to undo me. My throat tightens, my eyes burn, and my body instinctively sways toward him because no matter what he's done, no matter how many lines we've crossed, no matter how fractured and fucked-up we are or what the rest of the world might say, this is where I belong. Right here, with his hands cradling my face, his forehead almost brushing mine, his pulse hammering just as frantically as my own.

"She's... she's not okay," I manage, my voice hoarse, barely more than a whisper, as I shift slightly, revealing Meg still curled against me. Her body is boneless, and her skin is pale. "I can't, I can't get through..."

"I've got her," Thiago cuts in. He's at the other door, opening it much more calmly than Wyatt could have managed. My arms tighten around her instinctively, and Thiago notices. He lowers with ease, keeping his easy smile in place. "I'll take care of her. I promise."

It's not that I don't trust Thiago, but that my trust with Meg is shot for anyone. I want to be the one to help her, but then I look down and note the way she's curled herself away from me, only remaining in my hold because she's too weak to move away.

Swallowing, I ease my arms back, my heart splintering with every inch I put between us. For so long, I'd pictured a joyous reunion that she'd smile and tell me I did good. But that's a far cry from reality. I haven't done anything but fail her.

Thiago moves into the car, his movements precise and gentle as he scoops Meg into his arms, lifting her against his chest like she weighs nothing. She makes a slight, weak sound, barely stirring, and Thiago's lips press into a grim line as he turns, already moving toward the paramedics on standby.

Wyatt doesn't move, doesn't look away from me. His fingers ghost down my arms as if he's checking to make sure I'm in one piece.

"Can you stand?" he asks, something strained in his voice. It's like he's been screaming for hours and is struggling to return to an appropriate level. I nod, even though my entire body feels like lead, like every muscle is locked, like I'm barely holding myself together. Wyatt's arms slide around my waist to ease me onto the seat, and the second I feel his warmth and his unshakable presence anchoring me, I break.

Not with sobs, tears, or words. Just a shuddering exhale, my forehead dropping against his shoulder, my fingers twisting into his jacket, gripping hard enough to hurt. He doesn't rush me, nor does he say anything. Wyatt simply tightens his embrace, his hand pressing flat against the back of my head, his other arm locking around my waist, and keeping me right there against him, safe and steady.

The world beyond him is still spinning too fast and too loud, but Wyatt doesn't loosen his grip, even as the police swarm around us. Torch lights flicker over our faces in a twisted strobe effect.

Wyatt's fingers move, skimming my neck, threading gently into my hair. His touch is reverent, even though I can feel his entire body thrumming with residual rage and the aftershocks of almost losing me. He swallows hard, his Adam's apple bobbing.

"I saw you," he finally says. It's a strangled sound, as if he's afraid something will shatter between us. "Through the windscreen. I saw you attack him. If you ever do something that reckless again," He cuts himself off, his jaw tightening, his thumb stroking over my broken cheekbone, like he needs the proof that I'm alive.

"I'm fine, Wyatt," I offer weakly, tugging his hand away. "I knew you'd come for me."

"I'll chase you down. Every damn time." Wyatt grunts without hesitation. A warming feeling blossoms in my chest, the strain I've been harboring for weeks finally easing. I reach up, tracing the sharp line of his jaw and the tension locked tight in his muscles with my fingertips.

"And I'll always find my way back to you," I whisper before I can second-guess the weight they hold. Wyatt's breath catches, just slightly, but then his head dips until his lips are pressed against mine. A single, sweet kiss that contains a world's worth of promises. Wyatt has come to mean more to me than I ever expected, and now that we've stopped pushing each other away, the possibilities for us are endless. Our future actually stands a chance.

A sharp voice breaks the moment, and I barely process the uniformed figure crouching beside us until Wyatt lets out a low, reluctant sigh and pulls back.

"She needs checking over," the paramedic says, and Wyatt doesn't argue, helping to shift me to the edge of the open car door, allowing her to take my vitals, check my wounds, and ask questions I can barely answer. I let her work, but my attention is diverted. I'm searching for Meg.

I spot her just as the ambulance doors are shutting, Thiago's figure lingering beside her stretcher, his face grim. For someone who is usually so upbeat and casual, the look doesn't bode well. The vehicle pulls away, sirens wailing into the night, and it might as well rip my heart out with it. Meg has been saved. She's going to be okay, but I have the sinking feeling that I didn't really get her back.

I'm coaxed out of the car, Wyatt's arm around my middle supporting me when all I have is an oncoming headache and a pair of jittery legs. A foil blanket is wrapped around my shoulders to block out the cold seeping into my skin, the jumpsuit doing nothing to protect me from the night's air. But I hardly feel it.

We make it to the ambulance when two more police cars skid to a stop down the road. The driver catches sight of who I imagine is his superior and holds up a hand, mouthing, *'Don't ask.'* Garrett jumps out first, quickly followed by Huxley. Dax hangs back to check Axel is okay, but even Axel is moving quicker than I've seen in weeks. I want to tell him to slow down, that there's no rush, but it's pointless. I want them to be here as quickly as they can manage.

Wyatt steps aside but doesn't go more than arm's length away, which is lucky because as Garrett barrels straight into me, he manages to grab Garrett's collar and drag him back a step. On a second attempt, Gare approaches gently, sinking onto the step at my feet and clinging to my shins.

Dax's hand lands on my shoulder as he eyes me to ensure I'm still in one piece. Hux unapologetically strides straight in to embrace me. Taking my hand in his, Axel lets out a quiet, shuddering breath before brushing a stray strand of hair from my face.

The street is a blur of flashing lights and shifting figures, the sirens and radios blending into a distant hum, but all I can focus on is the warmth of their bodies surrounding me, anchoring me to something solid. My knees are bent, my feet planted on the ambulance's step, and my arms wrapped tightly around Huxley's torso as he holds me close, his heartbeat thudding against my ear. His grip is secure but gentle, his breath stirring the top of my hair as he presses his cheek to my head.

The others are close, so close that I can feel their body heat, their steadying presence keeping me from spiraling any further. The tension in their muscles hasn't fully eased, their bodies still rigid from the fight or flight instinct that none of us have shaken yet, but the way they lean into me, into each other, is enough to quiet the tremor in my chest.

For a moment, we just sit there, huddled together in the middle of the road, the weight of the night pressing down on all of us, but then, one by one, they start speaking, murmuring soft words that sink into my skin.

"We've got you, Peach," Garrett says first, forcing himself to keep his tone light despite everything.

"You're safe now," Axel adds, his hand resting over mine, his thumb brushing over my knuckles like he needs reassurance just as much as I do.

"We are never doing this again," Dax mutters as a quiet promise that settles deep in my bones. Then Huxley exhales a breath that shakes slightly, his arms tightening around me like he can't bear to let go.

"I love you, Swan," he breathes, pressing me harder into his chest. As if he holds me tight enough, he can make the last few hours disappear.

A huff comes from beside me, and Garrett nudges Huxley aside with a little more force than necessary. "Don't kid yourself, Hux. I love her more."

Dax scoffs, shifting so he's angled toward me, his knee knocking against mine. "I loved her first."

Wyatt grunts in disapproval, his grip on my waist flexing, his fingers pressing firm like he's staking a silent claim, daring them to challenge him.

"Let's not start that fight now," Axel grumbles, rubbing at his temple. The blood has been cleared from his face but it lingers in red smears along his cheekbones. I swallow down the bile that threatens to rise, remembering whose blood that is, and Axel drops his eyes knowingly. However, when he tries to withdraw his hand, I cling on tighter.

I force a smile, hoping to reassure us both, but the second the expression stretches across my face, a sharp sting flares in my cheek. I hiss, twisting away from the pain on instinct, and instantly, every single one of them releases me, hands hovering like they're afraid of making it worse.

"It's fine," I mutter, bringing a tentative hand up to my face, feeling the raw scrape of skin where the impact of an elbow has done a number on my cheekbone. The wound throbs under my touch, but it's nothing compared to what it could have been. "It was worth it."

The worry in their eyes doesn't lessen, but I force myself to meet each of their gazes in turn, letting my fingers brush against Axel's one last time before dropping my hand. "I love you all, too." The words hang in the air between us, and for the first time since this nightmare began, I feel like I can breathe again.

"That's enough," the female paramedic worms her way through my guys to stand before me. "We need to get you to the hospital. Who's riding with her?" Four hands shoot into the air, which Garrett takes full advantage of, punching each of the Souls in their balls. He jumps into the ambulance, easing me up from behind to lie on the stretcher. A round of curses and groans fills the air, but Garrett only winces when Axel calls him a lowlife bastard.

"Sorry, Axe. These things don't have favorites, but since I'm Avery's, I'm sure you'll understand. We'll catch up with you guys later." Without waiting for a response, Garrett jumps onto the stretcher and wriggles all six feet of him to fit on it with me. I huff a quiet laugh, shaking my head against his chest as the paramedic mutters something under her breath about juvenile delinquents and starts prepping the ambulance for departure.

Outside, the others are still groaning, Axel clutching his stomach like he's been mortally wounded, Dax flipping Garrett off while wincing through gritted teeth, and Huxley glaring murderously at him from the sidewalk. Wyatt, of course, is standing stiffly with his jaw clenched, probably calculating how long he needs to wait before exacting revenge.

"You can really be an asshole sometimes, you know that?" I reach down and pound my own fist into his dick. Garrett yelps, but it doesn't lessen his grin. He just tightens his arms around me as the ambulance doors swing closed behind us. "Yeah, but an asshole you love, so who is the real fool here?" he drawls, smug and self-satisfied, his breath warm against my temple.

I roll my eyes, feeling the exhaustion begin to creep in now that the adrenaline is finally fading. Allowing my eyelids to flutter closed, I sink into the steady rise and fall of his chest, the distant sound of sirens, the warmth of his presence pressing in from all sides. For the first time in what feels like forever, I don't have to fight. I don't have to run. For the first time in months, I can finally rest easy.

AVERY

We pull up the curved driveway and come to an easy stop, all six of us eager to escape the limo that picked us up from the airport hanger. During my short stay at the hospital, Axel was checked over and cleared to fly, to which Wyatt instantly started making plans. Removing the latest cold pack from my cheek, I nudge Garrett to wake him up, his head the weight of a bowling ball on my thighs. Despite the length of the vehicle, Gare stretching out and a muscled Huxley invading my space has easily made it feel small.

The Souls have not left my side for a single second in the past few days, including timing their showers with my need to use the toilet. There is no sanctuary from them now, and I can't say I mind. It helps to have them close, like yesterday, for example. I'd been so careful to avoid thinking of Nixon until the grief hit me like a ton of bricks out of nowhere. With it, the pain of losing Cathy resurfaced, and I was unconsolable until I cried myself to sleep. There is no doubt that it will happen again, even if Wyatt refuses to acknowledge what we've both lost. He won't even say Nixon's name.

Harrison managed to get away. He was injured, his blood splattered across the road, but somehow he managed to slip into the night and avoid all of the police searching for him. His accomplice was shot dead on sight. I've been receiving regular updates from the chief investigator, but instinctively, I know Harrison is done with me. He got the bloodshed he wanted.

Wyatt pops the car door, exiting first, with Dax and Axel just after. Hux shifts, holding his hand out for me, and when Garrett tries to follow, Hux shoves his face back into the limo and slams the door shut. The whole dick-punching situation has yet to be forgiven, especially since Hux had to be examined by a handsy doctor when he was worried one of his testicles had rescinded into his body. They haven't.

Garrett pushes the door open again, not phased in the slightest, and whistles at the manor in the glory of the midday sun. The central doorway is rounded, carved into a gray brick building adorned with flowerpots on each windowsill. On either side of the central building, dark wood runs the length of the extensions, with a garage located at the far end. The limo pulls away, rounding a fountain undisturbed by the gentle wind as it trickles water from a three-tiered spout.

We merely stand there, taking in the warm glow spilling from the house and the faint scent of something delicious wafting through the open windows. The front door flies open, and a short, rounded brunette woman rushes out, moving with more energy than her small frame should allow.

"Wyatt!" she cries, whipping her arms around his middle. Her dress is patterned with tiny flowers and sways around her calves, her small black flats barely making a sound against the stone porch. An apron is tied neatly around her waist as if she left something simmering on the stove when she heard the car pull up. "You've finally come home."

Wyatt's smile is unguarded, the sight temporarily stealing my breath. He folds her into his arms, resting his cheek atop her head. "I promised I would."

"And Riot is getting rather good at keeping his promises lately," Garrett quips, casually stomping all over the moment without a hint of self-awareness. The woman releases Wyatt, and he turns her by the shoulders to face us.

"Rachel, this is my family. Dax, Garrett, Avery, Hux, and Axel. Guys, this is Rachel. She's my mom." The sheer pride that beams from Wyatt has my heart squeezing. I barely hear the following greetings because I'm too caught up in the sweet grin he's sporting and the way Rachel gazes up with unabashed love, the kind that asks for nothing in return. It's like catching a glimpse of the man Wyatt could have been if someone had always loved him as unapologetically as Rachel. It's evident in how her eyes gleam when she peers into his face.

Remembering herself, Rachel claps her hands together, snapping me out of my thoughts. "Well, don't just stand there! Come in, come in! You must all be exhausted." She shoos us into the house and directs us towards the kitchen, throwing questions along the way.

"Are you all hungry? I've been cooking since Wyatt called and said you were coming. You'll find new clothes in the wardrobes upstairs. I hope you don't mind that I allocated your rooms, but Wyatt tells me you all rarely sleep where you're meant to, so feel free to just use the rooms as a base. This is Wyatt's house, after all."

"It's *your* house," Wyatt corrects, but his attempt at sternness is undercut when Rachel simply waves him off and continues moving. Entering the kitchen, two freshly baked pies are steaming on the side, and another set is in the oven. Garrett is a goner, helping himself while the rest of us remain polite. Rachel guides me to a dining chair and sits beside me, taking my hands in hers. They're warm, slightly calloused, and so familiar in their motherly touch that my throat tightens unexpectedly.

"Oh, Avery. It's so lovely to have you here, especially." Her eyes search mine with quiet affection. She doesn't stare at or comment on the bruising spreading across my cheek and seeping into my left eye socket. The throbbing is constant, but luckily, the X-rays didn't show extensive damage. I should heal within the next few weeks with just ice packs and painkillers. I just need to avoid all mirrors until then.

"Wyatt has told me so much about you." Rachel smiles kindly.

"He has?" I ask, blinking. A blush starts creeping up my neck, but my embarrassment is nothing compared to Wyatt's. His entire face flushes red, and suddenly, I don't even care what she says next. Just seeing him like this is worth it.

"We really don't need to talk about that," Wyatt mutters, shifting his weight like he's contemplating making a run for it. Garrett, of course, is instantly riveted. He joins us, stuffing a forkful of hot apple pie into his mouth and puffing his cheeks around it after the fact.

"Tell us *everything*."

Rachel's eyes brighten, and she is delighted to oblige. "Well, for a start, he wasn't lying about how beautiful you are," she says, touching my hair and rubbing it through her fingers.

"Rachel," Wyatt groans in warning, scrubbing a hand down his face like he might physically wipe this conversation from existence.

"He adores you, you know," she continues, undeterred. "He told me that when you dance, the entire world stops. I'd love to see it sometime." My eyebrows shoot up, my mouth parting slightly. Wyatt actively avoids my gaze.

I try to process the fact that Wyatt said those words and when and in what context, but all I can manage is a quiet, "Anytime." Then, my smile falters. "I haven't danced in forever." Rationally, I know it's only been a few months. But at this moment, it feels like a lifetime. Clearing my throat, I force the tilted slant of my mouth to return. Rachel gently squeezes my hand, her joy wrapping around me like a comfort blanket.

"Well, that's a shame," she says, light but meaningful. "I hope you'll find your way back to it soon. Something tells me it's a magical sight to behold."

My throat tightens again, but before I can find the right words to respond, Garrett groans dramatically, rolling his eyes back into his head. "Fuck, this is a good pie. I don't want to make it weird, but I'd *do things* to this pie." He lifts his fork pointedly at his plate, only for Huxley to swipe it straight out from under him. Axel comes up behind and smacks the back of Garrett's head, warning him to watch his manners in front of Wyatt's mom.

"Oh, I don't mind," Rachel chuckles, watching Garrett protest loudly and lunge for his stolen pie. "It's nice to have people to bake for again."

Wyatt lightly grips her shoulders, still recovering from his attempted public humiliation. He finally meets my gaze again; his green eyes are stormy, but his lips twitch into a smirk. Dax suddenly appears, a glass of water and my next set of antibiotics in his hands. I thank him, leaning into his side after I've swallowed them down.

Rachel watches all this with something knowing in her gaze, but instead of commenting, she rises from the table, smoothing her apron. "Eat as much as you like, and when you're ready, go get some rest. There are clean towels in the upstairs bathrooms, and I put extra blankets in the rooms, just in case."

"Thank you, Rachel," I say earnestly, meaning it more than I can possibly express. She just smiles, patting my hand before she leaves.

"Oh, honey. You don't have to thank me. You're safe here." I frown at Wyatt, wondering just how much he really has told her. On cue, a yawn escapes me, and my eyes feel heavy. Dax gives me a slight nudge, offering to find me somewhere to rest. Huxley accompanies us, and just before we leave the room, Garrett shouts around a mouthful of food.

"No naughty business without me," he muffles. I give him a narrowed glare over my shoulder.

"We can't make such promises. You'll have to choose between sex or the pie."

I wish I could capture the stunned yet pained look that claims Garrett's features as he looks from me to the pie and then back again. I walk away laughing, climbing the staircase flanked on either side.

I'm not sure whose bedroom we enter, but it's the closest one with a king-size bed. Dax helps me peel off my sweatshirt and tank top, carefully lifting the fabric over my head without catching my cheek. Shimmying out of my leggings, the men strip off, and a twinge of longing filters through me at the sign of them both comfortably and gloriously naked.

Turning to face me, Hux catches the glint in my eyes and shakes his head, leading me to the bed, still in my underwear. We curl up beneath the covers, me lying on my right side to spoon Dax while Hux spoons me. The three of us are asleep within minutes.

CHAPTER FORTY NINE

Sometime later, I rise to the smell of something rich, possibly spicy, and definitely filled with garlic. My stomach rumbles before I'm even fully awake. For a second, I don't remember where I am. Only that I'm warm, wrapped in the steady rise and fall of Dax's breathing in front of me, Huxley's arm still draped securely around my waist.

But then, awareness trickles back. Rachel's house. The safety of these walls. The way exhaustion had pulled me under so swiftly that I hadn't even fought it.

Shifting carefully, I wiggle out from between them, my muscles stiff but no longer screaming with the sharp pain of overuse. Dax makes a rumbling noise but doesn't wake, rolling onto his back and spreading out like a starfish, while Huxley only tugs the blankets tighter around him. I smile, shaking my head as I grab a hoodie and sweatpants from the wardrobe and slip them on before padding quietly downstairs.

The house is quiet in the way a home is after a long day. The lights are dimmed, and there's the faint hum of a radio playing in a distant room. When I step into the kitchen, I spot the plates left on the side, covered with foil to keep them warm.

Garrett is perched on the counter, swinging his feet, and finishing off what is probably his second helping. "About time you woke up, Peach. Thought we'd have to drag you down." I roll my eyes but head straight for the plates, lifting the foil to reveal what looks like slow-cooked beef stew with thick slices of crusty bread on the side. My stomach clenches with hunger.

"This looks delicious, Rachel," I compliment the woman standing at the sink, drying her hands. She waves me off.

"Wyatt cooked, actually." I freeze, glancing at him where he leans against the fridge, arms crossed, watching me carefully.

"You cooked this?" A slow smirk tugs at the corner of his mouth.

"Rachel is a good teacher. When I stayed here before, she taught me a few of her special recipes."

Garrett snorts. "If we'd known you were so easy to domesticate, we'd have started making use of you years ago." Rachel swats him on the arm with the dish towel, making Garrett yelp and leap off the counter.

"Enough out of you." I can't help my grin. Rachel has understood quickly how to deal with Gare, and I can tell already that she will be like a mother to everyone. Just before she sets her towel down, preparing to leave the room, her brown eyes flick over my outfit, and she grins at Wyatt knowingly. "You're right. Orange really is her color."

I look down at the clothes I dragged on in the dark, only now noticing the vibrant orange shade of the hoodie. Just like Wyatt's one that I've been stealing since I arrived at Waversea. Gaping at him, Wyatt shrugs, feigning innocence.

"I don't keep secrets from Rachel. It's a new thing I'm trying." Nodding, I take my plate and pause to take him in, appraising him with my eyes.

"I like that."

I slide into the same dining chair as earlier, happy to find I have Axel for company. He's working on something on his phone, brows pinched in concentration. I don't bother him, but I nudge my foot forward to touch his. He briefly flashes those beautiful hazel eyes my way and smirks, meeting me halfway beneath the table.

Carefully lifting the spoon to my mouth, Wyatt steps forward to cast me in his shadow. "Once you've eaten, we have a surprise for you." I glance between him and the others and lower the spoon, suddenly suspicious, but it's not me who speaks first.

"A surprise?" Huxley asks, appearing in the doorway with a blurry-eyed Dax. The pair of them exchange a look with Garrett, who mimes zipping his lips and then eating the key. Axel avoids my gaze completely, clearly in on whatever this is.

"Eat," Wyatt repeats, and the way he says it makes my stomach twist with anticipation. So, we do.

The stew is as delicious as it smells—rich and hearty, warming me from the inside out. The bread is perfect for sopping up the thick sauce, and despite how sluggish I'd felt moments ago, I finish nearly all of it, albeit rather ungracefully. The ache in my face forces me to chew excruciatingly slowly, since most of my meals up to now have been liquified. I manage it though, feeling sated and full at last.

For a beat, I glance around the table, taking in the faces of the people who have become my family. The exhaustion, the hunger, the bruises, the scrapes, and the shadows under their eyes are all still present. But for a rare moment, it no longer matters.

I let my mind drift back to the hospital. To the room that Meg is currently occupying in the psych ward. Upon arrival, she only spoke five words, and they were enough to convince the doctors that I was detrimental to her recovery.

Keep Avery away from me.

Those words continue to cut through me like a knife, slicing deeper every time they echo in my head. Five words, each more painful than the last, each twisting inside me like a blade I can't pull out. No matter how much I want to. No matter how much I *need* to.

Meg is lying in a hospital bed, curled away from the world. She believes, with every ounce of what's left of her shattered soul, that I'm the reason she's there. I squeeze my eyes shut, but it doesn't stop the images from surfacing. The dull, broken look in her eyes in the back of the car, the way she flinched from my touch as though I seared her.

I swallow hard, blinking back the sting behind my eyes. I should have been able to save her. I should have been able to do *more*. Instead, I made questionable choices, and ultimately, I was too late. Now when she looks at me, she sees nothing but the worst moments of her life.

My chair scrapes back against the floor, jarring me back to the present, and I realize that Wyatt is watching me. His sharp green eyes narrow slightly, his jaw tightening. Always so perceptive, always so *aware* of me.

He knows. Of course he knows.

Wyatt has spent years picking me apart, learning every flicker of my emotions and every small shift in my posture. He doesn't have to ask what's wrong. He already understands. But that doesn't stop him from trying.

"You're in your head, Angel." He leans down to speak into my ear. The others can hear, but it's nice to pretend that it's not so obvious when I check out and allow my mind to drift. "Come back to us." They all know I can't shake this feeling that it will creep up often. Axel reaches over, his fingers brushing over my knuckles. A silent reassurance. A quiet promise. The rest of the table picks up the conversation they were having, giving me the space to break in peace.

But breaking won't fix this. Breaking won't change the fact that Meg doesn't want me near her. Breaking won't bring her back to me, but hopefully, time will. I have to trust that she's in the right place now, and Thiago has vowed to keep me updated. For whatever reason, Meg has listed him on her visitation list. Apparently all they do is sit, watch movies, and eat vending machine snacks in silence.

Prying the spoon from my hand, Wyatt deems me finished. He removes my plate and then guides me further into the manor. I've left to explore, and I wish I could say I was taking any of it in. Another time, maybe. Garrett comes up behind me, his hands on my waist urging me onward, and when he speaks into my ear, it's a giddy sound that lifts everything that was sinking inside of me.

"You're going to love this, Peach." Excitement flashes in his dark eyes. That only makes me more suspicious, but I let them lead me through the house and down a hallway. Wyatt stops in front of a closed door, glancing at me instead of reaching for the handle. His throat bobs with a swallow before he finally clears it, his hands restless at his sides.

"Before we go in, there's something I need to say." His voice is quieter than usual, strained with something I can't quite place. He drags a hand through his hair before meeting my gaze head-on. "I'm not going back to Waversea. I'm staying here."

I search his face, reading between the lines, but all I see is determination, unwavering, and final. So, I lift a shoulder in a half-hearted shrug. "Okay. Then we'll stay here." Wyatt shakes his head, his brown hair shifting with the harsh movement.

"No. I want you to go back with the Souls." I blink several times, my heart tightening. Is he seriously going to push me away now? After the hurdles we've jumped together, the obstacles we've maneuvered. I thought we were over this shit.

Licking my lips, I try to keep myself calm. "Wyatt, I—"

"Without Fredrick and me looming over you, you'll thrive there," he quickly says, rushing to speak over the thoughts tearing through my mind. What did I do wrong? Does he not feel the same way I do? Wyatt shifts closer, his fingers twitching like he wants to reach for me but doesn't trust himself to. "Avery, I want you to dance and graduate. I want you to party and be happy, and just *live*."

"I thought we weren't going to separate anymore," I murmur, struggling not to feel the sharp sting of rejection. "Not after everything." Wyatt's jaw tightens, and I know he's fighting with himself, fighting the part of him that wants to be selfish. But he's already made up his mind.

"If you still want to come back after, I'll be right here. I'm not going anywhere. But I won't have you resenting me, all of us in fact, later down the line." I'm shaking my head, lips parted with an argument, but Wyatt holds up his hand. "You've spent so long cooped up inside, hoping that the world will forget about you. But you're meant to be seen, Angel. I see you, and you're fucking incredible. Now it's time to spread your wings, and if you feel like coming back afterward, you know where to come."

"I will come back," I vow without needing to even think about it. I know what I want out of life, and Wyatt is part of that. Squaring my shoulders, the stubborn part of me decides I'll show him. I'll make a cute freaking vision board, and he'll be pinned right in the middle of it. At least I'll have the rest of my men with me, keeping me on the right path.

"I'm staying too," Axel announces, his voice quieter than Wyatt's but just as resolute. My head whips toward him. The silence is so tense, it could be snapped clean in half. This time, it's Garrett who starts to argue, seemingly caught off guard too.

"Axel," he frowns, so serious that I could cry for him. For us, because I feel exactly the same. Axe strokes Garrett's arm gently, but he struggles to meet his lover's gaze.

"I've been through a lot, and I need time. I need to heal without a thousand eyes on me. Space to breathe and to go through therapy without feeling like I have to hold myself together for everyone else." His gaze flickers away for a moment, his throat working as he swallows hard. "It won't be pretty, but I want to heal. Please let me do this without..."

"Without me," Garrett groans, realizing who and what exactly Axel needs space from. He loves Garrett; there's no question about that. But some things can't be solved with a sarcastic joke or a quick fuck. Distracting him from the issues isn't helping to confront them. Axel exhales sharply, forcing a weak smirk.

"Plus, I've been looking at switching my major to psychology. There's an option to study remotely, and honestly, that'll be better for me."

"I don't understand why we can't all do that," I mumble quietly. In fact, I do understand. I can see the opportunity that Wyatt is giving me. I just don't know if when the time comes, that I'll actually be able to walk out of the door and leave them behind. But this isn't just about me. Wyatt and Axel have demons they want to face and ideas of the men they want to become. I can't hinder that, but I'm also going to be a whiny little bitch about it until I leave.

Garrett clearly isn't happy, but for now, the subject is set aside. Hux and Dax are listening to the conversation from behind, keeping their opinions to themselves. Wyatt takes hold of the door handle, exhaling all of the tension from his shoulders.

"But before you go back, there's a certain right we need to wrong. Something that you can remember us by." Wyatt offers a small smile and his hand.

I tentatively take it and brace myself as the door swings open. Inside, the office has been shifted around to accommodate a tattoo artist who is already setting up, placing ink bottles in neat rows along the desk. A chair sits before her, empty and patiently waiting. I blink, my heart skipping a beat. Turning to Wyatt, I find him watching me closely, something unreadable in his gaze.

"You're a Shadowed Soul, Angel. You need your ink." A breath catches in my throat. Of all the things I expected, this wasn't it. Tears prick at my eyes, but I don't let them fall. I just stare at him, at the man who has broken and bled for me, who would tear himself apart if it meant I could be whole.

Wyatt leads me into the well-lit room, his hand a firm weight against the small of my back. The scent of antiseptic and ink lingers in the air, punctuated by the snap of gloves being pulled onto the artist's hands. A lamp casts a focused glow on the transformed workstation, illuminating the prepared equipment, the gleam of the machine, and the sketch laid out across the wood.

My breath catches.

Wisps of curling smoke rise from the base of a skull, its hollows deep and endless. A whisper of everything I've endured, every version of myself I've buried and let die. Resting atop the skull is a queen's crown, tilted slightly as though it belongs to someone who has *earned* it. My throat tightens as I reach out, brushing my fingertips over the paper, imagining how it will look inked into my skin.

"You like it?" the artist asks, her face tilting up. She is covered in ink herself, the red hair on her neck pulled back by a bandana, and metal studs forming dimples in her cheeks. I swallow hard.

"It's perfect." She's pleased, beaming as she asks me to choose where I want it and sit accordingly. I remove the hoodie, baring my inner forearm. I want it somewhere I can see it every day and wear it like a piece of armor. I never want to forget the trials I've been through and the woman I've become. One who is loved by five amazing men, who are all currently looking at me as if I'm their entire world too.

"Fitting, isn't it?" Axel murmurs to no one in particular, a smirk tugging at his lips.

"She's been our queen since day one." Huxley agrees. With Dax and Gare close, I settle into the chair, shifting slightly as the artist preps my arm, cleaning the skin before pressing the stencil into place. The coolness of the transfer makes me shiver, but when she peels it away and I glance down at the purple outline, something fierce blooms in my chest.

This is theirs as much as it is mine. This is for every drop of blood, every night spent sleepless, every time we've fought, fallen, and risen again. This is their brand, a declaration that I am one of them and that I have always belonged.

The machine hums to life. Wyatt crouches in front of me, his hands bracing my knees, his thumbs tracing absentminded circles over my skin. "You sure you're okay with this?" he asks, searching my face for any lingering hesitation. I meet his gaze and smile.

"I've never been more sure of anything in my life." My response makes Wyatt grin wider, and my heart trips over itself. His grin is something I'm not sure I'll ever get used to, but every time I see it, I get butterflies all over again. Nodding, Wyatt shifts to the side, out of the artist's way. "If at any point it starts to hurt too much, you can use Garrett's balls as a stress reliever."

I snort a laugh as the first press of the needle stings—a sharp, buzzing pain that quickly dulls into something rhythmic and grounding. I breathe through it, letting my eyes flutter shut, letting the sound and sensation of it settle into me, etching their trademark into my skin. The Souls don't speak much, but I feel their steady presence at my side. Dax leans across the table to hold my hand, and Huxley soothingly holds my shoulder. Garrett is leaning lazily against the wall but watching with rapt attention. Wyatt stays in front of me the whole time, his hands never leaving my knees.

Minutes bleed into an hour. The pain never fades, but it transforms, shifting from discomfort into something else entirely. A mark of endurance. A testament to survival. When the artist finally leans back, wiping my arm clean with a damp cloth, I inhale sharply, blinking against the sting of antiseptic. She angles a mirror toward me, and I take in the sight of it. The deep blacks, the shading that makes the skull look hauntingly real, the delicate but powerful linework of the crown. It looks meant to be there, as though it has always belonged on my skin. I exhale slowly, the pride in my chest swelling so large it nearly chokes me.

"Holy shit," Garrett and Dax mutter in unison.

"It's perfect for you," Axel nods.

"You wear it well, Swan." Hux's gaze darkens with approval.

Wyatt doesn't say anything, but his fingers tighten slightly on my knees, his jaw working as though he's swallowing down words he would rather give me in private. I trace a careful finger around the fresh ink, already imagining the way it'll heal, the way it'll sit beneath my skin for the rest of my life. I belong to them. And now, I carry it for the world to see.

A short while later, I'm in the living area, stretched across Dax and

Wyatt on the sofa. I can't take my eyes off my new ink, wanting to admire every millimeter of it. Wyatt is running his thumb just beside the raw ink as if testing its longevity. Hux and Axel are discussing various universities that offer home learning, sitting on armchairs across a coffee table, which Rachel insists on keeping littered with soda and snacks.

We're in our own, peaceful ravine, content to simply be in each other's company when the tattoo artist reemerges, carrying a case with all of her equipment. Garrett is trailing just behind.

The Souls barely react at first, happily relaxing when Garrett clears his throat dramatically. Standing in a place we can all see, he hesitates for only a moment before reaching for the hem of his T-shirt and dragging the material over his head, exposing the ridges of muscle I've come to know, but the others haven't.

No one knows how to react at first, so shocked by Garrett's reveal that we don't know what to say. Then he points a finger to a fresh piece of ink sitting just over his heart. A singular peach in vibrant color. My mouth drops open.

"Garrett," I breathe, drawing myself to sit up and peer closer. The fruit has been purposely made to resemble the shape of a heart. His first tattoo that has a meaning. My pulse skips a beat as warmth blooms in my chest.

"I know, I know," he interrupts, grinning. "It's incredibly romantic, and you're absolutely obsessed with me now. I get it." I let out a short, breathless laugh, shaking my head.

"I was going to say, you finally don't have a shit tattoo!" A roar of laughter sounds, and Garrett being Garrett, he doesn't give a shit about being openly mocked. Climbing to my feet, I approach him for a better look. I press my palm lightly over the ink on his chest, just as he reaches for my arm, fingers ghosting over the crown-topped skull. My brand for his brand. Lowering my voice, I bat my lashes sweetly. "I love it, thank you."

Garrett steps closer, his teasing smirk softening into something real. "You're my Peach. You always have been." Dragging me into his arms, he pulls me in for a deep kiss, uncaring of who's watching. A few cheers and whistles follow, laughter filling the room. I've never felt so light, so filled with love, and simply at peace with myself.

As I look around at them—my Souls, my family, the ones who have carried me when I could no longer do it myself—I realize just how *deep* their claim runs. No matter where we go next, no matter who returns to Waversea and who doesn't, none of us are ever walking away from *this*. I love them all with everything that I am.

Turning back to Garrett, I step back, making a show of looking over his torso in finer detail. "Wait, where's your tattoo for Axel?" Garrett grins, and I know instantly, I shouldn't have asked as he starts to whip his pants down.

"Oh, Peach. You haven't seen my cock yet."

AXEL

Two Years Later

Upping the speed on the treadmill, I push myself into a full run, sweat dripping from my chin. I relish in the feeling of my lungs expanding, banishing Doc Marcus' voice from my head with each step. I'm at the peak height of physical fitness without a trace of asthma in sight. Mind over matter, and all that. My muscles burn more intensely with each heavy pound of my sneakers on the rubber, my mind clearing of all thought, and my eyes trained on the horizon.

Through the floor-to-ceiling windows of the penthouse, the skyline stretches endlessly as the city landscape twinkles like stars trapped behind the glass. Below, the streets are thrumming with life, even at this hour.

Wyatt and I moved into the penthouse two weeks ago, overseeing the renovations and ensuring everything was ready. Some of the home comforts we've been spoiled with at the manor have filtered into the decor, given that Rachel has her own apartment on the floor below and she can't help herself from making suggestions. She decided a while back that her manor held too many memories and it was time for her to move on, but Wyatt wouldn't let her go far. I reckon she'll be in our gourmet kitchen more often than not.

My phone pings through my headphones, disrupting the music I was vibing to. Not that I care when the notification lighting up the screen is Dax from our group chat, informing us they will be arriving in around twenty minutes. I exit the home gym, wiping the sweat from my head with a small hand towel.

Passing Wyatt in the art-lined hallway, I tell him to get the wine ready before climbing the spiral staircase to our open-plan bedroom. One huge space with a custom-made bed and separate walk-in wardrobes for each of us. A photo frame sits on the bedside table, an old image of Avery and Meg hugging and smiling behind the glass. A bittersweet pang tugs at my heart, but I know Avery will appreciate the gesture. We need to hold our memories close to remember how and why we're here, and what we have to live for.

The connecting bathroom is just as lavish, with a jacuzzi bathtub fit for six in the far corner. I shower quickly, pausing in the mirror whilst drying off. A satisfied smile grows across my face, the man staring back at me, one that I'm finally happy to accept. My head is freshly shaven, and my hazel eyes are no longer shadowed by exhaustion. My shoulders appear broader now that the constant pressure and unbearable guilt have lifted, leaving me standing taller than I ever have.

I run a hand over my chest, feeling the steady beat beneath my palm, the rhythm of a heart that no longer feels like an anchor. Therapy has been brutal. An unrelenting occurrence tearing me open and forcing me to face the things I had buried deep. To confront the death of someone who was supposed to have been my mother but never acted like it. To accept the abuse I've suffered and understand that it doesn't make me weak. It makes me a survivor.

A knock at the door pulls me from my thoughts. "Hurry up, Axe," Wyatt calls through the wood. "They're almost here." I huff a quiet laugh, shaking my head as I exit, a towel pinned around my waist.

Nothing has changed in Wyatt's stalking ways, but at least he uses an app to do it now. Avery had the chip removed from her neck before she returned to Waversea, cutting ties from his obsessive, toxic behavior and encouraging him to try a different approach. One we all consented to beforehand.

Once back in the bedroom, I pull on a black T-shirt, the fabric stretching over muscle that wasn't there before. I clip Avery's compass bracelet around my wrist, knowing I should have given it back a long time ago, but its weight feels like having a part of her with me at all times, even when the distance between us is vast. After tugging on some dark jeans, I find Wyatt pacing near the kitchen island, rolling his shoulders. He's gone a step more formal, a white shirt collar parallel to the sharp line of his jaw. Pushing his hands into the pockets of his navy slacks, his dress shoes make a clipped sound against the marble floor.

"Relax, man," I tell him. "Everything's perfect, and she wouldn't care even if it wasn't."

"I know that," Wyatt sighs, shaking some of his nervous energy. Planting his hands on the islands, I watch him make a conscious effort to calm his jittering. His hair has grown out and is no longer forced into submission with products, the brown strands falling around his face. Those green eyes, though, haven't lost their edge one bit.

Handing him a wine glass, he accepts it and clinks mine, sipping in silence. I feel the same anticipation curling through my gut, a sharp-edged thrill at the thought of everyone being under the same roof again. Everything is set. Three bottles of wine are breathing on the counter, the scent of garlic and rosemary still hanging in the air from the meal Rachel helped us prepare earlier. Candles flicker in glass holders on the dining table, and a ridiculous amount of flowers take up nearly every available surface.

"One bouquet would have sufficed," I offer, eyeing the various colors. Wyatt snorts, his meaning loud and clear.

Avery deserves every flower under the sun, and I'm going to give it to her.

Anyone who thought Wyatt and Avery's feelings were a passing fad was quickly proven wrong. For the past two years, we've all eaten dinner together over video call, sent care packages, and visited during the holidays, but those two are in constant communication.

Where the others get her on a physical and comfort level, Wyatt gets her mind. They're on the phone for hours, sometimes all the way through until morning. Any achievement, any inconvenience, or triggering counseling session, she's straight onto the phone, needing Wyatt's opinion. Wanting him to console her. In all of the years I've known him previously, I've never heard Wyatt just talk and open up and be so honest. I suppose they have a lot of missed time to make up for.

I, on the other hand, received what I needed. Space. I know it hasn't been easy on Garrett, and at the end of each visit, we have the same argument. *Why can't you come with us? When will you be ready for me to love you?* But he understands, truly, even if he doesn't like it.

Sipping my wine, the crispy liquid easing down my throat, I wonder how I'm going to put into words that I'm finally ready. I'm finally the man I want to be for him. For Avery. For myself.

A buzz sounds through the penthouse, resonating from the elevator. Wyatt and I exchange a look before he strides to the control panel and grants access. A moment later, the doors slide open. My smile couldn't stretch any further.

Between the bundle of suitcases, Avery stands tall and proud amongst her men. She's cut her hair to just below her shoulders and recently had her outgrown brunette roots merged into the blonde tones further down. She's wrapped in one of her oversized sweaters, a box of books in her hands. Her eyes sweep over the space, taking in the high ceilings, the open-plan layout, and of course, the flowers.

Dax is the first one off, dragging two duffel bags behind him, his grin wide and easy. "Home sweet home!" Huxley steps out next, rolling his suitcase, his lips twitching. Garrett follows, balancing a box labeled *'Shit I Probably Don't Need'.* His dark eyes settle on me instantly, like a laser beam spearing straight through to my heart. He looks over my bulkier physique, one that rivals Huxley's now, and curses beneath his breath.

"Fuck, you're so hot."

I smirk, closing the distance between us to take his box and set it aside. He's in my arms in the next second, arms banded around me like he never wants to let go. I nudge my cheek against his, peppering his face and neck with light kisses. It's so good to have him like this again, knowing I don't have to say goodbye anymore. Pulling himself back before we get carried away, Gare twists back to face the elevator, still bundled in my arms.

Avery exhales a breathless laugh, last to enter. "Holy shit. This is incredible. And... it's *ours*," she beams at the five of us staring at her like she's the center of our universe, and she is. Wyatt, who had been frozen at the sight of her, finally moves. He strides toward her, his hands settling on her waist, and dips down to press a kiss to her forehead.

"Welcome home, Angel." Her blue eyes flick to mine over his shoulder, and I smile.

"Feel free to put your womanly touch on it. But maybe ask Rachel for advice here and there. She's not stopped saying how excited she is to have a daughter." Warmth blossoms in both Wyatt's and Avery's eyes, and they step aside, needing a moment in private. Dax and Hux take themselves on a tour while I tug Garrett along and guide him towards the wine. Accepting a glass and downing it in one, Gare proceeds to throw himself on a large sofa facing a roaring fire and the city rooftops beyond.

"I can't believe we've finally graduated. I thought we were gonna be in that school *forever*." I snort, resting against the back of the sofa.

"I know," I exhale, watching the flames dance in the fireplace. "Feels surreal that we're all together again."

For a short while in the middle somewhere, when the calls were streaming in about how Garrett and Huxley were constantly bickering and forcing Avery to act as their mediator on a regular basis, I didn't think we'd get to this point either. After pushing him away time and again, I was on edge, waiting for the news that he'd done something reckless, whether it was to drink himself stupid, get arrested, or go on a sex spree with half of Waversea. But he surprised us all, reigning it back in and focusing his energy on the basketball team he became captain of, in Wyatt's absence.

Garrett stretches, his shirt riding up to reveal a sliver of tattooed skin. "You're lucky I came at all," he smirks at me. "You know how I feel about therapists. But I figured as least you can fuck my body whilst raping my mind, and I couldn't miss the chance to call you Professor Axel."

I snort, ignoring the rest of that sentence. "I won't be a professor for a long time yet." Eventually, though, that is the goal. The last two years have been about personal growth and not just the physical kind. Through healing and pushing myself towards meaningful, I took every online class I could, chased every credit, and now I have my degree in psychology. But I'm not stopping there.

"I've been thinking about taking it further," I admit, swirling my wine glass. "I want to focus on creative therapy. Helping people work through trauma in ways that feel natural to them. Art, music, dance.

Maybe even something more experimental." Garrett raises a brow, and his smirk widens.

"Something like nude still life drawing? Because that's something I can totally help with." He starts tugging off his T-shirt, and I reach out to stop him. Since working through his self-consciousness, Garrett has become a nudist for the most part. I rarely get a photo with his clothes on these days, ever since Avery convinced him to do a meditation course called '*Embrace your Body.*' It was a bunch of hippies hugging trees and swinging their dicks in the wind, and he loved every second of it.

"You're gonna be too busy playing basketball, Mr. Hotshot." I wiggle my eyebrows, still holding the hem of his T-shirt down by his waistband. Garrett's smug grin doesn't falter.

"Still got time to model for you," he winks. I roll my eyes, but there's pride swarming in my chest. We had no idea what Garrett would do when he came upstate until a few weeks ago, an agent saw him play and offered him a contract. He's worked so hard, invested so much time in bettering himself, and now he's about to go pro. Dax joins us, making a choked sound at the sight of me grappling to keep Garrett from removing his top.

"At least wait until after dinner before you start stripping off," Dax chimes in, dropping onto the couch beside him. My Brazilian friend has also let his hair grow out, a wild blond afro spilling from the top of his head and hanging past his shoulders in a mix of tiny ringlets and unruly waves. It suits him, as does the relaxed smile on his face. He looks at home here, his arm slung over the back of the couch and his body stretched out loosely.

Dax didn't return to Waversea in the same capacity as the others, since his scholarship was revoked and he didn't feel like jumping through hoops to get it back. Instead, he took up a biomedical engineering apprenticeship at a nearby facility, using the frat house as his base, and after working his ass off, has landed a real job in the city below us.

"You excited to start at the lab on Monday?" I ask him, sipping the rest of my wine and setting the glass on the coffee table. Garrett nudges up to make room for me to sit and curls himself around me. Dax is still grinning.

"Just excited to finally be living. Feels like we've all managed to get our shit together." Huxley scoffs, strolling into the room.

"Some more than others," he narrows his eyes at Garrett, who in turn flips him off. I laugh, my gaze settling on Huxley as he moves to stand near the windows, silhouetted against the city. It doesn't take long for Wyatt to filter in and stand at his side, the pair muttering in hushed whispers.

They've been working on their plans to start up a charity together for months, putting their business degrees and money to good use. The concept is to give kids a way to escape dangerous homes and start over, no matter what background they've come from. Rich, poor, abused, manipulated. They will all be saved and placed with well-vetted, loving families, receiving the best care both through court cases and afterward.

Wyatt nods as he talks, his sharp green eyes flicking to his new partner. Huxley crosses his arms, a satisfied glint in his gaze. I reckon Wyatt is filling him in about a call he took earlier, setting up a meeting with some potential solicitors who are interested in joining.

Avery steps into the room, tucking her hair behind her ear. The light seems to radiate around her, shining like a halo and filling the space with the warmth it was missing. She may have only just arrived, but she effortlessly belongs. The thought fills me with satisfaction. After everything—after the fights, the bruises, the nights spent wondering if we'd make it to morning—we've made it. We built something better. Something that's ours. We've found our home.

Her eyes snag on the fireplace and for a moment, her smile falters. Wyatt notices too, swiftly stepping in to guide her closer. On the mantelpiece, a thin vase holds the only flower in the entire penthouse which won't wilt and die. Afterall, Wyatt spent the best part of three days building the yellow rose out of lego. Confusion flickers between Avery's brows and Wyatt takes her hands.

"If you want me to get rid of it, I will. But it's taken me two years to come to terms with what was done to us, and this is my way of making peace with the past. For Cathy and Nixon, and even Fredrick. They manipulated us, molded us, lied to us, but they also brought us together. They brought me to you."

Avery is speechless, her eyes flicking between Wyatt and the flower, until she throws herself at him. Her arms wind around his neck, her lips crashing against his. Wyatt catches her effortlessly, his hands gripping her waist as if he never intends to let go. Their mouths move in perfect sync. Hungry and desperate, years of tension unraveling in a single kiss. Avery clings to him, pressing closer, her fingers tangling in his hair. A low sound rumbles in Wyatt's throat, his grip tightening as he steals her breath, owning every inch of her.

I turn my attention back to Garrett, stroking his neck with a coy smile. This feels right, all of us here. No one has to hide how they feel in this penthouse; it's our space to be free.

Contrary to expectation, Wyatt didn't make it his mission to reveal Nixon's secrets. He didn't burn Avery's adoption certificate or run to the media about their relationship. After long reflection, Wyatt decided to turn Hughes manor into a museum. Cathy's film career is immortalized in those walls, her awards and memorabilia on full display. Somehow, he decided it's what the Hughes would have wanted. Nixon and Cathy worked so hard to create the illusion of their reputation, and in death, it made sense to give it to them. To let the world believe the show they put on. All of the ticket proceeds go to charity.

I, on the other hand, sold my childhood mansion the second the deed was put into my name, making sure Richard didn't get a cent. Sharon's death was ruled an accident, but unfortunately that didn't put an end to the auctions. Last I heard, Top Knot Taylor had taken the role as head organizer, using his experience and connections with the clients to run them elsewhere. As long as everyone is consenting and fully aware of what they're getting into, it's not my concern anymore.

Remembering the rest of us are here, Avery extracts herself from Wyatt's hold. He tenses, contemplating whether to let her go but relents eventually. Brushing her lips, there's a gleam in Avery's blue eyes, something playful about the way she twirls with her hair. Sliding her feet over the marble floor, Avery accentuates her long legs past the sofa and towards the staircase.

Her body hasn't changed over the years, but she appears stronger. Every movement is calculated and well placed, her posture putting the most experienced models to shame. That's why she's been given a place at the Royal Juliet Dance School a few blocks away. It's the best in the city, a place that will push her harder than ever. But she's ready.

I've been to every one of her performances, whether for the

Waversea showcases or an external competition. Somewhere in the bags, her small collection of medals is ever-growing, quickly boosting her into a career she never thought achievable.

When I blink back to reality, I find her halfway up the stairs, her fingers trailing the golden banister.

"I hope you all don't mind if I skip dinner. I'm just going to make myself comfortable and wait for whoever is planning to eat me instead." The room stills on a sharp inhale, and then we're all moving, scrambling towards the staircase. Avery squeals and runs the rest of the way upstairs while we fight it out just below.

Wyatt somehow flies across the room and gets to the first step, but we're right on his heels. Garrett snatches the back of his white shirt, yanking him hard enough that he staggers back, cursing under his breath. I take my chance, gripping Garrett's shoulder to shove him back too, but Dax, the sneaky bastard, grabs the waistband of my jeans and hauls me down a step. Wyatt recovers fast, shouldering into Dax, so he almost eats the marble floor. Huxley comes in like a damn linebacker, bulldozing through us all, his muscled legs giving him an unfair advantage.

"Not happening, assholes," he grunts, powering forward. Garrett hooks an arm around Huxley's waist, dragging him backward as he lunges forward at the same time. I manage to mostly avoid the tangle of limbs, dancing around the grunts and curses that follow. Hands grab at shirts, belts, anything to slow the others down.

Wyatt nearly makes it, his fingers grazing the gold railing before Dax lunges and locks an arm around his middle, sending them both crashing back into Hux. They go down hard. Garrett stumbles over them, a hand launching out of the mass to grab his ankle and take him down too. I'm left laughing as I sidestep the pile of bodies.

A giggle echoes from above, where Avery is perched at the top of the stairs with her knees bent up to her chest. I fly up the steps, grabbing her hand and launching her to her feet in one smooth move. Avery yelps as I scoop her up, throwing her over my shoulder like she weighs nothing. Her fists drum against my back, laughter bubbling up between her half-hearted protests.

"Axel!" she squeaks, wriggling in my hold.

"Should've thought about the consequences before teasing us like that, Swan," I rumble, striding toward the bedroom. Behind us, the others are groaning, still tangled in their pile at the bottom of the stairs. Their curses and threats echo through the penthouse, but I ignore them, focused solely on the woman in my arms.

The back wall of the bedroom is made completely of glass, fitted with blackout blinds that start to lower by the push of a button, blocking out the city lights. In its place, I flick on softer lights trailing the edge of the ceiling, casting long shadows over the luxurious bedding. Avery gasps when I toss her onto the mattress, her blonde waves fanning out as she bounces slightly, her sweater slipping off one shoulder.

She props herself up on her elbows, watching me with wide, heated eyes as I crawl over her, pressing her into the plush covers. My fingers trail up her thigh, pushing the fabric of her sweater higher, exposing the flawless skin on her stomach beneath. I've been waiting too long to do this—to have her in a space that belongs to the Souls, a place where she can be treated like the queen she is.

"You wanted this, little minx," I murmur, my lips grazing the shell of her ear. "All of us fighting over you, turning us feral with that naughty little stunt you just pulled." Her breath hitches, confirming my suspicions. I lean down, capturing her mouth in a slow, teasing kiss, coaxing a soft whimper from her pliant mouth. She arches into me, fingers gripping my shoulders, nails biting through my shirt.

A scuffle sounds behind us, the mattress dipping in various places.

"I let you win that one, Axe," Huxley grumbles.

"Yeah, yeah," Dax mutters sarcastically, his attention distracted by Avery panting beneath me. He strokes her hair out of her face and trails a finger along her throat.

"Turns out Axel has found a selfish streak while we've been away. I wonder how Wyatt feels about that." Garrett's grin is all mischief as he falls onto the bed beside us. Wyatt is the last to approach. His green eyes burn as he slowly stalks forward, rolling up his sleeves.

"I'll forgive him," he murmurs, "if he moves over." Avery's whimper is drowned out by Garrett's.

"I've had a wet dream just like this for *soooo* long," he groans, biting his lip. I smirk but shift back slightly, allowing Avery the space to sit up, though she doesn't get far before Garrett catches her chin between his fingers, tilting her face toward him. His lips ghost over hers, teasing, before he claims her in a deep, slow kiss that has her melting against him.

Huxley kneels behind her, his fingers slipping into her hair, tilting her head slightly to press his lips to the exposed curve of her throat. Dax slides his hands beneath her sweater; his fingers drag slow, torturous lines over her bare skin. I watch her shudder, watch the way her breath hitches when he presses a kiss to her neck, his teeth scraping just slightly. She lets out a quiet moan, her body supple, lost in the heat of their touch.

Wyatt settles beside me, watching with darkened eyes, his thumb grazing the corner of his mouth. "I hope you know what you've started, Angel. We're extremely pent-up and aching for you. There's no telling what can happen." He says slowly, directing his words to Avery. She pulls back from Garrett just enough to catch Wyatt's gaze, her lips kiss-swollen and pink. She releases a sultry smile, her eyelids already hooded with desire.

"I guess we're about to find out."

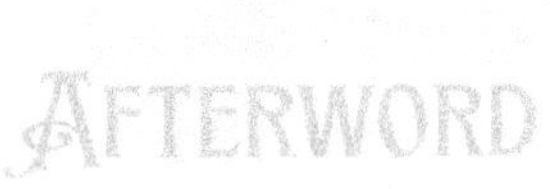

Afterword

You made it!

The Shadowed Souls series has come to a beautiful, fulfilling end in which all of the deserving bastards died, and the heroes (even the morally gray one) got their happy ending. I understand you have some questions yet to be answered, which is why you can expect:

Two bonus chapters from the Shadowed Souls!
For anyone who needs more of Garrett's humor, Axel's newfound strength, Hux's hotness, Dax's beautiful mind and Wyatt's obsessiveness, those extra two chapters will be available in my newsletter for you to download.

You can join my newsletter through my website:
www.authormaddisoncole.com

Also, as you may have guessed, **Meg will be getting her own story!** All of that trauma has to go somewhere, and you will get extensive flashbacks to fill in the gaps of her kidnapping. What actually happened to Fredrick? Will Harrison come back? Will Thiago be a part of her future? (I can already confirm that one for you.) It will all be wrapped up in a spinoff series for your reading pleasure. Look out for updates later in the year, after my heart has taken a little hiatus from the Souls.

Thank you again for sticking with me during this series. A special acknowledgement to Daisie Mae for editing, Bianca and Victoria for being my betas, and Kris and Ella for being my emotional support blanket throughout. This story is a testament to these lovely ladies.

If you loved the ending to this trilogy, **please leave a review** on Amazon and Goodreads. Your support is fundamental to indie authors like me. Then, make sure you're on my socials. The Shadowed Souls will be creeping up now and again!

ABOUT THE AUTHOR

If you're a new reader to Maddison – welcome to the Mole's Burrow!!

Maddison is a married mum of two, and a serial daydreamer. As a huge fan of all romance tropes herself, it was time to pen the stories which consume her mind most hours of the day.

As a child, Maddison was a jet setter and has lived all over the world, only to return to the south east of England, where she is now happily settled. With a double award in applied arts and art history, Maddison is a creative with a dark passion for feisty females and spicy stories.

For regular updates, check out my website on:

www.authormaddisoncole.com

and/or catch me on socials.
www.facebook.com/Maddison.cole.314
www.Instagram.com/authormaddisoncole

Other Works

If you'd like to keep reading from Maddison's backlist, please check out...

Shadowed Souls Series – (set in Waversea)

RH Dark Academy Stepbrother Romance

Forged by Shadows

Bound by Obsession

Haunted by Secrets

Billionaire Brothers RH (set in Waversea) – Standalone

Beautiful Delusions

I Love Candy

Dark Humor RH - Completed Series

Findin' Candy (novella)

Crushin' Candy

Smashin' Candy

Friggin' Candy

All My Pretty Psychos

Paranormal RH with mutants, ghosts and demons - Completed Series

Queen of Crazy

Kings of Madness

Hoax: The Untold Story (novella)

Reign of Chaos

Bound by Fate

Fated Mates RH Shifter – Standalone

Moon Bound

A Deadly Sin

MMA Fighter BSDM RH - Standalone

A Night of Pleasure and Wrath

A Wonderlust Adventure

A Twisted Menage Retellling Duet

Descend into Madness

Embrace the Mayhem

Billionaire Badboys

Con Artist/Billioanire RH Romance – Uncompleted

Wreckin' Amethyst

The War at Waversea

Basketball College MFM Menage - Completed

Perfectly Powerless

Handsomely Heartless

Beautifully Boundless